THE PRICE

D0097008

THE
CIRCLE of DESTINY
1

The PRICE

A NOVEL

by Jim & Terri Kraus

TYNDALE HOUSE PUBLISHERS, INC. | WHEATON, ILLINOIS

Library of Congress Cataloging-in-Publication Data

Kraus, Jim.
    The price : a novel / by Jim and Terri Kraus.
      p. cm. — (The circle of destiny ; 1)
    ISBN 0-8423-1835-6 (softcover)
    1. California—History—1846-1850—Fiction.   2. California—Gold discoveries—Fiction.
  3. Clergy—New England—Fiction. I. Kraus, Teri, 1953- II. Title

Printed in the United States of America

06   05   04   03   02   01   00
7   6   5   4   3   2   1

Shawnee, Ohio
March 1842

The cabin, with its odd angles and pitches, hulked beneath a cluster of pines. A soft mist glistened on their outermost branches and on the brown needles that carpeted the ground. Nature quieted, becoming almost somber.

A thin curling of smoke pushed up from the stone chimney, struggled into the heavy air, and hesitated a few feet from the edge of the roofline. It cleaved to the lower branches of the pines for an instant before twisting and slowly inching upward.

A lone rider perched on a black mule plodded along the rutted, muddy path to within a few feet of his destination, then dismounted with a grunt. As he knocked on the door of the cabin, each rap sounded as hollow as a thump on a ripe pumpkin.

The door swung open, stretching its leather hinges. A young man with angular features and bright eyes peered out from the dim interior.

"You Joshua Quittner?" the express rider said, then coughed.

"I am."

"Registered letter. Here."

A pale envelope fluttered from the rider's breast pocket and fell neatly into Joshua's open hand.

"Hope it ain't bad news. Got to go so I git home by sundown."

Joshua thanked him and shut the door by leaning hard against the rough planks until the wooden latch clacked into place.

"Who was that?" his mother, Mae Quittner, called out from the smoke-draped kitchen.

"It's a letter. From Harvard."

"From whom?"

"Not from whom . . . from *what*. The Harvard seminary. The letter I've been waiting for."

Joshua's mother entered the room. She was a short, rounded woman with dark, determined eyes. As she wiped her hands against a threadbare blue apron, she peered up at her son.

"From who?" came a bellow from the loft.

"Harvard," she shouted back at her husband. "It's the letter!"

Joshua's father, Eli, leaned over the railing. His dark hair was scattered in a dozen directions. As he studied, he twirled his hair and would finish with a bird's nest that resisted the most determined combing. In his hand was a worn Bible. He had just begun his message for the Sabbath and his congregation at the Shawnee Church of the Holy Word. It was now Friday.

"Harvard?"

His mother glared up at her distracted husband, then dismissed him with a wave. The sound of an envelope being torn drew her attention back to Joshua, her only child.

Joshua's eyes darted back and forth across the page.

"Well? What does it say? What does it say?" his mother asked excitedly.

Joshua's huge grin could not deny the contents.

"You've been accepted?" she shrieked. "You've been accepted?"

He nodded, and she dove at him, embracing him fiercely. He held the letter close to his face, the paper smooth and beautiful with elegant black spins and swirls.

"You'll study hard, won't you, Son?" his father shouted from above, adjusting his suspenders. "You'll study hard and come back to us. You'll come back here to work for God, won't you?"

Joshua smiled, a curious sidelong smile, but did not answer.

CHAPTER ONE

Harvard Divinity School
September 1842

HIS journey to Cambridge, Massachusetts, took three days.

Three sunrises.

Three sunsets.

Hundreds and hundreds of miles.

On the dawning of the fourth day, Joshua awoke to the train's rattling and chug-cough-chugging along the banks of the Charles River, a few hours west of Boston. The long journey–his first train ride on the "iron horse," as his father called it–was, at the outset, intensely exhilarating, with only dreamed-of sights and sounds. But now he was bone tired and ready to be off this noisy railway car. He wanted to begin his new life.

As dawn's steely light glinted off the ripples of the slow-flowing river, Joshua tried but could not see to the far side of the Charles. It was too foggy. Cambridge lay in that direction. Cambridge, just north of Boston, was home to both Harvard College and the Harvard Divinity School.

He looked down at the Bible–his father's–that lay unopened on the seat next to him. When Joshua had left Shawnee, his father had given it to him and had instructed him to read it every day, as both knew he would. As Joshua now ran his hand over the leather cover, worn to a skin's thickness, he closed his eyes. He could almost hear the chorus of a thousand church choirs, trembling together as one reedy voice. The thousands of sermons he'd heard since birth echoed in his father's voice.

His palm rested flat against the book, and it warmed to his flesh. He lifted the Bible, still unopened, and hefted it into the air, feeling its pull. In Ohio, the words felt as if each had dimension and weight. Now, nearly at his destination, the words grew light, as light as gossamer, a fainter and fainter echo, almost pulling his heart heavenward, like the thin white chords of a dandelion head loosed by the wind. Without knowing the reason or searching for one, Joshua felt less encumbered than ever before. Even the carefree and light days of childhood were weighty and grave in comparison to the lightness of his heart on this particular morning.

He smiled. Soon he would be walking on the hallowed grass quadrangle of Harvard as a divinity student. Walking among the same great ivory towers, the same tall stacks of books, as did John Adams, Samuel Adams, and John Hancock. *The noble thoughts that must permeate the very air of Cambridge,* Joshua thought.

He was young for a divinity student; most of his fellow classmates would have gone to college first, at least for a few years. But Joshua did not have the time or resources for such a leisurely approach. And he was already an accomplished student, most of his learning self-taught.

As he watched the rising sun, his gray-green eyes brightened further. Realizing his long blond hair lay thick and matted from the journey, he ran his hand through it, smoothing it as best he could. When he combed it back from his forehead, the sun highlighted the slight streak of red in the blond locks. Rubbing the sleep from his eyes, he was unaware that other passengers were watching him. For Joshua Quittner, from the hamlet of Shawnee, Ohio, was a man who often drew long looks from blushing young women.

Drawing little comfort from the stale air trapped in the crude sleeping car, he slipped the Bible into his leather bag, drawing the drawstring as tight as he could. Then he stood, rocking to the sway of the railcar, and looked out the dirty window as ashes and cinders rained down from the locomotive's smokestack.

Other words from southern Ohio echoed in his head.

"Don't need to be goin' off to some fancy school out East to learn truth from the Bible, boy," his uncle Hiram, *also a local preacher of sorts, had forewarned. "You're a smart one, sure. But there ain't much they can teach you that you can't be learnin' right here. Besides, I hear tell that school is run by a bunch of Unitarians."*

Joshua had merely nodded in deference to his uncle's admonitions and replied quietly, "Then perhaps I am needed there to be a beacon of the Truth."

"You're a leader," his uncle had added, growing more avuncular. "You lead people right, they'll follow you—even if you don't think they will. They'll be able to see the Truth in your eyes. You look to the Lord, and others will look to you. That's your callin', boy. That's your destiny. To lead . . . and to be a servant of the people and serve the Almighty."

Joshua shook his head to clear the memory, then opened the door to stand outside on the platform between the railcars. He breathed deeply of the air, spiced with the taste of coal dust, and stared out, his hands loose on the dew-slick railing. The train clattered past clusters of farms and villages nestled in fog-shrouded vales.

"We'll be setting into Boston in an hour," the conductor called as he stepped past Joshua on the rattling steps. "That's your stop, isn't it?"

Joshua nodded. "Well, Cambridge, actually. Harvard Divinity School."

The conductor, a bulky man with an enormous mustache, narrowed his eyes. "Well . . . I wouldn't have taken you for a preacher. Something about your face that don't take to being set off in a church."

Joshua offered a puzzled smile in return. *Just what does a preacher look like?* he thought.

The conductor squinted again, his hand on the forward door. "Then again, I've been told that traveling as much as I do in this blasted wheeled rattletrap will addle a man's mind." As he started to pull the door shut behind him, he paused for one last comment. "So be it, I always say. If I'm addled, don't pay me no mind. You'll be a fine preacher some day, if that's what you're to be."

Blinking against the acrid fingers of smoke around him, Joshua smiled, then threw his head back and laughed—the kind of rolling, bubbling merriment that came from his heart and soul. Startled, the conductor nearly tripped as he slammed the door behind him.

From the ladies' car forward, Joshua heard the muffled words, "Boston—next stop. End of the line—Boston!"

Joshua had procured a Boston city map from the land office of the courthouse of Shawnee County, Ohio. Now he bent closer to make out the details. According to the map, the distance from the center of Boston, where the train depot lay, to Cambridge was no greater than the thickness of his little finger.

But that short distance on the map had become a hard-edged, expanding geography because of the heavy theology books that lay evenly divided between his two satchels. By the time he made the crest of Boston's first hill, his arms were crying out in pain.

He passed horse-drawn rockaway carriages, gaily painted wheeled contraptions that ran in narrow tracks laid right into the cobble-stones. Each massive carriage, pulled by a team of large horses, groaned under the weight of a dozen or more passengers.

Elegant plum-colored broughams clattered past him, carrying smartly dressed city folk, their coachmen calling to the horses for more speed. A steady stream of shiny hackneys also passed. No doubt they could be hired with a whistle, but Joshua knew such an extravagance was too dear for a person of his meager financial means.

Regardless of the fare, walking will be easiest on my wallet, he told himself. *In Ohio I would walk for miles and think nothing of it.* But walking here was different. The main streets were of cobblestone or paving bricks, bumpy and uneven. Where there were walkways, the boards were uneven.

Since Boston was near the ocean, Joshua had imagined the waters would provide cooling breezes to the city. But where he now walked, the sun bore down without interruption of tree or cloud. The air was still and had a cloying, sweaty wetness. Joshua had grown up living next to cows, pigs, and chickens—each with an earthy muskiness of their own. But Boston smelled different. There were horses, to be sure, but also the scents of neighborhoods—the aromas of food stalls, the produce peddlers, alcohol, and waftings of tobacco pipe smoke. This heady combined fragrance promised something more . . . more exotic, more foreign, more enticing.

Joshua wiped his brow with his sleeve, shifted his bags, and walked on.

Boston was noisy. Wagons clattered on the hard streets, horses' hooves clopped, and whistles and sirens sounded behind him and from a distance. A peddler cried out, his voice only a bit louder than the clattering of the tinware pots and kettles stacked high on his wagon.

"Milk! Fresh milk!"

Another offered fresh oysters. And another held up the morning newspaper, calling out the headlines, "Labor Unions Legalized! Massachusetts Supreme Court Rules Labor Unions Legal!" Among the peddlers were young boys and girls—*mere children,* Joshua thought—selling matches, toothpicks, and flowers.

Just underfoot was the steady hum and clank of a city—a city alive and breathing. As Joshua walked upon its streets and felt Boston's pulsing breath, anticipation quickened his pulse but also nicked his heart with fear.

This is what I've dreamed about all my life, he thought, *and I cannot believe it has all come to pass.*

To his left was the golden dome of the state capitol. Harvard lay to the north of that, he knew, across the Charles River. A church spire reached up over the city's buildings, most of them red brick or white clapboard. Neat and tidy houses, crowded shutter to shutter, flanked Joshua's walk. Verandas with shiny painted railings and flower boxes lined the street. He turned left, then right, then left again.

Stopping at a corner, he lowered his bags, flexed his fingers, and massaged his sore arms. He took a step forward and, through a narrow gap in the buildings, could see a bridge and the glimmer of water. Turning toward a man who leaned against a cart stacked high with potatoes and cabbages, Joshua pointed toward the river.

"Is that the bridge one would take to Harvard?" he asked, careful with each word, avoiding the slurred and loopy speech of backwoods Ohio.

It was obvious the short and swarthy man couldn't see what Joshua gestured toward. From his mouth came a torrent of clipped words—none that Joshua knew or could begin to understand.

"Cambridge?" Joshua asked loudly and slowly, pointing again toward the north and the river.

The dark-eyed man chattered off a dozen unintelligible words, then said, "New bridge. Craigie's Bridge." He nodded in a most friendly manner, pointed, and added, "Cambridge three mile."

Joshua smiled back. "Thank you."

The little man touched the bill of his cap as Joshua walked past.

Cambridge, Massachusetts

Nearly an hour later Joshua stood in the center of Cambridge, at Harvard Square—the hallowed home of America's first institution of higher learning for two centuries.

To his left was the new astronomy observatory he had read about. To his right was the tall clock tower, complete with cupola and bell, over Harvard's imposing administration building. With the dozens of granite columns flanking the building, it looked every bit like a heathen Greek temple Joshua had seen once in a drawing.

Joshua tried to feel a sense of awe but could not. He was too tired and sweaty and thirsty and hungry, and more than a little confused. He wiped his brow with his sleeve, spun completely around, his eyes searching for a clue as to where to begin his new life.

Ten minutes later Joshua stood on the street where his new home was supposedly situated, a mere two and a half blocks from the clock tower and the school commons. Yet even in that short distance, Joshua had made two wrong turns and asked three people for directions—none of whom seemed eager to stop and talk.

They move so fast here, he noticed. *Like farmers before a harvest rainfall.*

"619 Follen Street," he said aloud. He looked at the house numbers, then down at the penciled address on the back of his acceptance letter.

To Joshua, the choice of housing had been nearly as important as the school. His tuition was underwritten by a scholarship funded by a group of rural churches in Shawnee County that pooled a fraction of their tithes every week to train local pastors' sons for the ministry. Joshua was the first son to have asked for the scholarship. In the small world of southern Ohio, Joshua's intelligence and ability burned brightly.

But living costs were to be borne by the student or his family. Joshua's parents had saved for years, but it had been a penny here, a nickel there. Joshua had only the sum needed for train fare and his first two months' rent. After sixty days, he would be on his own.

He knew that was proper. After all, he'd be having an easy time at school compared to his father and mother, who would have to work twice as hard on their tiny plot of land to make up for his absence during the fall's harvest and spring plantings.

Now Joshua stared up at the rambling, three-story white clapboard house before him. It looked crisp and tidy—at least at a distance.

As he walked closer, he saw the front of the house was an inviting jumble of dark-green shutters, wide porches, railings, stairways, and doors. Ivy covered much of the first floor and curled its way to the second.

The petite and thoroughly wrinkled landlady, Hazel Parsons, was expecting him. They made their way painstakingly up the first floor stairway, where Mrs. Parsons stopped, breathing hard, then continued on to the third floor.

Joshua spoke up. "I could take the key, Mrs. Parsons. I'm sure I could find it."

She did not stop her trudge upstairs.

"Mrs. Parsons?" Joshua called out, more loudly this time, reminding him of the number of deaf farmers in his father's church. But Mrs. Parsons still didn't stop. By the time he decided to try again, she'd made it to the top of the stairs. Apparently winded, she clutched at her chest with one hand and pointed with the other toward the porch at the rear of the house. Joshua saw a door almost hidden by the branches of an elm tree that had grown close to the roof.

"You'll have to push the branches aside, Mr. Quibbner. Haven't anyone to prune them back just now."

"It's Quittner, Mrs. Parsons," he called out, almost shouting. "Joshua *Quittner*, not Quibbner."

"Quibbner. That's what I said, young man." Mrs. Parsons muttered under her breath, "Nice boy, but can't hear worth beans." Unlocking the door, she stood aside, ushered him in, and gave him the key. "Rent's due the first and fifteenth. No liquor. No women. No hooliganism."

"You don't have to worry about that, Mrs. Parsons," Joshua called out. "I'm attending the divinity school."

She eyed him closely, leaning toward him. "Divinity school?" she said, sniffing. "Don't look like a preacher to me."

And with that, Joshua was left alone. He lowered his bags and glanced around the twelve-by-twelve-foot room, noticing the one wall that stood short due to the roofline. The walls, covered with wide, inexpensive planking, had been painted white years prior, and now threads of dark brown wood and knotholes peeked through. The floor, partially covered by a braided rug, glowed the color of a butternut squash in the sun. There was a washstand with a pitcher, a basin, and a long looking glass. A large, ancient bed with a quilt of reds and browns stood under the eaves, and a bedside table held a globe-shaded lamp. A single wardrobe and fireplace took up much of the free wall, and a plain desk with an oil lamp and a chair filled the other wall.

The room was nearly twice the size of his at home. And he had his own window, even though it was only a dormer! Joshua felt powerful and free as he first stood in the middle of this space—his space—and drank in his surroundings.

He walked over to the window, parted the starched white cotton curtains, and gazed out at Cambridge. Bending to the sash, he forced it open, the dry wood squealing. With the door open a crack, a slight breeze washed through the room, and coolness began to replace the hot staleness.

He stripped down and washed the grime of the last three days from his body. *Amazing what soap and water can do for a man's soul,* he thought.

Now clean and wearing a fresh shirt and trousers, he faced another challenge. Not simply hungry, he was famished. He vowed that, regardless of the cost, he would eat until he was full this day. He might scrimp tomorrow, but not today. Making sure his door was locked, he headed toward the stairway.

At the bottom of the steps stood a young man who would play a part in changing his life forever.

⁂

"Careful there, my good man!" boomed a voice from downstairs.

Joshua leaned over the third-story railing on the street side of the house. Parked in front of 619 Follen Street was the largest and most laden livery wagon Joshua had ever seen. Men swarmed around it, lifting steamer trunks and wooden cartons, hefting them to their shoulders and staggering toward the house.

On the second-floor landing stood a tall fellow, near to Joshua's age, wearing a white suit with silver buttons and a brightly striped cravat. He turned, and the afternoon sun outlined his profile:

classically handsome, Joshua would recall later, with a chiseled nose, strong jaw, and a shock of dark hair.

Joshua's hard-soled shoes must have sounded loud, for this fellow suddenly squinted up the stairs.

"Say, you must be the new fellow," he called out, bounding up the steps three at a time, extending his hand before he was halfway to the top. "Gage Davis," he said. "Actually, I'm Gage Davis the second, though I never use that appellation. Too pretentious, don't you think?"

Once at the top of the steps, Gage grabbed Joshua's hand and pumped it with a surprising, refreshing vigor.

"Joshua Quittner," Joshua replied. "From Ohio. Shawnee."

Gage's dark eyes pierced Joshua, knowing, yet unthreatening. "Never heard of it," he replied. "Shawnee, I mean. Ohio I have heard of . . . once or twice at any rate. Indians out there, right? Tomahawks and scalpings and all that?"

Joshua fumbled for a reply.

Gage clapped him on the shoulder, as one would a long-lost brother, and laughed. "You must get used to my feeble attempts at humor, Joshua, now that we share the same address. I am jesting, I assure you. I've been to Cleveland—a right smart city it is, I must say. I've just never heard of Shawnee before. Southern part of the state?"

Joshua felt tumbled over, washed along by a raging river of good-will and immediate camaraderie. He could manage only a nod.

"Well, then, that's settled," Gage said. "No Indians at all—just a burg in the southern counties. Shipping? Logging? Factories? Which is it?"

Oh, he must mean my family business, Joshua thought.

"Uh . . . farming, of a sort . . . and preaching."

"Preaching?" Gage questioned.

"I'll be studying for a three-year term at the divinity school starting Monday," Joshua said, finally getting out a complete sentence.

"Divinity school? Well, I'll be . . . ," Gage said, his voice trailing off. Then, placing his arm about Joshua's shoulders, he leaned in close. "This is a perfect serendipity. You'll be here, above me," he said with a sweep of his other arm, "making sure I do nothing too dangerous, foolish, or illegal." He released Joshua's shoulder. "It will be like having a conscience. Won't that be grand?"

Feeling as clumsy as a new foal on a field of spring ice, Joshua gathered up his poise to ask a question. "I was on my way out to find a restaurant . . . that isn't too dear. I haven't had a decent meal since I left home over three days ago. Perhaps there is a place you could recommend?"

Gage brightened. "Another serendipity. I am feeling most peckish myself. And, yes, I do know of a wonderful place close to here. I trust you don't think this too forward, my inviting myself to dine with you. But we are sharing the same address."

"Why, yes, of course. I would welcome the company," Joshua said, hoping his words sounded as polished and sure as Gage's.

Despite being dazzled and overwhelmed by this fast-talking, somewhat brash young man, Joshua also began to feel a growing sense of ease for the first time in many days. He'd worried about fitting in at Harvard. After all, he came from a town no one had ever heard of.

Gage called out some last-minute directions to the stevedores and teamsters unloading his myriad trunks from the wagon, then whispered to Joshua, "I have a tendency to overpack a little."

They had walked a block from the house when Joshua asked, "What is this place we're going to? It's not a saloon, is it?"

"Land sakes no, Joshua," Gage said, laughing. "I won't so soon lead you into temptation. The place is one of my favorite haunts. You'll love it, just you wait. It's called the Destiny Café."

⚜

After plowing through a hearty portion of a rich stew of corned beef, potatoes, carrots, cabbage, squash, and turnips, a hunk of Boston brown bread, three steins of a tart cider, and two tasty apple dumplings, Joshua sighed with satisfaction and pushed away from the table.

Gage had ordered a cold roast beef sandwich and stein of ale. He grabbed it when delivered and wandered about the room, greeting others, sitting and talking at this table, then another. It appeared to

Joshua that his housemate knew just about every person in the café. His newfound friend had been right about the food. It was plentiful, palatable, and, even for a small-town boy like Joshua, surprisingly affordable.

Only three blocks from 619 Follen, and a few from Harvard Commons, the Destiny Café seemed to be a most popular spot for returning students. The large room, filled with a happy clattering of voices and plates, was pleasantly worn and faded. Round wooden tables scarred with use and mismatched chairs were arranged haphazardly. The walls, mellowed to a light umber, bore the scrawled signatures from generations of Harvard students. The tin ceiling was covered with a smoky haze from oil lamps, and cozy leather-seated booths lined the walls. Joshua guessed there was no one over the age of thirty there, save for the sour-faced owner. He was perched on a tall stool by the counter, a locked cash box at his elbow.

As Joshua finished his last bite the waitress sauntered past and asked, in a honeyed voice, if he might like a cup of coffee or an ale. Joshua looked up into her face and flushed. He'd never been comfortable around women, and the waitress was comely, with big brown eyes and an inviting smile.

"Uh . . no thanks, miss," he stammered. "I think I've had enough for today."

She hugged her serving tray, crossing her arms.

"Are you a new student at Harvard?" she asked, flashing that smile again.

He knew his face was reddening, and he struggled to hold his voice in check.

"Yes, I am . . . or will be . . . at the school . . . I mean the divinity school."

The waitress arched her eyes in surprise. "Well, that's a pity. But I'm sure I'll see you again. Everybody comes to the Destiny. My name is Melinda."

"J-J-Joshua," he replied.

And with that she headed back to the kitchen.

Melinda, Joshua thought. *That's a pretty name.*

A second later two thoughts popped into his mind:. *Why didn't I say that to her?* and *What should a divinity student look like?*

After a moment of silence, he surprised himself by grinning. *I'm going to like it here.*

⚜

"A very good place to eat," Joshua said as he and Gage walked back to Follen Street. "Lots of food and inexpensive. We don't have anything like that in Shawnee."

"Next time try the clam chowder," Gage replied. "It's delicious. There are better restaurants in town, of course, but the Destiny is close and convenient."

"Is this your second year at Harvard?" Joshua asked, knowing it could not be Gage's first, since he was so familiar with the place.

"My second, less a half. There was a bit of disagreement after my first year as to which courses I passed and which I did not. Yet now I've settled into a firm routine. Business classes mostly, which my father approves of. Philosophy, which my mother thinks will improve my cultural standing. And the study of poetry, which neither of them wishes to understand."

Much more relaxed now that his hunger was satisfied, Joshua felt less frazzled and unnerved. Cambridge was still a long way from Shawnee, but even after these first hours, Joshua had a growing sense of peace.

"When do you think the others will be moving into the house?" Joshua asked as they turned onto Follen. "I haven't seen any yet, have you?"

Gage smiled. "There won't be any others."

"But there must be a half-dozen rooms on the second floor alone. Surely Mrs. Parsons would have them rented by now."

"She has."

"But you said there won't be any more fellows arriving," Joshua said. "I don't understand."

"I've rented them all," Gage replied.

"A dozen rooms?" Joshua asked incredulously.

"Actually, it's fourteen rooms—but it's more like one big suite of rooms now. I had my carpenters open up doorways and move a few walls last year."

"But . . ."

"I was actually looking for a house to buy during the last term," Gage said matter-of-factly, "but the closest one was nearly eight blocks away. And that would not do. I like to sleep late in the morning."

Joshua stopped and stared at Gage, who had walked ahead several paces. "And the whole second floor is your apartment?"

"No, not the whole second floor . . . alone. I use the rest of the rooms on the third floor, too—for storage mostly. Don't know why I overlooked that small room in the corner . . . but apparently Mrs. Parsons did not. That's the room you have now."

"You've rented out an entire floor and a half of that big house?" Such expansiveness was rare in Shawnee.

"Well, yes," Gage replied. For an instant, Joshua thought Gage looked a tiny bit sheepish. But the moment soon passed.

"It's a great residence. School is close, the Destiny is a pleasant stroll away, and best of all, Mrs. Parsons is deaf. I don't think she sees very well after dark, either. If you're careful, you can do anything you want."

Joshua had not taken another step. "Gage, just what does your family do? I mean, as a trade."

As soon as the words poured from his mouth, Joshua realized he had no business asking such a private question. Back home you didn't inquire about such things until the other person brought it up. Even so, you could guess farming and be right 95 percent of the time.

"Well, Joshua," Gage replied, without the slightest hesitation or discomfort, "we make money. Lots of it."

FROM THE JOURNAL OF JOSHUA QUITTNER
OCTOBER 1842

How absolutely delicious, yet often puzzling, these first two months have been—a whirlwind of experiences, ideas, and emotions. To put them onto paper is to do a disservice to the richness of this time, but yet I must.

On my first Sunday on campus, I sought out a church in which to worship. There is a large Presbyterian church several blocks from 619 Follen Street. Perhaps it will be my church home away from Ohio. It was comforting to slip into a pew and to experience a familiar service, though more polished than I'm accustomed to. The music, swelling out from an immense pipe organ, was grand, and the preaching infinitely more erudite and studied than back home in Shawnee. The pastor, in a black flowing robe and purple vestment, spoke on Paul's letter to the Corinthians. Up to this point I had considered myself well schooled in the Bible, yet I struggled to keep pace with the sermon. If this is what's considered preaching here, then I have much work to do. To be a preacher such as this, speaking with power and theological authority, stirring the hearts of men and women to uphold the Scriptures, and to impact their minds— that is, and has been, my dream . . . and my father's dream for me, as it was his father's dream and his father before him . . . a family legacy of dreams.

But after the first week of classes, I despair over my dream ever coming to fruition.

To be certain, every student, save myself and other obvious rustics, must have had the luxury of growing up coddled—attending the best of schools, with money, privilege, and all extravagances. These students possess an ease of knowledge I dare not dream possible. I must delve into my books until the gray shank of dawn colors the sky, burning the midnight oil merely to stay abreast. Most fellows in my class seem nary to crack the spine of a book, and the facts roll off their tongues in melodious, studied tones that the professors appear to lap up.

And the professors—liberal to the core, from what I can glean. I have heard the word *universalism* often whispered at the edges of students' conversations. I admit some remarks made in class lead me to believe that some of my professors harbor views that allow man not one path to God but many and say that the Scriptures allow for a road to heaven that perchance does not enter through the door of Christ.

Even writing these words, I feel a tightness in my heart. These learned men are misguided, and even though I'm a new student, I can see the error of such words. Will I continue to sit quietly as they espouse such ideas? Should I speak out? Or should I learn what I can and discard the chaff?

Such are the trials and tribulations of a first-year divinity student. In time, no doubt, I will have these weighty matters sorted out.

Yet there is more than simply attending classes and studying. Much, much more.

What of simpler matters–like living and eating and the rest?

It is certain that Gage Davis, the fellow who shares the house with me at 619 Follen, has taken me under his wing. He's instructing me in the basics of the cultured life and proper behavior on this cosmopolitan campus–including what is, and what is not, proper to wear. Joshua Quittner, late of Shawnee, Ohio, is now puzzling over style and cut, rather than hoping the frayed edges of his attire will not be noticed. Gage, in a fabulously generous gesture, has lent me a veritable gentleman's wardrobe–perhaps two dozen topcoats, waistcoats, and trousers, with shirts, vests, cravats, and socks to match. "Since we are of the same stature, you may as well enjoy them. I will never need them all," he said. Then he confided in me that he has a weakness for good tailoring.

I've never met such a wealthy person. The richest man in Shawnee County, as far as I know, was Spider Jeffreys, who owned five hundred acres of good bottomland near the river. He seldom ventured far from his tract, chasing off strangers with a rusty flintlock. From what my father preached from the pulpit, I imagined a rich man might be more imperious and taken with himself. That does not seem the case with Gage. I like him.

On more than one occasion I have descended the stairs with a "borrowed" ensemble of clothes, feeling grand. Gage steps out from his suite, looks me over, and either nods–and I go on my way–or he raises an eyebrow and grins. It's that look that causes me to return and alter my choice.

I must admit that, dressed in stylish attire, I have begun to feel more at ease here at Harvard, and in some ways, more sophisticated. Perhaps my rough edges have become, or are becoming, less visible.

Such is the way of the world, is it not?

And did not Paul say that in Rome, he acted as a Roman might act. Is that not what I'm doing?

CHAPTER TWO

Cambridge, Massachusetts
November 1842

JOSHUA blinked at the sun, rising red and gold to the east. He stretched, then sat upright. Even though it was a Saturday, it meant no rest.

The sky, billowed with clouds, was bluer than it ever had been in Ohio, Joshua thought. He speculated that the deep color was caused by sea breezes that often slipped up the Charles River, cleaning the air, carrying with them a hint of salt and adventure. Although he knew it would probably be warm by noonday, he slipped on his old trousers, a thick wool shirt, his coat with its patched elbows, and comfortable boots.

When he left his room, he took care not to make clumping noises. No one in the house rose early, so Joshua went to great lengths not to disturb them on his way out.

Back in Ohio, Uncle Hiram had been convinced a small-town lad such as Joshua would fall quickly to the devil's charms in the big city.

So far, Joshua thought to himself on occasion, *I see no greater depravity in Cambridge than I saw in Shawnee. They simply describe their sins with a better vocabulary.*

Yet his uncle had been absolutely right about one thing: Ohio money was not the same as Boston money. Ohio money was smaller, Joshua painfully realized, and it didn't travel as far as it did back home. Uncle Hiram had insisted that Joshua's purse would soon be as empty as a farmer's cider jug at the end of a day of plowing.

Books were more dear than Joshua imagined. And studying as hard and long as he did brought out a fierce appetite in him that required three meals a day, if not more, to satisfy. Though the Destiny Café was inexpensive, the cost of three meals times seven days added up quickly.

He had tried, on several occasions, to purchase raw foodstuffs and put them together himself, with his fireplace as a cookstove. But after cleaning the grease it created off the floor, the pot, and himself, he realized that his effort to be thrifty actually cost him twice: once to purchase the food, only to throw it out as inedible because of his limited cooking abilities, and then having to slink to the Destiny for food that was palatable.

During his first week at 619 Follen, Joshua had arranged a reduced rent with Mrs. Parsons in exchange for carpentry and handyman work. His energy and willingness to work had garnered her recommendation to other widows who owned large houses. Thus, by the end of October, he had secured five other handyman positions, earning a few extra dollars. It was just enough, he calculated, to arrive at the end of the month with at least pocket change remaining—and a full stomach.

Joshua spent the early morning chopping, splitting, and stacking firewood for Mrs. Bowder, a young widow who lived on Berkelye Street. It had become warm, as he'd expected, and he removed his coat. Mrs. Bowder closely supervised Joshua, flittering about him as he carried the ricks of wood into the house to fill the wood boxes for the kitchen stove and three fireplaces on the first floor.

"Please be sure the parlor fireplace has enough wood," Mrs. Bowder said. "I'm having my spiritualist circle meeting here tonight, and we mustn't be cold."

Joshua had heard whispers of the use of "mediums," who conducted séances to contact departed loved ones. It was a practice not of God—of that he was sure. He wondered if he should say something to her about this deceptive practice.

She must be lonely now that her husband has passed on, he thought as he glanced up at her face, faintly lined with grief at so young an age. *Next week perhaps . . . I will tell her next week. I have too much to do this day, and I do not know this woman well.*

When he left, he brushed the wood chips from his clothing as best he could and shook his head to clear the chips from his hair. He knew he needed a bath and a change of clothes. When Mrs. Bowder gazed at him intensely, he thought, *In Ohio, I could wear this outfit for another week, and no one would care or notice. In Cambridge, people definitely notice. Though most are too polite to mention it, I can read their thoughts by their wrinkling expression.*

He didn't realize it wasn't his clothing Mrs. Bowder was staring at.

His task completed, he headed back toward Follen Street, then stopped, frozen nearly in midstep.

Coming toward him, from the direction of the house, was Gage Davis. For a Saturday morning, that alone was a rare sight. On weekends Gage rarely, if ever, awakened before noon. Joshua knew by the length of his shadow that the hour was well before twelve.

But what was more arresting, what had stopped Joshua in his tracks, was Gage's companion.

The young blond-haired woman wore a dress the color of pond ice; a gossamer lace shawl was draped about her fine shoulders. Later, as Joshua attempted to describe her attire, all he could recall were two most delicate arms wrapped in a perfect white haze. While her dress was not cut too daring, Joshua felt his eyes drawn to the expanse of her fair skin below her throat. He willed himself only to look upon her face.

It was a most difficult task.

If she wore a bonnet, Joshua did not remember. Her eyes captured his own before he could see farther.

She was not classically beautiful or powdered like many of the

Boston ladies Joshua had noticed before this day, but she was more memorable than all of them combined. Joshua was sure, even after a glance, that any man would remember her days, weeks, even years later: the quick smile, flawless skin, and eyes the color of dark, wet moss beside a shaded brook.

Joshua barely remembered Gage hailing him and performing the introductions. What he *did* remember, with a vivid shock, was the warm touch of her hand through its thin glove as she extended it to his own. And when she smiled, it was the wondrous light of approval.

"Morgan Collins," Gage said, "though I am certain she uses the 'Morgan' merely to confuse and confound."

"The gentleman speaks not a word of truth," she said, laughing.

Joshua must have stood mute as he held her hand.

"Close friends call her Hannah–that's her middle name," Gage added.

Her laughter flitted into the chilled air as if the sun had come from behind the clouds and a chorus of birds had graced the air.

"You will call me Hannah, won't you, Mr. Quittner?"

When Joshua mumbled yes to her query, she returned her arm to Gage's arm.

"We are on our way to meet Hannah's uncle at the Boston train depot," he explained. "He's come all the way from Philadelphia for a firsthand report on his niece. His shameless niece, I might add."

Hannah gently elbowed Gage and shifted her eyes away as a hint of a blush crept onto her cheeks.

Gage laughed, then said loudly, enjoying his own theatrics, "My sweet Hannah has signed up for, and is actually attending, the course in human anatomy offered by the Harvard medical college–with its consequent intimacies. I'm sure they only admitted her because they thought the 'Morgan' on the enrollment list was a man. And when this demure young woman showed up . . . well, need I say more?"

She giggled. Joshua did not know why, but *he* began to blush. Hannah looked back up, finding his eyes again.

"Perhaps you will join Gage and me at the Destiny this evening."

"If your uncle doesn't rescue you from a dangerous life at Harvard, spiriting you back to your home and the blue-blooded society in Philadelphia, that is," Gage said, chuckling, as they stepped off toward town and the hackney stand on the main square.

Joshua watched them walk away. Hannah turned back once and waved a gloved hand. It was only then that Joshua became aware of his jaw, hanging open.

FROM THE JOURNAL OF JOSHUA QUITTNER
NOVEMBER 1842

Today I have abandoned my tasks. Even my books lay strewn across my unmade bed, unopened. Instead of spending time in serious studies, I must write in this journal.

A whirlwind has descended, I'm afraid.

I have met a woman, Morgan Hannah Collins of Philadelphia, Pennsylvania. Her wondrous appearance defies my feeble attempts at description. It's curious. I'm sure I've met more beautiful women, but there is something about the combination of her features that alone or singularly would be unremarkable but together add up to a remarkable visage.

Gage introduced us (and me in my worn work clothes!) and made light of the fact that she has registered for a medical anatomy class. I've come to find out, from reading the course offering in the Harvard catalog, that a cadaver will be dissected. I am shocked, I think, that a woman as gentle as she plans on attending such a class. A young woman peering at an unclothed body—perhaps even a man's—and then lifting a keen blade to cut beneath its skin?

Such an idea would be most scandalous in Ohio.

Such an image shakes my sensibilities.

Are she and Gage old family friends? He did call her "my sweet Hannah." Was that indicating an advanced level of intimacy?

I might pray—even though such a matter is not to be prayed about—that they are simply friends and that Gage's language is an example of his usual hyperbole.

I've stared out the window for most of the afternoon. The shadows are beginning to lengthen.

Perhaps I shall take her up on her kind offer to meet later at the Destiny.

⚜

"Gage! Miss Collins!" Joshua called out. "Over here."

Joshua stood, motioning to Gage and Hannah from a corner table at the Destiny. He had sat there for nearly an hour, hoping that each time the door opened it would be them.

His heart sank a bit as a second young man followed them inside.

Then Hannah smiled again, and for Joshua the rest of the room disappeared, as if an autumn fog had fallen about the place.

"Did he attempt to spirit you away?" Joshua asked as he rose and drew out a chair for Hannah.

"Spirit me away?" she replied, confused.

Joshua immediately wished his words could be withdrawn. He tried not to wince in embarrassment, knowing how inept he felt in her company.

"Your uncle . . . Gage said he might try and . . . you know . . . take you back to Philadelphia."

Their second meeting was but seconds old, yet was going so absolutely wrong that Joshua wished he could step outside the Destiny and begin again.

Then Hannah tilted her head back and laughed.

Joshua panicked. Was she laughing at him? Was she making sport of his country ways? Gage, now sitting next to her, joined in her laughter.

"I'm sorry, Joshua. I misled you. You've been a casualty of my ill-placed humor again. Uncle Winthrop's visit concerned her trust fund—nothing more than boring dollars and cents." He glanced over at Hannah. "If you were ever to meet Uncle Winthrop, you would understand the reason for our laughter. He is not a man who could spirit anyone off. Not now. Not ever."

Hannah laughed even harder. "He is a wisp, Joshua. To him, even the train ride from Philadelphia was a journey of Homeric proportions. He actually had his case handcuffed to his wrist for fear of highway banditry. He'd think that traveling on a train from Ohio, like you did, my friend, would be akin to traveling over Niagara Falls in a barrel."

Relief swept over Joshua like a cooling shower. Now Hannah's laughter was sweet to his ears.

The fellow at the far end of the table, who had been silent while they were being seated, now caught Joshua's attention.

"It seems my well-mannered and well-bred friends have taken leave of their upbringing," he said, his voice somber and dark. "I'm Jamison Pike."

Joshua reached over and shook his hand. "The 'J. Pike' of the *Crimson Review?*"

Jamison looked pained, then tried to smile. "He and I are one and the same."

"I always look for your name when I read the newspaper," Joshua replied. "Your work is so well written. The rest of the paper pales in comparison."

Gage watched with amusement. "Harvard's premier cynic, hailing from Pittsburgh's smoky inferno, meets Harvard's most pure and unsullied student from Ohio's green cornfields." Then to Hannah he added, "You'd have thought there would be greater emotional disturbance when the two shook hands, wouldn't you?"

"Neither of you should pay him any mind," Hannah chided. "If the Davis and Collins families had not been socially acquainted before, I would have nothing to do with this horrid person."

Gage signaled for the server. "It's true, Hannah. You know it is. Joshua is the embodiment of everything right with America. Pure of heart and mind, strong of body, noble in purpose, divine in aspirations. What more could the nation ask for?"

Jamison listened with a wry smile. Joshua was simply confused.

"And Mr. Pike is the antithesis of all that. Despite his strict, pious upbringing, he sees nothing noble in man's aspirations. Thinks that moral betterment is an oxymoron. I'm sure he secretly harbors desires for a better world but knows that, if it were to happen, he'd have no subject matter for his writing."

"You're terrible," Hannah said. "Our Mr. Pike is not the soulless wretch you describe. Say you are not, Jamison. Tell him the truth."

Hannah's eyes lit up as she defended Joshua and Jamison. Her cheeks flushed, not in anger, but in delight of this intellectual combat.

Picking up his coffee, Jamison sipped loudly, then spoke. "He's right, Hannah. I am a soulless cynic. If there could be heaven on earth, there would be no need for writers like me. I need both man's moral aspirations and his inevitable failures in order to exist. Simple folk need me to trace the well-intended fool's ascendancy as well as his plummet back to earth. If noble people like Mr. Quittner did not attend Harvard, I'd no doubt vanish like a puff of smoke in a storm."

Hannah looked shocked for a moment, then broke into peals of laughter. Jamison held his stern grimace a second longer, then began to laugh as well.

Joshua could not help but chuckle with Hannah, feeling a light-heartedness at this shared experience. He knew they were, in a gentle manner, making sport of him and his rural, naive ways. But yet, to be part of such a smart and cosmopolitan group allayed any pain of being politely mocked.

⁂

A single lamp illuminated the table. The rest of the Destiny was deserted. From the kitchen behind them, they could hear the soft clatter of tableware being washed. All four were currently silent, having talked for nearly five hours. Joshua enjoyed the easy banter as they discussed such diverse subjects as theater, steamboats, the potential of the telegraph, the use of anesthetics, and the tales of Nathaniel Hawthorne. Such topics would be unimaginable in Shawnee.

Well, Joshua reconsidered, *maybe telegraph lines, but only so one farmer might complain to another about the poles along the roadway.*

Hannah sat up straight in her chair and adjusted the patterned silk shawl around her shoulders. Though they sat near the fireplace, a hint of chill prickled the evening air. Joshua watched the fabric drape across her arms and fall into delicate folds.

She looked up and met his eyes.

He prayed this evening might never end.

She studied him, then Jamison, then Gage.

"Gage," she asked, her voice edging to a feminine low, "what will you do with your life after Harvard?"

Gage appeared surprised.

"Has no one asked you this question before?" Her voice had grown soft. Her hand touched Gage's forearm with the lightest pressure, then traveled to his starched cuff.

Gage pondered the question, then replied, "Why, no . . . they haven't, really. I suppose it's always been assumed that I'll work for my father, someday taking over the family's concerns." He pushed back from the table, his brow furrowed. "It's not that I resent that presumption of my future, but . . ."

He sipped at his cold coffee. "I suppose I'll do what's expected, for the lure of wealth is strong indeed. And I must say I find the accoutrements of wealth to be most satisfying. Perhaps it's shallow of me, but I do enjoy crisp white linen sheets, boats, opera, and champagne now and again, and find actual manual labor stultifying. It's hard to combine the two." He looked down at his hands. "And, of course, having as much fun as possible every day."

No one spoke for several moments.

Hannah turned to Jamison. "And what of our heartless cynic? What will you do?"

He snorted. "There is a future? Are you sure?"

She reached over and shoved at his shoulder with a childlike playfulness. "Being a cynic is surely too hard of a vocation for a gentleman like you," she responded lightly. "You must hold other dreams. Travel? Adventure? Romance?"

Jamison shook his head. "Women!" he said. "How well they know the desires of a simple man."

Surprised, Hannah said, "So it's true what I thought, is it not? You are like a little boy, I imagine. You want to travel the world, have grand adventures, find romance. You are like that little boy, aren't you, Jamison?"

He nodded. "Maybe not a little boy, but that's what I want. And it's not just simple adventure. I want to see what is out there, and I want to write about it—perhaps for a New York newspaper. I want to see the world while there are mysteries left to explore—before nature is sullied by man. I want to see what no one else has yet seen. I want to tell the truth of what I see—unvarnished and uncolored—warts and all. Not like the tripe you see in most newspapers."

"And that's why you carry a notebook with you always?" Hannah asked. "I see the hard edge protruding from your waistcoat pocket."

Joshua watched her face carefully as her eyes coyly probed Jamison's frame.

"One must write to remember," Jamison replied, tucking the notebook out of sight. "And an unremembered life will come to vapor at the end. Stories need to be told."

"And what of you, Joshua? What will your story be? What will you become—our sweet innocent?" Hannah asked, reaching out and touching his wrist with the tip of her long, elegant fingers.

He fought the urge to shiver. There was no way he could resist answering her with anything but the truth.

"Why, I'll become a preacher and serve God—like my father and his father before him. I'll serve in the church like they've done. That's my destiny. That's what I'll do with my life."

Joshua's three new friends grew quiet.

"It's a most noble calling," Joshua insisted.

No one spoke.

"It is."

"Joshua," Hannah finally said, with a pause after each thought, "it truly does sound noble. . . . However, it . . . and forgive me for saying this, but your words sounded . . . rehearsed. As if you've said those phrases a thousand times before this day."

"It was *not* rehearsed," he retorted, tension nipping at his words.

More silence. It was apparent no one believed him.

Jamison broke the uncomfortableness and leaned forward, the

chair legs creaking. "And our lovely Miss Collins . . . what of your future? What will become of you following our graduation from these hallowed walls?"

She looked past him into the darkness, her hands drawing the shawl tighter around her throat, then fluttering like swallows to the table. As she lifted her head high, the lamp's glow tinted her graceful neck to a pure alabaster. After some hesitation, she smiled strangely, as if she were about to reveal a significant intimacy.

The three gentlemen held their breath in unison, waiting for her reply.

It was then that Joshua felt his heart tighten, and he became acutely aware of two fears: that he was falling in love with this woman, and that Gage and Jamison felt exactly the same way.

"I should not tell you of my foolish ambitions."

"No, please," Joshua said, almost pleading. "We've shared, and you must also. No one will find amusement in your dreams."

"Do you all promise?"

All three men nodded solemnly.

"I truly wish I might become a doctor."

Gage brightened. "For truth? A real doctor who slices into people's abdomens with shiny knives and all?"

She giggled. It looked as if Gage enjoyed making her giggle.

"Yes, a real doctor with a sharp knife . . . and I would first operate on your vocal cords."

Gage wrapped both hands about his throat in mock defense, making gagging noises.

"But yet, there's something even more." She looked at each man for a heartbeat, then lowered her eyes.

"It has to do with children . . . unfortunate children, such as those laboring in horrid factories like slaves. I know this isn't a popular cause, but my heart breaks when I see them in the streets, alone and dirty and uncared for. They roam about on their own, unsupervised and unloved. I imagine their injuries and diseases go untreated for lack of compassionate medical care. I want to help them."

Again, silence reigned at the table.

"A noble goal, I'm sure. But, Hannah," Jamison offered, "Harvard will not offer you a medical degree, despite your obvious intellect, your pedigree, and your noble dream. You may be a woman pioneer at Harvard, but you must remember that not all pioneers make it to their destination."

Hannah's eyes grew hard.

"I'm not alone. Remarkable women are fighting for the rights of women—to vote, own property, and receive higher education. Women like Elizabeth Stanton, Lucretia Mott, and . . ."

"Women whose pursuits I've written about myself. But I'm telling the truth, Hannah," Jamison interjected. "Despite my confidence in your abilities, you must know the impenetrable walls that exist to inhibit the advancement of the fair sex in the field of medicine. The ones in this institution may not crumble just yet. You may fight the good fight and still end up disappointed. You may be angry at this message, but I'm not to blame."

Hannah snorted. "You are not to blame, and he is not to blame, and he is not to blame," she said, pointing at her three friends. "Men! Every one says he is not to blame." Her words sounded shrill in the darkened restaurant. "I'm not accusing anyone. I simply want what I want."

The three men sat back, shocked, leaning from the light into the safer shadows.

"I've heard Oberlin may allow such things," she said calmly, lifting her chin, her words precise.

"Oberlin? I'd not spend the night in Oberlin, much less four years," Gage remarked with condescending finality. "No offense to Ohio, Joshua, but Oberlin, well, that's another story."

She glared at him, then softened. "I know, I know . . . it is a dream that may prove most impossible." Then she added darkly, "Most likely I'll find a rich young man and settle down in a fine house with all the right furnishings, do needlework, attend teas and charities, and raise proper, civilized children. That's what everyone would suspect I'll do with my life—family, friends, society." Agitated, she implored them, "But none of you feel that way, do you? Do you think I could be destined to do something extraordinary? Might I pursue my dream despite the obvious barriers? It's not impossible, is it? You agree I should try, don't you?"

To a man, all three agreed.

"But then again," she said, breaking the somber mood with a laugh, "I may run off with the circus. After all, I'll have had practice dealing with nature's oddities after spending my college years with the likes of you three for friends."

Standing, wrapping the shawl around her, she bent over to lower the wick of the lamp. Outside the window of the Destiny, a gas light glowed faintly along the deserted street.

"I'm such a libertine. It's much too late for a proper lady to be out. Will you three gentlemen escort this fallen woman back to her residence this dark evening?"

Joshua rose and stood next to Hannah, who took his arm. He was flanked by Gage on his right and Jamison on Hannah's left.

As the four walked out, Joshua continued to pray this night would never end.

CHAPTER THREE

Cambridge, Massachusetts
February 1843

IT was February–a cruel, cold month in New England.
A harsh wind flicked at the window of Joshua's room, hardening
further the thick coating of ice that had formed across the bottom
sash. Although his breath came in puffs, Joshua was yet too preoccu-
pied to tend to the fireplace.

He lay on the bed amidst a scattering of papers and books.
Propped up next to the pillow, spread open, was his father's Bible.
Next to it was a sheaf of papers, marked with bold, scrawled handwriting–notes from his Old Testament survey class. The book he
held was a turgid discourse on the role of the minor prophets. Yet
while he worked through the notes in preparation for an upcoming
examination, Joshua fought to keep Hannah's image from flooding
into his mind and taking over all conscious thought.

Finally he let the book fall against his chest and stared out the
frozen window. His studies faded from his thoughts and turned to
more warm, pleasant matters.

Since meeting Hannah that wonderful November morning, Joshua
felt privileged to enjoy dinner with her five other times at the

Destiny Café, though never alone. Three times Gage was a member of their party; the other two evenings Jamison had sat with them. He would admit to no one but himself that those evenings had been the highlight of his time at Harvard. Her words, her smile, her laughter were to Joshua a perfect light in a dark world.

One recent evening, over the same table where they had first dined, Joshua had asked Gage about Hannah.

"She relates so little of her past," Joshua had said, "and yet she knows so much of us. It appears you know her well. I am . . . curious to know of her life."

Gage had offered a soulful smile, as if he knew Joshua's innermost longings.

"My friend," Gage had said, "it's true that the Collins and Davis families have been in acquaintance for some time. But as in many–if not all–social relationships like this, the knowledge is superficial at best. We meet at parties and make minor pleasantries, never going beneath the surface."

Gage had leaned in closer.

"I hesitate to say what I'm about to say. This is a confidence, my friend–and I know you above all other people would never betray a confidence."

Joshua had looked apprehensive but nodded.

"It's true our families have known each other for years. But we are not equals."

Joshua had bristled. "You honestly assume your family has more value than hers?"

Gage had held up his palms as defense. "Not better as people, my sensitive friend, but gauged by cold, hard resources. Hannah's father was once among the wealthiest members of Philadelphia society. They made my family look absolutely bourgeois."

Joshua's eyes had widened.

"But he lost it . . . well, at least most of it. Risky speculation, bad investments, land deals gone awry. I've heard they've let go of all their servants but two. The summer home in Rhode Island is empty. The family manse in Philadelphia is leveraged to the hilt. This is what one hears if one listens at the edge of parties, talking to the black sheep and scoundrels. Of course, those are the very people I'm most likely to find interesting," Gage had finished wryly.

"But then how could she attend Harvard?" Joshua had asked. "She looks every bit a member of a prosperous family."

"Trust funds set up before the losses. You must have noticed that she wears last year's fashions."

Joshua had not. In fact, until now, he hadn't known that women's fashions changed on a yearly basis. He had seen no evidence of it growing up in Ohio.

"I've heard rumors—from that same group of ne'er-do-wells—that her parents agreed to a Harvard education precisely so she might meet a rich husband who might offer salvation for their fortunes. 'Old money' provides great security in this troubled world, my friend."

"But she can't be as calculating as that, can she? She's not that type of woman."

"She's not," Gage said confidently. "In her heart and soul, she's not. But she also must eventually face reality. It's as easy to love a rich man as it is a poor man, so the saying goes."

Joshua had sat stunned for the remainder of that evening. Even back home, he knew, some married for love, some married because it was the proper time, some married because the arrangement offered both parties security and convenience. But he'd hoped Hannah was above such base motivations. He'd hoped she would look for the pure, righteous love of a good, solid man—no matter his financial state.

Now he pulled his quilt up to his neck and thought, *Perhaps it's hopeless, but I'm not without hope.*

⁂

Joshua's reverie was interrupted by a furious banging on his door. Peering out the window, he saw Gage standing there without a topcoat, rubbing his hands together for warmth.

"Come in," Joshua said, opening the door. "Why aren't you wearing a coat? It's freezing outside."

"And it's cold in here as well." Gage blew into his cupped hands. "We're friends, aren't we?"

Surprised, Joshua nodded.

"And friends help each other out, don't they?"

Joshua nodded again.

"Then you've got to be a real friend today. I find myself in the most precarious of predicaments."

Joshua's thoughts raced. *What predicament? How could I help a man with Gage's resources?*

"You mustn't tell Hannah," he whispered loudly.

"Tell Hannah what?"

"You mustn't tell her anything."

Is he asking me to lie for him? Why? Joshua thought.

Draping a confiding arm about Joshua's shoulder, Gage said in a conspiratorial tone, "I have a young lady in my apartment."

In the past, Joshua had observed other young lady visitors in Gage's company, and as near as Joshua could tell, their visits were cordial and polite—with no hint of wanton behavior or any manner of lasciviousness. Of that he was fairly certain. Even Mrs. Parsons had not objected. But then again, she may not have seen Gage's guests come or go. He was certain she had never heard anything.

"Yes," Joshua said slowly, "but you've entertained female guests before. Why now is it a predicament?"

"I hate to appear as a bounder," Gage replied, "but I've never made a similar commitment with two ladies simultaneously."

The predicament finally lodged in Joshua's thoughts. He began to understand the prickliness of Gage's situation.

I understand, but I'll not offer sympathy or acquiescence.

"You have a lady friend visiting?"

This time Gage nodded.

"And Hannah is involved somehow?"

"Yes," Gage said sheepishly.

"So . . . Hannah is expecting to spend the evening with you."

Gage nodded again, his head bowed slightly, though Joshua saw the hint of a smile.

"And the young lady downstairs has shown no inclination to depart?"

Gage gave up and let his smile fill his face. "She has given no hint of an immediate departure . . . not that I find such hesitation on her part objectionable in the least."

Joshua fought the urge to smile back, forcing a judgmental frown in response.

"Please, Joshua, no lectures right now. I know I deserve one, and I know what you'd say. I've heard it before. You can save it for me until tomorrow when I'll repent and promise to do better. But today, well, this is where friendship is tested. I'm in an awkward bind, and only you can help."

Joshua shook his head. "Gage . . . how could you . . ."

"Hannah is a friend—a great friend. And I know she'd understand. But I can't leave her out there in the cold. Nor can I leave here. There's no way to get a message to Hannah . . . except you, good friend."

"Me?"

"You must take my place. Be her escort in my stead."

"Escort? Hannah? To what? Tonight?"

Joshua's heart quickened as he tried to hold his excitement in check.

Gage slapped him on the back as if his reaction were agreement enough. "That's grand, Joshua. Just grand. Hannah will be at the Commons under the clock tower at 4 P.M. There are tickets to the Bach recital at the King's Chapel in Boston waiting under my name. I've arranged for dinner reservations at the Harvard Club at 8 P.M. She'll expect you to be a gentleman and provide civil, polished companionship. That I am certain you can do."

Joshua listened, yet found no words for a cogent response.

"This is a family obligation from months and months ago, when my parents and her parents were together at a soiree. She has a distant cousin or some such shirttail relative in the recital, and they decided together that I'd be Hannah's gentleman escort for the evening. But now I cannot attend. I truly cannot."

"But . . ."

"Joshua, you can easily take my place. I'm sure Hannah will be happier with you than me, if the truth be told. I find recitals to be a total bore, while you seem the type to enjoy them. Hannah will appreciate your enthusiasm over my yawning boredom. Now you must get ready. Wear the burgundy waistcoat, black trousers, the cream shirt with the black-striped stock, and the black overcoat with the fur collar."

As Gage stepped back outside, he reached into his pocket and pulled out a thickness of currency, slipping the bundle to Joshua.

"But what shall I tell her? Why would I take your place? Won't she think it odd for me to be there instead of you?" Joshua queried.

Gage shrugged and raced toward the steps. "I'm sure you'll come up with a story that makes sense. And for tonight, you are to be an absolute rake with my money. Spend it all if you have to. I trust you, above all others, Joshua, to be the man you say you are. You'll treat her with Christian decency."

Just before he was out of sight, Gage turned and called back, "Have a great evening."

As Joshua stood in the chilling breeze, he looked down at his hand. Unfolding the bills, he saw that Gage had given him one hundred dollars in ten-dollar bills. He whistled softly.

I could live for a year on this, and he wants me to spend it in one night?

Before he closed the door, he peered to his left. The clock on the church spire read 3 P.M. Dusk was edging close.

I am compromised. I must weave a fabrication to protect my friend—and Hannah's sensibilities. And he's asked me to squander more money in one night than my father's annual income.

Shaking his head, he walked toward his closet. A minute later he held up the burgundy waistcoat and began to brush specks of lint from the collar.

FROM THE JOURNAL OF JOSHUA QUITTNER
FEBRUARY 1843

How do I recap such an evening?

If words are to be my livelihood, they've now failed me.

I arrived at the Commons a few minutes early, and when Hannah arrived, I stood mute, seemingly affixed to the earth as she looked about, searching for Gage, her intended escort.

I'm awkward in describing feminine details, but I must try. She was wearing some sort of green velvet cloak with a fur-trimmed hood. Her hair was twisted up in an intricate fashion and festooned with pearls, or so I imagined them to be. She shimmered as a shooting star in the fading light.

Eventually I found my voice and called out to her. I do not recall what I said, or even the nature of the excuse I fashioned for my friend. I truly do not. But at some point in my stammered response, she laughed, and–heavens above–reached out, unbidden, and placed her hand about my forearm.

I am a rube through and through. I stared at that gloved hand resting on my arm much like a rabbit fixates on a snake.

She saw my surprise, gave my arm a squeeze, and giggled.

Giggled!

Squeezed again.

"Accompanying you this evening is unexpected, but most happily so," she said, and I remember each word with absolute clarity and fidelity.

Yes, I've been at a dinner table with her in the past, but this was different. This was a man escorting a woman on a proper social occasion.

While I know it is not, I felt the evening might be thought of as the first step . . . dare I say . . . on a long–a very long–path to courtship.

As I write this, I must disavow that notion. Hannah is wonderful, but to even think she might consider someone like myself . . . well, such is beyond comprehension.

I've stopped writing to catch my breath. It is near dawn on Sunday morning. In a few hours I'll need a somber countenance as I step to the pulpit of a Presbyterian church of Cambridge and read the Scriptures–a task that helps fulfill the practicums–the requirements needed to obtain a Harvard degree.

I do not know if I can be somber today.

I recall only scattered bits of the evening, such a whirl were my thoughts. Traveling down Brattle Street from Harvard Square to Boston, I recall the sound of bells on the horses that pulled our sleigh. Her hand rested on my arm as we walked into the church with a lofty pulpit and cushioned pews. I believe the performance was adequate, yet I remember no musical notes other than her whispered comments. We encountered Jamison there, notebook in hand, and he appeared surprised at our pairing. Later Hannah entwined her arm with mine as we strolled in the crisp winter night to the Harvard Club. Crisply starched white table linens. Silver services glinting in the candlelight. Throughout the elegant dinner she listened to my prattle as I described Ohio and the curious people of my acquaintance. We ate, among other things I cannot recall, fricasseed oysters, roast beef, and fruited pastries.

At the end of the evening, having spent more than a quarter of Gage's bankroll—a king's ransom (and I enjoyed every moment)—I saw her home. From the Commons, we walked rather than rode to her boardinghouse. Upon reaching her doorstep, she turned to face me from the shadows.

"I had a most pleasant evening, Mr. Joshua Quittner from Shawnee, Ohio," she said softly.

She smiled, and the moon disappeared.

"Tell our duplicitous Mr. Davis that I assume the woman he stood me up for was worth it."

My jaw dropped. Her smile increased.

"You are very sweet, Joshua, but a poor liar. I like that in a man."

She turned back into the door, opened it, and slipped inside, like a fragile apparition.

An hour passed as I meandered back to 619 Follen, a distance of only a few blocks. The sound of sleigh bells passing made the night's magic last a bit longer for me.

I am vexed by her charms, and I must endeavor to hold her at arm's length lest I lose sight of my calling.

CHAPTER FOUR

Shawnee, Ohio
Summer 1843

IN the shade of a chestnut grove and by a stream, six
long sawbuck tables made from pine planks and X-shaped trestle
legs groaned with food and drink. The grove was no more than a
two-minute walk from the center of Shawnee. Ladies, men, and
older children made their way there from both the church and
community at large. They carried platters, wooden bowls, and
chipped and cracked crockery piled high with roasted mutton and
venison, succotash, loaves of thick-crusted bread, pickled beets,
Indian pudding, and fruit pies. Several men handled wheelbarrows
laden with barrels of cider and one keg of ale. Others carried wheels
of cheese or baskets brimming with apples, strawberries, and vegetables only an hour or two past harvest.

Most of the town of Shawnee and virtually every member of the
Shawnee Church of the Holy Word were gathering to thank the
Lord for his goodness and the growing crops. They were also cele-
brating both the return and the all-too-soon impending departure of
Shawnee's most famous student, Joshua Quittner.

Seminary and final examinations had kept Joshua in Boston

through the end of June. Then, during an unusually hot July, he had sweated his way back west, leaning out a smoky train window for hundreds of miles. For the remainder of July and August, he'd worked diligently beside his father and uncle, tending the wheat and corn, grown high and green, to ensure a good harvest when it was time. However, Joshua could not help bring in that harvest since his classes were to begin within the week.

He would leave after his father's sermon the following day.

Joshua's emotions were mixed. He didn't feel out of place, exactly, but realized he had indeed been changed by his first year at Harvard. There was an element of polish to his bearing that had not been there before. His eyes saw the world afresh, and there was a widening difference between who he once was and who he was becoming. The roughness of his home in Shawnee and the farming life contrasted sharply with the smooth civility shown in Boston and Cambridge. Yet despite this newly formed sensibility, he remained silent about which location he preferred: Shawnee or Cambridge.

On this day of expansive celebration, Joshua found himself surrounded by a group of young men from the village. None had found previous opportunity to inquire of Joshua about the lures of the big city.

Joshua sat on a tree stump and first looked around to make sure his father and uncle were not within earshot.

"Tell us, Josh," clamored young Zebulon Morris. "Tell us what Boston is like. Is it true the houses and buildin's are smack-dab together, and they run that way for miles?"

"Is it true the women are most beautiful there?" asked another, followed by a round of eager laughter.

"And I heard tell the females are so forward they do most of the courtin'," another called out, his voice indicating he desperately wanted to believe the statement.

Joshua laughed and then held up his hand. He lowered his voice to a whisper, as if launching a conspiracy.

"Not all of what you hear is the truth, nor should you believe most of it," he said, watching the eager grins of his audience turn to sad frowns. "But some of the truth is so fantastic that even seeing it is hard to believe."

Every young man, without exception, leaned forward in rapt attention. Joshua had them in the palm of his hand.

He spoke at length, describing the energy and pace of Boston–the elegant carriages and mansions, the elaborate parties, the well-dressed people, and the tall buildings, some even six stories tall.

"Why, a man can find a meal even past midnight. Or go to a play or music hall if he prefers."

"Who on earth would stay up till then?" Zebulon called out.

Joshua just winked. "You'd be most surprised."

"Man alive!"

"What I wouldn't give to go to Boston!"

"And the women, Joshua. Is it true they are fancy and powdered and beautiful like we've heard? Do tell!"

Feeling like an explorer who had traveled to the outermost limits of the earth and was now reporting his findings to his backers, Joshua realized how hungry these young men were for news. Most of them would close their eyes for a final time without ever having traveled more than a day's walk from Shawnee.

He shut his eyes for a moment. Hannah's face came into view. With little hesitation, he decided to tell them about the evening Gage had sponsored. As he began to tell the tale, he inserted Jamison's name rather than his own. He knew that a small-town preacher had a reputation to protect–and there would be few in town who would hear this story and think it a simple and innocent dalliance. The story poured from him with practiced ease and great enjoyment. As he spoke, the images became more and more real, almost acquiring flesh with each sentence.

Mouths dropped open during his discourse–especially in his description of Hannah's physical attributes. Some nearly toppled over in their eagerness to catch every word. Near the end, he mentioned the money Gage had commanded Jamison to use in courting Miss Collins.

"Pshaw! He spent more than a double sawbuck on just one

evenin'?" Zebulon cried out. "What in blazes did they do–buy gold plates and throw them away?"

"Well, ain't that a huckleberry above a persimmon!" another voice called out.

Joshua held his hand out, trying to shush the hubbub that swept over the group when he mentioned the amount.

"Shhh," he warned, "not so loud." In their eyes Joshua saw a mixture of admiration, envy, and extreme astonishment that one of them could have entered such a rarefied atmosphere as Joshua had done.

As he whispered, he noticed several young women had gathered in a loose circle no more than a stone's toss from where he sat. He wondered if they could hear him as he told his story. He was sure they could–and did. A few bolder girls gazed directly at him, willing him to stare back and offering smiles in return. Had he not spent a year in Cambridge among men and women of style and breeding, he might have missed their intentions. But now that he was a "man of the world"–at least polished and cultured in the narrow environs of Shawnee–he knew these women were vying for his attention.

So the women in Shawnee are shy and unassuming? Joshua thought to himself with a smile. *No, it's just that they have a different way of expressing their interest.*

⚜

From near the tables, Uncle Hiram bellowed out, "Joshua! Joshua Quittner! Get over here so you can ask the blessin' on the food. Do it now, son, for we are powerful hungry."

Joshua stood up, brushed the bark and grass from his trousers, and walked over to the assembling crowd. The people formed into a ragged circle and, after a time, quieted. On Joshua's first word, every head bowed, and almost everyone clasped their hands together.

"Almighty sovereign and omnipotent God," Joshua began, using his most stentorian voice. "We, your indentured servants, assemble now at this most beautiful locale in order that we might solemnize and venerate thy divine approval. We beseech thee that, penurious sinners that we are, we might be completed and filled with thy heavenly nature. We know that it is not propitious to entreat thee respecting thy sanctified grace, but that thou proffer such largesse to us without encumbrance. We covenant to be beholden to thee for all thy gifts eternally. Amen."

The crowd, hearing at last the familiar *amen,* lifted their heads and began to move as a wave toward the tables.

Lines formed like legs radiating from a spider–the longest at the meat table. People snaked along the vegetables and wound their way to the pies and sweets. Joshua hung back, allowing the crowds to pass before him. Then, from behind him, he heard the unmistakable coughing bark of Uncle Hiram.

"Listen, Joshua," Uncle Hiram said, wheezing, "I know they taught you a lot at that fancy school, but bein' highfalutin as you were in that prayer ain't the way to impress these folks. You should know that. You're from here. And you'll be comin' back soon enough. I bet ain't more than a handful of people here understood more than a word or two of that prayer . . . that is, until you got to the 'amen' part. That they understood."

Startled, Joshua pondered how to respond until his father broke through the crowd, put his arm about his son's shoulder, and pulled him even farther from the tables.

"Let's me and you sit awhile. There's more than enough food for twice the crowd. We can wait till the line shortens."

Joshua followed his father, sitting beside him on a fallen tree. As conversation flowed around them his father looked off in the distance and spoke in a controlled voice. Later Joshua remembered thinking his father seemed close to tears. But for a man such as Eli Quittner, tears would be unthinkable.

"Son," he began, "I'm proud of you–being the first in our family to head off to college–and the first one in all of Shawnee as well. No doubt they're teaching you a good amount there."

"If it's about the prayer," Joshua interrupted, "Uncle Hiram already told me. I apologize for using a few too many five-dollar words. But that is what they teach us. God requires us to think, you know."

His father did not turn to him, nor did he frown.

"No, it's not the prayer, though that's part of it. We've been working side by side for nearly a month now. You learn a lot about where a man's heart and soul is at by working next to him."

Joshua was about to protest again.

"And it isn't your work that's suffered. You still can work harder than any two men I know. I'm not questioning your arms or your back."

"Then what?" Joshua asked.

The older man placed his hand on Joshua's muscled shoulder.

"You're a smart boy. But don't stand above them–the people you minister to. You have to be with them–standing shoulder-to-shoulder as you do the Lord's work. Men or women will suffer through a lot and support you with all their hearts if they think you're living the same life they are. But if you stand above them, looking down, you won't be serving God. You'll be serving yourself."

"But I haven't changed. I still want to serve God."

After a pause his father stood up, as if such open talk embarrassed him. His eyes fixed on the horizon.

"Son, I hope you're telling the truth. I know about serving and choices. And I know you'll be facing both of those soon enough. I never told you about this, but I had a chance to move away from Shawnee–a long time ago–just after your mother and I married. There was a bigger church up near Cleveland that asked me to consider their call. And I did. I considered it hard and long."

Joshua watched as his father reached up and wiped at his eyes.

"A big church–with a proper organ and Bibles and real hymnbooks. With a salary that meant no more farming–no more calluses or ruined crops."

Astonished by his father's secret, Joshua just sat there.

"But I looked around and saw these poor souls who really needed me here. I guess I started to love them even so soon as that first year. Each one of them looked to me to bring the Word of God to them. I knew that if I left, my brother, Hiram, would be their only preacher, the only man of the cloth within fifty miles of Shawnee. I couldn't see condemning these innocent souls to such torture!"

As a grin broke over his father's face, Joshua stared back in amazement.

"You have to be true to your heart, Joshua. And a young man needs to tame his heart to do the Lord's bidding. You have to decide, Son, if these poor folks are worth your heart and soul and mind. God asks for your all, Joshua, your all. You have to be able to give that to them."

A long silence followed. Then Joshua chanced a question.

"Have they been worth it, Father? Have they been worth your all?"

His father took a step toward the food tables, then stopped and looked down at his hands. In a soft voice he replied, "I hope so, Son. I hope so."

And then the moment was gone. His father slapped him on the back and called out in his best preacher's voice, "Let's eat before Uncle Hiram has fourths on everything."

From a shaded spot across the glen a voice called in almost angry reply, "I heard that! I'm only on my thirds, so you take that back!"

Joshua's father replied with great laughter.

Cambridge, Massachusetts
September 1843

Joshua's second trip to Boston bore scant resemblance to his first. True, the train and the distance remained the same, but no longer did he feel like a lost country bumpkin in a confusing city maze.

And if his thoughts be known, he was eager to be away from Shawnee and in the more uplifting and cosmopolitan setting that Cambridge provided. He leaned back, lost in thought and lulled into introspection as the train clattered over the rails.

He loved his home in Shawnee and the people there. Yet as much as he loved them, he also loved his new life, his new friends, and the view of the world that such a life offered. As the scenery clicked past, he wondered if it truly mattered to God where one served. Did God truly care about geography, or just a man's heart?

With long, purposeful strides he hiked from the train depot to the

Harvard campus and 619 Follen Street, eager once again to be a student.

As long as you offer him your life, Joshua concluded, *that is what he wants. That's the Almighty's desire.*

❧❦❧

His room remained unchanged. Mrs. Parsons scuttled out to greet him with an almost angry wave, then gave him a list of chores that required his immediate attention.

Joshua took the list in hand, thinking, *This feels so much like home to me now. Will I be able to tame my heart like my father said? Can such a comfortable feeling be thought of as a trial from above?*

Joshua had arrived in Cambridge on a Saturday afternoon. It was apparent Gage had not returned yet—nor had Jamison or Hannah—as he made his way to the Destiny that evening.

He entered the dimly lit interior and sat at his usual table in the back, by the window, facing the door.

Melinda, her hands full of plates and glasses, greeted him with a huge smile.

"Joshua Quittner," she called out, her voice happy, "a sight for sore eyes indeed. I'm so pleased to see you're back among us."

Joshua smoothed away the crumbs from the table.

"And I'm glad to be back, Miss Melinda," he replied.

In a moment she swung back out of the kitchen, empty-handed, and let herself drop into Joshua's lap. As she embraced him boldly, he felt his face flush. *Do I hug her back? Do I push her away?* He struggled to know what to do with his hands.

Oblivious to his dismay, she continued to hug him. He had seen her greet Gage that way on occasion, and while he knew such an action was almost bawdy, he had said nothing about it to her or Gage. But he was sure Gage was aware of Joshua's disapproval of such wanton actions.

Finally Melinda seemed to sense his reluctance. She spun away and sat in a chair next to him, elbows on the table.

"Tell me of your summer. Did you see any Indians way out west in Ohio? Gage said you would, but I don't know if I trust him or not."

Joshua's head whirled. He had never embraced a woman who offered such an enthusiastic hug, nor had he expected such an intimate greeting in full view of other diners. Thankfully none of them had the poor taste to look up and pay attention to the public spectacle.

"Well, Miss Melinda . . ."

She slapped him lightly on the hand.

"I really like it when you call me Miss Melinda. No one else does that, you know. I like it."

Maybe it is true, Joshua thought, embarrassed, *that Eastern women take the first steps in courting.*

In quick fashion he told her that no Indians were spotted on this trip and that his weeks away were most uneventful. At the end of his short story, Melinda sagged.

"Land sakes! I never get to leave this place, and then when others do, their stories are as boring as mine. Doesn't seem fair."

"Gage's will be better, I'm sure," Joshua replied.

Melinda smiled hopefully. She began to walk back to the kitchen, for the cook had bellowed out her name three times now. Then she turned back, narrowing her eyes at Joshua.

"I don't want to, but I'm supposed to tell you that Hannah was in here yesterday looking for you. She said if you were in today, I was to see that you stay until half past eight. She said she would be here then."

As Melinda stepped off, she added quietly, "Consider yourself told, Mr. Quittner."

Hannah? His thoughts raced. *What could she want with me?*

Then another thought clanged into his head. *What time is it?*

"Why didn't you send me a note this summer?" Hannah said, her voice husky, her eyes flashing in a combination of joy and anger. "Even Gage sent me a note, and Gage never writes to anyone."

Trapped, Joshua attempted a shrug, but that gesture felt small and scared. So he simply sat there, motionless.

"Tell me why," she repeated. "Why didn't you write? You must have received my letters."

Joshua nodded. One had been delivered to him in Cambridge, the other found him in Shawnee–and both were filled with chatty news of Hannah's summer activities. Joshua began to mouth a reply, then thought better and almost shrugged again, feeling as if the walls were closing in on him.

Finally he stammered, "I've been busy–with the end of school and finals–and the harvest at home and all."

He hoped no one else in the Destiny was paying attention to their discussion. But with what Hannah was wearing–a lilac bell-shaped dress with embroidered sleeves and matching cashmere shawl– Joshua was certain every male eye had turned to watch her as she'd made her way with deliberation and poise through the room to his table.

The women here do take matters into their own hands, he realized, *and while it is true, no one at home would believe this scene. No one.*

"Busy?" Her eyebrows arched in disbelief. "Busy? Balderdash."

I should have left when I had the chance, he thought. *But that would not have been the chivalrous thing to do.*

Joshua wished he could pluck his words out of the air and return them to his mouth.

"All summer–every night–and you were too busy?" she continued.

He watched her mouth form the words and then noticed the way her eyes sparkled and danced in the dim light. Thinking back to the young women in Shawnee, he knew he'd be comparing the stars to the sun, so brightly did Hannah's beauty glow.

"I did not think I had any news of great interest to report. I knew that any letter I would write would be a tedious and boring affair," was all he could think of to say.

"Tedious? Boring? Joshua, you are a friend, and I would have appreciated news of any manner. Honestly."

She folded her arms across her chest and harrumphed in a most ladylike way.

"For a man who wants to preach the Word to people, Joshua, you certainly have much to learn about half of the human species."

FROM THE JOURNAL OF JOSHUA QUITTNER
SEPTEMBER 1843

I was trapped. Like a wolf bound by piercing steel teeth, I was pinned to the ground. I had no recourse, save to lie emotionally prostrate before Hannah, in her beautiful lilac dress, and apologize like I've never apologized before.

As I did, and even though I had promised myself to hold Hannah at arm's length from my heart, I found myself failing at that vow. I know I should remain apart from her, but, alas, I cannot.

Not after tonight.

How does one remain apart when the vexation is flesh and blood before you? I'd forgotten just how attractive Hannah is.

I know the Scriptures state there is no temptation save that which is common to man (yet here I must add that if Hannah is a temptation–and my resolve on that determination is weakening–she is no common temptation at all).

So as I apologized and groveled, Hannah slowly offered me forgiveness. And such forgiveness is not only sweet but a soothing balm to my heart.

After the chasm had been bridged, we sipped at our coffee for hours. I told her tales of my short Ohio summer, and she slipped often into hearty, soulful laughter, which brought about menacing glares from Miss Melinda.

The evening had grown much too late for a proper lady to be alone on the streets, so we walked back to her rooming house.

"Joshua, now go back to 619 Follen and send me a proper note–an invitation that we enjoy some occasion together."

Her words were like honey in lemonade. I must have nodded, though I scarce recall that action after what occurred next.

I'm not sure whose arms opened first. I'm not sure whose lips leaned forward first. I'm not sure of the duration of the indescribable embrace and even more indescribable kiss.

All I know is that on the walk back, I could have traveled by way of Bolivia, so little could I concentrate.

Such vexations. Such temptations.

⚜

Gage rested his chin in his palms, his elbows on either side of his half-empty plate. The murmurs around him were lost as he stared at Joshua.

"And then you simply walked home?" Gage asked, his words edged with incredulity. "Just that one embrace?"

Joshua sat back. He nodded.

"Was there anything more?"

Knowing a gentleman does not speak of such things, Joshua blushed. For the last few days he had come close to bursting with the need to speak of that evening with someone.

Gage smiled knowingly.

"But I do have a question to ask, Gage," Joshua finally said confidentially.

"Anything."

"You are a man of the world, are you not?"

Gage sat back in his chair. "So they tell me."

"Well . . . after that night, that kiss," Joshua said, his voice no louder than the feathery movement of a bird's wing, "is that the first step on the road to matrimony?"

Gage hesitated, as if letting the question sink in. A wide grin grew. He reached over to pound Joshua's shoulder and began to laugh.

CHAPTER FIVE

Cambridge, Massachusetts
November 1843

MORNING light filtered through the tall Palladian windows of the deserted classroom where Joshua sat. When the bell's clanging had drawn the day's instruction to a close, the other students, jostling and laughing, had stampeded out the door. Even the instructor had seemed eager to leave, shoveling a sheaf of papers into a well-worn leather case.

Joshua leaned forward so the clock tower came into view. He always sat so far back in the room that he could not easily see the hands make their slow progress. Only if he tipped backward could he observe the clock—just in case his waiting for the bell became unbearable.

It was now just past eleven o'clock in the morning.

Joshua gathered his papers into a neat stack, wiped his quill clean, and slapped the inkwell closed. He looked down at his notes, marked with bold, harsh writing and dark underlines.

The notes gave away his feelings about the class. Professor Wilcox had become an admirer of Ralph Waldo Emerson since hearing the popular writer's address at Harvard Divinity School four years prior.

Since then the professor had veered closer and closer to what Joshua saw as outright universalism, the belief that man alone could engineer his own path to God and ignore the narrow way of salvation. The growing denomination of Unitarians derived its doctrines from revisions of Calvinism. Joshua also knew Professor Wilcox attended King's Chapel in Boston, which had removed all references to the Trinity from its liturgy some fifty years prior. Wilcox often quoted from the liberal *Christian Register* and the writings of William Ellery Channing, whose sermons were the bedrock of Unitarian belief. It was rumored that the professor was a secret proponent of William Wordsworth's outrageous social beliefs as well.

But if this is false doctrine, Joshua told himself, quietly outraged, *then I must learn about it in order to combat it. An uneducated pastor stands as fair game for a scholarly satan.*

So Joshua endured the beguiling rhetoric of the class, took notes, and would be able to answer the questions on any test—according to how his professor had presented the truth.

My father would find such accommodation of this heresy on my part scandalous indeed—but this course is a required one for all seminarians. So since I am in Rome . . .

Just then, from out in the hall, he heard footsteps, then a rapid, suppressed giggle, and hushed tones of mock outrage. Turning, he saw two faces through the glass panes of the rear classroom door. Visible for only a second, he knew who was attempting to hide.

"Hannah! Jamison!" he called out. "It will do you no good to conceal yourselves. I am aware of your presence. You have lost the element of surprise."

The door fell open, and Jamison tumbled to his side on the upper landing. Hannah stood up quickly behind, trying her best to maintain a solemn countenance, but failed, dissolving into laughter.

Joshua shut his eyes, and in that moment, vowed he would not spend the rest of his life recalling the golden, liquid sounds of her joy. He felt a tautness in his heart. Hannah, after their one shared intimacy, had never mentioned it again, nor did circumstances allow Joshua to think that the evening's magic might ever be repeated. Hannah seemed drawn to Joshua, seeking out his advice, his counsel, his company—but now always on a purely platonic level. What he feared most was that the difference in their backgrounds was what caused the gulf between them. Recently Gage had comforted him by explaining that a woman could be like that—wanting a confidant, drawing a man into her orbit, then keeping him at bay, teasing his emotions.

Joshua tried hard not to believe Hannah could be so predictable, yet what Gage said seemed to be true. Hannah appeared to all the world as if that single, pure, most wondrous kiss had never happened. Yet Joshua could not forget it or understand how she might live as if she could not remember it. Still, as a gentleman, he had never mentioned it to her again—as she did not to him—nor had she behaved in any sort of way that might indicate their shared intimacy. He would not sully the memory of that glorious event.

Joshua's reverie was broken by Jamison's cry. "She wanted to kidnap you from class, and I prevented her from that, my friend."

Hannah thrust her hands to her hips, her elbows flared out to the side. "*I* wanted? *I* wanted?" She pretended to kick at his feet. "You are such a play actor, Jamison." Then, when she glanced up and caught Joshua's look, she said hastily, "It was his idea, Joshua. He said since it might be the last of the temperate weather of the year, it was much too nice a day to waste indoors—especially in some stuffy classroom. He alone hatched this scheme to pirate away all our friends for a long walk to the river. He said no one must miss enjoying Indian summer. And we all know how few this man's buoyant moods are—so I felt obliged to participate."

Jamison spun on his back and grabbed out at her feet, laughing. "You are a prevaricator and a beguiler." As she moved to avoid them and her dress fluttered about, more than a hand's width of her bare leg slipped into plain view. Joshua's eyes were drawn to that spot like a beggar to a gold piece.

At that moment Professor Wilcox stepped into the hall from his office, only one door away from the classroom, and stopped, bewitched by the scene before him: a young woman with red face, a young man on his back, his hands about her ankle, and one of his seminary students, wistfully watching the tableau. The professor was about to speak, then simply smiled and walked away, his heels echoing down the hallway.

A crimson shame swept over Joshua's face. Hannah lowered her chin and giggled.

After a minute, Jamison said softly, "Well, at least he didn't ask for any names."

Did Wilcox think I was part of this . . . ruffianism? Joshua wondered. *He must have concluded that I lead two lives—one befitting a seminarian and one at the edge of proper behavior.*

Joshua's thoughts ran wild as Jamison stood up and dusted himself off. Then Hannah made all his worry vanish as she took Jamison's right arm and Joshua's left.

"I think we should take our scandalous acts outside, gentlemen, and pirate ourselves away to the banks of the river as Mr. Pike planned."

⁂

The shadows had begun to lengthen as the three friends sat on a park bench near the riverfront, watching a sculling team practice in the smooth waters of the Charles River. Jamison, his mood buoyed by tweaking the sensibilities of a seminary professor, was expansive. He bought thick, hot pretzels from a street vendor and coated them liberally with spicy mustard. Soon the only sounds to be heard were the gentle lap of water at the shoreline and the trio's chewing.

For November, the sun was unusually warm, its light filtered only by the skeletons of the trees above them. Jamison took off his topcoat and walked to the edge of the river, kicking pebbles into the water. The ripples were pulled into the current and twisted as they headed downstream.

"I wonder where this water will wind up? Africa? China? Maybe the North Pole?" he pondered aloud.

Hannah swallowed her final bite. "All the places you plan to visit?"

"Perhaps. I hope so. Ahh, the sweet lure of adventure."

"And romance," Hannah called out. "And don't forget mystery and intrigue."

Joshua turned to watch Hannah speak, to watch the curve of her throat, to watch the sunlight glint off her full lips. Then he closed his eyes. For almost three months he had guarded his heart carefully. He had worked hard to rebuild the walls about his heart following their one kiss. He knew he was called to do the Lord's work back in Ohio. Joshua was also certain of another fact: that Hannah would as much consider a life there as could he imagine turning his back on his calling.

But here by the river, in the buttery sunlight of a late fall afternoon, when the warmth was real and made of flesh, Joshua felt a tremor in his soul.

He became aware again that a battle raged within his heart. One portion of his heart wanted to shed its prim cloak and passionately pursue Hannah. The other half realized that Hannah and the pastorate were undeniably incompatible.

Every day started out with Joshua reminding himself of these verities. Yet, in spite of this resolve, there was always the faint spark of hope for a different future scenario—a future that included this wonderful woman. And this battle was fought over and over, with no victory in sight.

After Hannah dabbed away at her lips with a lace-trimmed handkerchief in case of any mustard, she said, "So tell me, Joshua. Our Jamison sees the flowing water and imagines exotic locales and mysteries. What do you see when you gaze off into the horizon as I often see you do? Are you imagining faraway places? Africa? The Far East?"

Joshua thoughtfully replied, "No, I do not. I see my future in the town of Shawnee. That's still where God has called me to serve."

"Are you certain of that? Still?" Hannah asked intently.

He nodded. "Nothing has occurred to change my intentions."

Hannah stared at him. Joshua wanted to jump up and down and shout out the truth: knowing Hannah had happened to him. Yet he knew it was not a truth that could be shared.

She smiled and patted his hand. "How I envy your certainty. The rest of us bob and float along with the waters of the world, and you remain an anchor. Such faith you have. How we all wish we could be that sure."

He wanted to shout, "You can be!" but only offered a slight smile and then averted his eyes.

The sun dipped an hour closer to the horizon as they ate and talked. From the far edge of the park, a private carriage with a uniformed driver clattered to stop, and a young man stuck his head out of the window.

"Hannah! Joshua! Jamison!"

Hannah jumped on top of the bench and began wildly waving her hands over her head. "Gage! Over here! Come join us! We're playing hooky from classes."

Gage trotted over to his friends. Joshua, now observant to such matters, noticed Gage's attire—an impeccably tailored waistcoat with velvet lapels and gold buttons, matching trousers, and a dazzlingly white shirt set off by a stunning cravat.

"I've looked all over campus for you. I even tried to bribe Melinda into telling me where she had spirited Joshua off to—but she wouldn't crack."

Hannah giggled and Joshua blushed.

"Where were you?" Jamison asked. "We attempted to break into your poetic literature class, but you were nowhere to be found. And you know we can't tolerate anyone skipping class if they did not invite us along."

"I've just returned from home. Pressing business, I'm afraid."

"Anything serious?" Hannah asked. "I mean . . . not that we could help with a business matter, I'm sure."

"Well," Gage responded with a grin, "yes, you *can* help."

Hannah looked up, surprised.

"The pressing business I attended to was seeing my dear mother and father off on a pilgrimage back to the Continent. Father has several business matters to attend to, and Mother has always wished to spend Christmas in London—Charles Dickens and the Regency Balls and all that, I suppose. They sailed on a new type of ship—a clipper ship, I believe they called it. Promised to cut the sailing time in half."

All three friends looked blankly at Gage, certain they had no idea of where his conversation was heading.

"And while on the ride back to Cambridge, I had a flash of inspiration."

"Inspiration?" Joshua asked, thinking he may have had a spiritual awakening of sorts.

"Yes, inspiration indeed," Gage replied. "The family manse will be empty, save for my older brother, who is totally unlike myself—a complete bookworm. And am I not correct in stating we have a long week's break from classes the week after this?"

The three friends nodded.

"I read in the New York papers that President Tyler suggested that families might take time to share in a season of thanksgiving for God's blessings. And for my friendships with you three, I am most thankful."

They waited, still uncomprehending.

"I'm suggesting we spend the week in New York City, with you as my guests, and take in the culture—both high and low—that the city offers. And also that we share a time of thanksgiving."

Hannah exclaimed happily. Jamison smiled broadly. Joshua was the only one whose trepidations showed plainly on his face.

"All week? The four of us together?" Joshua asked. "But what of chaperones? The three of *us* can share sleeping quarters, but not Hannah. Such liberties I could not allow to occur. You are my friend, Gage, but I must draw the line somewhere."

Gage stopped dead in his tracks—and then began to laugh.

⚜

Joshua hoped the final week of classes would pass quietly. He was knee-deep in papers and studies and needed to concentrate. Yet, as he sat in the library, with the sunlight slipping from red to purple, all he could think of was a week with Hannah. True, he knew Jamison and Gage would be there too, but their imagined presence in his daydreams was so slight as to be negligible.

As Joshua stared into the darkening sky, he heard a rattle of papers and the gentle scrape of a chair to his left. He turned and faced Professor Wilcox.

Joshua mentally began ticking off his shortcomings in class—obviously they were so great that a professor deemed it necessary to walk among the student stacks to talk to him.

"Uhh . . . Professor Wilcox . . ."

Professor Wilcox waved his palm.

"Joshua, you are not in trouble. I've not come creeping into the student's library with mayhem in mind."

Joshua tried to formulate a reply, and no logical word or phrase came. He truly was in awe of his professors. Some were less interesting and dynamic than others, but each one, with an array of letters following their names and diplomas covering their office walls, had earned the right to be held in esteem.

"I simply saw you here alone and thought I'd stop and spend a moment or two in conversation with one of my brighter and most earnest students."

Joshua was sure his heartbeat could be heard. Never in his wildest dreams did he imagine himself to be a keen and well-respected student—by a professor, nonetheless.

"And I wanted to know how your kidnapping went last week. The young woman who helped make off with you was indeed attractive."

Joshua reddened, not simply from the reference to Hannah, but the fact that the professor had noticed her beauty. Till this moment, Joshua held a secret belief that Hannah's beauty was only noticed by himself. To have others share in it was somehow unseemly and base.

"Umm . . . I guess it went well. We had a picnic by the river," Joshua replied, trying to smile, hoping he had concealed his anger.

"That's grand," Professor Wilcox said. He waited a moment till speaking further.

"I wonder if you . . . or perhaps your friends . . ."

Without knowing how, Joshua immediately realized that the professor meant Hannah.

"I thought you or your friends might find my new church

interesting. I thought I might invite you to attend a service. Perhaps you've heard of it. Hopedale Community Church?"

Joshua was well aware of its existence. Many of the seminarians had whispered about it. It had begun a year prior and was said to be looking to begin a community of utopia on earth. The group had purchased a tract of land in nearby Milford—some 250 acres—and planned to establish farms, small industries, a school, and a library.

"I've heard about it," Joshua said evenly.

Professor Wilcox smiled. "Then the whispers from around campus have penetrated the seminary as well?"

"Whispers?" Joshua asked, feigning innocence.

"I know there are many who consider us foolish for thinking man can achieve perfection. But I truly believe it can happen. And when I saw you and your friends . . ."

Again Joshua knew he was referring to Hannah alone.

"I thought, 'They would be such wonderful people to invite to our meetings . . . to get to know about the Hopedale Community dream.' You would be our future, Joshua. You and your friends."

Joshua felt light-headed. How could a respected seminary professor believe man could achieve perfection apart from God and outside of heaven?

"You would so appreciate our guest lecturers, Joshua. They would provide great stimulation. Why, just last week we had Mr. Emerson. When he speaks, I find my mind spinning about, new thoughts coming in flashes, like that comet recently seen at the Astronomical Observatory. I know man's native intuition about God is often the most correct. Emerson spoke about how worthy we are as individuals and that if we progress as a society—especially in social and humanitarian terms—then the foolishness of strict doctrinal issues will be forgotten."

Joshua struggled to keep up with the professor's words.

"Forget doctrine, Professor Wilcox? But wouldn't that be much like forgetting the Bible?"

The older man placed a hand on Joshua's forearm.

"No . . . and you will soon learn that doctrine is not how one finds enlightenment. In fact, it's just the opposite. Doctrine and narrow legalism cloud a man's mind with trivial rules and regulations."

The clock in the Commons chimed eight times.

"I'm nearly late for a faculty meeting," Professor Wilcox said. "Do pay us a visit next Sunday, Joshua. And bring your friends. You'll be challenged."

As Joshua watched his professor make his way past the darkened book stacks, he spread his palms flat on the table and took several breaths to calm his jangling thoughts.

I will never attend that church, and I'll never bring Hannah within so much as an arm's reach of that man again.

New York City
Thanksgiving 1843

After his unsettling meeting with Professor Wilcox, Joshua busied himself with studying and daydreaming about the upcoming trip to New York City.

His initial, and somewhat naive, concerns about chaperones and sleeping arrangements proved to be unfounded. Of course Joshua had known Gage was from a wealthy family and had taken over many rooms at 619 Follen. But he had not considered the reality of Gage's home in the city. Perhaps it was Joshua's humble beginnings that made it difficult for him to even imagine the expansiveness of the rich and powerful.

The four friends arrived at Gage's home as the sunset colored the cobblestone streets, reflecting off the wet stones to cast ripples of gold against the windows of a massive three-story building. Enormous pillars and carved stonework adorned the facade with a breathtaking stateliness.

Joshua gulped as he stepped from the hansom cab to the curb. "This is your home?" he asked incredulously.

Gage nodded.

"It's not a hotel or bank or a private residence for some crowned prince of a large European country?"

Gage laughed. "It's just the family home, friends, and it was not of my doing to be born into a family that likes its good fortune visible to all passersby as in the Greek Revival style here."

The trio was greeted at the door by Henry, the Davis family's butler, who led them through the public rooms of the mansion—a three-story foyer with black-and-white marble flooring, an oak-paneled library with nearly ten thousand volumes stacked floor to ceiling, a ballroom that could hold an orchestra and up to five hundred guests, a kitchen that could prepare meals for hundreds of visitors at a time, and endless room after room, it seemed to Joshua. Each was adorned with sumptuous draperies, carved mahogany Belter furniture with imported upholstery, and chandeliers and *objets d'art* from around the world. There was even a classical statue that stood nearly two stories tall, gracing the front entry and grand double winding staircase that led to the private rooms. It was taken from an abandoned temple near Athens, Greece, Gage said.

Carpets, handwoven in Turkey of the finest wool, were layered about the halls. Each possessed a thousand tones of gold, blue, and burgundy in designs that reminded Joshua of a book on Arabia he'd once read. The gas lamps were on gilded hangers in the shape of a lion's paw, each holding a finely etched glass cylinder. Their faint light charged each room with a hint of mystery.

The dining room contained a table that might hold all of Shawnee proper if fully extended, Joshua imagined. In the center was a grand silver candelabra with myriad candles—made of wax, not tallow—sweeping down in ornate arcs. The wooden inlaid surface of the table, polished to a bright sheen, reflected the dancing of the candlelight. Apparently servants had lit the candles moments before the young master of the house had arrived, for none had burned more than a finger's length.

To have servants anticipate such things! Joshua marveled.

Joshua's bedroom suite was large enough to hold all of his home in Ohio, even leaving room for a garden if desired. For the first hour after his arrival, he wandered about the space as if in a trance, walking a pace at a time, his fingers tracing the elegant carving of a black walnut dresser and bedframe, the gilding of an immense mirror, the purple and gold damask drapes that flowed from ceiling to floor. Each window was bordered by a waterfall of the fabric, glinting in costly richness as it fell into pools on the floor.

The bed was three, perhaps four, times as large as any bed Joshua had ever seen, with an amply stuffed feather mattress covered in monogrammed starched linen sheets and a rich damask counterpane. Joshua lay enveloped in its softness for a moment. And he was expected to sleep an entire week amid this amazing opulence! The top of the chest of drawers offered an enticing selection of splendidly scented toiletries.

The suite also had its own bathroom, its floor and walls covered with marble tiles and complete with a Roman bathtub with massive bronzed feet.

Joshua stood in the doorway, his eyes taking in the elaborate space. *Does one get immune to such a style of living,* he wondered, *or does one simply get infected with a desire for more riches?*

Just as he finished hanging up his clothing in the cedar-scented wardrobe, he heard a faint shouting emanating from deep within the house. He stuck his head out the door. From down the hall, he saw Jamison peering out from one of the many doors.

Jamison shrugged and called out, "The voice sounds like Hannah—but from where?"

Joshua shook his head. Her shouts echoed about the house. It could be from behind them—or in front of them.

"Let's head back the way we came," Jamison said, pointing, and the two set off. "Although I wish I had a pocketful of bread crumbs to mark the way back to our rooms."

"When I was a boy in Ohio, we often took an ax to a tree to chip out a trail. I suppose that might be frowned on in New York?"

Jamison stopped, surprised by Joshua's easy humor.

"I have a penknife," Joshua continued. "Do you think that would do?" He took the blade from his pocket and made a show of unfolding it and acting as if he were about to chip a groove into an ornately carved sideboard.

"Joshua," Jamison said in a tone near to shock, "you would not dare."

"I am jesting, my friend," Joshua said, clipping the blade back together. "Am I that humorless that such a joke frightens you so?"

Then they heard the plaintive wail: "I'm lost!"

"Hannah!" Jamison exclaimed. "Keep shouting. We'll find you."

Hannah had been given a room in the far west wing of the home, nearly a five-minute trip, it seemed, from the front door. Jamison and Joshua kept walking down a long hall adorned with oil portraits of Davis ancestors until her shouts grew louder.

"There you are," she called out, scurrying down a rear staircase. "It seems I dismissed the chambermaid prematurely, believing I could find my own way. I thought I'd waste away without finding either of you again." Lowering her voice, she said, "Have you ever seen anything like this before in your lives? There must be a million dollars worth of bric-a-brac in this place."

She offered a shy, hesitant smile as an explanation.

"It's not to say I have never seen wealth before, but even I am overwhelmed by all this. Bric-a-brac can be overdone."

"*Bric-a-brac?*" Joshua whispered back, puzzled. "I've never heard that word before."

"It's a rich man's word meaning 'I purchased this expensive object, and I don't know what it is or what to do with it, so I'm putting it here on display so others can see how wealthy I am,'" Jamison said, laughing.

At first Hannah scowled, then said reluctantly, "That is what it really means, I guess."

"But the Gage we know is nothing like this," Joshua said as he swept his arm in a circle, indicating the opulence that surrounded him. The three of them made their way toward the library that faced the front street and entrance. "For sure, he dresses well and has more money than I can imagine, but he's not as ostentatious and showy as this house portends."

"Who is not ostentatious?" Gage called out from the balcony that encircled the library.

Joshua tried to stutter an apology.

"No, my good friends, you are correct. This house and its possessions are ornate and overdone. But that is how my parents prefer to
live. And in their circles, this is the norm."

"And it doesn't bother you?" Hannah asked with a hint of bitter-
ness. "To have so much while so many have so little? Why, an entire
village could live within these walls."

As she spoke, Joshua knew that at this moment Hannah had again
painfully confronted the new realities of her life–recalling the privileges that her family had lost. Even though, in comparison to most,
Hannah was still wealthy, she was no longer a member of Gage's
circle.

A scowl slipped across Gage's face.

"Ahh, Miss Hannah," Gage said. "And I see you've given up your
fine dresses for sackcloth and your tuition money to the needy."

A hush of awkward, almost angry, silence filled the room. Hannah
looked about ready to blurt out a barbed reply, then pursed her lips.

Gage stepped to the spiraling wrought-iron-and-rosewood staircase and clattered down to the ground floor. "Please . . . let us not
talk of wealth and substance and material possessions right now. Perhaps after we've all had a good dinner we'll continue this discussion.
And even though my family has means, you must remember that all
of us in this room are wealthier than most people of the world."

No one, it seemed, was willing to comment further. Footsteps
sounded out in the hall, and Henry preceded Gage to the door, pulling it open.

"Ahh . . . my elder brother, Walton, has arrived home," Gage said
with a smile. "Come in, Walton. I want you to meet my friends."

Afterwards, Joshua recalled that Walton Davis possessed a singularly pinched and sullen look, as if he found pain in the sound of
human laughter.

They never returned to the subject of wealth. Joshua knew they
would not, given the chilliness of Hannah and Gage as they rode to
the site of the evening's meal.

But Gage was a superb host. His knowledge of the city of New York was voluminous. That first night, perhaps in response to Hannah's pointed question of wealth and fairness, they had their evening meal at a dark, raucous, smoke-filled neighborhood haunt near the docks, populated by longshoremen with muscled arms and chiseled shoulders and by sailors from a score of foreign ports. Many languages ebbed and flowed about them. The four of them dined in a back corner booth draped for privacy, enjoying fresh clams and oysters on the half shell and thick steaks and slices of heady cheese from England. Jamison, for the first time, drank a thick stout from Ireland that smelled of peat. Joshua could not imagine anyone finding the taste pleasant—and that was just from the smell of it alone. Gage ordered an ale cocktail, but Joshua and Hannah sipped at cider.

Just as they finished the expansive, though relatively inexpensive, meal, a trio of wobbly Irishmen took to a makeshift stage to serenade the crowd with a concertina and pennywhistle. Not long afterwards most patrons were on their feet, dancing an impromptu Irish jig.

Joshua remained seated, hoping he would not be called on to join any group in any form of dance, no matter how innocent.

The days following proved to be a whirlwind of culture—both high and low, as promised. Gage's family had a box at the opera, in which the four struggled to hold their laughter in check, much to the consternation of neighboring box holders. Afterwards they found themselves at an inviting restaurant with only four tables and a friendly bear of a waiter. That evening marked the first time Joshua ate food from the country of Italy. He would have cut his spaghetti with a knife and fork, but the waiter intervened, demonstrating the real Italian way to eat the thin, slippery noodles. He was introduced to many other culinary delights as well during the meals that were prepared by the Davises' cook.

They toured elegant museums resplendent with brooding European masterpieces, then visited drafty garrets stuffed with a confusion of painted canvases stacked floor to ceiling by the artist who glowered at them from the corner. They walked through stores that glowed with brass, sparkled with jewels, and glittered with high fashion, fingering exotic silks and tweeds. Then they bought roasted chestnuts from a short muscular man pushing a wooden cart that trailed smoke from a small fire.

So varied and wide ranging were the experiences that Joshua felt he could not capture them all—not in his heart, not on paper, not in his mind. The sights and sounds flowed so fast and furiously about him that he was afraid to look too long in one direction lest he miss a hundred other sights from the opposite view.

With each step taken, Joshua felt two steps farther from Ohio, farther from the earthen landscapes of his youth. In the lobby of a palatial theater, while waiting for a concert to begin, Joshua looked up into the enormous chandelier, hung with heavy chains from the ceiling. A thousand gaslights pecked at the darkness, their glass and crystal facets reflecting more billiantly on the richly painted walls than the dark skies punctuated by the stars Joshua remembered gazing at as a boy. It was as if the heavens were condensed in this one spot. Joshua stared, unabashed, at the sophistication of this new world.

The buildings. The people. The traffic. So much excitement. So much to discover.

I hesitate to admit this, he thought to himself, *but I truly like it here. And I know such thoughts are not right, but could I find a life of service in New York, or Boston, or Philadelphia? Each has a preponderance of churches, and I'm sure one would have need of a Harvard Divinity graduate. And if I could stay here, then perhaps Hannah might consider . . .*

And as that thought entered his mind, he shook his head, forcing his mind to turn away from it.

No. I shall not be deterred, Hannah or not. I'm certain of my destiny.

⚬⚬⚬

Nearing the end of the week, Jamison and Gage tumbled out from their beds early, hastening to the offices of the *New York World,* a newspaper in which Gage's father had a substantial interest. Gage had insisted on an introduction to the editor, knowing Jamison desired a newsman's position once his studies at Harvard were completed.

Hannah and Joshua were left alone in the expansive house. They spent the morning perusing the vast book collection and reading in the library. Hannah was interested in the many sailing trophies that adorned the shelves. From an elegantly framed membership certificate that hung over the trophies, the two learned that Gage was a member of the exclusive Castle Garden Amateur Boat Club, "a club restricted to young men of the highest respectability, who are determined to combine with pleasure the utmost propriety of conduct." Upon reading it, Hannah said, "A fitting description of our friend."

It was nearing noon. Unwilling to ring for a servant to prepare them lunch, Joshua suggested a walk toward Central Park. He had a few dollars in his pocket, and the thought of a quiet luncheon with Hannah, alone and unencumbered, was of such promise that the pain of spending his last few dollars would not stand in his way. Hannah donned a cape the color of blueberries and a matching silk scarf. Joshua thought she never had looked so beautiful.

They strolled together, relishing the sun's warmth. Just at the edge of the park, they came to a café. As they entered, Joshua gave a furtive glance at the posted menu. With a sigh of relief, he realized Hannah could order the most expensive item on the bill of fare, and he would have enough money left over for a less costly bowl of stew.

As the food was served—both had ordered the lamb stew with autumn vegetables—Hannah peered out through the steamed windows with a pensive look.

"Do you find all this enjoyable?" she asked.

Startled, Joshua looked about. "Well, the restaurant is not much, I admit, but it looks clean, and the food smells delicious."

Smiling, she took his hand. "No, sweet Joshua, not this place. That's not what I meant. I meant . . . well, all of this. New York. The opera. The museums. The concerts. Do you find it enjoyable?"

Joshua was puzzled. Throughout the week, each of them had remarked over and over about their absolutely extraordinary time and that, without Gage, they never would have come near to experiencing such wonders. He looked at her and realized she was wistful over all this–wistful that she once was the same as Gage in prestige and wealth but was no longer.

"Enjoyable? I thought we all found this time to be enjoyable. Don't you?"

Hannah fussed with her teacup. "I do, and I have . . . but there is something sad about this as well."

"Sad?"

"I look at the four of us and how much fun we have together. I look at you and realize what insight you have into our hearts–that's good for a minister, I'm sure."

Insight? She said I had insight? How seldom do I feel insightful, Joshua thought.

She sipped her tea and continued. "But when I stop and think, I realize we will all go our separate ways as we graduate. I do not know how I'll fare without you to point me in the right direction . . . without Gage to make me laugh . . . without Jamison to tell me the truth. Without you my life will be so . . . empty."

Yes, Joshua thought, *I could stay here and find a church. Then we could all still be together in a fashion. It could work, couldn't it?*

As she spoke, Joshua's heart swelled. He'd loved Hannah since the moment he saw her. He'd never shared that knowledge with any-one–nor would he ever. From that first gentle peal of her laughter, his heart had been hers. Though his heart claimed love for her, his head repeated over and over that such an outcome could never be.

Joshua nodded. "I will miss this, too."

Hannah looked up. "Really? You will miss us? But you have a call-ing to follow. We may laugh at the simplicity of that, but we are all so very envious. How could you miss us if you're fulfilling your destiny?"

Joshua shrugged. "I don't know, but I know I will."

"You'll miss me, too? All my endless questions? All my feminine shortcomings?"

I'll miss you most of all, he thought, but did not voice.

"Yes. Yes, Hannah, I will miss you."

FROM THE JOURNAL OF JOSHUA QUITTNER
NOVEMBER 1843

The glittering world of New York City that I've experienced this week seems a fantasy, a mere fleeting figment of an overworked imagination. So many sights, sounds, tastes, that I can scarce catalog them.

I will forever remember the brilliant universe of lights that bejeweled the streets as bright as the raiment of a thousand stars.

I will forever remember the music emanating from a dozen public houses, washing into the street and filling the air with a chorus of a thousand voices, though none discordant, like a cacophony of earthly angels.

I will forever remember the greatest art in the world, hanging on tall walls, free for me to luxuriate in. I was often struck senseless and mute by such brilliant creativity. To stand before the masterpieces of Michelangelo and DaVinci is a treasure I could not have imagined a year ago.

I will always remember walking side by side with Miss Morgan Hannah Collins, sometimes arm in arm, in the crispness of a fall day in the city. I will recall her laughter forever.

My heart skips a beat as I write this, but . . . could I stay here in the East? Could I find a church that needs a country-born-and-bred man like me? Could I break two people's hearts—my mother's and my father's—in order to salvage my own?

Oh, Lord—how much shall you have me sacrifice to serve you?

CHAPTER SIX

Cambridge, Massachusetts
December 1843

A DUSTING of snow had fallen softly during the night. Joshua left a single line of powdery footprints as he made his way to the woodshed behind the house on 619 Follen. He made three trips, carrying in armfuls of dried firewood that he stacked carefully inside by the fireplace. Mrs. Parsons, who was spending the Christmas holiday with her daughter in Providence, had left Joshua in charge of keeping at least one fire going at all times on each floor of the house. He stoked the massive grate in the first-floor sitting room with an armful of wood. Soon the coals remaining from the night's slow fire caught, and the logs began to smolder, then blaze.

Taking a step back, he turned his palms to the fire, rubbing them together. He felt the room's chill slip away with the flames' warmth.

Save the crack and hiss of the logs, the house was silent, as was most of the Harvard campus. Gage was back in New York with his older brother and "a motley assortment of cousins and shirttail relatives we have all but abandoned, all looking for two things—a huge banquet, and more important, no meal tab presented to them at the end," in Gage's words. Hannah was with her parents in

Philadelphia, and Jamison was on his way home to Pittsburgh and his family.

Joshua claimed his studies held him to campus. In truth, his money reserves had dwindled too low to afford a train ticket back to Shawnee, and, in reality, the length of the trip would have permitted only a day or two of visiting.

The fire's light kept the gray of the morning at bay as Joshua listened to the rhythmic ticking of the marble clock over the mantel. It struck the half hour with a gentle *dong*.

Joshua looked about to see if anyone was watching, then sat on the faded tufted settee near the fireplace. Weary to the bone, he leaned back and closed his eyes.

He hoped the image of Hannah would not soon come to mind.

For the past three weeks, Joshua had spent his Sundays, not just as a participant in worship, but as a leader. Much to his surprise, he had been recommended by several of his professors to provide temporary occupancy of the pulpits for a number of smaller churches in the village of Cambridge that, for a variety of reasons, were missing a preacher.

He did so with trepidation at first, certain that his rough-and-tumble demeanor would be laughed at by the polished congregations.

But no one laughed. After the echoes of his sermons drifted to silence, people approached him, hands extended, eyes wet with a trace of tears, and congratulations and thanks flowed easily.

The first week Joshua had been befuddled at such praise. After all, he was a farm boy from a rustic, backwater county of Ohio. He recalled his uncle's advice about not adding "too much book learnin' to your preachin'." Rather than complicate his message and the truth of the Scriptures by tangled, obscure words and phrases, he spoke in a simple narrative, telling stories of his childhood that he hoped would introduce and explain biblical truth in a fresh and engaging way. And it did.

On the cold December Sunday before Christmas, at a church a few miles north of Cambridge, filling in for a pastor who had come down with what he'd called "consumption," Joshua told the story of Christmas as seen through the eyes of a five-year-old child. He told of the joy and wonder of the unexpected gifts tied with gaily colored ribbons and the visits by friends and family from far afield. He spoke of the anticipation in the whirling, delicious scents of ham and sweet potatoes and brown bread cooking in a flurry of smoke and steam on the cast-iron cookstove in the kitchen. He spoke of the beauty of a frozen farm field under the pale skeleton of moonlight on Christmas Eve. He spoke of the wonderment as he looked heavenward, in the dark, for the dazzling light of Christ descending to earth. He spoke of never physically seeing that light but feeling it pour, like a waterfall, into his soul.

At the end of his message, he focused on the faces in the first few rows and was shocked to find trails of tears marking many of the men and women's cheeks.

He scarcely remembered his ride home that day, so awed was he by the emotions of those who had listened to his words.

If this is what it means to preach with power, he'd thought to himself in the chill of an open coach, *then I understand what draws men to illuminate God's Word. It's not pride I feel but a hint of the power of God's truth. It is intoxicating to my soul.*

Joshua now opened his eyes and sat up. He walked over to the fire and snugged the screen closer, holding back any threat of a spark or jumping ember.

Then, like a rushing wind, Hannah came to mind. He fought against the vision. Since returning from New York, he had scarce seen her—only in passing while walking to classes. He knew that if he were to spend more time with her, he would be further lost in the powerful, drowning whirlpool-like force that she exerted, unknowingly, on his heart.

A loud pop from the fire brought him out of his reverie again, but the screen held the spark in check. Joshua breathed deeply and began to make his way to his chilly room on the third floor. He had to draft a sermon to be presented at the Christmas Eve service at a Baptist church that lay within view of the ocean in the town of Revere, just north and east of Boston, along the curve of the harbor.

He grabbed his pen and willed himself to start the task—and to not think of Christmas without Hannah.

Christmas Eve 1843

After the service had ended, and after the congregation had slipped out into the brisk air, their breath clouding toward the heavens in a joyous mist as they returned to their homes, Joshua sat alone in the first pew, his hands folded about his father's Bible.

The stove finally had begun to chug off ripples of heat, and for the first time that evening feeling had begun to seep back into his toes.

The head of the deacon board had requested a short message.

"We're going to sing a small selection of hymns, have a prayer, hear your words, then return to our homes for dinners and celebrations. No sense in keeping these good folks from their eggnogs and plum puddings longer than necessary on Christmas Eve."

Joshua had indeed kept his message brief. He finished speaking in less than ten minutes. He told the story of a young girl who came to her time of delivery alone, with only the help of a husband whose hands were calloused by the sawing and sanding of wood.

He asked them to imagine an evening, perhaps only a little warmer than the one tonight. The night would be even darker, the sky a vast circulation of distant stars. Imagine two people, Joshua said, scared, far from home, apart from friends and all that was known to them.

Her time grew short. A sharp nudging of pain filled her being.

Her husband must have grown increasingly uneasy.

The inn offered them no room.

"What about the stable?" he must have asked.

The innkeeper shook his head.

"The stable is full of paying clients," he said with a snort. "I repeat, there is no room here. Go elsewhere."

The Greek words, Joshua explained, indicated that the Son of all creation was to be born outdoors, in a rough enclosure of rocks and timbers. There were no walls or roof. All this shelter offered was an ineffective break from the chilling winds—nothing more. A tiny flame may have flickered at their feet. Oil for a lamp was costly.

Joshua continued his story, saying that the Son of all creation entered the world alone, in the cold and dark, born to a frightened young woman and her husband who could provide scant comfort save their loving arms.

And this child born in such humble beginnings—more humble than any man alive—would grow to be the Savior of all mankind. That was the gift of Christmas—the only gift any man would ever need. It was the gift of eternal life.

Joshua was happy with his sermon. It avoided religious clichés and only once mentioned obscure and unknown Greek words.

He felt, as he spoke, that the people gathered before him needed to hear this particular message on this particular night.

And now, after the glow of preaching, Joshua sat alone in the church, in no hurry to be anywhere, thanking God for the abilities he had given him and asking the Lord once again to provide some reassurance to ascertain if his calling to the ministry was true to God's plan.

Just then a soft scraping echoed from the rear of the church.

Joshua raised his head, whispered, "Amen," and turned to the rear.

The door swung open, a chill swept through the room, and a shadowy figure entered, cloaked in a thick green woolen topcoat and scarf. The figure slowly unwrapped itself, and the scarf fell away.

"Professor Wilcox!" Joshua exclaimed when his professor's face came into view. "What on earth . . . ?"

The man stamped his feet, clearing snow from them.

"Joshua, don't be alarmed. I live not far from this church. And I heard you speak tonight."

"Heard me? From where?"

The professor walked down the center aisle. "I was in the back. I heard you were to present the sermon, and I could not resist hearing you come before a congregation—among which are some professors at the college."

If Joshua had known Wilcox was in the audience, he would have spent a much longer time polishing and refining his message.

"I left immediately as you finished and was halfway home before I was stopped. I knew I had to come back. I felt a powerful pull to tell you this."

"Tell me what?" Joshua felt sick. He was certain Wilcox would launch into a criticism as to the horrid flaws of his message and how his point was overlooked or underexplained.

How could I have sullied the Christmas message so? Joshua asked himself, alarmed.

"I know we share our differences in theology, son. Maybe God's heaven is big enough for us all. But if it isn't, I still need to say one thing to you. You have the gift," Professor Wilcox said, his eyes on the floor as if embarrassed to admit the words.

"The gift? Is that what you said? I don't understand."

The professor looked up, and Joshua thought he saw a faint tearing in the man's eyes.

It's from the cold night air, he thought with certainty.

"You have the gift. In my days at Harvard I have instructed many students. Some are glib at first and receive from us a little polish. Some students are rough, with jarring edges to their words, and we help smooth their delivery and tame their thoughts. We try and help them become better. But only rarely have I heard a student such as you. You excel in classwork, indeed, but tonight was impressive . . . no, much more than impressive. Tonight could have been life-changing for anyone who heard the words."

Joshua waited, stunned at what he was hearing.

"As you spoke, I felt my heart breaking for perhaps the first time since I was a young man, as the Nativity story was told. I have heard it a thousand times and remained unmoved until tonight, when you explained it from the perspective of the young Mary, alone and scared, in the dark, birthing the Son of the living God."

"I tried . . . I tried to . . . to keep it short," Joshua stammered, not knowing how to respond.

"You are indeed gifted, young Joshua Quittner. The Lord sometimes blesses a man with knowing exactly the right words to say and how to say them. There was not one word I could ask you to have removed tonight. Every word built a bridge further and further into my heart."

The professor's gaze became piercingly honest.

"I should not tell you this, but there is nothing I have that is worthy of teaching you. If you tell others this story of the Truth as you have done tonight, then you will win souls, my friend. That is your gift."

The professor bundled his scarf around his neck. "Thank you, Joshua. And have a merry Christmas, son." With that, he stepped back out into the cold and dark.

Joshua stared at the closed door for a while. Then he found his coat, tucked the Bible under his arm, and began to walk to the nearby hackney stand.

As the horse-drawn gig made its way through the streets, he gazed up at the winter sky of stars above him, listening to faint echoes of Christmas carols, laced with laughter, from the voices of a hundred hidden church choirs and a hundred Cambridge parlors, each a song of love and warmth.

Christmas 1843

On Christmas Day snow began to fall, and the temperatures dropped. Snow continued falling for seven days, accompanied by a fierce, flesh-cutting wind from the ocean that sliced like an icy knife across the open ground.

My second Christmas alone, he thought wistfully. *I do miss being home for the holiday.*

The streets of Cambridge remained deserted for days. Harvard's classes, scheduled to begin soon after the turn of the year, were postponed until the weather broke.

Joshua remained alone in the house. Gage must have remained in New York, and Mrs. Parsons managed to send word that she would be detained until the middle of the month—and would Joshua please attend to all household matters for her?

In the still whiteness of the first two weeks of 1844, Joshua studied, read, wrote letters, and watched the wind whip snow through the bare trees. He broke through waist-high drifts on the second day of the storm on his way to the Destiny Café. According to the sour-faced owner, he and two other very chilled patrons had been the only customers that day. He bought up as many provisions as his purse allowed and trudged back to 619 Follen.

Since the snow halted activity, Joshua had a time of enforced and unexpected reflection. Professor Wilcox's words echoed and re-echoed in his thoughts.

You have the gift.

But if it is a gift, Joshua thought, *why then am I not more perfectly settled on what I must do with such a blessing? I close my eyes and see Hannah's face before me—smiling, laughing, holding her hand out to me. Can I make use of this gift and stay here? Would she consider a man who has received such a calling?*

Joshua paced for miles in his room, praying aloud to God while he looked out at the blanketing whiteness.

"Lord, I ask that you guide my steps. I am overwhelmed by the words of Professor Wilcox. Such a refined and learned man who claimed to be softened by my preaching! I trust you are working in his heart. I know he and I have disagreed on many things, but I pray he returns to the risen Lord."

Joshua waited, as if unwilling to present his next request to a patient God.

"Lord, I ask that my path may somehow run alongside the path of Miss Morgan Hannah Collins. I find my heart light and joyous in her company. I ask that you show her the way to me, me the way to her, and both of us the way to you. I will continue to seek your guidance in all I do. Amen."

When he rose from his prayer, the moan of the wind stopped for a long moment. The silence that followed was disconcerting. Joshua looked out the frosted window. The tree limbs, often bent to near breaking the last two weeks, trembled a bit but were no longer bent. And at the far corner of the horizon was a patch of brighter gray, as if the sun were slowly overtaking the clouds and attempting, at long last, to break through.

Could this be the sign—the answer to my prayer?

But as he thought those words, the wind huffed once more, the moans began again, and the brief brightness was swept away as if the sun were but a hesitant illusion.

⁂

It was cold where he stood, with winter creeping into the church and his bones. Joshua smoothed the Bible open with his left hand. He pointed to the heavens with his right, aiming his forefinger at where he thought the sun might be.

"Do we stare at the heavens long after Christ has ascended? Do we stare and watch him as he disappears from our sight? Even the angels ask, 'Why do we look for him in the skies?' They know we must be about his business here on earth. We must not be still while we are waiting."

He resisted the urge to slam his open palm on the pulpit as punctuation as he had so often seen preachers do in order to amplify a weak point.

He looked down into the 250 faces. It was the largest congregation Joshua had ever preached to, and he was amazed at how much animation and invigoration such a large grouping provided. The most his father had ever preached to numbered no more than seventy-five, perhaps eighty. And now Joshua, even before his official ordination, was preaching to more than thrice that number.

He knew the crowd was listening. He knew the powerful Truth was breaking into their hearts.

As coached by his Public Oratory professor, Joshua stared at the back of the room, making eye contact with every person who returned his stare. As he did, his heart lurched in his chest.

In the back pew, at the farthest corner of the church, nearly hidden from view by the shadow of a massive column, sat Hannah, a bonnet covering her head and all but hiding her face.

He was certain it was Hannah. No other silhouette matched hers. No other set of eyes or nose or mouth looked as hers did, even from a distance of thirty-six pews.

Hannah! His thoughts jumped to match his heartbeat, now clumping as if a horse galloped in his chest.

Has she been here all along? Has she come just to hear me? Is she a member here? No . . . that cannot be . . . for did she not once say her background was Presbyterian? But is this church . . . no, it's not a Presbyterian church. Or is it? I cannot now recall the name of this place!

Silence washed over the congregation.

And now, where am I in my message? Have I concluded? Was there one more point to discuss? And what time is it? How long have I been talking?

Joshua lowered his arm, grasping both sides of the pulpit as if looking for an aid to find his balance and prevent a bad case of vertigo from causing him to tumble to the ground.

What do I say next? What do I say next?

Just then, as if God heard his troubled heart, the church clock in the spire began to peal. While not overpowering, each sounding was clear and sharp.

He sighed. *It's noon. It's time to end this message.*

He waited until the clock sounded its twelfth chime, then lowered his head.

"Let us pray," he said and lifted his arms in a brief and somewhat disjointed benediction, then nearly stumbled as he made his way off the platform to the main door of the church.

As he walked by, Hannah greeted his look with a wide smile. He nearly tripped again, catching himself with a hand at the end of the pew.

Hannah waited until the church was nearly empty to greet Joshua. With a slight hesitation, she extended her hand to him as if she had not known him prior to this Sunday.

"Hannah," he said. "I did not know you attended this church."

She lowered her eyes. "I don't. I came to hear you. All this time you have spoken of your classes in ancient Greek and exegesis and doxologies and all those terms that sound so foreign, and none of us has ever heard you exhibit some of the skills you are studying. You speak so eloquently of God and faith at the Destiny, and I wanted to hear your theorems presented in their native setting–a church."

Please do not say you're disappointed. I could tolerate such a critique from anyone else, save you, he thought wildly.

But aloud he said, "I am pleased, then, that you came. I only hope you were not disappointed."

She looked into his eyes for the first time this day. "Disappointed? On the contrary, Joshua. I was near overwhelmed. You preached with such power and conviction, I felt a stirring in my heart. I truly did. I am most amazed that our rough-and-tumble frontiersman could be so erudite, so scholarly, so polished."

His heart jumped at her praise.

"In fact, while I'm not a devout churchgoer, today was the most potent message I've yet encountered."

He could not hold his smile in check.

"I was captivated by your words and your delivery. I felt as if you were speaking to me alone. That is a gift. And, until the very end of your message, you held me in the palm of your hand. The last point was interrupted by the clock, was it not?"

Joshua could not help but nod, hoping she would not guess the real reason for his early truncation of the final point in his message. The two stared at each other for a minute. Hannah broke the gaze to look down at her delicate boots, then back up.

"Joshua," she said softly, "if you are not busy this evening, might you mind . . . no, I mustn't impose on you like this."

"No, no, please," he said quickly. "Impose on me. I will not mind, I'm certain."

"Well . . . there is a banquet I've been invited to–a boring, stuffy affair in honor of my great-grandfather's contribution to some venerable charity. I have an extra invitation. If you are not doing anything this evening, I thought . . ."

Before the words stopped, Joshua said, "I would love to be your guest. I really would."

Is this the answer to my prayer? his heart called out in happiness.

CHAPTER SEVEN

Boston, Massachusetts
January 1844

WAITERS swirled about the room, holding ornate silver trays high and balancing them on upturned palms. The lights from a thousand candles and gas flames reflected off the precious metal like a sky sparkling with diamonds.

The spacious banquet hall, complete with elegantly carved wood furnishings, reverberated with the sounds of glittering cutlery nicking against white china. Fine teacups touched lightly to delicate saucers, and the crystal rims of wine glasses clinked as joyful toasts were made.

Joshua sat, nearly slack jawed, next to Hannah, only two tables from the head table. Those guests, resplendent in silks and velvets, their seats raised above the floor on a twelve-inch platform, enjoyed their meal in a sort of royal isolation.

Joshua would be the first to admit he was by no means a man of the world. The past year and a half at Harvard had done much to burnish his worldliness to a shine—but still he often felt the rural bumpkin. Even though he knew Hannah to be a poor blue blood, this banquet served to further delineate the difference between his world and hers. The two main tables, each peopled by twelve guests, included three United States senators, the inventor Samuel F. B. Morse, a former U.S. vice president, and most astonishing, a former president—the very frail John Quincy Adams.

As they entered the hall, Hannah moved about freely, talking with those of her acquaintance whom she passed on the way to the table, introducing Joshua with great decorum and style. He struggled to keep names and faces together. While no one looked familiar, he recognized the names of some as being carved on the facades of banks or factories or mentioned often in newspapers.

The conversation at their table leapt from the presidential election campaign to the newly formed political party to the U.S. concern over the growing interest of France and Great Britain in the Hawaiian Islands. There was much discussion of the troubles brewing near Texas and Mexico and the state of the European nobility and finally the growing discontent among the young people of the nation. Joshua was asked if it were true that the youth had grown disenchanted with hard work and the goals of their parents. He tried not to blush as he answered.

"I cannot speak for all, but I know I've worked hard to pay my way through Harvard Divinity School, and my friends are dedicated to knowledge and the Truth."

A few of the guests around the table nodded as if they appreciated the young man's hard work and resolve, yet a few others narrowed their eyes as if wondering what this lower working-class man was doing sullying Harvard's reputation of class and culture.

Hannah whispered, without breaking her smile, "And what about the time Jamison locked his journalism professor out of the room?"

Joshua had to bite his lip to keep from a loud guffaw. Jamison told the story often, and each time when he described the professor coming back with the constable and a score of members of the fire brigade in tow, no one could help but dissolve into laughter. Hannah managed to elbow him gently without being seen. Joshua held his starched napkin to his mouth and pretended to cough, hiding his laughter.

A man with a flowing white beard stood at the head table and began to loudly hit the table gong, while holding in the other hand his crystal goblet, half-filled with wine. Some splashed out with each tap. Hannah quickly stood.

"Joshua, would you be so kind as to accompany me outside for a moment?"

Puzzled, Joshua stood obediently and pulled out her chair.

"You will all excuse us for a moment, will you not?" Hannah asked the table guests and received a murmured yes.

Hannah took Joshua's arm and navigated him along the wall and through the massive double doors in the rear of the hall that led to the lobby and coatrooms. Heading toward a set of winding stairs, she took his hand and began to walk fast, then almost run, causing her dress with its crinoline underskirts to swish with each long step. At the first level, she turned a corner and pointed to a door.

"Through here! Quick!" she whispered.

Joshua threw open the door and stepped onto a balcony closed off by a brocade drape. Through a slit in the drapery, Joshua peered out and saw that it was a private box above the banquet hall floor.

"I had to escape before they start with the speeches," Hannah said, gasping for breath. "Up here, I can listen and relax, and if anyone asks, I will be able to relate much of what was said tonight—as if any of it makes a difference."

"Hannah," Joshua replied, unsure of how much surprise to show, "how can you be so cavalier about this? There is a former president at the head table!"

She peeked out between the slit.

"Oh, him? I have heard him before. He can be very dry."

"Dry? Just like that? A former president? Dry?"

Hannah giggled. "Don't be such a stick-in-the-mud, Joshua. Life is short." She peeked out at the group again. "Hand me one of those candies I saw you pocket."

Joshua's cheeks grew hot. He was certain no one had seen him palm the handful of toffees that were ignored by everyone else at the table.

"Please, Joshua. I know you have them."

He shrugged, reached in, and withdrew a candy. She snatched it from his hand and opened the slit in the curtain an inch or two further. Grinning like a tomboy, she looked back at Joshua, then pitched the candy out onto the crowded banquet floor. Joshua, stunned, was too late in leaping to restrain her arm. She snapped the curtain shut and hissed, "Get down! They'll see you!"

Joshua had no time to think and ducked behind a velvet-covered balloon-backed chair. He had visions of a team of constables charging up the steps in an effort to find the ruffian responsible for hitting John Quincy Adams in the forehead with a toffee.

He shut his eyes and waited. He heard no commotion from the floor, other than the gentle hum of conversation. Then he heard Hannah begin to laugh, soft at first, then louder and faster. After a minute he could restrain himself no longer and joined her.

She held a hand over her mouth and looked out.

"I think I missed. Hand me another."

Joshua stood up. "I most certainly will not. I will not become a cheap ruffian."

Hannah turned to him, hands on hips, her face twisted in mock outrage.

"So I'm now a ruffian, am I? Well, Joshua Quittner, perhaps I should take my nasty and evil disposition and turn it on you to teach you a lesson." She held her fists in front of her like a caricature of a pugilist and danced from side to side.

Startled at this action, Joshua began to laugh harder.

As she took a step forward, a louder clanking of the table gong began from below, and a deep voice broke over the hum of conversation, calling for attention and alerting the crowd that the speeches were about to begin. Hannah jutted her jaw out defiantly.

"You've been saved by a speech, Joshua. Or else you would have gotten a sound thrashing for certain."

He had never seen Hannah so playful, so animated. A tiny part of him was shocked by her gleeful breaking of decorum and rules, but a larger part of him reveled in her loosened inhibitions.

They rearranged the chairs in the darkened box, each having a seat as well as a place to rest their feet. Hannah leaned back and offered a grand, relieved sigh.

Joshua looked into her eyes and, despite the dim lighting, saw a revealing glance. It was as if she had clearly said, *I enjoy your company, Joshua, and we have fun together . . . and I feel no threat of the amorous kind. We are simply friends and no more.* He tried his best not to shudder.

After a few announcements, the first speaker began his remarks. Some minutes later Joshua leaned over closer to Hannah.

"Thank you."

She turned and smiled. "Thank you for what?"

"You were right. These speeches are boring. And it's indeed more comfortable here."

She reached over and patted his hand. "Think nothing of it, my friend."

He could do little else but stare at her in the dark. His chair was set back just so that his fixed glaze could not be construed as intrusive. It would appear he was only gazing at the slit in the curtains, the only source of light in the box. It just so happened that Hannah was in the path of his vision.

Despite the distinguished and esteemed speakers that paraded up to the dais, Joshua found himself unable to concentrate. His thoughts charged off in a hundred different directions, like the scattering of snowflakes in a December wind.

Does she have any idea how much she captivates my heart? I'm certain she does not, for I've never had the courage to even hint at my feelings. I can share my faith but not my emotions–and such is my struggle.

But then what are my feelings?

I look upon these years and months at seminary and with my three wonderful friends as the happiest and most rewarding time of my life. How can I bear to leave our happy camaraderie? How can I bear to be without our late-night discussions? How will the iron of my ideas and theories be sharpened without my companions and their questioning?

Is there not a way we might stay together?

Gage will be in New York, that's certain. His wealth will tie him to that city– as will his family and business. Jamison will most certainly work from New York as well. That's the locale of the truly well-respected newspapers. He's so skilled with words, he'll have no trouble finding a position. Hannah . . . perhaps she would prefer to return to Philadelphia, but I'm certain she finds New York more cosmopolitan–with more amenities and culture than any other city in America. She could be happy there.

That finds the three all in close proximity to each other.

Then what of myself?

He hesitated, taking in Hannah's silhouette once again: the sparkle of her eyes, the careful lips, pursed in thought and quick to laugh, the long elegant neck, the graceful white shoulders.

And what of me? I've made promises to family and friends, to be sure . . . but would they desire me to suffer a fate God has not ordained? Could he not be leading me to stay here, in Boston or New York? Did not Professor Wilcox claim I have the gift? Should I not use that where the most people can be reached?

He looked away from Hannah.

I do not want to think about this . . . but I could stay out East. I could be a ministerial candidate at a large church. Such a congregation would provide a higher amount of support so that I could then offer a certain level of comfort to a well-bred lady such as Hannah. I could find a calling here. I could keep Hannah and my friends within arm's reach.

I could do that. I truly could. I could serve the Lord here and wait until Hannah falls in love with me.

Just then Hannah said, "Give me another toffee."

Joshua reached into his pocket, then withdrew his hand quickly. "I will not. I will not be, this time, a willing accomplice to your devious tricks."

She giggled. "Sweet Joshua, I promise not to do anything untoward. I simply desire a sweet right now."

He narrowed his eyes, then slowly reached back into his pocket and withdrew a candy. "You promise?"

She nodded, taking the candy, then pretended to throw it through the curtains again. Joshua lunged after her arm, catching it midthrow. He held it tight and flicked the candy backwards. She opened her mouth wide, and it sailed in.

"I told you I promised."

He held her arm a few seconds longer than necessary, enjoying the feel of his hand encircling her arm, even though it was wrapped in a thick velvet sleeve.

Hannah swiveled her chair toward him.

"This is most pleasant. I wish it could always be this way."

And I do, too, Hannah, more than you can ever know.

⁂

A chorus of applause rose up from the hall below.

"It's over!" she said emphatically. "We must get back downstairs." With that she took his hand, and the two raced out the door and down the steps, just as the main doors opened and a stream of people poured out.

Hannah stood tiptoe, scanning the crowd as it parted around them much as a river parts about a stationary stone in the current.

Then a man's voice called out through the chatter, "Hannah! Over here! Hannah, it's Robert!"

Threading through the crowd, Joshua watched a tall young man with dark hair make his way toward Hannah and himself. He was impeccably groomed and dressed in a fanciful damask waistcoat and curved top hat.

"You have to meet Robert," Hannah confided. "You two will get along famously."

I don't like him already, he thought as Hannah extended her hand to Robert and Robert brought it to his lips. *While I've heard such a greeting is the standard in Europe, he's taking a great deal of liberty with Miss Collins.*

"Robert," Hannah said, turning and indicating Joshua, "this is the Joshua Quittner I've told you about. Joshua, this is Robert Keyes."

Robert extended his hand to Joshua.

He best not attempt to kiss this hand!

The man with brooding eyes took Joshua's hand and pumped it sternly.

"Nice to make your acquaintance. Hannah goes on and on about you. She has spent hours detailing your escapades in New York and your clever antics at Harvard."

Joshua could think of no reply to this stranger who knew more about him than most people did.

Robert focused on Hannah, almost ignoring Joshua, and said, "I looked up to your table and, like a wisp, before the speeches began, you disappeared. Hannah, if I were your father . . ."

Hannah tapped his chest with gentle fingers.

"Then I'm most gratified, Mr. Keyes, that you are not. You are jealous that I've found ways to make these events tolerable, I'm sure."

"And I am sure that I am not," Robert added, his words a bit cold. "It is just that one must be aware of appearances and decorum. There are things we all must endure with a glad heart."

Joshua wanted to defend Hannah but was unsure what to say. And if he did so, would that be admitting he was with Hannah? And would that be a breach of manners as well?

"Hannah, my dear," Robert began.

My dear? Why is he addressing her with such an intimate appellation?

"You need be aware that people are watching at all times and that people will talk. I admit this gathering has few of the earmarks of a proper society function, but nonetheless . . ."

As Robert went on about the acceptable methods of behavior at such functions, Hannah nodded in all the right places. Finally Robert stopped and looked about.

"Now, you two must forgive me. I must return to the side of my dear aunt who had begged me to be her escort this evening. And once again, Hannah, I express deep regrets that I could not be your escort tonight. Nice to have met you, Mr. Quibbnor."

And with that Robert disappeared into the milling crowd.

⚜

"He is a very old friend of the family, Joshua—a very proper young man—from a family we've been acquainted with for ages. I find it amusing that my parents have told me on many occasions how fitting a suitor he would be."

Joshua's heart thumped and missed a beat.

A suitor? Why is it that I've never heard his name? A fitting suitor?

As she continued, her words rose to a higher-pitched chatter. "But I've told them *I* am in charge of my own destiny, just as you've always said, Joshua. I have replied that, perhaps, in a few years, after I attempt to see this medical training to its fruition . . . I might consider such an idea. But now? Really, Joshua. My parents can be such inopportune people at times. To talk of suitors and all."

Joshua felt as though he were floating in a dream, and Hannah's words were drifting up at him from far below, somehow escaping his hearing.

"When I'm finished with my schooling, then he and I . . . well . . . perhaps he might consider calling on me. Perhaps by then he will be richer and a tad less pompous, don't you think?"

She glanced at Joshua. His face, he was certain, was pocked with anger and betrayal.

"I mean," she hurried on, "that he is a handsome boy . . . and you know, comes from an upstanding family with a great financial future. He makes his money doing something with stocks . . . or bonds . . . or something like that. I'm never quite sure, and when he tried to explain it to me, I must admit I was baffled."

She paused, looked down, and with a single finger fussed with the lace trim of her dress.

"I always intended to tell you about him. But since all of this was so off in the future, I thought it best not to. And Gage said—"

"Gage knows him? He's met him? He knows about this arrangement?" Joshua's words were measured carefully, and he tried, without much success, to keep anger from coloring them harsh and cruel.

"Well, they do travel in some of the same circles, I imagine. You know . . . stocks and bonds and all that . . ."

"You mentioned his line of work previously."

Hannah stared at him, her expression unfathomable.

That's when Joshua made his decision: *I'll not show her anything that is in my heart. Not now. Not ever again.*

"He seems like a nice fellow, Hannah. He does indeed," Joshua said shortly, and, without waiting for a reply, he reached into his pocket and retrieved a token. "Wait here, and I'll fetch our coats."

He walked away, hoping he was out of eyeshot before the pain in his heart found flesh as a tear.

CHAPTER EIGHT

FROM THE JOURNAL OF JOSHUA QUITTNER
CAMBRIDGE, MASSACHUSETTS
FEBRUARY 1844

I'VE resolved that Hannah will no longer occupy so many of my thoughts. I understand Robert Keyes is not her "intended" officially, but I'm well aware he is farther up the list than I am—even if I dared dream I'd be on such a list.

I berate myself for having this anger, for Hannah never promised more than she has given. And to be honest, I'm an interloper into her world—a country boy attempting to pass myself off as a potential sophisticate. I fear it will never happen. And it is not fear, but resignation. And not really resignation, but acceptance.

Now on to things that are less confusing.

I recall being so worried about the scholarship needed at Harvard. I observed that many fellow students sounded much more learned than I, but the fact is I'm every bit their equal—and often their superior.

Last night was a case in point. I was sitting in the library (which is much warmer than 619 Follen, and I do not have to stoke the fire), working on my Greek vocabulary, when Giles Barthlemon came up and asked for my help. Giles is in several of my classes and has no sterling reputation for his studies. Many fellow students have described him as being an unrepentant bounder. His activities, in fact, have led him to be considered somewhat of an outcast among seminarians; no one wants to be painted with the same brush he is tinted with, so most avoid him. I have noticed the odor of liquor and smoke on his clothing, which must be a testimony to his off-campus activities.

But there is something about him that evokes my pity. And a Christian is in the business of helping others, is he not?

After a few questions, I realized he had fallen woefully behind in Greek comprehension. My quick quiz resulted in him naming perhaps 50 percent of the words correctly.

"What will you do?" I asked. "There will be a test within the week on several chapters."

He shrugged. "The fellow who sits across the aisle–Michael something or other–has the largest handwriting you might wish for. I can always glance over and check my work as I go."

Imagine my shock. A seminary student blatantly admitting that cheating on an examination was permissible and acceptable.

I should turn him in to the professor–but I will not. He'll suffer his own punishment in due time.

MARCH 1844

Giles met his match. Professor Graham, from the rear of the classroom, observed his attempts at "borrowing" from his classmate's paper and physically ejected him from class, amidst many gasps. Most students feel that, at last, Giles has gotten what he deserved.

I had warned him, and now he must face the punishment. As the two scuffled out and down the hall, the word in the classroom was that Giles faces immediate expulsion. "Wasn't the first time he copied," said the fellow whom Giles was copying from. "Felt his stare on every test."

And yet Giles is from a prominent, upstanding New York family. His father is a preacher, of all things. How will his parents bear this terrible news?

Our own Jamison recently won the coveted (at least some say coveted) Oak Leaf Writing Award for a story on immigrants living in Boston. Jamison refused to enter it on his own; it was the *Crimson Review* advisor who submitted it behind his back. Jamison acts aloof, as if it does not matter, but I can detect a hint of pride in a story well told. In fact, the state legislature is looking at the conditions described with a possible law as response to his story.

Jamison scoffs at such action. "As if they can actually accomplish something with their laws," he said derisively.

Gage and I have talked long into the night on many occasions. He's fascinated by everything. He asks about the Bible and its teaching on money—often. Maybe it's because gold, to Gage, is the only yardstick to measure life.

"It's how one keeps score," he once said.

I told him, for a poor boy from Ohio, money is simply a way to stave off starvation. There is not much scorekeeping going on.

Gage laughed. "If a rich farmer bought up a huge spread and started hiring hands at top dollar, wouldn't everyone pay attention to him? Wouldn't the church elders seek him out as a new member?"

I bristled, but he made me think about it. I dislike admitting it, but Gage is right. That sort of money would carry a lot of weight—even in innocent Shawnee.

Gage asked if a rich man had more of God's blessing because he was rich. Or was it the devil, corrupting an innocent man? I told him the Bible says the rain falls on the just and unjust. Money can be a blessing but also a curse. I think I saw a wistful expression in his eyes, but I'm not sure.

Does he want more money or less?

APRIL 1844

This afternoon Hannah appeared at our residence unannounced, totally unexpected, and almost in tears. Gage and I were both at home, and for the sake of propriety (and convenience—as Gage had not cleaned his parlor in days) we used the downstairs parlor.

Mrs. Parsons hovered in the kitchen, rattling saucers on teacups to let us know she could burst into the room at any moment.

Hannah sniffed as she related the story of being told not to come to the following week's anatomy class. This would be the first time an actual male cadaver would be autopsied, and the instructor had said her presence would make the other students uncomfortable.

Gage took great offense. "The college takes her tuition money for the class, then prohibits her from accomplishing its goals? Preposterous!" He stormed out, leaving me with Hannah to cry on my shoulder–literally.

I never thought she was that fragile or truly cared about her scholarship. Gage had remarked she was at Harvard to land a rich husband, and while it made me angry at the time, I was forced to agree with him. There were worse ways for a woman to spend her time, I guessed. Now her tears made my considering her a gadfly appear spiteful.

I don't know how Gage accomplished it, or if money was passed from hand to hand, but the following day, Hannah was back in class. The professor offered her both an invitation and an apology.

How was the "delicate" matter to be handled? A draping of cloth would be added to the cadaver, and Hannah had to promise to be absent from the most sensitive dissections, but as Gage said, "A lung is a lung, and a kidney is a kidney. You'll see 99 percent of the insides of the poor fellow–and I bet that's more than enough."

It was a small victory for Hannah, and her spirits were strengthened.

As we spent those anguished hours waiting for Gage to work his magic with the powers that be, I read her the Proverbs 31 passage. I believe it was the first time she'd heard or, at any rate, truly listened to these Scriptures. Admittedly, this portion of the Bible is not the favorite sermon topic for many pastors. (Just as I've never heard a sermon on the Song of Solomon, I've never once heard my father read these proverbs from the pulpit.)

Hannah was effusive in her praise for both Gage and me. How delicious I find her company, even though I know the truth of her situation. If she only knew of my feelings, perhaps things might be different.

MAY 1844

I have fewer and fewer moments to record my thoughts in this journal. School and classwork progress at a frantic pace. There's so much to learn from books and so many long hours of discussions with friends. Which is the most rewarding? I will know when I actually take over a pulpit. But right now my soul delights in these friendships.

And spring is upon us. The first greenings and warmth descend on a gray, chilled-to-the-bone Cambridge. And I admit the campus has become a tad bit on the eccentric side. All manner of people are out and about in their fancy dress gamboling and frolicking.

I know the love of money is an evil that true believers should shun, but having a friend with such resources as Gage makes it difficult at times.

Last Friday, as a warm breeze was blowing in from the south, Gage assembled the four of us and spirited us off in his carriage to a wharf on Back Bay. Then we boarded a trim, gleaming two-masted schooner, thirty-six feet long and twelve feet wide, that he had commissioned for the day. On board, the entire crew was there to satisfy our every desire. Such a wondrous time!

Yes, I know that back home in Ohio people are struggling to plow fields, working long, painful hours. But that afternoon, as we glided over silver water, a hint of summer in the air, and with the galleymen bringing out trays of oysters and—a first-time taste for me—caviar on crackers, how could I resist its allure? (The caviar, I can resist, for certain. It tasted like an accumulation of the ocean's raw brine in a single bite.)

Yes, I struggle. Yes, such luxuries can be seductive, and I pray I'll not succumb to their ultimate destructive lure. But for now I have allowed myself to enjoy them.

Hannah was alone on the bow, the wind blowing her hair about her shoulders. I saw her lips curve into a wonderfully inviting smile, and I was set to make my unsteady way to her for a private word or two when I saw Jamison, a hesitant smile on his face, making his own way to Hannah.

My heart skipped a beat. Could he be as interested in her company as I am? As they talked, I admit my heart twisted nervously. I wondered if Jamison had displaced me from her affections—though I know such a thought is ridiculous since neither of us can possibly figure in her future.

SHAWNEE, OHIO
JUNE 1844

I had forgotten how hot Ohio can be. No wind, little rain, dust everywhere, sun unrelenting. Crops look promising despite the lack of water. Farmers are optimistic for a good year.

The first Sunday back, I stood with my father at the front of the church and shared in worship duties—the reading of the Scriptures, the announcements, and the like. As I sat in the front looking out over the congregation now numbering nearly one hundred—new families arriving and farms springing up—I have to thank Gage for his instructions on the complexities of life and (I nearly blush as I write this) on women. Several of the young unmarried females of the congregation have chosen to stare at me during the service rather than look at my father or listen to him preach. It's most amusing, for I sit on the right side of the church, on the deacon's bench, and every single woman had chosen that day to sit on the right side as well. If Gage had not told me the workings of the feminine mind, I would have thought no more of this. Or worse yet, thought each woman was focused in horror on my appearance. No, I've become more sophisticated (though I'll never reveal this learning to my mother), and I realize those women are merely stating their interest in me.

From a purely aesthetic viewpoint, none of them surpasses Hannah in a comparison of physical features and how they are arranged, though a few come close—specifically one Constance McArthur. The McArthurs are new to the county, from Gallipolis on the river, and have purchased the old Larimar land. That means they are not of trifling means. And Constance is most comely, though still young.

I'm certain she would not be Hannah's equal in learning, conversation, and social skills.

I remind myself that pairing Hannah and myself in the same breath approaches a high level of ludicrousness.

It's hot, and a sea of hand fans gently sway as I look out. Constance, although not formally introduced to me yet, smiles invitingly. Following Gage's admonitions against giving too much away too early, I smile back, in a smaller fashion, and offer an imperceptible nod. Constance must have seen it, for her smile broadens, and she bends forward in the pew.

Perhaps there will be a dinner invitation forthcoming. If Gage were here, he'd whisper that he'd "wager a month's interest on it."

And on that particular Sunday, he would have won.

JULY 1844

Work has been difficult. I see my father growing quickly into an old man. Until this summer I felt that his work and output always surpassed mine, such was his vigor and stamina. This summer, however, I know I've worked harder and longer and have produced more. This is not written as a complaint—just facts.

No one mentions it, but I believe both he and my mother know it. Such is the inevitable outcome of any life. No man can live forever—in this world, that is. Eternal life is only to come in heaven.

We've received a good amount of rain this month, and all signs portend an outstanding crop.

One evening, after supper, my father nearly fell asleep at the table. Till this day I would have thought such tiredness unthinkable for him. Caught in the act, he roused himself and took his coffee on the front step of the house.

"If your mother and I could find a way to increase our income by a few hundred dollars a year, we could live off my pastor's stipend and not have to worry about the hard work of farming ever again," he mentioned as I joined him on the porch.

If the land was ours and not rented, he would sell it in a heartbeat, I'm sure. The few acres we do own, with the house and the chickens, would not return enough money to be invested and yield sufficient interest.

I'm certain that when graduation comes, he expects me to return, perhaps build a house on this land, and help support him and my mother as they age.

I know that such a course is proper . . . but do I admit my darker thoughts? Being tied to this patch of ground may be my future, but could there be a time when I'm unfettered?

Hannah will remain out East, as will everyone else. And here I am, forced to take this pastorate as if it's the only pastorate in which God can use my services. Is that truly his will for my life?

I've read these lines and wanted to cross them out in an angry scrawl. But I will not. Yet my heart has been convicted. These dear people gave me life and sacrificed for me with no desire for their own well-being. The least I can do is support them as they've supported me.

AUGUST 1844

The heat of the past fortnight makes preaching on eternal damnation easy. "You think this is hot? Want more of the same?" my father called. "Then keep your sinful ways, and you will live for eternity in Ohio in August." The congregation, sweaty and limp, laughed heartily in spite of the terrifying admonition.

In the midafternoon, when no breath of a breeze is to be found, I've often slipped to the stream near the house and the deep pools hidden by shade trees. Shedding myself of all constraints (and I choose not to explain further for good taste), I slide into the cool water and float in its gentle embrace, feeling the currents remove sweat and grime as well as my cares.

I have been correct about Constance McArthur. The Sunday after I first saw her, Mr. McArthur, a robust, broad-chested man with an immense beard, grasped my hand with the powerful grip of a hard worker and invited me to share dinner with them. My mother, from several feet away, was beaming. She has declared that the McArthurs are most sophisticated—head and shoulders above any other Shawnee family that includes an available young lady. How could I refuse his offer?

I was surprised they are using the old Larimar house only on a temporary basis and are having a larger and much finer house built next to it. This means Mr. McArthur is more than a simple farmer and must have found other means of investment. The new home is designed smartly and will be the envy of even a Bostonian. There will be etched-glass gas lantern shades, silk draperies, and fine uphol-stered furniture. There will be a clavichord in the parlor, now on order from a firm in New York, I'm told. Constance is skilled in musical endeavors.

She is also indeed pleasant and agreeable. She and her mother joined her father and me on the porch after a delicious meal. She smiled easily and seemed interested in the affairs of the world, though she remained mostly silent, as might be proper on a "first meeting." (Yet I must admit that her silence made me yearn for Hannah's gregariousness.)

Mr. McArthur was interested in my studies at Harvard and even more fascinated when I spoke of Gage Davis. It appears he has heard of the Davis family and may have had some dealings with freight and shipping interests in Gallipolis. He asked me all sorts of ques-tions about what Gage and his father were planning on doing in the business world. I admitted complete ignorance of their plans.

As in church, Constance watched me throughout the afternoon, offering a smile every time I looked her direction. It was a pleasant afternoon. Indeed, I scarce thought of the heat.

CAMBRIDGE, MASSACHUSETTS
SEPTEMBER 1844

Back to seminary and Cambridge—and on this journey I am a man of two hearts. One is heavy for having to leave my parents with half the harvest still to be brought in. They have much work ahead, and my father looks unwell at times. (Despite his tiredness, he insisted most forcibly that I must return to school.) He is most dogged that I complete what I've begun.

Yet another heart beats in my chest, and it rejoices at my return East and to the refined culture and sophistication. There are no chickens to be fed or slaughtered. There are no pigs to be slopped. There are no cows to be milked twice a day. Instead of dirt, there are educated people in great abundance.

I feel most at home in Cambridge.

I am not being a snob but a realist. The people in Shawnee are simply not the intellectual equals of the people here. I missed the challenging and witty conversations. Gage has been back for nearly a week, Jamison for a few days, and Hannah is due tomorrow. Gage is anxious to have us together again. He said he despaired of laughing the entire summer, not having myself or Jamison to provide him with smiles.

I asked him of his summer. "I attended meetings, I sat through insufferable luncheons and interminable dinners, and I signed endless contracts. I think I made a lot of money for my father. But I could not wait to get back."

I nodded. While my summer and Gage's summer were universes apart, I understood what he meant. Here feels like home and family, and we accept one another as we are. Back home, whether in Ohio or New York, there are family or others who expect you to behave in a certain manner. And we both behaved as expected.

I always thought that when God had a plan for your life and you followed that plan and did his will, then your heart would feel settled and sure. In fact, I'm certain that's how God communicates at times— by providing a peace and a calm to one's emotions.

So how am I to figure God's plan now? In Ohio I know there is a calling and a need for my abilities as a pastor and a son. Shawnee needs me, as do my parents. They love me and want me home. Yet it is on the tree-shaded streets of Cambridge and in the shadow of the ivy-coated walls of Harvard that I truly find my heart at peace and . . . somehow most alive.

Where are the Scriptures that address this conundrum?

OCTOBER 1844

After being on campus now for what seems like many years, I thought I'd seen everything. Students here are nothing if not extremely inventive in their pranks.

Last night two students (and I'll not reveal their names here, but Gage and Jamison are intimately acquainted with them) "borrowed" a horse from the local hackney service, dressed it with bells and ribbons and a lady's bonnet, and loosed it in the administration building. Where they found the key, I'll not even ask.

I was alerted to their plans before sunrise. So were many others, apparently, for a crowd had gathered near the venerable building at the beginning of the school day. Within minutes the president stormed out of the building, red-faced and sputtering, arms gesturing in the air. He immediately spied the larger-than-usual number of students on the front steps and accused us all of complicity. This set off a howl of protest, and the constables and janitorial crew were called. We sprinted off to morning classes, hiding snickers as we ran.

Yes, I know laws were broken, but no real harm was done.

A week later Gage was actually threatened with expulsion—but not for the horse prank. He somehow arranged to delay the arrival of a professor and dressed the part himself as a substitute. He managed to convince the members of the freshman class (a humanities lecture) that they would be holding the lesson outdoors. He had them snaked, arm in arm, in a long line halfway across campus when his ruse was uncovered.

This time I'm sure some monies traded hands, and Gage was left to stay with only a reprimand on his record—as if that would truly hinder his future successes.

Mentioning successes—I too have had my share. Because of the unsolicited endorsements of Professor Wilcox, I have been more and more engaged as speaker at a number of churches whose pastors are ill or on leave. I do not consider myself a polished speaker, but perhaps it's my "homespun" approach that appeals to congregations. I've been asked back to do additional services by several of them. In fact, one Baptist church in the heart of Boston has asked if I might consider serving as assistant pastor after my seminary duties. I said I'd think and pray on it.

I know what my answer must be, yet I hesitate to close the door.

NOVEMBER 1844

As my divinity school training goes on, I feel more and more sure of myself in the pulpit. When I stand before a congregation, despite my natural reticence, the words flow, and my stories reach the listeners.

I know this is not my doing but God's truth revealed through me. And for his gifts, I am most grateful.

After one evening service that I presided over–at a small but wealthy church in Beacon Hill overlooking the Back Bay–Gage presented himself to me. It seems that every time friends attend one of my services, they need to remain hidden in the back pews or balconies until the end. I'm never sure if they do so because they do not want to hurt my feelings if my sermons prove truly awful–and thus can slip out unnoticed–or perhaps, like I think with Gage, they are uncomfortable with God's truth and seek to be inconspicuous. I know God sees them, but they must believe that sitting in the shadows protects them from his scrutiny.

On this evening it almost appeared Gage *had* been affected, for his eyes showed a vulnerability. "Your words touched me, Joshua. I've never heard such things before," he said. I thanked him and pressed to see if he truly understood what a relationship with the living God might mean in his life. He stiffened, then smiled. "I'll not have you saving my soul just yet," he said, laughing. Then he added softly, "But let me know if there's ever anything I can do to help you. Anything."

And with that he slipped away again. What does his "anything" really mean, I wonder?

And later this same month, Jamison and I happened to be walking back from the Commons to the Destiny. Jamison can be the happiest pessimistic person I know, often reveling in the most horrible news, as if that somehow confirms the vitality and truth of his own existence.

I shared with him the reason I have confidence in the future. He scoffed. "The future is for idealists and dreamers. All I believe in is today—what I can see and taste and touch. Tomorrow may never happen, my friend. I've no use for that which may never be."

Even though he presents a thick wall of indifference to things of a spiritual nature, there are flashes of hope that sometimes break through Jamison's despair. Perhaps I'll have a chance to reach him someday. I know his eloquence with the written word is unsurpassed. God could use that talent in a mighty way.

And with him coming from a family that serves the Lord, I find his indifference, often verging on outright hostility, to be perplexing. His anger is an anger I've also seen in other Harvard Divinity School students—some, in fact, from homes of preachers. I wonder if it's a hazard of growing up too close to a higher standard and observing the gulf between perception and reality.

DECEMBER 1844

Once again I'll forsake Christmas at home and the wondrous activities and celebration to stay within the confines of 619 Follen. Both time and money are in shorter supply this month than ever before, so a trip home is out of the question. I did send my father a commentary on Romans, although, unlike his preaching, this writer's work greatly emphasizes God's absolute grace. My father believes in grace but finds it hard to believe that horrid, abject sinners will be offered the same "easy grace" as moral, upstanding people. I will not argue the subject with him anymore, but I thought this volume might give him pause to consider. My mother will receive a rather elegant scarf that I purchased at a smart women's apparel shop in Boston. With those two gifts, my wallet has grown slim and will provide for no other holiday expenditures.

I've not mentioned Hannah often in these pages of late. That is by choice. We are still the best of friends—the four of us, that is—and she often dines with us at the Destiny. She regularly has us in stitches of laughter as she describes embarrassing moments in her medical classes. At a recent demonstration of a surgical technique on a cadaver, two strong, virile men in her class fainted dead away, clumping to the floor like wounded ducks, she said. I so admire her pluck for going through these horrid-sounding classes where flesh is sliced and organs taken out for inspection. The mere thought of it makes me queasy, but when Hannah tells her tales, her face flushes, not with embarrassment or queasiness, but with excitement.

I do not mention Hannah often, for when I reread the lines, my heart twists ever so slightly for the prize I think I've lost. But one cannot lose what one never has owned, and I have never owned the prize. So I avoid the subject and its attendant confusions.

Speaking of surprises, however, and confusions—Jamison stopped in at the Destiny last week with a tattered, well-worn book in his hand. It was a guide to Oregon and California written by an army scout or some such person. It was filled with descriptions of men fording rivers and crossing mountains and fighting off red savages along the way. It sounded frightful, if the truth be told.

With a gleam in his eye, Jamison asked if I might like to come west with him on a grand adventure to the Pacific Ocean. I must have appeared startled.

"Gage has no need of adventure," Jamison said. "And he would not come with me. I could not ask Hannah, of course. That means you and I must go."

But while I have often daydreamed of such adventure, to actually do such a thing is unlikely.

"Don't they need God out there as well?" he asked. "Wouldn't that be a mission field for you?"

I wanted to respond, but I did not.

JANUARY 1845

As has been the custom for the Quittner family ever since I can remember, New Year's Eve is spent on one's knees, asking for God's blessing and praying for his continued guidance. While hundreds and hundreds of miles separate us, I've continued the practice. Gage and Jamison each invited me to separate functions: Gage's was an elegant soiree at the Harvard Club, and Jamison's a much more rollicking one to be held at the Harvard Rowing Club.

As I explained my reason for declining, both men seemed to soften and then asked quietly if I'd include them in my prayers. Of course I agreed. Perhaps my behavior is making an impact on their hardness. I hope so.

As I prayed, I heard from outside the sounds of the New Year echo in the darkness—shouts and explosions and trumpets. And I felt God tugging at my heart. I could not discern a specific message, but I know he has my life in his hands and I will follow him.

My last semester is about to begin, and while I'm assured of God's guidance, I despair at knowing where his path will lead me. I assume that, in time, it will be made clear.

Near the end of the month, Gage gathered us together and hustled us via his carriage to a pond not far from campus. There we donned ice skates, which we clamped and tied to our boots in a most ungainly manner. But once on the smooth ice, it was like flying. I have seen others skating before but never knew it was such a liberating, intoxicating experience to glide on the surface like a seabird swooping along the shore.

Arm in arm the four of us glided about in the afternoon light, the blades of the skates skimming over the ice, the wind slapping our cheeks to a robust redness, our laughter spilling about in the frigid air. As I looked down the line at the faces of my three special friends, I realized one reason for my deep affection. It is that I do not believe any of them truly knows Christ as Savior and Lord. Perhaps Hannah does, but in an infantile way. Jamison knows the way to salvation, but his heart is absent. Gage has other gods and goals, I believe.

Yet on this frozen afternoon, I knew I wanted them as friends forever.

Will God's plan include any of them in my life after graduation? Is it fair of him to have given them to me for such a short time, only to have me lose them?

FEBRUARY 1845

This short month can be most cruel. The days are brief, the sun is barely visible, the snow and wind nip at one's every step. And when the temperatures do warm a bit, the debris in the streets festers, and the slush and wetness seep into the most snug of boots.

Rather than becoming more difficult, classes appear to have become simpler. Perhaps it's because I now know what answers and attitudes my professors desire; perhaps it's because the truly difficult Greek and Hebrew courses are in the past; perhaps it's because I've become smarter.

Gage has moped about 619 Follen for several weeks. He ended a relationship with a wealthy young beauty from Stockbridge. This sort of affair-ending process had occurred a dozen times in his time at Harvard, and always Gage has emerged with renewed vigor to continue the hunt. This time, however, the loss has laid him low. Part of me is sad for him, for as he despairs, one light is gone from our circle of four. But part of me is encouraged, for often because of pain in this life, man admits his need for a greater power. Perhaps because of his pain, Gage will turn to God.

Jamison hounds me to accompany him on his trek across America. He purchased a map of the territories—the latest printed—and has set about marking trails and even writing to guides mentioned therein for costs and availability. We talk and I resist his exuberance, but it's difficult. The way he spins such tales of wonder and grandeur about the trip! He has practically worn out his *Emigrants Guide to Oregon and California*. Will he actually go? I would guess not, but Jamison has surprised us in the past.

Hannah is nearing completion of the medical studies she has been allowed at Harvard. Gage now believes Oberlin is her best chance at actually receiving a medical degree, and he has made inquiries for her there. The lone female among the nearly seventy-five men in her class, she holds the top position scholastically. She claims it is a woman's intuitive sense that makes her understand sickness and pathology better than most less-sensitive men. I agree with her on this. Most men are often ignorant of all but the obvious answers. It's why I'm certain most pastors need to be married. Their feminine mate can help point out what their less-aware sensibilities overlook.

Yet if Hannah is indeed so sensitive, so very intuitive, why, then, has she up until now ignored, or at least, overlooked, my feeling for her? How can she not see what is in my heart? Or am I so skilled at hiding my emotions now that I've practiced for nearly two and a half years?

MARCH 1845

Divinity school goes on. My opportunities in various local pulpits continue. I'm always working to improve upon my preaching skills. I do not wish to brag, but I'm aware of a greater fluidity on my part.

But what I have not overcome is the problem my heart encounters every time Hannah and I are alone. I've made quite sure that such a situation seldom occurs–and never occurs as a result of my own planning. Until this month, now nearly the end of winter, I've kept good on my promise that I would not allow Hannah to vex my heart any more than she already has.

Yet this one night, at the very end of March, Hannah and I found ourselves at a quiet table at the Destiny–alone. Gage was in New York, and Jamison out with a new lady friend (much to our collective surprise. Until now, Jamison had never mentioned women in that way).

The Destiny was uncrowded, and no casual acquaintance was handy, so Hannah and I dined privately.

I will not hold back my thoughts. She simply sparkles, and in the dim interior of the Destiny, her light filled our dark corner.

She related to me the latest news of her education. She has managed to take nearly all the required coursework needed to become a physician, save a few classes and a prolonged stint of practical work at a local hospital. However, that practical experience is a huge stumbling block. No hospital I know will allow a female doctor. They allow female nurses, seeing as how they are well suited to provide compassionate care and succor. But a doctor of the female sex? Hannah's ire rose as she recounted the conversations with the "gray-hairs"–the keepers of all things academic–at Harvard. They have been obstinate in their refusal to see any rules changed.

Yet despite this, Hannah has been kind. I've heard Gage hint at a possible solution. Perhaps more money toward the endowment? I would not place such largesse past Gage, but Hannah did not elaborate.

She spoke more of this Robert Keyes fellow. That discussion I did not enjoy. She kept mentioning the need in her life for security, owing to the lessened financial standing of her parents and the fact that this Keyes gent will have bushels of money rolling in as he makes his mark on the business world.

How I yearn to tell her such a goal is nonsense. Money provides nothing but heartache–eventually, at least. Money does no one good. It will not purchase happiness or passage to heaven. But the things I should have said remained unsaid. I simply sat and listened, happy in her company.

I resolved that night to investigate the possibility of finding a calling out East. Here, in a wealthy church, I could provide Hannah what she seeks–in a minimal way, at least. If I stayed in the East, I would still be in her life.

That evening, before I slumbered, I prayed I'd be allowed to find a way to stay close to this woman. I prayed mightily that I'd be allowed to remain here in this world that feels so comfortable and right. I prayed all night that God would grant my innermost desires as the Scriptures promise he'll do.

APRIL 1845

This letter from home says all that needs to be said of my prayers and God's intervention in my life.

My dear son, Joshua,

Your father has all but forbidden me to write this letter, but for the first time in our married life I know I must disobey his wishes. He is sick, Joshua. Very, very sick. I do not know the specific name of the illness, and Doctor Seple is somewhat puzzled as well. His strength is gone, and dizziness overtakes him when he attempts to work. There is trembling in his hands and hesitation in his steps. His condition is slowly becoming worse, although Doc says these cases can linger on for years with no change in symptoms. He says it doesn't look good for your father to get any better. I know he'll not be able to do what needs to be done with this year's crop. Uncle Hiram has helped as much as he's been able to, but he cannot do his own job and his brother's, too.

Your father cannot keep the church, either, for his thoughts are often tangled and confused.

He needs your help. We need your help.

I know you are so close to graduation. Is there some way you could leave early and still receive your degree?

Your father has been a good husband, father, and provider all these years. We have sacrificed a lot for your education. I do not want to jeopardize your diploma, but you are needed here.

Please, Joshua, I have no one else to ask. And I know I cannot do this myself.

In God's love,
Mother

CHAPTER NINE

Cambridge, Massachusetts
April 1845

JOSHUA walked up the wooden steps of 619 Follen, listening to their familiar creak and groan. His fingers trailed along the banister, tracing the particular pattern of nicks and paint chips he had touched hundreds of times before. He rattled the key in the lock, and the door squealed open.

His room was not much different this day than the first day he entered it some two and a half years prior. He had added few personal items, lacking both the resources and the inclination to personalize the space. Packing was a simple matter.

Because of Gage's generosity, Joshua had been forced to purchase a large canvas leather-handled haversack that now held nearly three dozen suits and shirts and three elegant—though a year out of style—topcoats. His housemate's expansiveness had enabled him to spend only a pittance on attire. And it would enable him to live in Ohio for several more years before he would need to replenish his wardrobe. He folded each item neatly as he packed them in his bag.

Wanting to be done with such chores, he immediately packed all his books and belongings except the outfit he would wear on the long train ride west. As he packed each book and journal, he imagined he was packing away his memories of this place as well. Perhaps one day he would take them out and revisit them, but not for a long while. He feared the visions would remain too sensitive for too long. As the tangible souvenirs disappeared into the sturdy trunk, he slipped his emotional memories away, too, hiding them in what he hoped was an easily forgotten corner of his heart.

A man is not destined to receive all his heart's desires, for the heart is wicked, and many desires would lead to disappointment, to be certain, Joshua pondered as he tightened the leather straps about the trunk. *Perhaps in the years to come I will understand why the door to this world so suddenly snapped shut. Perhaps God in time will show me the reasons. But for now, I will simply make my way home in order to do his bidding. That is all. That is the life he has prepared for me, one of a servant.*

His face glum, he looked over at the expensive topcoat hanging on a nail near the window. He felt tired and empty and cold.

A man of God must fear nothing and be content in all situations. And if I cannot conquer my own fears and capture my desires, then I will be an incompetent minister of the Word. I must be joyful as I return to serve the Lord.

He set his jaw.

I can be happy where the Lord leads me. I can and I will and I am . . . happy and satisfied. My father was, and I shall be.

He sat on the bed and stared at the floor.

And I vow and resolve, from this moment on, to be an obedient servant of God who will be used of the poor people in Shawnee County. That is my destiny and calling. It is what a loving son can offer to his father.

He stood and, with a sweep of his hand, grabbed at his clothes more abruptly than needed.

And I'm praying God will prepare my heart for such a life. If I indeed have a gift, then let the gift be used for the kingdom in Ohio.

⁂

Joshua had said quick good-byes to Gage and Jamison. Both were concerned with his father's health and knew Joshua had to return home—even if his heart was not set on the matter. He did not tell Hannah or seek her out.

He had packed last evening, immediately upon receiving the letter. As the dawn broke, he was ready to leave, and he bid farewell to Mrs. Parsons, who actually allowed a tear to break her normally stoic exterior.

Joshua would not awaken Gage. Their good-byes had been said the night before. That was enough. To prolong the farewells would only add pain.

His mother had been correct. He would be allowed to graduate. After packing, he had hurried to Professor Wilcox's home and explained the situation.

"Even if you failed every test between today and graduation," Wilcox declared, "you would still graduate near the top of the class. I am sure every professor will see to it that your final grade is reflective of your work to date. Leave with a good heart, Joshua. You have been my most promising student ever. Thank you. I wish you Godspeed wherever you go and in all you do."

As the hackney made its way from Harvard Square down the now-familiar Cambridge streets and over Craigie's Bridge across the Charles River and on to Boston, Joshua carefully took in all that he passed this day. He wanted what could be his last sight of Cambridge to be etched in his memory.

Boston, Massachusetts

Later, alone at the Boston depot, waiting for the earliest train west, he sat, his heart heavy. He was concerned, of course, for his father but perhaps more over the life he was leaving. That in itself was troubling. *How could a good son and servant of God think of such horribly petty things at such a time as this?* he chided himself. *God heard my prayer and answered it. I am to go to Ohio, plain and simple. It has always been so and always will be.*

Just before the train was to leave the station, a messenger boy ran along the tracks, calling out a name, holding an envelope high in his outstretched arm.

"Joshua Quittner!" he called. "Letter for Joshua Quittner!"

Startled, Joshua took the letter, boarded the train, and as it chugged out of Boston, tore the envelope open.

He knew whom it was from. There was the scent of lilies of the valley on the paper. Hannah loved lilies. In the corner were the letters "MHC," written by a feminine hand.

He willed his hands not to shake and his breath not to come in shorter gasps as he read the words.

Sitting on the edge of a hard seat, the morning sun peeking under the cracked window shades, he unfolded the single page inside the envelope.

Dear Joshua,

This will be a short, short note.

I am furious that you refused to tell me the news of your father's illness and your sudden leaving. How could you! After all we've meant to each other, you steal away like a thief in the night.

I wanted to say good-bye to you in person, to offer a farewell embrace at the least. Now I will not have that pleasure. Perhaps I will show up on your doorstep in the future. I am a persistent woman, remember?

I understand your need to return home. I truly do, Joshua. Perhaps, though, you will find a way to settle matters there and eventually return to the East. God could use you here—I'm certain of that.

I know I'm angry with God right now for taking you from our wonderful circle of friends. Perhaps I'll understand it in time—about your faith and your call, your servanthood and all the rest. I'll admit no understanding of any of it this day, for my heart hurts too much. Heaven knows how often you tried to explain it to me. I'm hoping that one day it will make sense.

I know you and I have enjoyed a special bond. I will always remember you with much admiration and affection.

Please do your utmost to stay in touch. Please? Life without you will be most plain.

Always,

Hannah

Joshua remained statuelike as he read the letter, despite the rocking and jostling of the train car. He wrestled with one overpowering question: *Do I save the letter, or discard it, thus truly ending this chapter of my life?*

He gently folded the paper, slipped it back into the envelope, and placed the envelope in his breast pocket.

I will decide later what to do with it, he determined.

It was not until the moon was near its nightly zenith that his thoughts finally slowed, and he nodded off to sleep.

CHAPTER TEN

Shawnee, Ohio
May 1845

JUST as dawn broke, a rooster crowed. Joshua awoke with a start, slapping at the bed coverings. His thoughts swam, disoriented. He blinked and wiped at his eyes.

"I am home in Ohio," he whispered to himself. "And that was just a rooster."

For most of the last two and a half years, Joshua had been awakened by a different chorus of early morning noises—delivery wagons, pushcarts and the voices of street vendors, and the low reverberation of Boston a few miles south.

There in the darkness before dawn, Joshua would often lie in bed for a moment, trying to decipher the calls of the city. Was that a train rumbling across an iron bridge? Was that a new ship ringing its announcing bell? Was that a fruit seller hawking his wares as he pushed through the avenues? Was that the steady clip-clop of the milk wagon?

In the city the chorus of noise was built, one rumble upon another, until it sounded as if the entire town were stretching awake. No one sound took precedent; no sound was much louder than the next.

But here, back in Ohio, the morning noise was much clearer, much more distinct. First the rooster called his greeting to the sun. Then followed the mooing of cows, waiting to be milked, lifting their heads in unison. Then the bleating of the goat and the squeal of a rusty barn hinge.

Each noise was separate, distinct, and easy to discern.

If only his new life were like that.

As he returned home, Joshua had thought that, even under these unsettling conditions, he would have a true sense of God's leading, of God's guidance. He listened for God's whispers, he tried to make out his heavenly nudges. Yet each day brought more and more silence from above.

The first few weeks in Shawnee had been a whirlwind of visits and often hushed conversation only steps away from his father's side. Family, friends, and most of the congregation stopped by, offering their welcome and halting condolences.

At first his father's appearance shocked him. Always a robust man, Eli Quittner had withered. His face was lined and wan, and the voice that once could fill a barn to its rafters was diminished to a throaty whisper. But the confusion of his thoughts had given way to his former unclouded mental state, and for that, all were grateful.

Joshua wrestled with God's verdict, asking more than once in his prayers, *What has my father done to deserve such a harsh reward? Is this God's love at work?*

Uncle Hiram had stepped in to fill the pulpit at the Shawnee Church of the Holy Word. Hiram could match Joshua's father for volume and duration, but his sermon content always leaned to the sparse side.

While at church, Joshua sat in the first row and carefully masked whatever criticisms his face might disclose of his uncle's sermons. He was sure everyone expected him to speak, now that he was back, but the bylaws of the church forbade anyone but an ordained minister to fill the pulpit. Joshua might give announcements and read from the Holy Book, but unless and until Joshua was ordained, he must remain silent.

This sleepy corner of Ohio was changing. In the years since Joshua had been gone, Shawnee had begun to blossom. Over thirty-six families had begun farming in the county, and half of them had become members of the church. There was a sprinkling of new faces in the pews. And in the weeks after Joshua's return, most of the eligible young women in town had made their way to a church service. But as of yet, none had been so bold as to walk up and engage him in actual conversation, being content with smiles and long, uninterrupted glances.

North of the church, along the main road of the county, six stores had taken root. The smell of fresh-cut wood and paint hung thick and sweet in the air. A main street, albeit muddy and rutted, had grown along a one-block stretch. The stores and self-proclaimed emporiums offered tin wares, food stuffs, and other assorted merchandise. The tavern had even begun to serve meals and feature the music of a real fiddler or piano player each weekend night.

Joshua tried not to compare these ragged shops to the glittering stores and retail concerns of Boston and New York, but the differences were jarring and hard to ignore.

Uncle Hiram preached; Joshua's father rested. Joshua worked his father's land, setting to working the land and waiting to hear the voice of God announce his calling.

Joshua did not wait long. The board of elders gathered a few weeks after he returned home.

The decision to call him to the church was the easy part. Everyone knew Joshua was gifted with words—even before he went off and learned more about the Bible. All twelve elders agreed he would make a fine preacher.

Everyone in the congregation assumed Joshua would soon be standing behind the pulpit, in the exact place where his father had stood these many years.

"But he ain't married," Sam Iverson said, appearing uncomfortable stating such an obvious fact. "And I ain't sure an unmarried preacher is the best preacher."

A handful of the elders nodded.

"A single man in the pulpit–I don't reckon the Bible had that planned. Don't it say a preacher is supposed to be married?"

Another replied, "It says a man should be married to only one woman, but it don't say a preacher *has* to be married. Not at least in what Scriptures I've read. If it were, we couldn't even have a widower in the pulpit."

"Married or not, Joshua would make one fine preacher. I read some of the letters from his professors there at Harvard. They say the boy is gifted–truly gifted with preachin' the Word. One professor said he could tell God has blessed the boy greatly. A professor with a bunch of initials behind his name and all."

"We can't let him slip away just because he ain't found a woman yet. He will. There is a good number of nice young women in town who would make anyone a fine wife."

"We all know Hiram is fine for now, just like we all know we won't be callin' him for permanent. We need to make sure Joshua don't find another callin'."

Hearty agreement filled the room.

"But can we say he should be married before we offer the call?"

More than half the elders shook their heads no.

"We can call him . . . ," Sam added, "then give him a real hard nudge towards gettin' married. That would be acceptable to most of us. Let him know we want him to find a good helpmeet on the quick side of things."

Each elder pondered that.

"Besides," Sam continued, "if we hire a single man, it's cheaper for the church. We don't pay as much for a single man as we do a married one. If he takes a year to find a woman, all the better for the budget."

There were nods all around.

"And still bein' single, he'll have more time to fix up the new parsonage real nice, so a woman might want to live there. I know he's got to help his folks now, but he'll be needin' a place of his own to live. And the new parsonage and his folks' house is only a mile apart."

The church had inherited, just after Christmas of last year, a musty, ramshackle log cabin that stood kitty-corner to the church. Its previous owner, a bachelor farmer, nearing death from consumption, willed it to the church after finding faith at the last moment. The structure itself was sound, but the interior needed work.

"That's true. It would give him time to prepare the house for proper married livin'. And you know these young people—they expect to spend time courtin'."

"Then it's settled? We call Joshua Quittner to be our pastor at the pay of twenty dollars per month. That would increase to twenty-five dollars if he were to get married?"

"Plus the parsonage—don't forget that."

"Plus the parsonage. All in favor?"

"And the official ordination is when?"

The secretary peered at the calendar. "How about July 5? We'll already be set for the Independence Day festivities. We can keep the tables up from that."

All twelve men nodded, and the church secretary dipped his quill in the inkwell, scratching out the proper words to reflect their vote in the old leather-bound book containing the history of the Shawnee Church of the Holy Word.

"It's official, isn't it?" Mae Quittner cried out, hugging her son tightly. "I knew they would call you. I knew it."

She let him go, insisting he keep reading. From the first word of the letter, Joshua's mother was at the edge of tears. She listened as he carefully read the invitation from the elders of the Shawnee Church of the Holy Word.

Then, taking him by the hands, she said, "I have dreamed of this day since the first time I held you in my arms. You took so long being born, and I was in such pain. When I saw your little eyes blazing back up at me, I knew God was going to use you. Use you in a mighty way. I just knew it, and that's when I promised you to God."

Joshua could do nothing other than reflect her broad and grateful smile.

Everyone in Shawnee County also knew Joshua's uncle would have loved to have been offered that same invitation. But his gifts for oration and scholarship held but a dim candle to Joshua's flaming torch. Joshua hoped Uncle Hiram would understand and bear no grudge.

"So I've prayed every day of your life," his mother continued, "that you would answer God's calling on your life and be a preacher like your father. And now, this very day, God has answered my prayers. One servant steps down, and another servant steps up."

The tears began to flow, and Joshua gathered his mother in his arms as she sniffed.

This truly is my destiny, he admitted again to himself, *for how could I disappoint God and my mother?* Then he prayed, *I was meant to be here . . . this is right, isn't it, Lord? You have honored my parents with this calling. You have honored me. And I shall serve you to my best ability and sacrifice.*

⁂

Later, Joshua's father called him over to his side. They were on the front porch, and the warm breeze carried the gentle scent of corn, barley, and wheat.

The older man's decline appeared to have halted. In fact, his health had improved since his son returned home. He managed to walk haltingly with a cane, the tremor in his hands had diminished enough to allow him to hold a knife and fork, and his speech had remained clear and his thoughts sharp. Though he grew tired after any exertion, he was in no obvious pain.

The family rejoiced that God had spared him further suffering.

Joshua watched his father as he read the invitation from the church board. Gratitude etched the deep lines of his father's face as he finished the letter. Then he motioned for Joshua to draw closer and embraced him in a fierce hug. Joshua was shocked; this sort of affectionate display was unexpected from a man not given to physical outbursts.

Then his father began to tell his son how proud he was of him.

With his only offspring walking in his footsteps, his heart overflowed with deep joy.

But as they talked, Joshua thought he also saw a hint of sadness in his father's demeanor. Was his father saddened that this invitation marked the end of his preaching days—and his obvious usefulness? He had often remarked how wonderful it would be to be ministered to, rather than always ministering to others. Was that shading of eyes and voice a hint of jealousy or regret—or perhaps anger? After all, Joshua's initial salary was twice what they paid his father.

If it isn't any of those emotions, then what is it? Joshua thought.

That night as he lay in his bed, he began to fear the truth of his father's response. With a chill in his heart, Joshua realized his father was sad—sad for what his son had just done. Joshua was a young man with great promise and unlimited possibilities. And with that letter, he had tied his entire future to a one-horse town in a backwater county of rural Ohio. Shawnee, after all, lay far from the glittering capitals of thought and culture.

Shawnee thwarted the dreams of my father, Joshua thought with a sudden fluttering of his heart, *and that was the reason for his sadness. He sees the same gloomy future for me!*

Waves of dark despair began to crash against Joshua's soul.

But that couldn't be, Joshua argued with himself, fighting the thoughts, *for he wanted this as my destiny as much as my mother did.*

He tried to close his eyes and find sleep.

I'm simply imagining things. My father wants me here and has always wanted me here.

But his eyes were still open when the first rooster crowed, announcing the beginning of a new day.

⁂

There was no question in Joshua's, his parents', or the board's minds as to Joshua's final decision to the elders' invitation. Even though he waited nearly a week to inform the board of his answer, no one in town harbored any doubt.

Afterwards, each of the twelve elders made a point to stop by the

Quittner farm. They shook the hand of their new preacher, extending a promise to assist in every way they could.

Following one visit, his father nudged Joshua. "Enjoy this time, Joshua. Once you start preaching, you'll have at least one of them upset with you every week over something you said."

Joshua laughed, then turned serious as the warning became clearer. "Really? All the time? One a week?"

His father smiled. "Sometimes it's much more than one."

"You never talked about this before. All the time I was growing up I never knew."

"Son, I protected you and your mother from a lot. Didn't want my trials to become your trials. That's a good piece of advice for you, too. Just don't forget birthdays or anniversaries, and remember to mention that someone made a special contribution for a project or cooked dinner for you or gave you a set of cast-off clothing. I seldom got complaints about theology. It was everything else that was fair game."

Joshua saw relief soften the lines on his father's forehead.

"Don't get me wrong, Son. The preaching has to be right. But if you quote a Scripture wrong, you don't have a verse figured out completely, and you never see the obvious problem until you're in the middle of your message . . . Well, folks will forgive you for that—if they even notice in the first place. But you hurt people's feelings—that they'll remember forever. You wrong them once and make them feel unloved and uncared for—that's the biggest wrong for a preacher. There are a few folks who don't talk to me other than a nodded hello because of things I forgot ten years ago."

Joshua's eyebrows raised in surprise.

"But I know you're a smart boy. You know about the way people are put together and how they think. Just treat everyone in church like important guests, and you'll do fine."

June 1845

The parsonage was a pastor's home in name only. During the weeks before the ordination, Joshua spent long hours dragging out debris, crumpled rags, broken bits of furniture, leaky buckets, moldy canvas seed bags, and the accumulation of twenty years of hoarding.

A bonfire burnt continuously that first week. He scrubbed the walls and swept abundant cobwebs from the ceilings and rafters. He covered the dirt floor with puncheons–short, thick planks held in place with wooden pins–unwilling to walk in a thin coating of mud during the spring rains. He cut larger openings into the walls for wider windows, ordered in from a joinery in Cleveland. He borrowed his old bed from his parents and asked a local carpenter to fashion him a chest, a table, and a few chairs.

Within a few weeks of working late into the night, the parsonage at last felt comfortable. The new chairs and table stood ready to receive guests. White cotton curtains–not feminine, but not roughsack either– hung in each window. In the kitchen, Joshua built a washstand with a long counter out of smooth-sanded planks. With a few lengths of black pipe, he brought the pump right into the kitchen. No longer would he have to trek outside to bring water for washing or cooking.

Joshua stood in the doorway, watching the sun set fire to the tree-tops in the meadow opposite the church. He sighed. It had been a hectic return to Shawnee. Soon he would lead a service at his very own church. He had led other services in other churches but always as a hired hand. There, if things went well, he would be happy. If the service went awry and the congregation seemed untouched, he could take comfort in the fact that he would not soon return to that pulpit. But here . . .

Later, as he unpacked his books, most of which had remained closed since leaving Harvard, he noticed that one commentary–a book on the Gospel of John–bulged out as if something prevented its full closing.

That's odd. Did I spill water on it? he asked himself.

He lifted the cover, finding a thick envelope tucked in the opening pages. His name was written on the front. He tore the envelope open and stopped in shock.

Along with a single sheet of paper, a packet of bills had slipped out, sprinkling the floor with green.

In a heartbeat Joshua gathered them up, counting each one as he did. There were twenty-five one-hundred-dollar bills.

Joshua's head spun in confusion, and panic rose in his throat. He bent over to pick up the single sheet of paper that had fallen to the floor and recognized Gage's handwriting immediately.

My dear friend,

I hope I have surprised you. You've been the best friend I've ever had. You haven't expected anything. You've never tried to take advantage of what I have. That is a rare gift, Joshua. And you even tried your best to reform me. I'll never forget your kindness. Use this pittance for the ministry, to augment your salary or however your God leads you.

Don't even think about returning this. I don't need it and will disavow any knowledge of it should you mention it ever again. I don't want it back. And do not write with effusive thanks as I'm sure you think you must. Your friendship was thanks enough. When we see each other again—and I promise that we will—you can treat me to a fine dinner in Shawnee.

Until then, I remain your loyal friend,
Gage Davis

Joshua's mind refused to comprehend the gift, so he sat down and reread the letter while holding the bills in his left hand.

Gage's amazing generosity would provide a substantial cushion for both life's adversities and the meager salary a pastor commanded. In fact, if one were frugal, the amount would provide enough income for years and years.

When his thoughts cleared, he bowed his head, thanked God for this wondrous gift, and vowed he'd never use it unless he found himself in the most dire of straights.

Money will often change people for the worse, and while this cushion is a comfort, I will not let it change my life.

He tucked the bills in a deerskin pouch, wrapped it in an oilcloth, and slipped the package into a narrow cleft in the chinking of the roof. No one would ever find it there, he told himself.

July 1845

The Sunday of his ordination as pastor was a blur.

He found it hard to focus on the ceremony of his installation. His mother wept and smiled and wept again through the service. His father beamed from the front pew. Each elder offered his greetings.

His first message was a repeat of one delivered in Newburyport last winter. It had been well received the first time, and Joshua sought to make a good impression. Going through his handwritten copy, he had shortened sentences, eliminated long, pretentious words, and simplified thoughts.

He preached it twice, standing before a cold fireplace. The words felt right. The delivery felt right. The theology was sound.

Joshua was ready.

That day, at the end of his sermon, he offered a heartfelt thank-you to everyone for the glorious privilege of serving them in God's house in Shawnee. Then he bowed his head and began to repeat the Lord's Prayer. Most of the congregation joined him. When Joshua said "Amen," the congregation was smiling.

That evening, as the night's first shadows erased the color from the tall grass and wildflowers, Joshua's soul was calm.

This day marked a special occasion. It was the first Sunday in a thousand Sundays that would make up his destiny in this world. A destiny was not a single event, Joshua understood, but a hundred thousand steps along God's path to his ultimate destination—a life of service, prayer, study, worship, and devotion.

And this day was the first in Joshua's journey.

He bowed his head in the growing darkness.

Lord, I'm humbled you've called me here to serve you. I know you have. This has always been my place—to call others to you—others who do not know of your wondrous truth, light, and love. I am privileged to bring this Good News to them. Please bless me as I take the first step in this journey with you.

As he looked up into the last rays of the sun, he saw a fleeting image of Hannah's face.

Without hesitating, he fled into his parsonage, hand outstretched, seeking a match to purge the darkness from his eyes.

⁂

The following Sunday, his last words hung in the air like jewels on a crystal chandelier.

The church was near overflowing. Every member, save the infirm, was in attendance, as well as some curious non-churchgoing citizens of Shawnee. A new pastor with new stories, especially one who had just gotten back from Boston, was bound to draw a good crowd.

The sun streamed into the church like honey, and songbirds trilled a natural crescendo to his message. The air was ripe with the scent of a rich harvest.

Joshua held onto the edges of the pulpit. He could almost feel the warmth from his father's hands, which had grasped the same wood hundreds of times. Joshua held his smile at the continuation of a family's dreams.

This feels so right. I'm certain this indeed is where I belong.

As he greeted well-wishers that day, two impressions reverberated within him.

One was his father's words as they embraced on the church steps.

"You have the gift, Joshua. You truly do. God will use you mightily. But remember–keep the theology simple, and make these people your family. You belong to them now, not to us."

With that Eli Quittner broke the embrace, raised a sleeve to swipe at his cheek, and hurried away as fast as his cane would allow. Joshua knew he would always cherish that remarkably intimate moment. His father was giving his son to the Lord in his own way.

Yet the second impression reverberated in Joshua's thoughts in a much different way.

True, everyone had taken his hand and said they were moved by his message and were glad to have him in the pulpit. But there were a few in the congregation who repeated much the same words, yet

Joshua was certain they meant something entirely different. Those came from the twenty-four unmarried young women of Shawnee, still living at home with their parents.

They waited for an introduction, offered a curtsy, then took Joshua's hand and held it longer and more tenderly than did anyone else in the receiving line. After the twelfth young woman had taken his offered hand and subtly pulled it closer to her, Joshua knew he was not only being welcomed but squired.

Keep the theology simple, his father had warned, *and the rest of your problems will be simple.*

Now as the moon slipped out, Joshua smiled and spoke to the darkened sky: "Theology I can handle with ease. But these young ladies . . ."

God, protect me and guide me. Show me your path.

As Joshua got ready for bed, he could not help but let a smile linger.

CHAPTER ELEVEN

HAS it been over a year since I last handled these pages? I am amazed, yet the calendar does not tell falsehoods. I marvel at the passage of time.

At first I felt my life in Shawnee was too ordinary to warrant writing a daily journal. The days of a preacher in a small town are filled, but with small occurrences and small events.

And to be honest, now that I have pen in hand, I also hesitate to write because doing so reminds me so much of Harvard and my friends and the life I left there. For a long time, such thoughts were painful and hard. With the gentle passage of time, however, I now can view my past in a different light.

Yes, I admit to an occasional twinge, but I'm happy now. I do not regret leaving the East.

I truly do not.

I'm busy learning the ways of Shawnee. I thought I knew these people before. After all, I grew up here. I lived all my life here until going to Cambridge. But I was never a *student* of their lives.

Until now.

Before I recount some of the events in my life, I do want to pen a history of other events. I've heard reports of my friends.

While Shawnee is well off the beaten path, we do receive a newspaper once a week from Cincinnati. I've come across Jamison's byline on numerous occasions. He writes most often from New York, but the location of his dispatches have included an island in the Caribbean, along with Canada, Florida, and more states than I can mention. He must live a hectic life–always journeying from one spot to the next. But that was his dream, was it not?

Gage has been mentioned several times in the financial sections of the paper. If not Gage himself, it is Davis Enterprises. He's following his destiny as well–making money.

And I've seen, or at least think I've seen, news of Hannah, though this mention would not be pleasing to her family. There was a small demonstration in New York City, led by a group of women protesting an educational slight. A few ladies were arrested and sent to jail for a time, and among the list was an "M. Collins." True, there may be another M. Collins in New York City, but taking a stand like that sounds like our old friend Hannah. However, if she married this Robert Keyes, then it would be another M. Collins for certain.

How good it feels to be writing again–not just writing sermons, but writing for the sheer pleasure of placing words on paper. I know I'm leading a smaller life than the saints of old, but an unexamined life is not worth living. That's a sentiment I once read.

Perhaps one day I, too, will be famous for something. Then I'll be able to turn to this journal for my autobiography.

Though no one can see my expression, I'm smiling broadly as I write this last line.

No, I will not be famous, but I *will* keep a record, from this day forward, of my life and how it was lived.

Let me start where I left off, more than a year prior to this point.

I was ordained by the Shawnee Church of the Holy Word and took their pulpit in July of 1845. The first few weeks were indeed idyllic. For a time, I held the members of the congregation at arm's length, and they did the same to me. We would learn the intricacies

of each other in due time. In spite of the fact that I lived my childhood among these people, my being at Harvard has changed me in
their eyes, and they each must learn of a new person.

Knowing I had many prepared sermons, I spent much time at first
renovating both the church and the parsonage, which, until I
stepped in, was as habitable as a badger den. I have made no mention of Gage's generosity to anyone and have spent only a fraction of
his monetary gift—in an effort not to stir up too much speculation on
the source of my funds.

But rather than wait for years living in a poverty of furnishings,
I've managed to transform the former hovel into a cozy home. It's
light and cheery, the fire pit has an excellent draw, the water is clean,
and it's only a short walk to the church.

Once done with the majority of the renovation, I threw myself
into preparing a reservoir of messages. I like that luxury of time to
study without the bear of deadlines growling and nipping at my feet.
Even with the work in the fields, I have had enough free time in the
evenings to do the study that's required.

What takes up a pastor's time? Take, for example, the following
situation: I had no idea that planning and coordinating a potluck
feast marking our harvest celebration would be so complex. One has
to consider every angle, as I've been warned repeatedly. For instance,
Mrs. Sonners, a "newcomer" to Shawnee, is well noted for her mince
pies. But her neighbor, a longtime citizen of Shawnee, Mrs. Coates,
believes *her* mince pies are better suited to the church members'
hearty appetites. Mrs. Coates regards Mrs. Sonners as a too-recent
arrival to our soil (residing in Shawnee County only for a few years)
and has often stated so with a snippy edge to her voice.

(I do not wish to gossip about either fine woman, but such is the
talk at elders' meetings.)

So this posed a perplexing dilemma for me (for the board voted I
was best suited to make the call). Who should we ask first for mince
pies? Or could I skirt logic and ask them both? Would we then suffer
from a surplus of mince? Should I ask neither of them and opt for

apple or cherry instead? Even on the elder board, there are factions for both minces and a small band of those who prefer neither.

I've lain awake at nights pondering just such questions. I can imagine old crusty Professor Podderstein of Harvard in such a situation. I'm certain he would take the Scriptures in hand, bellowing loudly that there is no mention of mince in the Holy Writ, and God does not approve of such petty bickering.

But I also recall that Professor Podderstein never pastored a church. His only background lay in lofty academia. There was seldom a mention of mince at Harvard.

(Incidentally, I came to a decision—like Solomon, perhaps—and praised the efforts of both women to the skies and then requested both to make their mince offerings. If we have too much, then I will eat mince for weeks.)

What my father told me once is most certainly true. The theology of what I preach is important. But people's lives are even more important. And that course of study will occupy me for the rest of my life.

Every day is different.

Weddings, baptisms, funerals, and every manner of religious function has become second nature to me. Even town events and celebrations require a prayer to start, and they always ask the local preacher. (I'm sure they think I have a more direct line to the Almighty than they do.)

I've reconsidered one matter: Had I sought out the pulpit of a large church, I'd not have enjoyed such a varied experience.

What's also rewarding is that our church is growing. The population of the county has increased, and those new citizens are seeking out a place to worship, so our church has been the recipient of some of those souls.

But we're also seeing old faces in our midst—people who have been citizens of the area for years and years.

I shall not take credit for this growth. It's solely God's divine will for this place. But I do sense renewed enthusiasm. Perhaps, in some small way, my preaching has helped unlock people's latent desires to serve God. Sunday school attendance is inching up. The ladies have formed a sewing circle that will produce bedding and clothing for those less fortunate. And even the fiscally conservative elder board has dialogued in recent days about purchasing a piano—or even an organ—for the church. Such is music to everyone's ears. I enjoy singing, but I'm afraid the notes on a page are but obscure squiggles to me. I can only hope to start a song out on the right note. And when started, my voice quickly shrinks back, and I let the better-accomplished singers take over.

An organ would solve that problem and allow our worship to soar.

Seeing as how our tithes and offerings have edged up over the past few months, I see this as a real possibility. Just think—our little church complete with musical instruments and perhaps even hymnals.

In addition to the numbers, I'm convinced that believers are also growing in their faith. Such an observation is difficult to quantify, but I think it to be true. People seem eager to attend church, to participate, and to pray for one another. Gossip and such will always be a part of a church, but the tenor has softened as of late. My father said that, as a rule, one elder would be angry with him each week, but I've yet to experience such divisions. Perhaps I am more diplomatic, or perhaps God is allowing these men to mature in their faith as well.

I've hesitated to spend much time penning my thoughts on this next matter. But I'm certain it's of great interest to many. (Though I trust no one will ever read these words.)

If you asked any number of people in the church—especially my mother and her circle of friends—they would state that the greatest concern facing the church is the state of my availability—matrimonially speaking, that is.

Most folks had the decorum to wait until I was settled and the parsonage was presentable until their nudges became harder, more direct shoves. I expected the pressure would remain subtle, but it has not. I had only a month till the nudges began—and they increased with every passing month.

Numerous young ladies among the church family who are

endeavoring to find a mate view me as most suitable. But many of this initial grouping have already been spoken for by other young men in the county or have too wanton of a past to warrant my consideration, having been courted by several young men prior. Some of the young women have even been seen kissing in public! My mother had it on good authority that a few of the women had been kissed by as many as three suitors in quick succession.

Such women could not aspire to be the wife of a pastor.

How such wantonness spread to innocent Ohio is beyond me. In many ways, this is not the Ohio in which I grew up. But that is another subject and worthy of a full series of messages on Sunday on the value of temperance and virtue in courtship.

Hannah once told me that, for a man, I was attractive. I did not see her evaluation as accurate at all–especially as I peered into my mirror each morning. Yet I trusted her female intuitions, and now I assume she was expressing a typical female judgment.

(I have not thought of Hannah in months, and writing her name still pulls at my heart. I am learning to work past the memories and allow God to dominate my life, rather than my own petty feelings.)

At each social occasion of the church, and often after services, one or two of the group of five young women I consider as possibilities for a pastor's wife will be found at my side or near it. We chat about the sermon (and it's always the best they've heard) or mention the weather or an upcoming event. Between the five families represented, I have had twelve dinners so far, and four more casual invitations have been issued in the past week.

I've endeavored to show no favoritism that would indicate a choice being made.

If a mince pie creates hard feelings, I hesitate to imagine what a botched courtship might cause. So I have taken my time, finding this part of being a pastor most convivial. Meals have been splendid (though by no means the equal of the offerings of a Boston or New York establishment or the Destiny Café), and the conversation–for the most part–enjoyable.

I've found myself being called on to tell stories of life out East.

And to protect these young girls' feelings, I have exorcised myself from the tales of visiting New York (and the opera and the stores). Instead of making each story a personal recollection, I tell them these are stories that Gage recounted.

I tell them of the culture and elegance of the big city and how the women dress and act at social functions. Both mothers and daughters take a keen interest in this. I'm glad for Hannah's friendship, for she explained the inner workings of a woman's desires when it comes to attire.

And with the young ladies' fathers, I talk of how the heresy of universalism has crept into the staid institutions of Boston and its environs.

They ask how I came through unaffected. I tell them it was their prayers and my father's strong foundation of faith. They always nod solemnly and tell me what a fine man my father is. Despite his claim of making elders angry, there has not been one person who has spoken ill of him. Perhaps it takes time to appreciate a man's impact on a church.

But I have digressed.

I began this section writing of . . . matrimony, though I find it a bit mercenary to discuss it in such calculating tones.

Of the five women who have made their presence most known to me, I believe I have narrowed my choice. I hesitate to mention whom I have not selected, for they are fine young ladies. But in each was the absence of that special something. . . .

When I write this, I think of how I felt when I first saw Hannah. How my heart turned and twisted just so—not pain, exactly, but a delirious, aching anticipation and desire to know her better.

Of course, it was not to be. And I repeat to myself that such emotions are wrong and should be ignored. And I do.

The one for whom I felt a certain stirring when I talked with her is a fetching woman—whom I've mentioned before in the pages of my journal. Her name is Constance McArthur, a distant relative of the McArthurs who settled in the town of the same name south of

Shawnee. I first met her more than two years prior, and she has developed into a pleasing woman.

Constance is of middling height, about the same height as Hannah, and her hair is of a similar golden color. Her frame is a bit more solid than Hannah's—but one would expect that from a woman living on a farm. Of course her clothing is not as stylish, but she has made every effort to remain presentable.

Her laugh is similar to Hannah's—fast and musical to the ear. She's eager to please and knows her way around a kitchen—something of which I'm certain Hannah had no training. (Why must I compare so?)

Constance McArthur appears to be a woman with whom I could spend my days in contentment. However, I do not presume to usurp the Lord's plan for my life.

Constance is a decent and lovely girl. I am aware that I do need to have this loose end in my life tied and sealed. And why not Constance? A man could do much worse.

I shall endeavor to add this matter to my prayers. I am sure God will favor this—as he seems to have found favor with so many other matters of prayer in my life.

Shawnee, Ohio
October 1846

Joshua had been bent over his desk for close to four hours, working on his message for Sunday. He leaned back in his Windsor chair and stretched his muscles, twisting to the left, then right. He blew on the last page of notes, making sure the ink had dried.

Joshua closed his books and looked out the window.

The crisp colors of fall enlivened the meadow and the trees beyond. A scent of burning wood effused in the air. He could hear the calls of Garrison Riley as Riley and his team of oxen carefully plowed under the stubble of a just-picked corn crop.

This week had been calm. The only event on the church calendar was the regular midweek prayer meeting—and that had been sparsely attended. Most of his congregation were busy with the harvesting and storing of crops, and he would only see them for the few hours on Sunday morning and evening.

Joshua stepped to the window. The church, as well as the parsonage, lay less than a quarter mile south of the main street. The stage line running east and west crossed through it on the north side of town. There had been talk of the railroads extending a spur through Shawnee, south from Zanesville and running the whole way to the Ohio River at Gallipolis, but so far that had proved to be only speculation.

He pulled out his pocketwatch, an extravagance he had allowed himself with another portion of Gage's gift.

After all, a pastor needs to know what hour it is, Joshua had said to justify the purchase. *Rather than be alerted by grumbling stomachs as the sermon hour closes in on noon, a pocketwatch is a much better timekeeper.*

It was now a few minutes past two in the afternoon. The coach that ran from New Lexington to Logan usually rattled through about this time. If anyone in Shawnee was to get mail, it would be on this coach. In the year and a half since leaving Harvard, Joshua had the distinction of receiving the most mail in town. Jamison had written more than anyone, as Joshua would have expected. A few notes came from Gage. Yet Hannah, despite her final note, had not written once. He reminded himself several times that her silence did not matter now that he had settled in Shawnee. He led a different life, and Hannah would not be part of it. Joshua told himself he was grateful for her silence. After all, thoughts of her tended to confuse his thinking and rumble at his newfound peace.

If mail arrived by express, Charlie Wentzler, the proprietor of the new general store in town, would deliver it, owing to the proximity of the parsonage to town.

As Joshua settled back again in the chair to review his notes for his message, he thought he heard a vague rustling of voices. He strained to listen closer, but the wind must have pushed the sound away.

There it is again, Joshua thought. *Whatever could that be?*

He sat still and closed his eyes to listen more intently. They were voices, he was sure of that now, but they were only murmurs. There was also the sound of hesitant footsteps.

Just then a firm but polite knock sounded at his door. The noise was so unexpected that Joshua snapped shut his Bible and nearly tumbled out of the chair in response. He jumped toward the door.

It must be the mail . . . but what were those other noises?

Joshua fussed for a moment with the temperamental door latch. He pushed at the door with his shoulder and thumbed the latch up, then swung the door open.

What greeted him was the most unrealistic, impossible scene he could ever have imagined.

Standing in the doorway, in a shaft of autumn's honey-colored sunlight, was Morgan Hannah Collins.

CHAPTER TWELVE

Shawnee, Ohio
October 1846

"H ANNAH . . ." was all Joshua could croak out. "What . . . where . . . but . . ."

Dressed in a dark blue satiny dress and jacket, Hannah offered a dazzling smile and a feminine shrug. Even her eyebrows went up gently as if stating she wasn't sure how she happened to be here–but she was here, nonetheless.

Standing behind Hannah and her coiled hat with the blue plume was a ragtag half circle of people, including Mr. Wentzler. Behind Mr. Wentzler was his young apprentice, who was carrying a large suitcase and had two hat cases tucked under each arm.

Since Joshua appeared to have lost his power of speech, Hannah smiled again, turning her head to the crowd, then back to Joshua.

"Joshua, I know this is a shock, for I have not written of my intentions to undertake such a trip."

"But . . . but . . ."

"Actually, I have not written to you at all. I thought that was best, didn't you? I'm sure you did. Now, this journey was much longer and much more rigorous than I imagined."

The parade following Hannah had hushed, waiting to see how Joshua would handle this spirited and stylish apparition.

Neither spoke for a moment.

Then Hannah said, "Do you think you might invite a poor girl inside and out of the chilly weather . . . and maybe offer her a drink of hot tea or coffee?"

It took Joshua almost another full minute until he found the powers of locomotion and swept his hand toward his home.

"Hannah . . . do come in. I'm sorry . . . but I guess I was just a little . . . surprised."

She took his arm and squeezed it softly.

"Yes, I guess you were."

◆◇◆

The crowd milled about the parsonage, pointing and gesturing, speculating on who this brazen woman might be. Her elegant leather bags were stacked just inside the front door. When Mr. Wentzler was ushered outside, he gave Joshua a perplexed look.

"Anything else I can do for you, Pastor Quittner?" he asked, laying intentional emphasis on the word *pastor*.

Joshua was in no state of mind to consider the possible ramifications of such a visit and merely shook his head no.

"I will call for you if I require something . . . additional," Joshua stammered, his hand on the older man's shoulder. Joshua took a step back into the darker interior of his cabin and placed his hand on the door. He was set to close it, as any normal man might. Then suddenly, instead of closing the door, he left it open a ways, so anyone passing by would be able to see clearly all that was–or was not–transpiring within the walls of the parsonage.

Hannah stepped out from the kitchen with a tumbler of water in her finely gloved hand. She had found the glass and worked the pump herself. He watched as she brought the water up to her mouth and slowly drank the entire glass.

Joshua's thoughts were in an absolute whirl, as if a tornado had touched down and was ripping through his newly settled life.

Hannah held the now-empty glass at waist level. "Well, Joshua, my old and dear friend," she said, her words soft and sweet, "aren't you going to show me around this Shawnee I've heard so much about?"

It took Joshua another half minute to find the power to nod.

❧❦❧

As Joshua led Hannah back toward town, heads popped out from doorways and windows. Joshua heard a steady stream of murmurs as they passed by shops on the main street. From the corner of his eye, he saw young William Rebner run off to the north along the stream, as if on a mission.

With his thoughts rattling past his brain at breakneck speed, Joshua struggled to converse in a civil and cogent manner with Hannah.

There is no one along that stream for miles . . .

Then an image flashed before his eyes with bell-like clarity, and perspiration beaded on his forehead.

. . . except the McArthur farm . . .

His heart jumped.

. . . and Constance.

At the end of the plank sidewalk, Hannah turned, surveying downtown Shawnee.

"Joshua, this is a pleasant little village. Very quaint. Very . . . rural. How nice it seems."

He could do little but nod in return.

"Did we not pass a restaurant at the end of the street?" she asked. "I must admit to a certain peckishness since I've not eaten since daybreak. Would it be a terrible imposition if I asked you to accompany me for a light meal? Or is there some other establishment that might be more proper?"

Joshua struggled for composure. The tavern was the only place, outside of someone's home, where meals could be purchased. But it also was developing a less-than-savory reputation, owing to the drinking and dancing that went on—or so Joshua had heard.

But all I have at home is some beef dodger. I cannot serve Hannah corncakes with minced beef. That would not do at all.

He looked about, his eyes darting.

My mother would be able to place a presentable meal on the table in short order. But could I take Hannah there? And how would I explain her sudden appearance? No, I can't go there. Not yet.

He stared at Hannah's petite, high-cut leather shoes with ivory buttons that gleamed against the rough planking of the town's walkway.

How will I explain this to them? My mother will never understand.

He licked his dry lips.

How do I explain any of this to Hannah? I'm sure she wouldn't understand.

"There is a restaurant of sorts, Hannah," he finally found himself saying, trying to hide any concern he might have displayed to her. "Along with offerings of other . . . libations and all."

A coy smile marked her face. "And it will be acceptable if you . . . as the pastor . . . accompany me to this place? I do not wish to force you to do anything that would be upsetting."

His answer was a trembling smile—as he extended his arm to her and led her to Murphy's.

⁂

As Joshua slid Hannah's chair toward the table, he saw three faces duck away from their obvious stares and another two faces slip out of view along the front window facing the street.

Joshua looked around for the serving girl.

"I'm here alone," the bartender rasped. "But I can fetch a meal if that's what you need."

Joshua nodded. "Two servings of today's offering."

"And a glass of . . . lemonade if you have it," Hannah added. "It has been a dusty day."

She sat almost regally, tidying her gloves, smoothing imaginary wrinkles from her lace-trimmed sleeves. Joshua looked at her, then focused on the inside of the dim tavern.

It was as if a blindfold had been removed from his view.

What had been a fairly presentable establishment quickly changed into a soiled room with mismatched chairs and nicked tables. A handful of flies flitted about, and the puncheon floor seemed to be coated with a sheen of beer and tobacco stains.

The street outside was rutted, and swaybacked horses waited for their riders to come out from one of the shabby and meagerly supplied stores. A passerby's footsteps echoed on the warped wooden walkway.

The distance between Shawnee and any place of interest suddenly grew immense. Until that moment Joshua had felt growing pride in his town, in his position as pastor, in his new life. But seeing it reflected in Hannah's eyes made it all seem so . . . tarnished and coarse. Seeing it in Hannah's eyes made Joshua feel, for the first time since leaving Harvard, ashamed of his life–who he was and what he was becoming.

"Joshua . . . Joshua," Hannah called out softly, "are you all right?"

"I'm sorry . . . I guess I wasn't paying attention. What did you ask me?"

Hannah laid her knife and fork down.

Even this food is tasteless and plain, he thought.

"I was asking where I might find a room for the time I'm here. I know I did not give prior announcement of this visit, but it was unplanned. I left Philadelphia without a certain itinerary, other than to find Oberlin College. My parents are in a state of nervous apoplexy, but I told them it was my trust fund, and I must live my life as I see fit. So I set off and have seen much of eastern America in the process. I know it was well out of the way, but I managed to view the tremendous falls at Niagara in New York. Absolutely magnificent. Joshua, you should go there someday. I made my way to Pittsburgh . . . a horrible place of smoke and dirt and unsavory riverboats . . . and when there, I saw that Shawnee, Ohio, was not that far from me. I was drawn again to find you, especially since I never had the chance to officially state my good-byes. So here I am."

Joshua could only listen in stunned silence. She, a mere woman, had done more in a few weeks than he could hope to do in an entire lifetime. How fast he let life slip from his hands, he thought.

"So, where might that be?" Hannah asked.

Joshua stumbled. He had not heard half her words. "Where might what be?"

"Sweet Joshua," she said, placing her hand on his forearm. "A room."

"Uhh . . . this is the only place I know of that has rooms," Joshua said, then realized no lady of Hannah's breeding would find this crude place acceptable. "But I do not think you should stay here."

She narrowed her eyes. "Joshua, I've traveled many weeks and have found lodging in some, shall I say, interesting places. I'm sure the rooms here will be fine."

But I've heard rumors . . . indelicate rumors . . . of what transpires here after a night of raucous celebrating. No. Hannah cannot lodge here.

"You shall have my house. . . ."

Even though it's as unrefined as this place, at least there will be no illicit behavior going on, he affirmed to himself.

". . . and I shall take lodging with my parents during your stay."

Hannah raised her hand to protest, but Joshua held her back. "I shall accept no objections, Hannah. You'll stay at the parsonage. It's not often we get a visitor from the East, and we must make any guest feel welcomed and safe."

Joshua was certain Hannah would have protested longer and harder and eventually found a way to get her way, but she lowered her eyes.

"If you insist, Joshua. That's most gracious of you."

FROM THE JOURNAL OF JOSHUA QUITTNER
OCTOBER 1846

I could scarce have imagined a more surprising development than the one that has occurred this day. Hannah Collins—a woman I never expected to see again—arrived at my doorstep. Since she's on her way to Oberlin College, she must still plan to finish her medical training—although she grew recalcitrant and would not confirm anything more than a simple visit when I asked her. But to stop in Shawnee? That is not on her way, to be truthful.

She sidestepped all my queries of the demonstration I'd read about. She laughed, as if expecting the questions, then brushed them off, stating it must have been another M. Collins.

Curiously, I had made no mention of "M. Collins" as I spoke, so I now believe it *was* Hannah who was arrested.

As we chatted, I began to wonder: *Is there another reason for her visit? Can I bear to imagine she came to see me for a strictly platonic call? It's obvious she's not married.*

She has been nothing but gracious, even exclaiming how charming I have made my home and how peaceful the church is. I know she cannot truly find them that way but is averse to damaging my feelings. No, my life here, as seen through her eyes, must appear base and low.

She has related such wonderful adventures and sights, I cannot believe she has accomplished them all: the falls at Niagara, the lakes in New York, a long boat trip up the Hudson, stops in Pittsburgh and Albany and so many other places.

She appeared to be near exhausted by the first edgings of nightfall, so I bid her farewell and walked to my parents' home, stating I would return on the morrow.

The news had preceded me. I think it may have been young Mr. Rebner who alerted all concerned parties as to the arrival of my visitor. I have not, nor will I, think this night of the impact of such news on sweet Constance.

My mother near accused me of consorting with a wanton woman, a vixen who could destroy my reputation in a day. My father grimaced, saying that even a hint of immorality would cripple my effectiveness in my position.

I countered that she appeared, unannounced. What would they have me do–show Christian hospitality by sending her to a rattrap boardinghouse only one step above a bordello?

After some harsh words, everyone calmed down. My mother insisted that, starting tomorrow, she would stay with Hannah in the parsonage, thus avoiding any suspicion of my returning under cover of darkness for a midnight rendezvous.

I agreed, more to keep peace in the family than to admit the need for such action.

I am so vexed and light-headed that I must stop my writing.

***

Joshua hesitated outside the parsonage door. He had in his hand a basketful of warm buckwheat pancakes and bacon with a tin of syrup. He also had a glass jar of cool milk and a full pot of coffee that was growing colder.

He hoped Hannah was awake and ready to receive visitors.

Having my mother stay here would be a suitable idea, Joshua realized. *If she stays longer than a night or two, I will need to get to my clothes and books in a timely manner.*

The door swung open, and Hannah called out, "Good morning, Joshua. I heard you rustling out there and hoped you'd bring food. I've been up for hours and am famished. This clean country air and the peaceful night have done wonders. I highly recommend it to anyone who has struggled finding sleep."

She glanced about, then whispered, "Your bed is marvelous, Joshua, just marvelous."

She grinned as he went crimson. He was glad the one other indulgence he had allowed himself with Gage's money was a feather mattress. She took his arm as he stepped inside. The curtains were wide open, and the morning sun streamed in.

"Well, Joshua," she bubbled, "it's time to eat."

She slipped into her chair.

"I'll not compromise your standing as a moral pastor, at least not any further than I already have," she said. "So we shall eat in broad daylight by the window this morning."

After his frazzled emotions calmed down, he found breakfast to be most enjoyable—in the sun and in plain view of anyone who happened to walk by. And on this day, Joshua noted with a smile, many people found reason to stroll past the parsonage.

Some stopped, knocked at the open door, and all but requested an introduction to Joshua's guest. Upon each introduction, Hannah would repeat how noble it had been for Joshua to give up his home for an old friend who had arrived out of the blue. After the fourth time Joshua heard Hannah state the same words, in her sweet, yet sophisticated manner, he began to feel as though it was not as outlandish a story as his mother had assumed.

After the dozenth person stopped, Hannah chuckled. "I would stake my reputation on the fact that your reputation has not suffered too greatly."

Finding no suitable reply, Joshua merely nodded.

"I've kept up on our friends, you know. Have you heard from them?" Before he could reply, she continued, "I understand Jamison took his notebook and headed west, sending dispatches back to his newspaper. Not that I read much, but others claim he's a gifted writer."

Joshua waited for a break in conversation that did not come.

"And Gage, well, we knew Gage was going places, didn't we? He has taken control of much of the family's business, and I continue to hear his name mentioned even in the best circles in Boston. They say he'll be the richest young man in the East if he continues. A most eligible young man."

Suddenly Hannah leaned forward, gently tapping him on the forearm.

"Play it smartly, Joshua. We have company coming again. And please introduce me as just a friend from Boston . . . and not your *old* friend. Makes me feel too mature when you say it that way."

❧❀☙

The rest of the day was a blur. Joshua and Hannah tidied up from their meal, and she insisted they take a walk to his parents' house.

"I know they consider me a hussy. After all, I am a single woman traveling on my own. And visiting their only son, a pastor, and causing no end of gossip."

Hannah was nothing if not totally charming. She had the ability to make people feel at ease and instantly liked.

Both Joshua's parents bristled for the first few minutes. Then, with a bolt of awareness, Mae Quittner realized she had, in her home, a member of Philadelphia's high society. And Hannah's disarming charm soon had Joshua's parents laughing and admitting their fears.

If my mother and father can laugh with Hannah, Joshua thought with relief, *then there will be no ongoing repercussions.*

All three of them listened to Hannah's entertaining stories about her travels.

But what do I tell Constance? That thought kept creeping into Joshua's mind. *I know she does not have any claims on me, nor have I on her. How will she react when she hears about Hannah?*

Late that night, Hannah, Mrs. Quittner, and Joshua walked back to the parsonage. Even with Hannah's charm and blue blood, Mrs. Mae Quittner was not about to let her son face such a temptation alone.

Once there, Mrs. Quittner busied herself, redoubling Joshua's earlier efforts at cleanliness and order. Hannah sneezed, perhaps from the dust being raised, and immediately Mrs. Quittner sent her outside with her woolen shawl.

"Joshua, you accompany her outdoors. I'll only be a minute or two."

With a thick wrap about her shoulders, Hannah sat against the fence at the edge of the property and stared off into the diminishing sun. Joshua walked over and sat a few feet from her.

"I like it here," Hannah said. "I know you think I'm patronizing you, but the landscape is nice, and your parents are very pleasant."

"Rustic, though . . . and unsophisticated," Joshua added.

Hannah smiled. "Just like you a few years ago."

"No . . . I mean yes . . . I mean . . ."

"Please Joshua, do not make excuses. They lack the snobbish, proper Philadelphian reserve, but they are honest and wonderful. You should be proud of them."

"I am," Joshua replied. "It's just that with you here, I guess I was comparing them to a different standard."

"I know. I know you love them, though."

Joshua waited a long moment. Crickets began to call, and bullfrogs yawled loudly.

"Hannah," he said softly, "I'm flattered you are here. But Shawnee is a long way from anywhere. Our friendship was special, but I honestly never expected to see you again. . . . Why are you here?"

She was not smiling. "I'm on my way to visit Oberlin."

"That much has already been stated, Hannah. But why else would a woman make such an incredible journey?"

"I'm searching, Joshua," she said quietly, head down.

For the truth? For God? Do I tell her how to find peace with the Lord Jesus?

"Searching for what?" he asked.

It took Hannah several minutes to respond.

"For truth, I guess," she said firmly. "A meaning to life. You were always so sure. I wanted to talk with you once again. You always saw things so clearly, and I need to know what to do."

"To do? About what? School?"

"No . . . it's more than that."

"What then, Hannah? You can tell me."

"It's Robert Keyes. He has asked me to marry him."

Joshua blinked hard and, for the hundredth time that day, lost his ability to think.

CHAPTER THIRTEEN

Shawnee, Ohio
October 1846

HANNAH seemed unflappable and, to Joshua, completely unfathomable. Here she was, hundreds of miles from home, in an uncultured town at the edge of civilization with nothing of sophistication to offer, and yet she behaved as if it were the most natural and desirable place to be in the whole world.

Joshua's demeanor indicated his inner turmoil. Every hour with Hannah he was struck near to mute by the realization that she was physically in Shawnee. Her friendship was no longer a pleasant memory or mere apparition but a real flesh-and-blood relationship again.

Hannah and Shawnee did not, as Joshua once had figured it, seem to be able to exist in the same place and time.

But there she was.

Joshua had tossed endlessly during Hannah's first night in Shawnee, ensconced in his old tiny bedroom in his parents' home. Rolling the fact of her presence over and over in his mind, he despaired of ever finding rest again.

Hannah was as far from Ohio as Ohio was from the moon in its celestial orbit. In order to find peace, Joshua had told himself with finality that he and Hannah were never to be. She could not be part of his life. He was sure of that.

And then the second night she told him of Robert Keyes. How he hated that name. At first he felt dumbfounded, then angry. Yet as she exploded that name before him, he could not even sputter an answer, for his mother had bustled out of the parsonage and hurried Joshua away and back to his parents' house.

All he could mutter was a good-night and "I'm sure we'll talk of this in the morning, Hannah."

And with that he walked away in the growing darkness toward his parents' home.

Why would she have come all this way to ask me what to do about Robert Keyes? Does she want me to tell her not to marry him? She does not need my approval for this. Is she asking, in the feminine way, for me to consider such a question? I'm absolutely perplexed. I cannot think of any other reason. I have no hopes of more . . . do I? No, I'm sure of that. She's only confused and a little scared and wants an old friend to tell her she's doing the right thing.

The road wound through a quiet grove of trees.

Can I tell her that? In honesty, can I tell her that? I don't really know Robert at all. He must be a nice enough fellow for her to be considering him. And it is my duty as a pastor to help Hannah avoid temptation by marrying, rather than living as a single woman.

His eyes focused blankly off in the distance.

But she came all the way from Philadelphia to find me. To ask me a question such as this. . . .

He stopped and tried to clear his thoughts.

Would I truly consider asking her myself?

His heart hurt.

She came all the way from Philadelphia . . . for me. To find me. To see me. I am deeply flattered. And that is revealing, is it not?

The farmhouse was just now in view. Joshua sniffed the air. The smell of his mother's earlier cooking perfumed the vale with a pungent, spicy scent.

What would the elders and the congregation say? And how will I feel when I receive the invitation to Hannah's wedding to another man?

What had once felt settled in his heart proved vexing that night.

Joshua managed to eat a few bites of the food his mother had prepared before going to the parsonage for the night, but his appetite had vanished. And he barely spoke in response to his father's questions.

An hour past midnight, Joshua finally admitted defeat. He slipped out of his bed, gathered a thick blanket, and climbed down from the loft. Stepping onto the front porch, he marveled at the warmth of the October evening.

We'll have a hard winter to make up for such moderate weather, he reflected.

He sat and stared at the moon. From the fields he heard the lonely call of an owl as it swooped along the black furrows, searching for mice. In the distance, he heard the yowling yip of a fox.

Then he heard the slow creak of a floorboard from the weight of a foot. A door squealed open.

"Are you still up?" his father called softly.

"Sorry if I woke you," Joshua replied. "I couldn't sleep."

His father shuffled closer.

"No . . . I'm often awake during much of the night," his father said quietly back, even though there was no one else to wake. "The price one pays when the body begins to age, I guess."

Joshua let the air grow heavy with silence before he spoke again. His voice, too, remained little more than a husky whisper. "When you met Mother, did you know?"

"Know?"

"Know that you and she . . . I mean that . . . were meant to get married and all."

Joshua could not see his father's face in the darkness, could not see the look in his eyes, the crinkle at his temple.

"And why do you want to know that now?"

"I'm not sure. I was just thinking about it, that's all."

Joshua hoped his father would not ask about Hannah. It was not something he wished to discuss this night. His father's answer came swiftly.

"Yes, I knew before the first day was over. I knew that soon."

"How did you know? How could you be sure?"

"I had been praying about the situation for a long time—I mean, me being single and all. And when your mother showed up at the social, I felt a strong nudge to go over and talk with her. She was so pretty that I didn't want to risk it. I mean, such a pretty girl . . . and me, a poor farmer at best."

"Did she talk with you?"

"She did. I even heard her laugh that night. That was all it took. I knew she was the woman I'd been praying for. When she said good-night, I tipped my hat, and my heart settled in my chest—like it found the place it had been looking for all my life. I found home looking in your mother's eyes."

"You knew that soon? You didn't have any doubts?"

"About her being the one? No. I had doubts about ever deserving her—but not about her being God's choice for me."

"Really?"

"Really and truly."

Silence returned.

"Why are you asking about this, Son? Is it because of your friend, Hannah? Are you thinking she might be . . . ?"

"No, that's not it . . . really, it's not."

"She is a beautiful and polished young lady, Joshua."

Joshua did not want to talk more about Hannah with his father. Agitated, he stood up and walked to the edge of the porch.

"But she's from out East, Joshua. And you're from Shawnee. Those worlds don't go together. You should know that. A marriage includes some compromise, but not that much."

"I'm not thinking about marriage. And besides . . ." Joshua's throat tightened. "And besides, I think she's going to marry someone else."

"You need to pray about this, Joshua. It sounds like you still pine for her some."

Joshua shrugged and turned away. He did not want to hear any more advice.

"I think I'll try to get back to sleep now," Joshua said quickly, moving toward the door. Then, as he climbed the ladder into the sleeping loft, he called back, "I'll see you in the morning."

Eli Quittner said good-night to his son's back.

❧◆❧

Like a bear trying to hide behind a sapling, Hannah's marriage question had lurked behind Joshua's every move in the hours since. Yet as much as he wished to discuss it with her, there proved to be little time.

Now it was Saturday, a day full of activities: from Joshua helping to ready the church for the next day's services to an urgent call on an old woman of the church who had sickened and appeared near death. It was an hour ride out to the Simmons' farm.

As the sun waned in the late afternoon, Joshua made his way back to the parsonage after praying with Mr. and Mrs. Simmons. The anticipation of seeing Hannah rose within him, and he tried to push it down, reining in his horse to a slower gallop. As he crossed the road that led to the McArthur farm, he pulled the reins in so abruptly that he was nearly thrown forward off the horse.

Constance! I'm to have dinner with the McArthurs tonight! In less than two hours!

With the excitement of Hannah's arrival, he had completely forgotten.

What shall I tell Hannah? I'm sure she was anticipating a quiet meal together tonight in town. Do I say I'm merely going to the home of a church member and not give further details? I cannot possibly break my promise to Constance.

He patted the horse and gently tapped his heels against its sides, coaxing it into a trot.

What would Gage do in a situation such as this? I'm afraid I have no envoy to send in my place. And Constance has probably already learned of the arrival of a beautiful Eastern woman at my doorstep.

He slowed the horse even further. He could see the smoke from the chimney of the parsonage over the barren branches of the trees.

Think quickly, Joshua! his thoughts called out.

⁂

Hannah sat in the old rocker on the parsonage porch, reading *Godey's Lady's Book.* As Joshua approached, Hannah put down the magazine and called out sweetly, "And how is Mrs. Simmons?"

Joshua tied the horse to the hitching post and answered, "She is some better."

"Just seeing you would lift anyone's spirits," Hannah answered. "Your dedication is quite touching, Joshua."

"Nothing any pastor worth his salt wouldn't do," he replied, sitting down on the top step. He took off his hat and skimmed it against his leg, removing most of the road dust.

I will simply tell her the truth about Constance, he told himself. *She'll probably be marrying Robert Keyes anyway, so what difference will it be to her if I am courting another woman?*

"A Mrs. Sonners came by with a delicious mince pie about an hour ago," said Hannah. "I'm afraid I wasn't polite enough to await your return before enjoying a rather large piece of it."

"Aah, Mrs. Sonners," he answered with a smile. "I'm just surprised Mrs. Coates hasn't been here with one of *her* mince pies, too." And he proceeded to tell Hannah of the harvest-celebration dilemma.

When Hannah let out a long giggle, even the rosy sun on the porch floorboards seemed to brighten.

What is it about the sound of her laughter that vexes me so? he asked himself for the hundredth time since her arrival. *And how can I tell her about Constance?*

⁂

Joshua's troubled thoughts were interrupted by the sound of hoofbeats approaching at a rapid clip. When the horse and rider appeared around the corner of the church in a dusty cloud, Joshua immediately recognized Constance's father.

"Whoa!" Mr. McArthur called out, yanking at the reins and stopping near the porch. "All respects, Pastor."

"Hello, sir," Joshua replied as he stood up stiffly.

He watched the man's gaze go directly to where Hannah was sitting behind him. It remained there for several long moments before returning to Joshua.

"Sure are looking forward to having you tonight," said Mr. McArthur. "Constance has been cooking up a storm for days, and all your favorite dishes, too. Hope you come with a hearty appetite."

Joshua could feel his cheeks burn. He was glad Hannah couldn't see his face.

"Thank you most kindly, sir," he managed to sputter.

"Six o'clock sharp, then?"

"Six o'clock sharp."

Mr. McArthur's eyes returned to Hannah's direction, and an awkward silence ensued.

"Pardon my boldness, sir," she said evenly, "but it seems the tongue of the esteemed Reverend Quittner has lost its usual eloquence. I'm Hannah Collins, of Philadelphia, Pennsylvania."

"Glad to make your acquaintance, Miss Collins," Mr. McArthur replied, tipping his hat. "Well, I best be going. I sense a bit of chill in the air, and I've got to get the home fires blazing before tonight's feast commences."

He turned the horse and galloped off before Joshua could reply.

The next sound Joshua heard was the swish of Hannah's skirts as she hurried into the cabin and closed the door.

Saturday night was a blur to Joshua. He was almost sure he made all the proper responses during the evening's conversation around the dinner table. Constance had indeed prepared quite a feast, but Joshua could scarce recall even a bite of it.

There were no candles burning in the windows as he returned home by way of his cabin.

Hannah must be asleep, he thought, so he could do nothing but retire to the straw mattress in his parents' loft and listen to the sounds of the night as he wrestled the hours away until dawn.

As usual, his Sunday was filled with church services and pastoral calls on the homebound members of the congregation. Hannah did come to hear the morning message. Joshua found it difficult to ignore her presence as he strained to keep his attention on his place in his sermon notes. Her deep purple taffeta dress trimmed in white and matching hat stood out in the congregation as he struggled to keep his eyes in every direction but Hannah's. At dusk, with his stomach in rebellion against the variety of foods offered at each home he visited, he managed to return to the parsonage. His mother was sitting by the front door.

"Go home, Joshua. Hannah fell asleep an hour ago. You two can talk in the morning."

⚜

"You're leaving today?" Joshua all but cried out the next morning. "But you've just arrived. We've hardly had a moment to talk."

The two were at the table in the parsonage. Mrs. Quittner moved about the kitchen, preparing the breakfast. Hannah appeared tired, but Joshua could detect no anger in her demeanor.

"I know, Joshua, but in order to make it to Oberlin by Wednesday–and that's when my appointment with the dean is scheduled–I must take my leave now. I have a seat on the coach this morning. I'm sorry we've had so little time."

Joshua's thoughts roared past. *How can I get her to stay one more day? We need to talk.*

"And besides, if all transpires as hoped at Oberlin, I'll be only a short distance to the north. We could visit."

But what of my explanation of Constance? What of your question about marriage to Robert Keyes? Do I bring this subject up now? Do I wait for you to voice it again?

"But we shall have this pleasant breakfast together. It's not quite like our late nights at the Destiny, but it will do for today," she added.

As Joshua's mother fluttered about, cooking and serving their food, they chatted politely about inconsequential matters. At last Joshua suggested a final walk before she packed up.

While the last few days had been unseasonably warm, this day opened gray and chilled.

Mr. McArthur was right, Joshua thought. *There is a chill.*

Their breath could be seen in the air as they walked. When they stopped at the stream just beyond the parsonage, Hannah tucked the wool shaw around her and sat on the trunk of a huge fallen oak.

"It's so pretty here," Hannah said. "Living in the city makes one forget the wonders of nature."

Joshua nodded, then cleared his throat.

"I don't know how to begin," he stammered, "but I . . . Constance and I . . ."

She hid a frown and stared at the ground.

"You said that you and Robert Keyes . . ."

"I should not have bothered you with such a trivial matter. It's personal, and nothing for you to be concerned with."

"No . . . isn't that what friends are for? To talk about such things?"

She shrugged, then said, "He would be a suitable husband. He comes from a good family and already is on his way to being very rich. I could do so much worse, I imagine."

Don't settle for him, Hannah. Wait! Wait!

But Joshua did not voice his thoughts.

"What does the Bible say about this, Joshua?" Hannah asked, her beautiful face turned toward him. "You being a pastor and all. You tell me what God says about it. I've heard from every other side."

"What do you mean—'every other side'?"

"Well, his parents want it to happen. My parents are beside themselves that I would even want to spend another moment considering it."

"So they're in favor of the proposed union?"

Hannah half giggled. "A union . . . sounds so businesslike, doesn't it? Oh, yes, they would love for me to forget this whole Oberlin College affair, forget my dreams of a medical practice, and settle down with Robert's money. But this is my trust fund after all, and I can spend it as I see fit."

"Do you want to marry him?"

She did not answer but tossed a handful of pebbles into the stream.

"I suppose . . . it would make my parents happy." She looked up at him. "Aren't we supposed to honor our mother and father? The Bible says that, doesn't it? That's what love is about, is it not?"

Are we both honoring our parents and living our lives for them, he thought, *instead of ourselves?*

"Yes, the Bible does say that, but it says lots of things about marriage. Honoring your parents–that's important, but it's not the only thing."

"Isn't it? Isn't that what you're doing?"

Just then an echoed shout came from the direction of the parsonage. From across the field, they saw Joshua's mother waving a kitchen towel in the cold air.

"The coach . . . in town . . . hurry!" were the only words they made out.

Hannah stood and surprised Joshua by opening her arms and offering him a long, tender embrace. With her face nestled against his chest, his arms fit perfectly around her.

This feels so right, he told himself.

Then Hannah stepped back and looked up at him.

Tell her how you feel, his heart shouted, but no words came.

"Thanks, Joshua, for listening. I feel better now. It's nice to have such a friend as you. And I'm serious–Oberlin is not that far. You must visit me. You must. I'll write you with my address–if I'm accepted, that is. All the best with Constance. Your mother says she is a very fine person."

And with that she took his hand and drew him away from the stream, toward town and her waiting coach.

As the coach pulled away, Hannah looked back and waved good-bye. Joshua at last called out, "I'll write you, Hannah. Godspeed. Have a safe journey."

"I'll write you, Joshua. Thank you for everything."

As each step of the horses took Hannah farther away from Shawnee, Joshua's heart chilled.

I should have done what my heart told me! I should have followed my heart! I should have made a bolder case for love.

That thought rolled over and over in his mind and robbed him of sleep or even a peaceful daylight moment for more than a fortnight.

Would God surprise me like this? he asked himself over and over. *Could this have been the hand of the Lord after all? Would he move in such a manner in my life?*

CHAPTER FOURTEEN

Shawnee, Ohio
February 1847

A COLD snap chilled Shawnee for most of a week, and on its heels a day-long snowstorm added a blanket of white to the frozen landscape.

After sitting at his desk by the fireplace for several hours preparing for his Sunday sermon, Joshua got up to stretch and stoke the fire. After pouring a cup of coffee, he went to the window and watched the snow fall.

Most of the county's residents were holed up in their homes, staying close to their hearths. All was quiet save for the sound of a single sleigh's bells somewhere off in the distance.

So peaceful, he thought. *I wonder if it's snowing in Cambridge.*

He wrapped his woolen blanket tighter around himself and ran his hand through his hair. As he returned to his desk he thought he heard footsteps scuffle outside his door, then a murmur of conversation. He listened closely, thinking it might merely be the wind in the chinks of the cabin. He sat back down at his desk and snuffed his candle.

Since Hannah's unannounced visit in October, he had begun to dread any unexpected visitation. It was best, he thought, to remain in the known, the predictable, the sure. Visitors only offered a means of causing turmoil.

Then there was a loud rapping at the door.

Who could be calling in this weather? was his thought as he opened it.

For the next several moments Joshua could scarce contain his amazement.

Standing before him was his second visitor that year who had made the long journey from Harvard and the East.

"Gage Davis! Of all the people in the world I'd never expect to see at my door, you are the first and foremost. And in this storm?"

Gage grabbed his friend's hand and pumped it.

"Well, then, we're squared. For I never thought I'd ever venture to the bustling little town of Shawnee, Ohio, either."

Joshua happily pulled his friend inside. Dressed in a dark velvet-trimmed greatcoat and a red vest, Gage carried only a single leather bag with him. With his boldly printed scarf, chamois trousers, and gloves the color of honey, he was every bit the eastern dandy on a great adventure to the frontier.

"I'm telling the truth. It *is* a great surprise being here," Gage explained. "Only days ago I found myself in the port city of Gallipolis. We're expanding into shipping, and I'm exploring several sites and opportunities along the river, along with overseeing the construction of a new port and dry-dock facility. When I saw how close–comparatively–Shawnee was to the river, I could not refrain from visiting my old friend–especially since my business concluded earlier than expected. The snow made the going slower than usual, but here I am, none the worse for wear."

"And from here, where will you go? How long can you stay?" Joshua asked as he scurried about, finding enough odds and ends to put together a decent meal. After he put water on to boil for fresh coffee, he sat down as his friend ate the simple food.

"I'm actually on my way home. And to my sorrow, I've made plans to be on tomorrow's coach–if the snow does not prevent its arrival. My life is much busier now than when we could afford the luxury of lazy afternoons at the Destiny. But let us enjoy this day and evening at any rate. You must tell me all the news of Shawnee and your church. We have much catching up to do. And I have news of all our friends."

Joshua's smile appeared bittersweet.

"I miss them all, Gage. I do. I miss you, too."

Gage looked around the room, at the walls and floor, in one encompassing sweep. Joshua felt a prick of unease, as if Gage had just judged his life as shallow and coarse with that one single look. As with Hannah, he saw in Gage's eyes a reflection of how sparse his life was in comparison to what he had tasted back in Cambridge and Boston and New York.

It was clear Gage noticed Joshua's nervous look—and that he knew what that look meant.

"I saw Jamison in New York last month. He is building quite the reputation for himself with his writing from exotic places. He sends you his best."

"I've read many of his articles in the few newspapers that come to town. He is quite the adventurer."

"Yes, he is."

An anxious silence hung in the air as Joshua waited for Gage to continue.

"I saw Hannah, Joshua."

"Where . . . when?"

"I saw her in Philadelphia before she left. She told me of her plans."

The color drained out of Joshua's face.

"She was on her way to visit Oberlin, she said."

Gage shook his head. "She'll never go to Oberlin. This trip was as much to tweak at her parents' sensibilities as anything else." Gage paused, then continued, "She told me everything, Joshua. She told me about Robert Keyes and the rest. I think she made up her mind a long time ago."

"She did?" Joshua said, surprised. "Then this was a charade? She's going to marry him?"

"I think so. Joshua, I know you held her in a special place in your heart. I think we all did, but yours was most apparent."

"It was?"

"Don't be embarrassed, my friend. She is a very special woman."

Joshua's voice dropped to a whisper. "I know."

"She made the only choice she could. You always said you wanted to be a preacher, and now you are doing just that. None of us would have stopped you from following your calling. And she knows that her parents expect a lot from her—to marry well, to help them out of their new 'poverty.' She felt trapped, Joshua. Perhaps if things had been different . . ."

Joshua struggled to find the words. "Really, Gage, . . . could things have been different?"

Gage draped an arm over his old friend's shoulder. "Could you have been rich, Joshua? Could you be a member of some snobby blue-blooded eastern club? Could you learn to forget about your calling?"

Time seemed to stop. "No, I couldn't. At least I don't think I could."

"You see, Hannah knew that. I knew that. To have things different, you would have needed to be a different person. And we can't be different than what we are. Didn't you always say God has a perfect plan for your life?"

Joshua nodded.

"And this looks like a perfect plan to me. You have a church and a snug little home, and I'll bet every beautiful woman in Shawnee is after you."

Joshua could not help but smile in spite of his pain.

"I know I'm right. You follow God, Joshua. That's the life you are called to live. Let Hannah live the life she's called to."

"But what about love?"

"Love can grow, can't it? Love can happen when the heart's ready. Hannah will be fine, Joshua. I know you wished it to be different, but you picked the right path. You did. We all envied your steadfastness."

"You envied *me?"*

"Of course we did. We're still wondering what to do with our lives. But you have yours all signed, sealed, and delivered. We envy your faith and calling a lot, Joshua. A lot."

Joshua turned away. "Why did she come, then—come all this way and spend all that time if she already knew what she was going to do?"

"I'm not certain, Joshua. I thought I had women figured out, but I guess I don't. Maybe she wanted to test herself. Maybe she was waiting for a sudden, overwhelming urge . . . a voice. A voice from heaven, perhaps."

"A voice? Saying what?"

"Saying, 'Don't do it.'"

"Really?"

"I think so. Maybe she just wanted to make sure. I suppose she didn't hear it or feel it. So she left."

Joshua was silent for a minute. Then he asked, "Perhaps her head wanted it but not her heart?"

"Maybe something like that."

Gage stood up and rummaged in his bag. He pulled out a thin brown leather book and tossed it to Joshua.

"You weren't around to get your yearbook, so I got it for you. Been meaning to send it by messenger. Hope you don't mind the wait."

Joshua rubbed his hands across the cover of rich calfskin. He opened the pages, delighted at seeing etchings of Harvard's buildings and classrooms.

"This is wonderful, Gage. Thank you so much."

Joshua flipped through the pages.

"Look. There you are," Gage announced.

On the bottom of the page was a grainy picture of a grim-faced Joshua.

"I forgot about this," Joshua said, whistling. "I guess when I had to leave early, I thought they may not have included me in the book."

Then he looked up, surprised, at Gage. "What is this?" he asked, pointing to his picture.

Underneath his image and his name were the words "Destined to be surprised by fate."

"The yearbook staff puts those in," Gage responded. "We all have something written under our smiling or frowning faces. Mine is 'Destined to be a tycoon.'"

Joshua's smile had not returned. "But why this?" he asked.

"You want the truth?"

"Of course I do. You know I do."

"Well, we thought your goal of spending the rest of your life in Ohio was odd—truly odd—given what we saw in your eyes. I saw something in you the first time I met you. I think most people did, in one way or another."

"They did? Saw what?"

"I don't know exactly. But your eyes told me that you wanted to climb the next mountain to see the other side. That you wanted to keep going until you could walk no farther and see no additional sights."

"But why would no one say a word?"

"But lots of us did—in a fashion. Didn't nearly everyone you met express surprise over your choice of study and your goal in life?"

Joshua felt compelled to nod.

"And we saw how fascinated you became when talk veered to places we had visited and places Jamison planned to write about. I saw a certain wanderlust in your eyes but assumed it was held subservient to your calling."

"I suspect it was," Joshua said thoughtfully.

"You were so adamant about that calling and how your life would turn out, and your life has turned out just as you said. We were envious that you had such a clear image of what lay in store. Even your faith was impressive. That you could know being a preacher in Shawnee would be so rewarding," Gage said. After a pause, he added, "It *is* rewarding, is it not?"

Joshua replied almost too quickly. "Indeed it is. As much as I thought and more so."

Gage sipped at his coffee. "Very good coffee, Joshua. Not like you get on a riverboat."

Joshua tried to smile. Then he asked, "Is it exciting?"

"Is what exciting, Joshua?"

"Traveling on the river. Seeing all the places we used to talk about."

Gage nodded. "It has its moments. If you ever want to take a short spin on a riverboat, my friend, stop in Gallipolis and ask for a Captain Hopler. He works for the Ohio Exploration and Freight Company. That's one of ours. Tell him you're my old Harvard pal—and he'll see that you're treated royally."

Joshua brightened. "Do you mean that? I could take a short trip on a riverboat?"

"Short or long, whatever you have the time for. Just mention my name."

Joshua grinned.

"Thanks, old friend. Thanks a lot."

From the Journal of Joshua Quittner
February 1847

I'm sure there will be no end to the vexations I'll endure as a servant of the Lord. I've expected temptations, though I did not expect them to take the form of old friends.

When Hannah arrived, she totally disrupted my world. There is a part of me that refuses to forget her face, laugh, and smile. Yet I have prayed that my calling remain secure, and I believe that prayer has been answered.

Then Gage arrives and shakes the foundation even more. He claims they all knew of my wanderlust. And yet he claims that I, alone, of the four of us, have made the right decisions with my life.

I think Gage is romanticizing my interest in the world.

Before his leaving, I thanked Gage again for the extreme

generosity of his gift. He dismissed it, claiming, as he'd said he would, that he had no memory of it.

It's good to have friends as noble as Gage.

Perhaps one day I *will* journey to Gallipolis and take a ride upriver from there to Parkersburg. I've always wanted to be in a boat as it plies the rivers in that manner.

Captain Hopler–perhaps I will see you soon.

CHAPTER FIFTEEN

Shawnee, Ohio
January 1848

THE autumn of 1847 had been glorious and warm in southern Ohio, and the hardwood trees blazed with luminescent colors. But the winter that followed was frigid and lifeless, with long periods of gray days and bone-chilling nights. As the New Year of 1848 arrived, winds whipped along the ground, nudging the snow into sullen, white banks.

On the first three Sundays in January, Joshua struggled to the church, breaking through waist-high drifts to light a fire in the ancient iron stove. As the winds howled about the structure, Joshua practiced his sermon on an empty room. Gusts of snow slipped through open cracks around the windows, and the roof groaned with its shouldering of whiteness.

Each Sunday Joshua sat on the deacon's bench and looked out over the vacant pews, checked his timepiece, waited till half past noon, then trudged back to his parsonage. No one tried to brave the elements. Joshua could not blame them. The only folks he had seen in weeks were the nearby farmers who had to struggle with livestock in open fields.

The cold and emptiness matched Joshua's soul.

He told himself over and over that Hannah's visit had been a good thing, that he finally was able to close the door on that chapter of his life. During his visit, Gage confirmed Joshua's suppositions that Hannah would never be part of his world, that she was trapped by her social position and the needs of her family.

Yet, even as he closed that door and tried to bolt it shut, the fact that the door even existed brought an edge of worry and despair to his thoughts. He prayed, sought counsel in the Word, and sat alone by the fire, late in the evenings, telling himself over and over that his decisions had been sound and that the life he led now was most pleasing to God.

He was certain that, in time, the petty thoughts that called Hannah's name would become increasingly faint and disappear forever.

At the end of January he received a short note from Hannah, which he did not keep as he had done with her past letters. She informed him that Oberlin did not offer the training and schooling that she desired—not to a woman, anyway. She added that there might be a small college near Philadelphia that would accept her. She signed it with no flourish—just her name. She offered no other news, no further information on her life, no mention of her antici-pated marriage.

Joshua debated for a long evening on what to do. Should he respond? Should he wait? In the end, he slipped her letter reveren-tially into the fire, watched it burn, and decided that both for now and in the future, he would only respond to a letter from her if it contained urgent subject matter that demanded a reply.

Joshua paced and wrote and read during these weeks of silence. For exercise, he cleared a path to his parents' home, breaking through drifts that often topped his head. He had not been worried for them and did not need to be. They were well stocked for such events, having enough provisions for months of solitary living if need be. But during his visits he refilled their tinderboxes and built up their firewood stores.

His mother drew him aside at the end of one visit.

"You look thin, Joshua. Are you eating enough? Shall I pack you a basket to take back? I'll not be able to bear it if others say I'm neglecting the welfare of my only son."

He managed to smile in response and knelt to stoke the fire.

"No, I'm eating well. And yes, I have more than enough in my larder. There's a good amount of corned meat and some fatback and a whole wheel of cheese and squash and potatoes and turnips in the root cellar. Why, it's more than enough to hold me for weeks."

He poked at a log, and a shower of sparks flew up the chimney.

"But you still look drawn." His mother took his chin in her hand and lifted it so she could see his face. "Something's wrong," she said, a mixture of concern and anger in her words.

"Nothing's wrong. Really. It's just cold and dark, and everyone is ready for winter to be over."

She looked in his eyes. "It's that woman from Philadelphia, isn't it? After all this time, you're still thinking about her."

Joshua did his best to prevent surprise from marking his face. "What? No . . . it has nothing to do with her."

"Are you sure? I saw something in your eyes when she visited—and that look is back again."

"You saw the look of an old friend, that's all. And it is not back."

"Well," she said, sniffing, "she was a charmer, that's for sure. But old friend or not—she was not the proper woman for you. An East Coast hussy, if you ask me. Traveling all this way alone, to see a man, no less. Why, if she were my daughter, that would never have been allowed."

After Hannah had left, Joshua's mother had allowed her true feelings concerning Hannah's visit to bubble to the surface of their conversations. Even though time had elapsed, townsfolk (including Joshua's mother) seldom gave up on a satisfying tidbit of gossip.

"It was perfectly innocent, Mother. She was on her way to Oberlin College. We are old friends. That's all."

He sighed, tired of having to explain it one more time.

"Maybe, but I still say she stirred things up in your mind, Joshua.

You need to forget about her East Coast manners and social conventions and pay attention to the task God has called you to do in Shawnee."

"I have, Mother. But remember, she was a friend. That is all she was."

She sniffed again. "No matter really, but people closer to home should be occupying your attention. You need to be thinking more of that nice Constance McArthur, if you want to know the truth. She's a beautiful young lady, don't you think?"

Joshua fought the blush that spread to his cheeks. His mother had hinted at such matters before but never had been quite so direct until now.

"I suppose so."

"Suppose? She's a beauty. I know a pastor is always busy and has to neglect his personal life for a time. But no one gets younger, and you need to get busy."

"I am busy, Mother. I seldom have a free moment," he said as he lowered an armful of logs to a spot near the grate. "And with this weather, no one has been doing much of anything."

"I didn't mean today. And I meant you should get busy courting Constance. I thought you started a long time ago–then nothing. What's the matter with her? Don't you find her attractive? I know what men look for in a wife, and she's got that."

This time Joshua did blush, even though he knew his mother's comments were innocent.

"A pastor needs a wife, Joshua. You know that. The church knows that. The elders told you it would be nice if you were to marry soon. There's a raise as well, I'm told."

Secrets were rare in Shawnee.

"Constance would make a wonderful wife."

Joshua tried hard to think of a reply but could not. He knew that she was right.

"And I want grandchildren. Your father and I are not spring chickens, you know."

"I hardly know Constance, and you have us married and with children. Don't you think that's moving events too rapidly?"

"Joshua, you are a wonderful pastor and were a brilliant student, no doubt. But you know nothing about the female mind. When the weather breaks, you simply have to call on Constance. You must. She's wondering why you haven't been more diligent in seeking her out."

Joshua wanted to ask how she knew he must, and how she knew Constance desired his call. But then he realized it might be better if he didn't know the hidden mechanics of the situation. So he simply nodded instead.

"When the weather breaks," he said with a sigh. "When the weather breaks."

The final week of January brought warm winds from the south. The town, which prior to this day had been numbed to lifelessness, revived, and people ventured out in the sunshine. A torrent of members filled the church that first thawed Sunday, and the sermon Joshua had been practicing for three weeks was finally presented.

Constance and her family were sitting in their usual three-pews-back-on-the-right location. As he preached, she indeed stared at him and, on occasion, just as Hannah had done so long ago, caused him to stumble and lose his train of thought.

He was certain no one noticed the gaffe and, if they had, were too polite to mention it.

His mother's words echoed in his thoughts, even as he preached. He knew Hannah was out of his life. He knew a pastor should be married. He knew he wanted to be married, to have an intimate ally. Of all the eligible women in Shawnee, Constance was the most attractive. While not a bright student, she was cheerful and gregarious. She also was a woman with unquestionable morals—that too was important to a pastor.

I could do worse, Joshua thought, *and I do like her well enough. Perhaps my mother is right. I need to make progress in finding a mate. It is*

181

clear to me now that a chapter has ended in my life . . . the chapter that includes Hannah. And this division is as clear as the heavens can make such a declaration. It is time that I turn the page and start a new chapter in my life–the chapter which includes Constance. Hannah is the past; Constance is my future. And I can learn to embrace that reality with all my heart. I know I can.

After the service, as he greeted each member of the congregation, he held Constance's hand a few heartbeats longer. Then he leaned closer in to her and said softly, though he was certain others may have overheard, "Would you like to accompany me to a dinner at Murphy's this week? Perhaps Tuesday evening?"

Breaking into a smile, she quickly lowered her eyes.

"I would like that, Pastor Quittner. I would like that a great deal."

✦

While Murphy's reputation was somewhat south of immaculate, Joshua had no other choice. He would not take her to dinner at his parents' house–too many questions and unsettling looks, especially from his mother. He could not invite himself to her house for dinner, although the food was always excellent, since he was sure Constance was as uncomfortable with her parents in his presence as he was in the reverse situation. And he knew with dead-solid certainty that he could not cook dinner for her. While he prepared some of his own meals, the cuisine seldom rose above cheese and Boston baked beans and johnnycakes.

Murphy's would have to do. During the week the boisterous element that emboldened the establishment on the weekends was absent. And despite its intermittent lapses in morality, virtually everyone in town who had the means dined there on occasion. Even Joshua's parents had allowed themselves the luxury of a meal there every month or so.

Joshua struggled with his selection. The only other alternative was to travel to New Lexington, north of town and home to six such establishments. But it was a hard ride, and winter travel over the snow-packed or sloshy road could be hazardous.

On Tuesday evening Joshua rigged up his buckboard with sleigh runners and drove the two miles to the McArthur homestead. He had packed three blankets and a fur throw for the ride–even though the temperature that day brought forth a torrent of water from melting icicles.

Constance remained quiet on the ride to Murphy's, as did Joshua. He turned slightly as he drove the horse, in order to take in Constance's features under the felt bonnet that covered her ears and honey-colored hair. Her cheeks and lips, perhaps because of the chill, were rosy and alive with color. Her eyes, a deep green-blue, looked out onto the road ahead.

Constance offered an altogether pleasing visage, he decided, even if her features were fuller than Hannah's. As he compared her mentally to Hannah, he scolded himself, promising to forget such comparisons in the future.

Constance caught him looking, turned to him, and smiled easily.

Inside Murphy's it was warm. The flickering light of candles cast a golden glow on the room.

It looks more wholesome than its reputation, Joshua thought.

The two of them sat at a table near the fireplace, looking out onto the main street of Shawnee. As they dined, people walked by and nodded to them or waved. Joshua smiled and nodded back to each. Their meal–a lean cut of roast beef covered in a thick gravy with potatoes and the last of the fall's vegetables–was appetizing. As they dined, Joshua told Constance stories of his seminary days at Harvard. She giggled uncontrollably as he told the story of the horse in the dean's office and Gage's masquerade as a professor.

Her eyes widened as he mentioned Gage's wealth, but she did not ask for details. Joshua marveled at her restraint. So often people clamored for the tiniest morsel of information of a rich man's life and fortune.

While they ate their apple pandowdy for dessert, she asked him about his pastoral duties–which ones proved most satisfying and which ones, most troublesome? He was pleased at her willingness to listen to him and ask after his views.

Once again, despite his best intentions, he compared her with Hannah, and this time, however, she compared favorably. She may not have possessed the natural wit and delightfully wicked sense of humor that Hannah did, but the evening was a fine one.

Joshua! he shouted to himself, *there will be no more of this thinking. I have vowed to not set Constance against a perfect memory of Hannah–and that is a vow I will keep. Constance deserves no less.*

On the way home, despite the night's chilliness, Joshua pulled the horse and buckboard to a stop along a narrow curve of the road. Through the trees they saw a half-moon and heard a faint, crystalline sparkling–the sound of the stream as it passed over a rocky ledge. The water at the falls seldom froze.

Joshua loosened the reins, and the horse swept his head back and forth for a moment, stomped once or twice, then appeared to understand the reason for the interruption.

"This was a most pleasant evening," Joshua said.

Constance exhaled as if she were expecting a harsher assessment.

"Oh, Pastor Quittner . . . I mean, Joshua . . . I thought as much, too. The food was quite good, and your stories were wonderfully amusing. You should speak of them more often in your messages. I'm sure people would find them to be entertaining . . . not that you need to be entertaining . . . but, sometimes . . . oh I get so flustered when I try to explain things like this."

Joshua laughed softly. "I understand what you mean. Humor and God are not mutually exclusive. And perhaps I will include some of these stories. I'll have to use them carefully, for there are not that many of them."

She giggled. "At least you have stories. All I know is this small town, and everyone knows the same stories."

"That's not so bad," he replied. "It's nice being part of a bigger family."

"Why, that's a sweet way to look at it."

Just then the unasked voice inside tried to whisper the name *Hannah* again, but he pushed it away with finality.

Constance is a very nice girl, he thought. *And very attractive. This will be a most pleasing chapter of my life.*

"I really had a nice time tonight," she said, as the moon hid behind a cloud. Darkness was nearly complete, but he thought she tilted her head slightly and leaned against his arm a bit more, closing her eyes.

If this girl is the one . . .

After an agonizing debate with himself, he smiled, then bent closer for a quick kiss. It was not long or lingering as he would have liked. But it was just long enough to announce his intentions without being greedy.

Surprised for a second, she then softened and kissed him back with lips as pliable as fresh bread dough. He smiled as that image came to mind, and she returned his smile.

The clouds parted, bathing them both in a glow.

Slowly he sat up straight.

"I best be getting you home, Constance. Your parents will wonder."

"I guess," she murmured. "Well, yes . . . I suppose I should be getting home."

She slipped her arm through his and snuggled close, tucking her head against his shoulder so that he felt the soft scratchiness of her felt bonnet against his cheek. The horse whinnied, shook its mane, and began to trot down the road, hooves nearly silent in the wet snow.

He walked her to the door. A series of candles flickered from inside.

"I had a wonderful evening, Constance," he said as he held her hand. "We must do it again soon."

Her eyes sparkled.

"I would love that, Pastor . . . I mean, Joshua. I really, really would."

She opened the door, slipped in, and watched through a narrow crack as he turned, whistling, and stepped to the buckboard. He turned to wave as he slapped the reins, and the horse charged off into the moonlit night.

A most pleasing chapter indeed.

FROM THE JOURNAL OF JOSHUA QUITTNER

JANUARY 1848

I'd never before considered kissing a woman on a first outing such as this! What came over me? While I did so enjoy it, I have no idea of what possessed me to be so bold and so unlike a proper, moral pastor.

Is this a matter I should confess to God? Or is it an innocent first step in a normal courtship? Of course, this physical attraction shall never progress beyond an innocent kiss . . . or two . . . until we might be married, that is.

And here I am mentioning marriage. What sort of spark has nested in my flax?

Constance is a perfectly lovely woman, and she laughs easily. I hear a gentler music in her laugh than I have heard elsewhere . . . and I will not dwell on such laughter from my past. Constance and I have not yet spoken of spiritual matters . . . perhaps that should be top on my list of criteria. And I am sure we will, for conversation with her is most easy and sweet.

I intend on scheduling another evening with Miss McArthur as soon as our schedules allow. This situation is no longer a loose end that needs tidying up . . . but a real pleasure.

Shawnee, Ohio
February 1848

Constance and Joshua dined three times more at Murphy's during the month of February and appeared together at two church socials. They were never announced as a couple per se, but it was obvious to all present that they were.

At the end of a potluck dinner, Joshua's mother sidled up to her son.

"Constance looks lovely tonight," she said.

At first, Joshua was perplexed. Why should he be complimented on Constance's appearance? Then he realized it was his mother's way of nudging him closer and closer to this girl, and he smiled at her obvious ploy.

"So when will you announce your engagement?" she asked, her face a mask of innocence.

Stifling a gasp, he replied, "What makes you think we're close to such a thing? We've only been courting a few weeks."

She did not hesitate. "Mothers have ways, you know." Taking him by the arm, she pulled him into the shadows. "Why wait? You know she's a wonderful girl. Mrs. McArthur and I would love to plan a spring wedding. You'll get married. The church will give you a raise. You'll have children. I'll have grandchildren."

Joshua was still discomforted by what his mother was saying. Yet even as she spoke the words, he found himself agreeing with her assessment of Constance and nearly agreeing to her proposed timetable.

"But don't you think people will talk? It has been only a matter of weeks that we have . . . courted," Joshua said.

His mother waved away his reluctance.

"Most of the folks around here didn't wait much longer. When the time and the person is right—why not settle it?" She grabbed at his arm. "You have been praying about this, haven't you?"

Joshua nodded.

"Your father and I have as well. We know that taking care of the farm is a handful for a single man like yourself. With a wife, well, that will help a lot. We don't want to be a burden, and we'll help as best we can."

"I know, Mother. I know."

A gale of laughter carried across the room. Two of the elders standing near the dessert table were in animated discussion with a third.

"So you're thinking about this, Joshua?"

He nodded again.

"Think hard about it. If you want a spring wedding, we have a lot to do."

I will. I will think about it.

Constance insisted he walk his mother home after the church social. His father had not felt up to the evening, and Constance would not have Joshua's mother walking home alone in the dark.

"I'll ride home with my parents," she said as she squeezed his hand. "We can have time after you're done with your visitations tomorrow." Then she blushed.

Joshua knew what the blush meant. While Joshua's promise of no further intimacies held firm, they allowed themselves the pleasure of a lingering kiss or two after their evenings together.

He would miss the experience tonight.

On the way home from his parent's house, Joshua stopped and listened to the lonely call of a wolf. It was a rare sound since the farmers' lands now took up most of the wooded areas, save for a band near the river. The bark and melancholy howl swept over the snow-covered fields.

Looking up at the moon, he thought, *Lord, I think I'm doing the right thing. No . . . I know I am. My heart feels mostly at peace. Constance is a most agreeable woman. She is kind and considerate. I feel stirred when I'm with her. She would make a wonderful pastor's wife. I know her parents—and my own—would be so happy if we were to wed.*

Joshua kicked at a patch of hard snow at his feet. As he turned toward his home, a bitter wind licked at his face.

Lord, I'm not a man to call for fleeces—you know that. I think a man can find his way using your Holy Word and not be bothering you every moment for some sign or indication. But saying that, I'm on my knees asking for an indication of your will. Show me the way, Lord. Show me that I'm doing the right thing. Show me that Constance and I should marry.

He tucked his head lower, into his collar.

Just a little sign, Lord. Just this once, and that's all I'll ever ask.

March 1848

March arrived like a lamb and appeared set on exiting in the same manner. Farmers gathered around warming stoves and speculated on having crops in ground by mid-April, the weather having been so mild. Even the crocuses, the earliest of spring flowers, arrived sooner than ever remembered, their colors sprouting in protected hollows and vales.

Joshua sensed the congregation's nervous excitement. Most of Shawnee's citizens saw winter as a long travail in cramped houses, with little to do except mend tools, sew, or retell tales known by heart by everyone who listened. Colors of brown and gray and black filled their eyes. Day after day after day brought a monochromatic sameness.

When spring came and the colors burst from the earth, pulses would quicken at the sheer novelty of it all. As he preached, he felt that quickening. The windows, only cracked open an inch or so, allowed a breath of a spring breeze to waft in. Joshua stopped at one point to sniff, thinking he noted the scent of new grass.

People in the congregation shifted as he spoke. His message this day dealt with God's promises and how a believer can rest assured that God hears every prayer and answers every one.

"Sometimes we ask, and the answer is as plain as a cow in the kitchen. We can't help but see it. Then, at other times," he continued, gesturing, "God waits awhile before he answers. He wants us to think about our request. But someday, when he answers, you will know. It comes like lightning on a summer evening. The sky is pitch dark. Then, in a heartbeat, it's ablaze with light and rumbling with sound. The flash makes us jump and take notice. All of us need to remember that God will answer us. He will. Just ask. And wait."

And as he spoke those lines, the back door to the church swung open, and a figure–a male figure–walked into the back. The sun was at his shoulders, bathing him in a pearly, early-spring light that hid his face. It was as if an angel had settled in, its brilliance preventing a mortal man from gazing at its features.

Joshua blinked, wondering who might be arriving so near to the end of his message. He hoped it was not an actual angel, come to answer his prayers.

God doesn't send angels to answer questions of matrimony, I'm sure.

The figure took a few more steps inside. Then the door behind him closed. There in the vestibule, wearing an odd mixture of buckskin and velvet, as if he was the East Coast meeting the mountains, stood a sunburnt and whiskery Jamison Pike.

On his face was the smile of an angel.

⚜

That evening, after he had finished his promised pastoral visits and met every urgent need of the day, Joshua spurred his horse back to town, almost at a gallop.

As he rode, his thoughts galloped along as well. It seemed as though Jamison's arrival that day was the highlight of the week. "How could that filthy person be allowed in our church," one woman asked him. "Aren't you afraid of what he might do?"

Others shared the same observations of fear and distrust. They saw a stranger and evil and peril. But Joshua saw something else all together. *He has just returned from California. He has seen the Pacific Ocean. He has traveled farther in a few years than the whole lot of you will travel in your lifetime. Think of what he can teach us. Think of what you can learn.*

Perhaps Emil Pouter, a bachelor farmer from south of Shawnee, best summed up the mood of the church. "This church ain't for strangers, Pastor. It be for the family of God, and that's it. I hope no more of your 'friends' stop in to visit–especially if they ain't believers."

He and Jamison had shared but a handful of words this morning. The basic gist of the message was that Jamison inquired urgently after a bed and a bath.

"I've been traveling three days without sleep and longer without a washing up. I know a bath is needed, but if I do that now, I'll fall asleep and drown."

Joshua returned a few hours later with an apple pie from Constance, a cold shoulder of lamb from his mother, and a keg of cider from Mr. McArthur. He busied himself setting out the table. Jamison stirred from the bedroom, then emerged grizzled, wrinkled, unwashed, and grinning from ear to ear.

He startled Joshua by embracing him in a fierce hug.

"Good to see you, friend. For a while out there I never thought I'd see civilization again. And now I find the companionship of a fellow Harvard man who provides me with a soft bed and clean water. Such luxuries you cannot imagine." He peered down with delight at the food on the table before him. "Such decadence!—having food not crawling with maggots or surrounded by flies. I'm indeed famished."

He sat with eagerness and grabbed for the meat, taking leave of his Harvard social graces and table manners.

"Where were you?" Joshua asked incredulously.

Jamison stuffed a hearty serving into his mouth.

"California," he mumbled, trying to chew. "Got there in time for Christmas and left soon after. You can't imagine what I've seen. Indians, volcanoes, wild skies, buffaloes, and what I think was a whale. It's been incredible." He wiped a greasy hand across his chest and smiled. "Can't get any dirtier."

Jamison squirmed to thrust his hand into a hip pocket, then tossed something hard on the table in front of Joshua. It landed with a thump and rolled toward him. It was a yellow, gnarled rock the size of a baby's fist. "It's yours, friend," Jamison said.

"What is it?" Joshua asked.

Jamison swallowed his mouthful of roast meat, then offered a secretive smile.

"It's gold, Joshua. They discovered gold at Sutter's Mill. The streams are filled with it."

Joshua's jaw dropped.

CHAPTER SIXTEEN

Shawnee, Ohio
March 1848

GOLD?" Joshua asked, shocked.

Jamison took a long drink of cider, then nodded. "There's gold everywhere in California. I've seen it in a dozen places—and it's there for the picking. A man stands in the shallow part of the river, scoops out some gravel, swishes it around in a pan, and it's as though God himself is breathing on those rocks. Gold nuggets are what's left—sparkling, heavy gold nuggets."

"Gold?"

Jamison smiled, took another bite of roast, and said through his chewing, "You might want to find a different word, Joshua, my friend."

Joshua shook his head to clear it.

"Why haven't we heard of this before? Are you sure? Can anyone mine it? How hard is it to get to California? Why aren't you there digging it?"

Jamison held up his palms in surrender. "Whoa now. You went from one word to a flood in a flash. I'm still recovering from the journey. Take pity on me."

"Well, you can't start throwing gold nuggets around like they're some sort of worthless trinket and not explain."

Jamison sliced into the apple pie, removing almost a third of it, and slid it, crumbs and juice dribbling on the table, onto his plate.

"You're right. I guess a gold nugget does stir things up. It's just that I've spent the last month being hushed about it. I felt like bursting to see the effect the story would have on someone."

"Is it truly gold? And is it really everywhere?"

Shoveling a huge forkful of sweet crust and filling into his mouth, Jamison mumbled, "Yep, and the reason you haven't heard anything is because I'm pretty certain I still have the exclusive story. Sent back most of it to New York already by fast clipper ship. The story may have beaten me back to New York, but I left out a few details so they'll have to await my return to run it. I know that's driving my editor to distraction–or to the bottle. But I'll have the exclusive unless some other reporter followed my trail out there. It is truly amazing how fast one can travel with the resources of a newspaper– and a lot of its money–behind them. Money and gold–and a great deal of good luck–that's the reason I'm here so soon and not trudging out along the desert. If I were a believing man, I would have said that God smiled on my travels."

Joshua all but ignored his remark. Instead he picked up the nugget and rolled it about in his hand.

"The gold is real all right," Jamison said between bites. "I had it tested twice by a couple of chemists–one was a Harvard alum–class of '33. He said without a doubt it's some of the purest gold he's ever seen this side of a smelter."

Joshua held it closer to his face and stared hard at it, as if he were listening to it, trying to unlock some mystery in its history.

"And you say it's just lying in the rivers? On the bottom? Don't you even have to dig for it?"

"Hardly," Jamison replied. "I suspect some ore might take extra digging. But the first harvest is going to be easy."

"It costs a lot to buy the land, doesn't it?"

Jamison laughed, and bits of apple dribbled on his chin. "I don't mean to be rude, but it's a funny question since it hardly costs a thing to stake a claim. You merely find an appealing section of river-bank, register with whoever takes registrations in the territory, pay your five dollars, and you're in business. In the places where there is no one to register you, it's first come, first served."

"Five dollars? That's all it costs??" Joshua said, incredulous. "Then why aren't you out there getting rich?"

Jamison looked as smug as a cat with a mouthful of canary. He grabbed a battered leather satchel and tossed it to Joshua, who almost fell off his chair as it landed against his chest.

"What's in here?"

"You don't have to ask, do you?" Jamison replied. "You want to know why I'm not out there prospecting? To be honest, money doesn't mean that much to me. But while I was there, I managed to pick up enough nuggets, even bigger than the one you're still hold-ing, to probably match my salary from the newspaper for the next five years. Any more than that, and I would have felt most greedy."

Joshua showed his shock.

"The Bible—doesn't it preach against greediness? A few years' cushion . . . that's enough for me. It's not the money, Joshua, that interests me. It's the experience. That's the treasure. Not the gold."

Fed and bathed, with his dirt-cloven clothes finally washed, Jamison caught the early coach east. He admitted Shawnee was out of his way, but he could not resist the urge to pepper Joshua's life with some piquant episodes of his western odyssey.

Joshua could scarce believe his hearing as Jamison related being chased down a cold stream with the sounds of bloodcurdling war whoops and Indian arrows whizzing through the air above his head.

"I never knew I could run that fast," Jamison said. "But I can. And my editor will love the story. I may even write it up for a novel. Every man trapped in a small life back East would fall in love with the yarn—except it would all be true."

Joshua watched as the coach carrying his friend eastward clattered off into the distance; then he walked home, his steps slow and measured.

His three closest friends from Harvard had all managed to cross his doorstep. Each one had seen more adventure and excitement than Joshua would hope to see in an entire lifetime in Shawnee. Even Hannah had seen the falls at Niagara and stepped on the deck of a riverboat.

And what is it I've accomplished? he fumed as he rattled about the parsonage. *And what can I ever hope to do? Only more of the same? All I know is that my life offers no such excitement.*

He knew, and repeatedly told himself, that a life as a humble and obedient servant offered more rewards and gentle joy than any trip to exotic and strange lands. A life serving the living God was of more value than a sackful of gold nuggets. Gold would be lost and spent and cursed, while God's treasure would last forever. God would reward his servants—not always on earth, but in heaven. That's where the true reward lay.

This is my calling, Joshua said, trying to convince himself. *This is where God wants me to be. He calls his servants to various tasks, and he has called me here.*

But this time his thoughts did not calm his heart. Agitated, he paced around the parsonage.

And hasn't God brought Constance into my life? No one else—not one of my friends—has such a person as her. Not even Hannah, no doubt, if she marries Robert, will have a mate of such a good and gentle spirit, willing to sacrifice and willing to do God's work. No, the Lord is doing good work with my life. I'm sure this is the path he has chosen. . . . Or is it?

He slumped at the table, picking the gold nugget up for the hundredth time, rolling it about, gently tossing it in the air, and catching it again. From the corner of his eye he saw the leaves of a well-paged book under the lantern on the table.

Jamison must have left it. I'll have to mail it back by express.

He retrieved it and saw that it was a dog-eared, stained, and creased copy of the *Emigrants Guide to Oregon and California.*

Penciled in tiny script across the cover and continuing to the inside flap was the following message:

Joshua:

This is your copy. Maybe it will inspire you. I have a second copy, so I have no need of this one. I made some notes about my travels on some of the pages. Don't bother with Oregon–I hear it rains all the time. Perhaps one day you might consider the trip to California. Watching the golden Pacific accept the sun at nightfall is an experience not unlike seeing God, I'm sure. Follow the route–through New Orleans–as we talked about last night. They say it's quicker than my overland journey by months. Do not travel due west. The Indians in the vast plains are numerous and bloodthirsty. The mountains are treacherous, even for the most experienced. Both could spell your doom. You must go south–down to the country they call Panama–a distance below Mexico. It separates the Atlantic from the Pacific by the narrowest of areas. The entire distance from ocean to ocean can be traversed in a matter of days–a week at most. (At least that is what I am told by those I trust.)

When you go, you must promise me to take notes. Tell me if what I hear is true–lands filled with jungle people and exotic animals. My friend, this would be the adventure of a lifetime. What an opportunity to make the geography we studied at Harvard come alive! Don't wait too long, or the easy gold will be gone. I've marked some hidden spots along the best rivers on the map. There's gold there. And don't forget–they need God out there, too. I can't say I saw one preacher or one church–except for a Catholic mission–my whole trip. Everyone who goes there will need to hear from God, won't they? And while you're there, you can pick up a few pounds of heaven's pavement.

Take care, my old friend. Watch for my story in the newspaper.

Jamison

P.S. California is your destiny. Of that I'm sure. Do not ask me how or why–simply take my word for it.

⁂

Jamison had grinned and waved with a fool's smile as the carriage turned the corner north of the Shawnee General Store. He had laughed and shouted, "Remember the Destiny." Or perhaps Jamison had called out, "Remember your destiny."

Joshua could not be sure what he had heard.

Joshua felt that curious, empty feeling again—one of his close friends had entered his life for a brief moment, then withdrawn.

How I miss their laughter and conversation, he thought to himself as he trudged back to the parsonage.

Trying not to look, Joshua picked up the book and nugget and placed them in the top drawer of his desk. He had the key in his hand and deliberated over locking them up.

No one knows the gold is here, he told himself, *so what would be the sense in the lock.*

After a moment, he did turn the key and felt the latch engage. The locked drawer was not to prevent thieves creeping in at midnight to pilfer the golden rock but to prevent Joshua from reaching in and holding the cold metal in his hand.

Best left alone, he sniffed, and went about his preparations for his Sunday message as usual.

That gold nugget glistered in the dark for less than an hour.

Joshua became stumped over a verse in Romans about man's destiny and fate with God. He stood to stretch, then sat back down, fumbled in his vest pocket for the desk key, and unlocked the drawer. He reached in and found the nugget. It felt less cold and quickly warmed to his hand. He tossed it in the air and felt the heavy thump as it hit his outstretched palm.

After staring at it for several moments, he returned it to the drawer and closed the lock again.

Free gold . . . there for the taking, his thoughts whispered. *Free gold.*

The week after Jamison's visit passed quickly for Joshua. There was a wedding at church, and a funeral . . . an unchurched uncle of a church member had passed on, and Joshua was quick to open the doors of the church for his service.

No telling when I can reach someone with the Good News. This is a tender time.

Yet each day, after the sun dropped and the shadows and dark filled the house, Joshua would slowly walk to his desk and unlock the drawer. With a practiced hesitation, he would reach in and finger the golden nugget there, picking it up, staring at its odd angles and bumps.

Free for the taking, it whispered to him. *Free for the taking.*

As the days passed, Joshua felt his thoughts growing more confused. A whirlwind of images sprang before his eyes. He saw rushing waters filled with the glinting bits of gold shimmering just below the surface. He saw himself bending to receive this gold, filling a great bucket with bits of the yellow element.

In the darkness he would pad about his home. The moon was full and flooded the rooms with a gray, ghostly light. He walked from his desk to his bed to the fireplace to the kitchen—as if in a trance. Sometimes he would carry the golden nugget with him. Sometimes he would simply stare into the night sky.

He heard Jamison's words over and over. The words were but a soft murmur at first, then as each day passed, they grew louder and louder in his ears.

California is your destiny. . . . California is your destiny.

He opened his front door. It was well past midnight. The moon was as fat as an October melon in the sky.

He carried the gold in his right hand.

Lord, he called out in a whisper, *is what I am thinking a sin? Is it an unforgivable sin?*

He tried his best not to use words to describe his hidden thoughts—as if the mere hearing would give them permanence.

He shut his eyes hard. In that moment, he knew he could go no longer without voicing them.

"Lord, is California my destiny? I know you use different methods to show your children your will and your plans for their life. Are you using Jamison to show me your will? Shall I . . ."

He lowered his whispered words to a faint hiss.

"Shall I leave here for a time to find this gold so I may return and fully serve you with resources that will allow a proper church and books and hymnals and the like? Could you be directing me that way?"

After only a moment, he shook his head, angry and tense, knowing that God would not, or could not, do such a thing in his life.

"Shawnee is my calling," he told himself aloud as if to emphasize the truth of his words. "And this church is my calling, and this ministry is my calling, and Constance is the woman I will marry and raise a family with. That is my calling. I know that beyond the shadow of any doubt."

The night grew solid in its darkness.

Without thinking, he rolled and turned the golden nugget in his right palm again, and it made his words disappear from his thoughts like a vapor.

No more than an hour before dawn, Joshua gave up on his dark vigil. God had not answered with a thunderbolt of awareness. The golden nugget still rested in his hand, growing warmer and warmer with each passing hour.

⚜

The gold remained locked in the drawer for a full week. Yet each time he passed the desk, he would turn and try not to stare at the latch. He rarely succeeded.

I will not hold that rock again, he told himself over and over and over.

Yet his thoughts were becoming consumed.

California is your destiny. Gold free for the taking. California is your destiny.

One night he could stand it no longer. He slapped the key on the top of the desk, pulled on a pair of boots, and ran into the field behind his house–almost as if he was attempting an escape.

The thoughts of gold and his fate followed him. Jamison's words echoed in his mind–words that brimmed with enthusiasm.

California is your destiny. . . .

Joshua stared out at the dark landscape of Shawnee and then over to the silhouetted church that, all at once—at least in this moonlit darkness—looked oddly angled. Joshua fought at the familiar urge in his heart—and this time, the urge caught his breath short.

I could go to California—for just a short while—and come back a rich man. A man could take care of his whole family, build a big house for a new wife, and never lack for anything ever again. A man would be foolish not to consider this.

He shook his head, trying to rid those thoughts.

I am a man of reputation and character and nobility. I am a man serving God. I cannot allow my soul to be as tarnished and broken as this.

As the words filled his thoughts, he knew, with a sudden thud of awareness, that he could do exactly that. He could be a man who leaves everything and pursues a dream, no matter how foolish.

He knew a man's soul was a fickle thing—but he had never realized how thin his faith was.

Try as he might, the image of a man kneeling in gently flowing water, his hands forming a cradle brimming with gold kernels in front of his face, stayed hard and fast in his mind's eye.

Joshua knew what the Bible said of the sin of lust—flee. He ran across the darkened field, then stopped and ran back to the road. He half walked and half ran, first in the direction of Constance's house.

But what will I tell her? And how could she answer me?

He spun on his heel and reversed his direction, walking toward his parents' home.

No, I can't go there either. I know with scriptural certainty what my father would say. I would say the same thing—God's calling supersedes any golden dream man might provide.

He veered off and ran to the stream that flowed behind his house, still rushing and cloudy with the remains of winter snows.

I just need time to compose myself. That's all I need.

He sat by the waters and felt the tang of their chill snap at his face and nose. His heart beat a troubled cadence. Until this moment, he thought he could battle any temptation.

But this is one that is common to no man, he found himself whispering.

Jamison's story of gold lying free for the taking, sitting in quiet pools about a man's ankles—such words enflamed his heart and scattered their embers to his mind.

No, I cannot be swayed; it's only gold. I know that other men will be rich, and I will not; until now it has not bothered my soul.

Joshua would follow his father's footsteps and lead a quiet life, filled with contentment and earthly satisfaction.

It would be enough, he told himself. It would be enough as long as God was in it. He gulped a great lungful of cold air. The moon above him hung in the sky, the color of the nugget hidden in his desk. At that moment, a dam in his soul broke. A thick stream of troubled waters gathered resentment, and denied gratification poured out.

I could think of going. I could at least do that. Consider the journey. I could go—if I promised myself and all others—to journey for just one year—one short year.

Now that these thoughts had started, he allowed them to flow, freely and without restriction. He knew he could no longer hold back the flood.

Perhaps for just one short year—yes, just one year—I could leave now, get there by late summer, gather up enough gold for me and Constance and my parents, and return by this time next spring.

His heart beat faster and faster.

No . . . that is absurd. I'd have to leave the pulpit empty. But Uncle Hiram could fill in. That has been his dream all along, hasn't it?

He turned north.

But what of Constance? Would she wait for me?

He fretted and twisted his hands together.

Well, it's only a year. And does she not deserve a better life than that of being yoked with a poor preacher—never knowing if this is the year that the crops go bad and the children must suffer?

He stomped off toward the parsonage.

But I can't. This is a fool's dream. Yet I'm tired of being poor and tattered and threadbare. Does not a servant of the Lord deserve as much as anyone else? I see what Gage and Hannah and Jamison saw here–a poor preacher in an impoverished town who's going to live out his life with little else but rags on his back. That will not do.

Turning back to the stream, he fell to his knees, the wetness tightening around his legs.

"Lord, I despair. I'm lost," he called out in the stillness. "Like a storm that arrives quickly, I'm being swept away. *Gold.* The very word adds a beat to my heart. But I'm being split asunder. What would you have me do? A year gone, and I could return with resources to do your work in grand fashion. I could build your church. That must be pleasing to you, is it not? I am not forsaking my faith or my calling. I will always hold you in my heart, Lord. It's only one year. Can you find such an insignificant delay troublesome? Please, Lord, give me a sign."

He bowed his head and waited.

A single thought echoed again in his mind.

California is your destiny . . . free for the taking.

Joshua knelt by the water's edge for more than an hour, waiting for that sign, until the damp cold seeped into his knees and shins and the water pooled in a muck about his legs.

"There will be no sign, Lord?" he called out again.

He rose, stiffly, and bent to brush away the leaves and mud that clung to his legs. Walking back to the parsonage, his internal dialogue churned on, unabated.

A year, and I can return a man with wealth to build Shawnee a proper church . . . with a real organ and hymnals and padded pews.

A cloud covered the moon, and darkness swept across the town.

But I'm forsaking the elders' call. It would crush my parents.

He deliberately slowed his steps across the bare field.

Yet they did say that a few hundred dollars extra each year would spell the difference between pain and comfort. If I went, I could truly take care of them in their old age. And I could afford Constance a proper home, like the one she is used to. I could never–on a pastor's wage–afford the type of house her father built. And would she not always compare me with him? Does not love come at some price?

He shook his head, as if trying to throw off these disquieting images from his mind. Then, from nearly a hundred yards away, the moon cut through a narrow gap in the clouds and swept across the field like a broom. The winds swirled about, then stopped, and the shaft of moonlight stopped on the parsonage, as if God were shining the moon on that one specific location.

God is illuminating my house in the darkness. That's the sign I wanted. You have illuminated the riches, Lord. I have seen your heavenly sign.

And as he thought those words, the clouds closed, and darkness fell again on Shawnee.

Joshua barely noticed as he headed to the parsonage.

Where have I stored my haversack?

He began to sprint and leapt over the fence that defined his parsonage.

***

By nightfall, Joshua had sorted through his meager possessions and decided which to take and which to abandon. His haversack bulged with his sturdy clothes, his father's Bible, the marked and tattered *Emigrants Guide to Oregon and California,* and a handful of other personal items.

He sat at the table, smoothed the single page of paper before him, dipped his pen in ink, and began to write.

Constance,

I know my leaving will come as a surprise. While our relationship is young, I believe we both understood its inevitable conclusion–and my desire to see that occur.

I am leaving for California–for only a year's duration. I have been informed that gold has been discovered and that a man might accumulate great wealth in a short time. Of course, being a man of God, it is not wealth I seek. But I admit that, if our relationship progresses, I would want

*to provide you a life at the level at which you are now accustomed. A
preacher would find it hard to do so.*

I trust you'll wait for my return.

As always,

J. Quittner

He blew on the page to set the ink. Rereading the words, he was
not satisfied with their tone or their content. He contemplated a
moment whether to discard his effort and start anew.

"But what else can I write? What words can I use to mollify the
surprise?" he said aloud. "There are none. I've asked her to wait and
yet not demanded it so. She'll have to see my intentions are noble."

He stood, put on his coat, and walked outside into the darkness to
address the crescent moon.

"Do I write them . . . or say good-bye face-to-face?"

Rubbing his hands together, he returned to the table and pulled
out a second white sheet of vellum.

Dear Mother and Father,

*I know your hearts will be saddened and perhaps even angry. I'm leav-
ing at first light. Do not think you've failed. It is not your decision, but
mine. It is not a loss of faith, for I still trust God to lead my steps. He has
made it clear . . .*

And Joshua replayed the scene—of the glistening ray of gold in the
window—again in his mind, attempting to reassure himself it was a
handiwork of God. He was not totally successful.

*. . . that it is a path he has chosen for me. I will make my way to the
Russian River in California. Jamison reported to me in confidence that
gold, in great abundance, has been discovered there. It is nearly free for the
taking.*

*I know such an action seems wildly impetuous, horribly unplanned, and
woefully thoughtless. I suspect that each is partially correct. Yet a wave of
excitement and surety has swept over me. I've thought about nothing else
since Jamison departed. If God smiles on this endeavor, I plan on arriving
in California in late summer and will work until the cold prohibits further
exploration. From the report that Jamison provided, such a time will be*

sufficient to secure enough gold to provide for many years' worth of wages. Then I shall return. If all goes well–and I pray it will–I shall return next year at this time.

A year is not too long to wait.

And, Father, I know that the Lord requires our all. Months have passed now, and I hold back . . . waiting for something. I'm not serving these people with all of myself. I know it. God knows it. I'm offering them a disservice by staying and pretending. It would be better for all concerned if I simply left now and took my halfhearted ways with me. They deserve better.

Do not think ill of me. I'm including a large portion of a generous gift I received from an old friend. I have taken a pittance with me for supplies and the like. Use the remaining two thousand dollars as you see fit to live on while I am gone.

If the most unfortunate happens, invest the capital, and it will provide enough for your remaining years.

God bless you as I leave. I know that understanding will be hard to find, but pray for me. I will pray for you.

All love possible,

Your son, Joshua

He folded the letter and slipped the bills inside, then tied the package with a string. He ran to the darkened general store and slipped the envelopes under the locked front door. Tucked between them was a dollar bill. He knew that such a large amount would guarantee their quick delivery.

Joshua returned home, blew out the candle, and the room fell into an ethereal, moonlit darkness.

California is your destiny.

CHAPTER SEVENTEEN

Shawnee, Ohio
April 1848

THE darkness wrapped a comforting cloak of silence and secrecy about Joshua as he walked away from Shawnee, his church, and his home. Faint moonlight marked his steps.

Rather than wait for the coach and the to-be-expected questions and confrontations, Joshua decided instead to make the first part of his journey on foot.

Athens, a stop on the coach line, lay no more than a dozen miles to the south. If Joshua moved quickly, he could be there well before noon. From there, he would have to hurry to Gallipolis, the river, and a waiting boat. Joshua hoped Gage's invitation of free passage would be honored. If not, Gage would still provide. Joshua had $350 of his friend's donation hidden in a seam of his coat.

He prayed it would be enough for the entire trip and supplies.

With every step south, his thoughts grew more tumultous and confused, and his soul divided itself further and further. Half of him felt a euphoric sense of liberation, as if, for the first time in his life, he was acting on his own accord, making decisions based solely on his own desires. The other half of him grew more guilty. His inner voice admitted that only a coward makes an escape under the cover of darkness. Only a coward leaves a church with nary a farewell and only a vague explanation.

After penning letters to his parents and to Constance, he had written a brief note to the head of the elder board:

Dear Mr. Swathers,

This letter is to inform you that, as of this day, I am taking leave of my position as pastor of the Shawnee Church of the Holy Word. I greatly appreciate the considerations you have extended me. I am on my way to California and will return in a year's time. I do not expect for you to hold the pastorate open and unfilled until then. If God smiles on my enterprise, I will repay, with great interest, the scholarship you provided me to attend Harvard. In seeing as how you have not received your just compensation in regards to this arrangement, I am obligated to make reparations. I also ask that you forgive me for leaving in this manner.

Sincerely,

J. Quittner

Joshua wrestled with his actions. He was a man of God who was abandoning his calling; he was also a realist who knew riches would be forever denied to him as a man of God. And yet here was an opportunity to gain riches to do God's work. He was allowing himself to forget Hannah and fall in love with Constance, yet he was abandoning Constance in Shawnee.

I know all this defies a rational . . . no . . . defies a spiritual *explanation. I have not abandoned God. I have not. I'll witness to all I come in contact with about God's truth. But I'll do so as I journey to California and as I gather gold. I'll return to Ohio to take up that calling again. But for now I simply have to take advantage of this wondrous, glittering opportunity. I would be a fool if I did not.*

Looking to the east, he saw the first etchings of dawn. Coming to a crossroads, a crudely painted sign indicated that Athens lay only three miles distant. He smiled, shifted his haversack from one hand to the other, and redoubled his steps. If there was an early coach to Gallipolis, he wanted to be on it.

A fearful groan rent the air in Joshua's parents' home. His mother
had torn the letter open with a frantic jerk, and the bills had tumbled
out around her feet. She had stared wide-mouthed as they fluttered
about her like wounded birds falling to earth.

In the span of a few heartbeats she had scanned the letter. Then
her arm dropped limp to her side, the letter following the bills to the
ground. She shut her eyes to the tears that began flowing. She did
not speak but instead let an animal-like moan, twisting into a painful
wail, flow from her throat. The room began to spin as her husband's
voice called her as if from a distance.

"What's wrong?" he cried. "What's wrong?"

She lost the power of speech and sank to her knees.

"What's that money? Where did it come from?"

She wailed louder and finally formed words.

"My God, my God! Why have you allowed this to happen? He
must have gone mad! You allowed him to go mad!"

In the McArthur household, the wail was not as persistent or as
intense. Constance was not a woman given to great public demon-
strations of her emotions. As she read the short lines, tears welled
from her eyes and fell onto the paper, leaving tiny ink-stained drop-
lets. She put one hand to her mouth, the other to her heart, stood,
and ran from the room up the steps, flinging herself, now sobbing,
onto her bed. In a moment, her mother followed her up the stairs,
her tears more of anger than pain.

Her father remained in the parlor, his hand clenching the letter.
He had read it quickly, and his fist formed into a tight ball, the paper
giving way with a muffled crunch. He stomped from the room,
down the porch, and to the barn.

He could not have gotten far in just a morning's time, he calculated.

He would follow this unfeeling cad who broke the gentle heart of his daughter. He would teach this so-called pastor a lesson in respect and nobility.

As he saddled his fastest horse, he stopped for a moment, dismounted, walked calmly back into the house and, from a top drawer in his desk, removed a seldom-used revolver. He thumbed at it clumsily to make sure it was loaded.

With a sneer, he stepped back toward his horse, which was pawing at the ground.

No man–even a man of God–toys with the honor of my daughter. No man–not even Reverend Joshua Quittner. She would have no reason to cry like that if he had not abused his power and tampered with my poor, innocent little girl's heart.

⚜

Joshua's father read the same letter that sent his wife into a wailing storm of shock and anger. He crumpled the letter in his hands and threw it at the fire, missing by a few feet.

"Satan is trying to get his soul. He left the church for a promise of thirty pieces of gold. Satan–and his demons from the hell pit called Harvard–have beguiled him and are leading him astray."

He motioned to his wife.

"Come. We must kneel before God, humble ourselves, and pray for our son. We must ask that he recover his senses. He must not be allowed to do this horrible thing. Prayer is the only thing that can save him now."

Tears streaming down her face, Joshua's mother nodded, knelt beside her husband on the rough dirt floor, and bowed her head.

⚜

Joshua sat back and breathed a great sigh of relief. An early coach from Athens did indeed run to the river port of Gallipolis. The next coach was scheduled to depart in less than one hour. He hurried to the ticket agent, scrambled out the dollars for the fare, and nervously watched the minutes tick by.

The coach arrived. Joshua shared the cramped space, which smelled of tobacco and whiskey, with bags of mail and a short, rumpled man with a wobbly, black felt top hat.

The coach lurched over the deep ruts in the main street. In a few minutes, when the road smoothed somewhat, the other passenger grunted a greeting.

"Headed west?" he asked, wiping at his mouth with his sleeve.

Joshua hesitated.

"Ain't pryin', young man. I ain't. You go south or west or north or whatever, and it makes no never mind to me. Just conversin' is all I'm doin'."

Joshua hesitated again.

"You ain't deaf, are ya?"

Joshua could not help but smile. "No, I'm not deaf. And I guess I'm heading west . . . by way of New Orleans."

The little man nodded. "That's a fair enough answer. I'm headin' east—to Pittsburgh from here. The river's a lot smoother than goin' by coach, that be certain."

Joshua nodded, not knowing what more to say. He laid a hand on his haversack and leaned forward to look out the dusty window. The sun was just clearing the tree line along the road.

I imagine everyone has read my letters by now.

He tried to imagine what might be transpiring as the words became real, but his thoughts were lost in a disconcerting web of images.

Perhaps they will be hurt at first, but in time I'm sure they'll understand.

❦

Mr. McArthur figured Joshua had neither waited for nor taken a coach from Shawnee. The nearest coach stop was north of town, near New Lenox. But if Joshua had planned on heading for California, he would have sought the fastest route to the river. And the fastest route ran through Athens.

Mr. McArthur spurred his horse to the south.

But by the time he arrived in Athens, he had missed the early coach to Gallipolis by nearly an hour.

Do I return home? he wondered, his anger nowhere near abated. *Can I look upon my daughter's face knowing I did not do all I could to protect her honor from this cad?*

He grimaced, felt for the hard metal of the pistol at his waist, then spurred the horse down the southern road to Gallipolis.

Ohio River

As he traveled, Joshua told himself, over and over, that heaven was favoring him and his decision.

He arrived in the strange and tangled town of Gallipolis and had no idea of which boat might be Captain Hopler's. He knew there was no guarantee Hopler's boat was actually in port. From the coach stop, he quickly made his way down the hill to the wharves, where a bevy of riverboats lay tied to docks along the shore of the river.

"I'm looking for Captain Hopler of the Ohio Exploration and Freight Company," he called out to a man in a dark blue uniform standing on a second-story deck.

The man pointed downriver and called back, "Three boats down. She's getting ready to sail, so you'd best hurry."

Joshua sprinted off.

Three piers down, a team of stevedores was grappling with a heavy, moveable passageway that led from the dock to the ship.

"Is this Captain's Hopler's vessel?" Joshua gasped out.

"It is," one of the men answered. "And if you're gettin' on, get on now. We're fixin' to cast off as soon as we get this blasted gangway unstrapped."

Joshua did not have a ticket, nor did he know if the vessel was heading up or downriver. But he knew he must get on board and keep going. As long as he was moving, he felt right about his decision. But he feared that if he were to stop, spend a night or a day pondering what he had done, a black panic would overtake him and cause him to return home, contrite and broken.

My life is now, he thought as he jumped on the gangway and hustled to the deck of the ship, *and the time is now. I must do this.*

The stevedores shouldered hard against the wooden contraption, and it squealed free. Pulling on a series of ropes, they lifted it and tilted it back toward the ship.

"Call out to the captain," the stevedore bellowed. "You're free to set off."

And with that, Joshua felt the ship lurch once. Then a huge paddlewheel at the back end of the boat groaned and began to turn in the muddy water. Crewmen at the front and back, long poles in hand, began to shove off from the deck. Thick ropes, the size of a man's arm, were tossed back to the dock and, like a great sea beast loosed from its restraints, the vessel shuddered and began to move away from land and into the middle of the Ohio River.

***

By the time the riverboat was an hour south of Gallipolis, a rider on a nearly exhausted horse arrived at the crest of the hill overlooking the docks. He saw a stream of vessels steaming along the middle of the river.

He shook his head. Mr. McArthur knew he would never find Joshua among all these ships. No doubt he had jumped aboard the first ship heading south.

He had failed to find Joshua and offer a measure of retribution to what the bounder had done to his little girl.

At least I tried. And that will be some comfort to my poor Constance. And that fool-headed Joshua will have to live with the guilt over what he's done to my family—and all of Shawnee as well.

He turned his horse, then looked back at the river one more time.

I hope you get all that's coming to you, Joshua Quittner. In fact, I hope God gives it to you in double measure—that's what I hope.

Shawnee, Ohio

At noon Joshua's father met with a confused and angry group of church elders. News of Joshua's departure had swept through Shawnee like a grass fire sweeps across the fields pushed by a summer's tempest.

"The boy's gone off," declared Mr. Swathers, the head of the elder board. "And I say that if he could pack it in without so much as a word of how-do-you-do, then he has no business bein' a preacher."

Others around him nodded. No one was smiling.

Mae Quittner had taken to her bed shortly after reading Joshua's letter and only minutes after her husband launched into a long, impassioned prayer for the boy's eternal soul.

Eli Quittner, sitting by the fire, legs covered with a tattered blanket, was left alone to either defend his son or condemn him. He appeared most ill at ease.

"I can't say what might have possessed him. But it all started when those friends of his from that fancy Harvard school started visiting. He was right before they came, and this happened after they left. It was the last one who turned him. It was the last one who looked the oddest."

There were murmurs of acknowledgment.

"He was a good boy. You all saw him grow up. He was doing God's work. It was those Easterners who turned him so. I blame them. *They* caused him to hang up his fiddle. It wasn't Joshua at all."

After a moment, the elders concurred.

"And now it's up to us to be praying him back home. He'll come to his senses soon enough. I know that God is not in the business of forgetting his own. He'll be back. He'll be back—that, I'm certain of."

The elders nodded. Breaking the long silence, Mr. Swathers declared, "Well, we'll pray for the boy. That's the least we can do, seein' how it was those outsiders that caused him to stumble this way. We're all hopin' he comes to his senses before it's too late and the devil takes him from us forever."

Joshua's mother, still supine in the bedroom, capped the impromptu meeting with a wail.

Ohio River

Captain Hopler, a thin, pale man, greeted Joshua with a cold and tight expression. As he talked, his eyes darted nervously from shore to shore, scanning the cloudy water for dangers lurking just below its surface.

"Mr. Davis said that if you came, we was to allow you passage as far as you asked. He said you would be taking one of two trips. One would be a round trip to Parkersburg and back. And the other would be the whole way to New Orleans."

"He really said that?" Joshua asked, surprised.

Captain Hopler nodded. "And he told me he'd take a wager that if you did show up, it would be the New Orleans trip you'd be asking for."

"He said that?"

Hopler nodded again.

"Didn't take the wager. Figured that a man like Mr. Davis would know all the angles. Glad I didn't now. And to tell you the truth, you're about as lucky a man as Mr. Davis. You happened to find me on the very day we set sail for New Orleans. You miss this boat, and you have a week's wait on your hands."

He leaned against a worn brass rail in the wheelhouse and slid across the narrow span of the room.

Joshua could now see how the brass had been worn. The walls, floor, and instruments all glowed with a velvet patina caused by clouds of pungent pipe and cigar smoke.

"You can never let up watching this blasted river. She'll hide logs and rocks and sandbars on you. I don't want to be the captain on watch when the river tries to sink me. You lose a riverboat, and the owners don't take it kindly."

Captain Hopler barked to the man holding the great spoked wheel, "Set her a few feet left of channel. I have a feeling that the storm moved the sandbar farther midriver."

Again he leaned against the brass bar. A fellow at the front of the boat tossed a weighted rope into the murky water and waited till it touched bottom. Then he turned, called out the depth in a booming voice, and tossed the rope again.

"The water changes colors when it gets deep or shallow. See there," Captain Hopler said, pointing. "The muddy goes to dark. That's the sand and mud reaching up to grab us."

Joshua could discern no difference in any part of the river save for the very shoreline.

"So Mr. Davis said you would have free passage. The cabin boy will show you. You're lucky there ain't many paying customers this early in the season. Otherwise I'd have you bunking with the crew."

Joshua thanked him profusely, then followed the young boy, who led him from the wheelhouse to the passenger cabins.

FROM THE JOURNAL OF JOSHUA QUITTNER
APRIL 1848

I had almost decided not to bring this journal for the sake of weight, but I shall endeavor to write small and briefly, since I've promised–of a sort–to take notes on this journey for Jamison.

Captain Hopler tells me the Ohio River flows hundreds of miles from Pittsburgh, Pennsylvania, to Cairo, Illinois, where it meets the mighty Mississippi. He says the red men call it the "Father of Waters." This huge river winds its way to New Orleans and the Gulf of Mexico beyond.

The journey was most pleasant–at least after I banished thoughts of home, family, Shawnee, the church, and Constance from my mind. The first two nights along the river, I endured lurid and horrid nightmares of demons and all sorts of evil depravity. I woke in a sweat and pushed all remembrances of home comforts and the familiar from my mind. It's as if I'm being reborn as a new man–a stranger with no ties to the past, only the future to look toward.

I have read and reread Jamison's book in preparation. The words describe the journey overland. I'm embarking on a different journey–down south and across the narrowing of land between the great continents. These countries are backward, I'm told. Some of the sailors on this vessel have visited the ports and bestowed on me many facts that I shall need. The land has been called by some as the Central Americas, and I shall attempt to cross to the Pacific in a country known as Panama, which is part of Colombia, only a few degrees north of the equator.

The trip thus far has been uneventful. At Louisville, Kentucky, a canal recently built around the falls there now makes it possible for larger boats such as the one I am on to navigate the entire river. We stopped at numerous cities along the way as we plied our way through the waters, setting off cargo, adding on new cargo. In Mississippi we passed vast cotton plantations, and I saw working negro slaves for the first time. From the deck I could make out their bent black backs as they picked cotton up and down the rows of plants. Bales of cotton clog the walkways and cargo bays of the vessel. The bundles, wrapped in canvas or burlap hulk on the decks and stacked two and three deep, are as big as a room and as wide as a team of oxen. It's hard to fathom the wealth of the plantation owners and easy to imagine why there is increasing strife over the question of owning another human being.

I am told the chilly weather is a drawback for passengers. Yet every mile we travel, the air becomes more humid and heated, despite the earliness of the year.

New Orleans
April 1848

It is nearing the end of the month, and springtime here is much hotter and more humid than I ever experienced in Ohio. We arrived in New Orleans at sundown. The city announced itself with a rank, prickling odor miles and miles before any lights came to view.

New Orleans is a curious place—a combination of vile areas mixed with elegant neighborhoods. Wealthy merchants live in fancy Greek Revival homes with formal gardens next to areas of squalor and filth with ramshackle huts. If the devil himself were painting a landscape, he could do no better than to capture the docks in their fullest, where boatsmen carouse and brawl. Many kinds of people live here together, including West Indians, natives of the Caribbean islands, and free men of color, who often own their own slaves.

This will be my debarkation point. The vessel unloads, takes on cargo, and heads back upriver for a much slower journey against the current.

I asked Captain Hopler for the name and locale of a modest hostel for a night or two–at least until I can secure passage to Panama. He laughed and replied, "There ain't any in New Orleans, but I'll show you the best of a bad lot. Be prepared to wait a spell. Ships heading south may not be that plentiful."

The locals here slur their words. I've heard Southerners speak and have been charmed at their accent, but these citizens chew and digest the words before speaking. It's a mixture, I'm supposing, of French, Indian, and Negro tongues that comes out all but unintelligible to this Ohio boy.

I found the establishment to which Captain Hopler had referred me. He was correct. This place is only a step above a bawdy house– perhaps half a step if I choose to listen closely to the rooms beyond my own.

The fetid odor floats above the city like a cloud. If a breeze is present, the city takes on a more exotic air.

Looking for breakfast, I walked a fair distance and stepped onto a narrow street in the "Garden District," lined with balconies made of delicate wrought-iron work. I ate, for mere pennies, a delicious French concoction of flaky dough and jam with coffee strong enough to stand a stick in. I found the food to be urbane and civilized and a few of the citizens to be witty, from what I could understand.

MAY 1848

Using the good captain's name, I booked passage on a smallish sailing vessel that was leaving New Orleans within the week.

On that ship, we traveled through the "bayou" south of the city. A more tangled swamp and mysterious place I could scarce imagine exists in this world. Large trees, dripping with what the crew calls "Spanish moss," clutched at the masts and sails as we poled and drifted along the current to the gulf and sea beyond. Whole towns of people live among these marshes, swamps, and bayous–descendants of French explorers, I was told. I studied French some at Harvard, but these folks spoke a dialect such as I've never heard.

We have not seen any, yet there are tales of huge reptiles, big enough to swallow men whole, living in these swamps. As we turned a corner in the backwaters, we saw the skins of twelve scaled beasts next to a shack built on stilts above the marshy land. I imagine that, alive, each was nearly fifteen feet long. Their bleached skulls were displayed as well. Staring past the rows of sharp teeth and bones, I could imagine the terror one would feel coming upon these reptiles in the inky waters.

I shuddered, imagining worse and more vile threats as I travel south to the land called Panama.

PACIFIC OCEAN, PANAMA
JUNE 1848

I am now facing the Pacific on the western side of this narrow finger of land. I did not once retrieve this journal during my entire journey across and through the jungles. Walking was like swimming, so dense was the air with water. And the air was hot to match, so that a single step would cause a man to break out in a sweat. I kept these pages tightly wrapped in oilskin to prevent the mold and mildew that covers everything here from damaging the pages. I did not see strange animals like Jamison imagined, yet I heard, often in the blackest time of night, their screams and wails and shrieks from the void beyond our meager campfires.

I would not have managed or even considered tackling this trip alone. I spent less than a fortnight on that small trading vessel en route from New Orleans to Panama–and that was time enough. Panama is populated by Spanish peoples and native Indians, and I found, again by naming Captain Hopler frequently, a small business concern–run by former Americans–that offers guides and supplies across their narrows from the Atlantic to the Pacific.

Without their assistance, at a relatively modest price, I would have perished, I'm certain. And even with their aid, it took nearly a full month to cross the land that looked so narrow on the map. Many frustrating days were wasted as we camped, sweating and hot, waiting for the proper time to pass through certain territories populated by natives and bandits or both. Our guides seemed to have the situation well in hand, and we suffered no hostilities as did others whose stories were related . . . endlessly–around the nightly cook fires.

The land here–jungled and filled with clawing, clutching green tendrils that flow from the trees in a vast waterfall of leaves and shoots–is to me (a boy from the hills of Ohio) dense, cloying, and dangerous. Our guides provided us with caustic ointment (vile-smelling stuff) to spread on our hands and faces, thus avoiding the swarms of deadly insects and biting creatures often too tiny to be seen.

Despite the fact that our guides made this trip innumerable times prior, they tensed at every snap of twig and odd birdcall. Perhaps it is their knowledge of what indeed could occur in the darkness that makes them so aware and nervous.

And now as I sit by the bay, waiting for the ship that will arrive within a fortnight and provide passage to California and the bay of San Francisco, I again find myself lost in a wash of despair. I've left all I've loved and worked for–for what? The promise of easy gold? I'm sure I've crushed the heart of my parents and poor Constance. With the passage of time, such awareness breaks into my heart, and I'm certain all in Shawnee must consider me mad for this adventure.

Perhaps I am a bit mad. All I know is that I've forsaken everything for a flimsy promise of riches. I pray God will forgive my weakness and offer me his protection.

I do not fully understand why I have acted in the manner I have. Perhaps I never will. Man has free will–this I know–and is capable of making the most outlandish choices. But I feel at peace–in some strange way. I know that I have never felt such a strong attraction to do anything else. I am drawn and driven. I am now on this journey come what may.

JULY 1848

The ship bound for San Francisco has arrived a week early. The vessel is cramped, dirty, and barely seaworthy, but I have no alternative. I'm told that if I do not book passage now, it could be months before another ship calls at this out-of-the-way port. The price of my ticket secures a tattered hammock near the bow of the ship. I pray the passage will be quick, and I will not have to bear the sound of the water crashing into the wood only inches from my head for more nights than necessary.

I pray for swiftness, yet I am told the journey will take at least two weeks, perhaps three, depending on the winds.

CHAPTER EIGHTEEN

OUR ship struggled with poor winds, then too much wind, as we edged our way up the coast. The shoreline was seldom out of sight, which provided me a great comfort since I lacked any trust in the seaworthiness of the craft and the ability and dedication of the sailors themselves. Most of their time they spent drinking, gambling, and roaring their displeasure at each other. The few paying passengers huddled at the bow of the ship. Despite the fact that we took more dips there and were often drenched from sea spray, we felt safer there because of the distance from the crew.

Finally the territory called California came into view.

I have made it to California in record time, according to what Jamison related to me. I did seem to have God favoring all the particulars of this journey, though I will not test God as to thinking that the speed also conveys his blessing. Jamison said that an overland journey can take up to six months depending on weather, routes, guides, Indians, and Providence. Crossing via the Atlantic south around and through the Straits of Magellan by ship is most dangerous–and at least a four-month journey. Yet I am in view of my destiny–after less than four months traveling. Jamison made the journey to Ohio in a shade over two months . . . but by his own admission, that schedule was fueled by money and luck–and could not be repeated, he said, in another thousand attempts.

The land and coastline that surrounds San Francisco is beautiful. The bay is surrounded by wondrous rolling hills and promontories, each greened with a mixture of deciduous trees and firs. We arrived at noon on a clear, sunny day, and the sea and shore were intoxicating in their loveliness. The crew laughed and said such weather is infrequent, and fog is as much a part of this locale as is air.

Then the beauty of the coast gave way to a rat's warren of docks and piers that jutted out into the water. All manner of human refuse floated past us, as if the entire city emptied itself into the bay. A rotting stench hung over the calm waters. I've never prayed harder for a breeze than I did in that city.

In the bay, twenty-plus ships bobbed at their piers, sails furled, anchors dropped. Ghost ships, the crew called them, and the more superstitious among the sailors dropped to their knees and crossed themselves or carried out other odd rituals as we slid past.

"The ships are empty, and the crews gone. We hear some left for the rivers inland. They got the gold fever and jumped ship."

Yet it was plain that other crewmen subscribed to a different scenario–one where the crews had been spirited away by maritime demons and sea creatures.

None of the passengers spoke much during the trip. There were nods of greeting and a few words at mealtime, but not much more. Each had a secret to keep–myself included. Each of my fellow passengers had a certain set gleam in their eyes. I've come to believe that all have heard of the gold waiting for the picking and are set to find their due in the cold waters of the rivers of California.

From the deck of our ship, San Francisco appeared tattered and ready to collapse upon itself. The hills just south of the bay, denuded of vegetation, and the steepness of the grade allows a man to see the entire city in one glance.

There is not much that recommends the place.

I will endeavor to find a decent accommodation this evening—one that does not put my life in peril as I close my eyes. And on the morrow, I shall seek out the needed supplies for my future.

It has occurred to me that I thought I wanted to be east of Shawnee, and now I am as far west as a man can go. I imagine the surprise on the faces of my friends from Harvard. What would they say of my faith and my steadiness now? Until this event, I have been most predictable.

Now I'm not.

I am a surprise.

I'm not certain if that feels good or not.

San Francisco

"Joshua Quittner!"

To his astonishment, Joshua thought he heard his name being called and spun about the crowded market, trying to locate its source.

I must have imagined it.

The vast store, lit by braces of candles, was piled high with heaps of digging tools, sluices, tents, metal pots and pans, rope, dynamite, picks, canvas bags, and a thousand other implements. Joshua simply stared, feeling lost, and despaired of ever knowing how to begin outfitting himself for his endeavor.

"Over here!" came the voice again. "Joshua Quittner! You heard your name. That's right. Turn around. Look over by the shovels and picks!"

Joshua found the source and stared at the man who waved an arm enthusiastically over his head. The man's hair curled to his shoulders; his beard was a fierce tangle of red.

"You don't remember me, do you?"

Joshua found the eyes familiar but could not come up with a name.

"Harvard?" he guessed, knowing no one in Shawnee would be in San Francisco. Outside of Harvard and Shawnee, Joshua knew no one.

"Giles Barthlemon," the stranger said, extending his hand. "I was tossed out of Harvard for borrowing answers on a Greek test. Remember?"

Joshua broke into a smile. "Of course. I recall helping you study."

Giles laughed. "And a darn poor job you did, my friend."

Unsure if Giles were truly angry or simply making a joke, Joshua offered another smile in return. Joshua recalled Giles–and how so many of his friends were relieved when Giles was expelled.

"He's a beast and a vulgar boor," said one, "and Harvard is better off without him. He'll as soon pull you into his personal cesspool as smile at you."

When Giles smiled, his teeth–save one missing–gleamed through his beard.

"Don't worry, Joshua. I wasn't set out to be a preacher anyhow. Best thing that could have happened to me. Now, of course, if you ask my father about it, he will provide a different interpretation–one filled with expletives."

As Giles slapped him on the shoulder, Joshua was unsure of what to do. Was Giles still a horrible fellow? Had he changed? Or had Joshua changed?

"So, farm boy, what brings you to this godforsaken place? Looking for lost souls?"

Crowding around them, a few men offered their laughter at Giles's comments.

"If you have, you've come to the right place. This is prime territory for the lost and evil. Dastardly fellows, all."

Joshua sputtered, trying to think of a reply. "Well, no . . . I'm here to get some supplies. You see, I think I may look for some land . . . to farm. That's it, that's why I'm here–to farm."

Giles leaned in close. "Joshua, old chum, this is a Harvard man you're talking to. No need to lie to me. I can spot a falsehood a mile away."

Chagrined, Joshua said, "No, that's the truth. I wanted to find some farmland. I hear the weather here allows for year-round growing."

A fist formed in Joshua's throat. He knew lying was a sin, yet he was unwilling to share with this relative stranger the knowledge of the gold discovery.

I have not found a single nugget, yet I grow greedy defending what I might find, he chided himself. *I'm not sure how pleasing this attitude is to God.*

Giles smelled of fortnights without a bath. Besides that gamy odor, there was a swirl of whiskey about him, mixed with a tracing of tobacco.

He beckoned Joshua to follow him. Nervous, Joshua looked about at the other men in the store, trying to ascertain if any man had overheard or would offer a conjecture. No one had paid much attention to their words.

Giles stood at the door and called out, impatiently, "There will be supplies here in an hour, but I might not be. Come have a drink—for old Harvard's sake. What do you say? You can tell me of your farming plans—and I can tell you my life story. Sound like a fair trade?"

The tavern was darker than the store, if that were possible, with only two windows in the front and a pair of anemic lanterns flickering above the bar. The entire building leaned into the hills. So steep was the ascent to the front door that Joshua found himself nearly disoriented as he entered. The structure appeared to have been built in haste. Slats of wood, with wide, toothy gaps, made up the front wall. The floors buckled and swayed. The tables were sawhorses with planks drawn between them. The only furnishing of substance was the bar itself, of mahogany and mirrors, looking very out of place.

Joshua tried not to notice the sidelong glances that met them when they walked in—looks he could only describe as pure disdain as Giles passed the unsavory clientele of the place. Giles stood up to the bar and called out his order. Joshua stood back, wrestling with his proper behavior. Giles saw his discomfort, smiled, shook his head slowly, and took his beer and whiskey and sat at one of the tables.

"Order yourself a sarsaparilla, Joshua. I can be accused of doing many things in this town, but leading an innocent lamb astray is not one of them. Although you'll find few lambs in California, that's for certain."

Sipping at the sweet drink, Joshua tried his best not to stare.

"You're wondering why I'm here," Giles said, his words slurred. "Although I could be asking the same of you, farm boy. Weren't you going back to Ohio to be a preacher?"

Joshua winced. "I was. I mean, I did. I went back."

Giles didn't reply.

"And then I came here," Joshua finally added.

"I'm not prying, Joshua. But like I said, getting the boot from Harvard was the best thing that happened to me." He bent forward, conspiratorially. "You know there's no money in the preaching game. You found that out, didn't you?"

Joshua found himself nodding despite the fact that Giles's show of bravado sounded hollow.

"After I got the boot, I drifted around for a while. My father said he never wanted to see me again. So I packed up and left." He took a long swallow, then continued.

"That's why I'm here. I came west to find my fortune. It's here, I tell you. Opportunity. Treasure. The future." Giles tipped back, lacing his hands behind his head. "And you're out here to become a farmer? That's a good story, Joshua farm boy. A good story—except you're lying to your old class chum."

Joshua reddened. "No, I'm not . . . not really."

Giles's chair thumped hard on the floor. "I know why you're here, friend. It's why we're all here."

"You do? You know?"

Giles whispered, "It's the gold. That sort of news spreads like wildfire. I think everyone around here has heard by now. That's why this town is both a ghost town and a growing town. People stop for a minute, buy a pick and shovel, and head for the hills. You saw the deserted ships in the harbor, didn't you?"

Joshua nodded.

"Ghost ships, they call them. Golden ghost ships."

Joshua sipped at his drink, then replied, "If you've heard about the gold, why are you still here? Why aren't you heading for the hills?"

Giles finished his beer, then lifted the whiskey glass to his lips, careful not to spill a drop. As it splashed suddenly down his throat, he clamped the shot glass to the table and winced as if in pain.

"Ahh . . . there's the rub. I would be in the hills, as you say, except for one small problem."

"And what's that?"

"After I pay for this drink, I'll be dead broke, that's the problem."

⁂

Joshua insisted Giles share his room and bathing privileges, but it was uncertain whether or not Giles would be allowed to stay at the rooming house, such was the objection of the clerk when they approached the desk. It seemed that Giles had been tossed out of the place and was told not to return, but after Joshua slipped additional bills into the clerk's hand, they were led upstairs. Over a modest dinner that Joshua paid for, Giles expanded on his journey west and his current perilous financial straits. His words took on a confessional tone.

"Took most of what I had to get here. Cleaned out the funds that were meant for Harvard. The trip was horrible. Kansas and Colorado and then up north. It took months and months, and I wound up in Oregon almost busted. Nearly half the people I traveled with are dead, scattered like fallen leaves between here and Kansas City."

Giles shuddered.

"A trail of fresh dirt and rocks is what we left as markers. Every week, someone would sicken and then die on us. No doctors, and nobody knew much of what might help. I tell you, a man with faith is going to lose it if he travels out here. I saw such awful things."

Giles sipped at his coffee, a murky brew with a tongue-thickening taste.

"And the blasted Indians–they're no better than the devil himself. They have no souls, I swear. Two of our party were ambushed as they rode ahead. We found them, lying on the trail, their heads skinned down to the bone and their hearts cut out. I never want to see anything like that again. If I get a chance, I will as soon shoot a red man as take a breath."

Joshua's pulse quickened at such tales.

"The trail led to Oregon. I spent the last of my money sailing here–the new El Dorado, folks are calling it." He took the last bite of a wide slice of elderberry pie. "And now, here I am, knowing that gold is just over there," he said, pointing to the east, "and the mountains laced with cold rivers sprinkled with golden nuggets, and I'm not able to get at it."

FROM THE JOURNAL OF JOSHUA QUITTNER
JULY 1848

I'd have preferred to burn Giles's possessions, such was the rank smell they harbored, but then I'd be obligated to replace them.

So I opened the window to our room instead. After the raucous laughter and shouts died off from the tavern down the street, a quiet swept over the town. I heard the piercing cries of gulls in the dark and the gentle hush of the waves. It was, for a moment, peaceful.

Yet, I slept little. I tossed and turned, playing over in my mind Giles's terrible predicament and the absolute mess he's made of his life. If he is an outcast among the type of people that seem to inhabit this place, he must have done some despicable things. To attend the seminary at Harvard, he must have shown *some* promise for the ministry–otherwise he would not have been accepted. How then could he have fallen so far and so fast? As I write these words, I realize I, too, have fallen far. I was serving the Lord; now I'm in a bakery overlooking the bay of San Francisco.

How did it happen? Why did I decide on this course? I'm still puzzled. And much to my chagrin, I have not, as I had avowed, shared the truth of God with any man since leaving Ohio. Perhaps I found explaining my life too difficult, too painful. So rather than risk embarrassment, I offer no story at all.

I believe I've found a solution. Traveling into the hills will be a perilous business. One man alone runs great risks and faces more work, I'm certain. Two men seeking gold will divide the labor in half. When I return to the room, I will detail this plan to Giles. I realize that taking him in as a partner is a risky business, given his past, and it means doubling some expenses, but it also means having a traveling companion. I think that will prove most useful once we arrive at the American River and Sutter's Mill. And it also appears that Giles Barthlemon needs a witness to help him find the way. Perhaps I need such a man as well.

I awoke well before dawn and slipped out to find breakfast. Just down the street, toward the bay, a bakery was open. I purchased bread there, as well as coffee flavored with chicory and laced with cream. After so many weeks of eating food of dubious origin, it was such a pleasure to eat a breakfast, fresh from the oven, with the warm yeasty flavor filling my stomach.

I picked up a newspaper as I ate and scanned, as is my habit, the bylines for a familiar name. And there it was: Special Correspondent, J. Pike. I have copied the opening lines of his article:

"The very whisper of the word is sufficient to soften the hardest heart. In remote river valleys in the California territory flows not only water but gold. Yes, gold. It glitters and dances in the shallow water, requiring only that a man stoop to retrieve handfuls of the precious metal."

I smiled as I read it, hearing Jamison's breathless voice as he repeated the same words to me less than a half year prior.

San Francisco
July 1848

Joshua thought Giles was close to tears when he explained his proposed arrangement. Joshua would bankroll the two of them, and what gold was unearthed would be split 60-40, with Joshua claiming the larger share.

"It's only right that way," Giles readily admitted. "Without you, I would have no chance at riches at all."

With Joshua's money, he and Giles were outfitted with the necessities: picks, shovels, gold pans, a large canvas tent, blankets, extra canvas and rope, a coffeepot, three pans, and enough incidentals to fill two immense packs.

A mule would be too expensive, so the pair would walk to their destination. Joshua made certain he held enough money back for unanticipated needs and the price of a return ticket to the East Coast.

Joshua was sure, like the others who preceded him, that such an insurance would not be needed.

They sought out the services of a guide to the gold fields. Maps were scarce, and those that existed often proved to be wildly inaccurate. Even the *Emigrants Guide* had opined that a well-seasoned guide was of high value.

Of course, there were no guarantees that the guides could deliver on their promises. Stories had been told of miners being robbed of all their possessions within minutes of leaving sight of town.

That possibility was another reason, Joshua figured, that a two-man team made more sense than a solitary miner going it alone. The guide Joshua employed proved to be reputable, although rather unsavory.

At night, on their way to the river, they stopped in one of a series of temporary canvas cities that were springing up to offer accommodations and services to the miners. The towns appeared like sailing ships on the horizon, fluttering in the breeze, as if a gale would blow them out of view. They took on most colorful names, such as Hard Luck, Whiskey Town, and Hang 'Em.

Their guide, Robert Stough, a gangly man with large hands and thick lips, made certain each night was spent in or near a tavern and a brothel.

Joshua knew he should refuse to travel any farther with the man, but his money had already been paid and would not be easily returned. So Giles and Joshua camped out at the edge of town. Stough would return, near morning, smelling of alcohol and gaudy perfume. To make the trip more unpleasant, he would spend much of the following day detailing his exploits from the night before. Even Giles, who was jaded by his time in the world, became upset

with the daily report. Yet they held their tongues, and within a fortnight, Stough had brought them to the banks of the Russian River.

He stopped only a moment before turning back to San Francisco.
Joshua asked him one question as he filled his canteen with river
water.

"You lead people to the gold fields, yet you don't bother to prospect? Why?"

Stough laughed and spit. "Mark my words, there'll be only a few
rich men leavin' these rivers alive. The water's cold, the work's hard,
and you'll wind up spendin' all your money on expensive women
and bad liquor. It ain't been more than a few months that I been
doin' this, and I already seen it happen more times than I can count.
And I can count pretty high. No, the rich men will get rich by takin'
gold from the miners. And that's what I'm doin'—just takin' the easier
way to get rich."

FROM THE JOURNAL OF JOSHUA QUITTNER
AUGUST 1848

I've never been as cold and tired and miserable as I've been these past
weeks. Upon being left at the frigid river's edge by Mr. Stough, Giles
and I, not fully knowing which area might be most productive,
shrugged and headed upstream. We had the map marked by Jamison,
but we are not sure which river he indicated or the specific area.

We hiked along rocky terrain for several days, eating nothing but
flour biscuits and beans. We did not think to bring fishing equipment
with us, and we can see huge trout darting in the water.

It is late summer, and the rivers are at their lowest ebb, we're told.
That much is good news, for it allows us passage along the river's
edge. But for summer, the water's iciness is surprising. I would hate
to feel the chill of a winter's water. Oftentimes brush, boulders, and
sheer rock faces force us into the water. Wading along in water up to
our chests, with our packs held above our heads, stepping on treacherous and slippery rocks, is perilous. We've both been dunked several times, though we were able to emerge before our supplies were

waterlogged. I have wrapped and rewrapped this journal and my father's Bible to prevent their loss.

The river has remained empty of all but us, causing us to wonder if Mr. Stough brought us to the right location.

Finally, somewhere during the second week of walking–and our progress, despite walking during all the sunlit hours, has been slow–we stumbled on a small encampment of prospectors. They treated us neither kindly nor unkindly. They quickly stated that their claim ran down the river a few hundred yards. They had set up an elaborate sluicing machine, into which gravel and river sediment is fed, along with a supply of water, and a series of flumes and shunts separates the heavier gold from the worthless rock.

We did not ask of their success. And even if we had, I daresay they would not have revealed it to us.

They have been at this spot all summer, they said, looking haggard and worn. Three of their party had come down with a strange malady and quickly passed on.

We are concerned, for they said that summer has but six more weeks to run, then the chills of fall will set in. Most prospectors, they claim, will pack up camp and spend the winter in the warmer lowlands.

We know our funds will not allow us that luxury. Giles has a look of grim determination on his face. "We will travel farther upstream than all, and we will work from first light till dark. We will make good use of these last weeks."

I have concurred.

SEPTEMBER 1848

We have passed three more "towns" along the river. Some are made up of muddy streets, canvas tents, and wooden shanties. Yet for all their hasty nature, it's surprising the number of services that can be found. There is a barber in one as well as the expected tavern and restaurant. One boasted of a tailor; another had a large brothel and bawdy house.

We have encountered our first red men. Yesterday, as we passed through, three Indians sat in a stupor by the front of a tavern. They were not allowed inside with white men, so they purchased a bottle of whiskey and drank it with such speed that all were in a slovenly heap by the front door. Other patrons merely stepped over them as they entered. Such is man's depravity that wickedness follows him to the wilderness. I held Giles back from doing physical harm to them, so great was his reservoir of anger.

There is sin in abounding measure here. As we walk past tents, we hear cursing and loud, coarse laughter and talk. The difference between here and Shawnee is enormous. I continue to read the Bible and pray, not neglecting totally my spiritual needs. Giles and I have not yet spoken much of faith. I know we will.

RUSSIAN RIVER
OCTOBER 1848

We have set up camp and staked out a two-man claim on a lonely stretch of the river. The shores angle up steeply here, and we have barely enough room between the water and the rock to place our tent and meager supplies. If heavy rains come, I'm sure we'll need to scramble to higher ground.

The work is hard, and our backs and limbs hurt continually. We are no better here than pack mules, and we work incessantly. Armed with only large sluicing pans and no elaborate machinery, we are forced to bend at the waist, load up the pan with gravel, and swirl the water about. The gold nuggets remain at the bottom of the swirl. In the first five days of digging and swirling, we've found enough gold pebbles to fill one-third of a coffee cup. We are not sure of its value, but the metal is free. Each morning, even before the sun rises, we make flour biscuits and coffee and set ourselves to the back-paining labor.

This is, after all, what the American dream is about—men of humble origins staking a claim to riches and, by the sweat of their own labors, pulling their lives into a more privileged class. And while money is not an end unto itself, I know God's people would share in its blessings if I were to come upon a large abundance.

We felt our first frost last night, and this morning flakes of white drifted from a gray sky. The water is interminably cold, and after only minutes, great shivering makes us scurry to the fire for warmth. The cycle is repeated a hundred times a day.

We pray we will last the winter, which is certain to follow within a matter of weeks.

CHAPTER NINETEEN

GILES and I believe no man could ever be as cold as we were in autumn 1848–bending a thousand times in the chilled river, searching for a grain of gold mired in the gravel and muck. Soon the leaves turned brown and brittle, and the winds whistled in from the west, carrying a scent of the sea. The air became so damp and biting that we despaired of ever feeling warm again.

In November a hard freeze came. We knew we were much too late in the fields. Not a day in October had gone by that other miners had not passed our stake, mostly from upriver or the nearby Spokane River, all claiming no man could work the fields during the winter. We would agree, then find ourselves asking for one more day's worth of prospecting. And those "one more" days added up until we neared the end of November and were still at the work, cold and hungry and miserable. But we were finding gold, and neither of us chose to abandon the effort.

During the last few weeks of November, Giles and I spent hours collecting wood and stacking it in long ribbons along the frozen shore. Set afire, the coals would thaw the ground and allow us to keep digging.

I shivered so badly I thought my teeth would fracture.

Then came a heavy snowfall, just at the end of November. We gathered our scanty mining supplies and hid them in a secret location—the giant trunk of a tree well above the river's edge. We strapped our meager personal effects to our backs and began to trudge through the drifts toward the coast, toward warmth for the winter.

We exchanged our gold as soon as we arrived in town. The amount was substantial—not a king's fortune as we had hoped, but not inconsequential either. After settling some bills, I had nearly six hundred dollars, and Giles had nearly four hundred. It would be a small fortune in Shawnee, but not in San Francisco. I immediately sent two hundred dollars to my parents with instructions that they were to use what they needed of this. The remaining moneys I'll use to live until the snows have melted in the spring. I'm sure I'll need every dollar, as the costs in town are so high. Even in the short time since my arrival in California, the prices in San Francisco have nearly doubled—and, in some cases, tripled and more. We've found a room near the harbor. It's scenic, but the damp air slips through the thin walls. We add blankets upon blankets. There is no ice or snow in the air, but I'm as cold as I've ever been in my life.

We are among a fast-growing circle of prospectors who are working these hills and rivers. For the most part, these are good, hard-working men. Many have left wives and families in search of their fortune. Some have returned from the hills with much less than Giles and I had found, even in our short time in the hills. Perhaps a few dollars were sent to their homes, but the lion's share is eaten up by the necessities at hand and those supplies needed to begin work again after the winter is passed.

Many men spend wildly. A gold nugget of a substantial size will buy many things—a room, a dinner, a night's entertainment, an evening of drinking, and the like. And then there is that part of town populated by other recent arrivals—women of dubious virtue. I'm told prices there have not only tripled but tripled once again. There is a

scarcity of womenfolk in this territory. There are hardly any entire
families here, and the paucity of the more civil and tender ladies, I've
discovered, allows the environments to become harsher, more crude,
and aggressive. While I do not frequent any tavern or establishment
that serves only alcohol, even in restaurants men will squabble and
come to blows over a trivial offense. It's apparent there are no home-
town eyes looking over any man's shoulder. There are no mothers,
fathers, uncles, or even old friends. It is all new—and raw.

Last evening, as Giles and I ate a stew of fish and oysters, two men
began to argue as to the comparative worth and virtue of New York-
ers versus people from New Jersey. I myself had never thought that
the people in one area of the country possessed any more innate
qualities than another, save accents and occupations, but within minutes, these two men were rolling about on the floor, trading blows
and insults. Giles and I managed to grab our plates just before they
crashed into our table. What makes the incident worth reporting is
the incongruous fact that neither man is an inhabitant of either of
the mentioned states. They were fighting by proxy. Such is the tenor
of these days.

I have not returned, even during these days of relative inactivity,
to much reading of the Scriptures. When I open the Word, I'm
reminded of how much I've given up to seek this earthly treasure.
I know God will never abandon me, but at night, when the cry of
the gull is the only sound, and I hear the crash of waves against the
shore, I feel in my heart that I have abandoned the Lord and done
his kingdom a disservice that may not be forgiven.

But the lure of glittering riches is strong. We've heard of and actually seen men with buckets full of the golden mineral. If exchanged
for cash, they would be envied even by Midas.

Next year we will do so as well. Giles and I continue to promise
ourselves that such a reward waits for men like us who are not afraid
of hard work. It's clear we see America as a "go-ahead" country of
risk-takers, unafraid of backbreaking labor or failure.

Spring is deceptive in this land. It remains chilled and damp. Why
anyone would seek out this locale as a permanent residence is a

mystery. The calendar states that February 1849 is nearly passed, and Giles and I have nearly completed our preparations for the return to the river. We've lodged a new claim, farther north, where a small but strong stream intersects with the larger river. We think the action of this other stream will dislodge more gold.

Days before our departure, I received a letter by express from Shawnee addressed to me in care of General Delivery in San Francisco. It brought my heart to despair. I choose not to repeat it all, save to say my parents are still in deep mourning over my departure, and my mother often is taken to bed for days at a time, so disturbing is her sorrow and anguish. They do not mention Constance. They do not tell of the state of the church. It is a short letter stating that they are alive and are spending only a fraction of the money I left.

The guilt I feel over leaving them and the people in Shawnee intensifies with these words. Perhaps if we find our gold early, I may be able to return by next winter.

I realize I intended on returning this spring, but I cannot. Too little gold has been found. I would return poorer than when I left, and I cannot abide that.

As the cold lingers, I've had the luxury of reading the many newspapers that arrive here from all over the world. One item in a New York paper caught my eye. It was a brief excerpt from a book written by none other than my old friend Jamison Pike. The title was *A Western Odyssey,* and the brief account included stories of encounters with Indians, raging rivers, blizzards, and the like. What fantastic and amazing experiences he has had. A postscript at the end of the excerpt stated that the book is selling briskly, more than any other work to date. It appears Jamison has achieved two of his goals—adventure and authorship. Perhaps he mentioned romance in the latter pages of his book. I've asked repeatedly in town in order to purchase a copy, but no one has it. One merchant offered to order it. Perhaps it will arrive in less than a year.

Another article told of a group of women who held a convention in Seneca, New York, where they formulated the "Declaration of Sentiments," a document calling for women's "immediate admission to all the rights and privileges which belong to them as citizens of the United States." The organizers of the convention were Lucretia Mott and Elizabeth Cady Stanton. Their platform: temperance, the rights of labor, and abolition of slavery. Hannah mentioned their names often as we discussed such matters late into the night when we were students. I can't help but wonder if she attended such an event.

It's curious. I have not thought of Hannah for so long now that I have trouble conjuring up her face. Such erosion of memory can only be blamed on the passage of time.

Russian River
April 1849

In spring the stream was a rushing torrent of water. Giles and Joshua surveyed the scene from a bluff overlooking the confluence.

"We can set our tent here," Joshua said, indicating a flat area nestled under a trio of tall pines. "The trees will serve as a windbreak."

Their plan was to set up camp first. The water was still so numbing that even the warming of one degree would be a welcome increase.

Giles nodded. His behavior, Joshua had noticed with rising concern, had changed since the two had found each other last year. At first, despite the adversity he'd faced, his spirit was bubbly and confident. Now, greeting a new day seemed a taxing chore. Every day brought fewer and fewer words, although Giles was no less a hard worker. However, his visage seemed to harden and then set.

The first day back along the river, they cleared their tent site and laid in a large supply of firewood. Joshua was determined they would be warm, at least during the short time between the end of work and beginning of work.

Both Giles and Joshua had staked individual claims, thus covering twice the territory. This year Giles had insisted that the gold be divided on an equal basis.

As they worked those first days, setting up camp, building a rudimentary wooden sluice to aid in the recovery of gold, over ten teams of men passed them on their way upriver. The amount of men far surpassed the number who had returned last winter.

"Bet the entire river will be covered with stakes next year," Joshua said as he chopped at a fallen log. "Once the word spreads back East, we'll have a crowd of treasure seekers."

Giles hefted the log, turning it so Joshua would have a clean surface to cut. "They'll be coming in a wave. I can feel it. You saw in the newspaper that San Francisco expects an increase of 1000 percent this summer alone."

"I read it, but I didn't believe it. I have a friend who works on a newspaper back in New York, and he told me how the truth gets stretched once it gets to print. In fact, you may know him. He was at Harvard the same time you were–Jamison Pike?"

Giles shook his head.

Joshua lifted the cut log and nestled it into the short wall they were constructing. The cabin would be no more than ten feet square and only five feet high with the canvas tent stretched over the top until they had time to cut logs for the roof. But in the meanwhile it would offer them a drier, cleaner abode than a drafty tent.

"He said stories get made up from thin air all the time. The average reader has no way of knowing which are cut from real cloth– and which are from the reporter's imagination."

"But when lots of stories all tell of gold and the ease with which a man can get rich–well, no one will choose not to believe that," Giles said, wiping at his brow. "Who could resist that lure? America is a land that guarantees equality–yet reality proves only a certain few have access to wealth. This would prove that wrong. It's why I came. It's why you came. A thousand family men are going to believe that, too, and leave in a great wave from home and hearth."

Joshua agreed.

Is that why I left? But there was more than that.

He stopped working and stared out at the river.

It's that this was the first decision I'd ever made devoid of considering others–parents and family and friends. It may have been irrational and impetuous, but it was made by myself alone.

He picked up the ax and moved toward a tree.

Time will prove me right or wrong.

May 1849

Within three weeks of setting up camp, Giles and Joshua had found more gold than they had during the entire previous year. A glass jar brimmed with the glittering nuggets and flakes. They buried it several paces north of their cabin.

Since their arrival, a few strangers had stopped by. Some stayed for a morning, asking questions and seeking advice. Giles and Joshua were cautious with both. Others only paused on their way upriver, murmuring sullen words of greeting.

Joshua could feel it from everyone who passed. The strangers considered Joshua and Giles lucky to have arrived early and taken such easy spots on the river. From the comments a few of the prospectors made, they had perhaps another three days' hiking to get to their stake on the riverbank.

Joshua noted with alarm two things about this new category of prospectors. One was that many of them seemed to be woefully underequipped. Some came wearing the only clothes they had and carrying no more than a shovel and a pan.

I wonder what they'll eat and how they'll sleep. When darkness falls in these ravines, the chill is intense.

The other item Joshua noticed is that more and more of the miners carried weapons. Joshua had debated purchasing a rifle in San Francisco to use for hunting but decided against it. Wildlife was scant in this area: Joshua had seen bushy squirrels, and once a bear had crashed along the stream above him, but that was all. It was not enough to support the two of them for very long. So instead Joshua had stocked up on fishing hooks and line.

But these new prospectors carried a veritable arsenal with them—pistols, rifles, shotguns, and long curving machetes, as if they were on a journey into a dense jungle. Were the weapons, Joshua wondered, going to be used to defend their gold, or perhaps, to insure that others did not become too prosperous?

Joshua and Giles decided they would hide their riches, all collected and stored in jars, more often and in different places, so that no man could steal the entire fruits of their labor in one catastrophic swoop.

June 1849

Summer fell upon the land with a blazing intensity. Joshua thought no more of the cold and now sought to keep cool. Even the river's water failed to cool them for long.

Rains fell infrequently, and the river edged lower and lower, exposing more and more ground to easy prospecting. The sluice contraption they constructed had been refined, and now Joshua would bring buckets of water and gravel and dump them into a hopper. Part of the river had been diverted, and the water washed away the worthless rock. Giles would shake the sluicer, allowing the gold to fall into a bottom pan, and the water would spill back into the river.

Giles worked harder than any man Joshua had seen, belying the old notion that Harvard men were ineffectual at manual labor. Oftentimes, at night, Giles would moan and toss in his sleep, calling out for his mother and father.

As they buried yet one more glass jar, Giles spoke. "If this does not impress my father, I do not know what will. He'll at last see that I could make something of myself without his counsel."

Joshua put a hand on his friend's shoulder. "Is that why you're doing this? To impress your father?"

Giles's face turned angry. "I keep hearing the words that he screamed the night I left: 'You're a cheat and will die a cheat! You'll never amount to more than that!' He just shouted that over and over as I walked away."

"Giles, I never knew . . ."

"I never told anyone else about this. My father thinks I'm a wastrel and a conniver. The family has been disgraced, he said."

As Giles turned from the burial spot for the gold, a deep cough bent him at the waist. After a minute, he managed to stand again.

"I'm going to return to him rich. I'll laugh in his face, throw a bucket of gold at his feet, and then turn away, never to look upon his smug visage again. But I'll never disgrace him again, either."

"Giles, I'm sure he's forgiven you. He's a minister of the Word, isn't he? He knows forgiveness. You can go home again."

Giles laughed sarcastically. "He's not that kind of minister, Joshua. And no, I cannot go home again. No one can." He coughed again. "Not even you, Joshua."

Joshua had no reply.

"You say you're going back, my friend. But if you go back rich, they'll see you changed and want no part of you—except your money. If you go back without any gold, then pity and anger and recrimination will follow you like a shadow as long as you live in Shawnee." Giles sat down to rest on the stump of a pine tree. "No, neither of us can go home again. We have left and will come back changed; no one will know who we are. We might go back, Joshua, but we can't stay."

Joshua shook his head. "You're wrong, Giles. I can go home, and I will. I'll have enough to properly set up a church. I'll be able to buy an organ, and the church will be absolved of offering me support. I can go home. I believe that's God's plan for my life."

Giles offered a bemused, sad smile. "You're fooling yourself. We have been together for months, and this is practically the first time you mentioned God to me. I find that odd for a man who claims to be doing God's will. No, Joshua. When you left Shawnee, you left God at the same time. You won't go back to either."

Their conversation stopped as the two wrestled the freshly cut logs that would frame the roof of the cabin. Both were sweating by the time only a few of the logs were lashed into place.

Giles sat down and leaned against the wall, his breath coming hard.

After a minute's rest, he inhaled once, deeply, and wiped his face with his pine-stained hand.

"Thanks, Joshua," he said without much emotion.

"Thanks? For what?"

"Thanks for taking a chance on me. I know about my reputation at Harvard. I know that you were a preacher boy and all—I don't mean that to be mean-spirited, but you did get ordained—and yet you took a big chance on me. You bankrolled me. You let me share this with you. Not many others would have done that."

Surprised at his friend's gratefulness, Joshua replied, "It wasn't anything another man wouldn't have done. And I couldn't have done any of this without you."

Giles sighed and stood.

"That's not true, and we both know it, but I thank you for saying it. Anyhow, thanks again for taking that chance and for believing in me when no one else did. I guess that's what a Christian fellow should do. You may not be preaching, but what you're doing is saying just as much. You don't know how much your friendship means to me."

Then, as if uncomfortable with his admission, Giles stepped toward the pile of cut trees. "Let's get busy now. I don't want to sleep with only a canvas roof for any longer than I have to. We still have at least two hours till dark. I say we best get to it."

As the two of them made their way to the logs, Giles coughed again, holding an arm about his ribs as if each breath caused him sharp pain.

God, what Giles said wasn't true, was it? I can still serve you, can't I? I can go home again, can't I?

Their hands grasped another log and heaved it to the roof, nudging it into place.

FROM THE JOURNAL OF JOSHUA QUITTNER
JULY 1849

We have now buried twelve glass jars and other jugs of gold. Every day seems devoid of any major find, yet in bits and pieces, a thumbnail at a time, the jars become heavy. They are beginning to represent a small fortune, indeed—at least in Shawnee terms.

And here is the rub. We have accumulated a fair amount of gold. If we could be magically brought back to our hometowns, we would be as kings, perhaps. But that cannot happen.

Instead, we are forced, every fortnight or so, to traverse downriver to the tent city for supplies. There we are forced to buy flour, sugar, coffee, and eggs at a price twenty times, perhaps thirty times, higher than the same items would fetch only a hundred miles farther west.

If one complains, one is told, "Then take your business there. I have no concern if you do. I have other willing buyers."

And we are placed in between that rock and a hard place. We must have supplies to live—but we have no time to travel the long journey to cheaper prices along the coast.

We are fortunate. We've found a healthy vein of gold. Others are not as lucky and bring all they've found to purchase meager supplies so they might go back out and scrape more flakes from the ground.

Our guide was right. Few prospectors are gaining much wealth. It is the provisions and suppliers who rake in handsome profits. Perhaps we should take our reserves, invest them in flour and coffee, and resell these commodities to others.

Yet despite our successes, I'm greatly concerned. Giles's cough has worsened; heaving coughs shake his body. I've insisted a dozen times that we descend the river and find a doctor—even if it requires us journeying all the way back to San Francisco. Giles will hear none of this.

"We cannot leave the stake now. We'll go in the winter, when other prospectors cannot jump the claim. Leaving now would be inviting them to steal from us. I won't leave. I must show my father that his son has made something of himself."

I am vexed. I cannot force Giles to return. We have worked only partial days for the past week (and still have found a good amount of gold). I'm hoping the half days of rest will bring about a cure.

But nothing is working. Giles is racked with near convulsions as he attempts to clear his lungs.

Russian River
September 1849

As the days grew shorter, Giles and Joshua worked fast, drawing as much time from the waning sunlight as they could. More than once they crawled up the riverbank, feeling their way with an outstretched hand, so dark had the night become.

"I'll be grateful for a sliver of moon," Giles called out in anger after tripping over a hidden root on the trail.

Joshua's concern for his friend increased. Every day brought them more gold, but Giles's cough grew deeper, more racking.

"We could leave now and have all the gold and riches we might ever want," Joshua argued. "Your father would be impressed now. I know he would."

Giles shook his head.

"We can wait till the first frost. I can make it till then. No sense in letting a good thing go too early."

But as the days slipped past, September saw Giles occasionally unable to rise in the morning. He would have good days of labor, unencumbered with the cough, and other days weakness would flow over him like a crashing wave at sea.

Joshua returned one night and found Giles, doubled over in pain.

"We have to get you to a doctor, Giles. I'll not have you dying here."

Giles pushed his hand away.

"I'm not dying. It's just a cough from standing in cold water and eating your badly cooked food. Buy me a good meal at the Destiny, and I'll be fine."

Joshua couldn't help but smile at the mention of his old haunt and its pleasant memories.

Joshua busied himself heating a portion of stew made the day before. As it warmed on the fire, Giles sat up in bed and called out softly, "Joshua, you paid attention in Bible classes at seminary, didn't you?"

Joshua smiled again. Giles constantly started his questions on that note—as if he still wasn't sure of the quality of Joshua's education.

"Yes, I paid attention," he called back. "And I have the diploma to prove it."

"Diplomas can be forged, you know," Giles shot back.

Joshua laughed and handed Giles a plate of stew with a thick slab of hard bread. "And friends can be tossed into the river in the night too."

But this night Joshua saw a note of urgency in Giles's eyes.

"What is it?"

"I think I know the answer, but I want to hear it from an expert. And you're the only expert here."

"Answer to what?"

"If a man does terrible things in his life, turns his back on God, forgets his family, lives like a heathen . . . well, is there still time?"

"Time? Time for what?"

"To make it right," Giles whispered. "I've made such a mess of my life. Can God forgive that? Can I make it right with him? Do I still have time?"

Joshua was stunned at his friend's questions. They had spoken of spiritual things before, in the darkness of their cabin, but Giles's heart had remained as hard as the trunk of a redwood.

"You have time, Giles. But no man can say how much time."

When Joshua saw tears welling up in Giles's eyes, he fought back some of his own.

"Do you want to start over again? Is that what you're asking?"

Giles nodded.

"Do you want me to pray for you?" Joshua asked.

Giles nodded again, now mute with pain, unable to mouth the words himself.

In that cabin, lit only by a tiny fire, Joshua knelt. Giles laid his plate aside, pushed himself from the bed, and lowered to his knees.

And in that flickering darkness, Giles made his peace with God.

FROM THE JOURNAL OF JOSHUA QUITTNER

SEPTEMBER 1849

How bleak and horrid this September day is. How devoid of all good things. The sun is out, and yet no warmth reaches my heart.

Giles has died.

For the last three days, he claimed to be on the road to recovery. Even his actions backed up his promise. Yesterday we worked nearly a full day. Blast it all! Why could we not have remained at camp? It was a Sunday, which makes our work that much more a sacrilege.

On this, his last morning, Giles arose, ate a bit of breakfast, and coughed deeply. He then lay back against the wall of the cabin, watching me as I prepared coffee. He coughed again, then clearly said, "It's so cold here," and wrapped his arms about his chest.

As I turned to him, his eyes began to flutter. Seconds later he slumped over, and I attempted to revive him. Perhaps he breathed another moment, perhaps two. Then he was gone.

I stared at the wild, green forest about me, which had now taken on a sinister, horrible countenance. I wanted to scream. I wanted to run. I wanted to escape this dreadful event.

I was forced to bury my friend. I selected a quiet sun-dappled place in the midst of a grove of pines. I dug a deep grave. I prepared a shroud from his blankets. The solemnity of this day was broken—it's hard struggling a dead man into the ground. All sense of dignity and decorum was lost. My hands were muddy. Dirt was streaked on my face. I shoveled the earth back on top and placed a pyramid of stones to mark his final resting spot.

I'm still a pastor, and as such, knew the rites that had to be observed. I returned to the river and washed and changed into my one set of moderately clean clothes. At the graveside—to the north of the river for which he gave his life—I tried to say the proper words to mark Giles's passing.

But no words came. I stood mute as tears began to well in my eyes. My heart was torn with pain. I fell to my knees and wept—deep, wrenching sobs.

We've suffered through so many days of numbing work, and for what? A few bottles of gold. For this Giles has given his life. Giles and I already had enough gold to last a lifetime.

Now he and the gold are both buried beneath the cold earth.

An hour may have passed. Still no words came. I returned to the river, and without thinking, without knowing why, began to dig in the gravel again, and lower bucket after bucket into the sluice.

CHAPTER TWENTY

Russian River
Fall 1849

JOSHUA remained at the river's edge the rest of that day, wearing his best clothes, yet uncaring how the water and mud stained them. He worked without thinking as the sun traversed the sky. He worked without seeing, without sensing, without feeling.

He tried to pray as he put his shoulder to shovel, lifting large clumps of gravel, water, and muck into the buckets. But no words came to him as he worked.

An image flashed past his thoughts—that of a little boy who had wandered far from home. As the little boy walked farther and farther into a dark forest, the shouts of his parents grew fainter and fainter, until all sound stopped. Even the sun was hidden by the canopy of leaves and vines. Suddenly the little boy turned to face home and realized he had lost sight of that place. He called out but heard no response. With a glum look, the little boy continued to walk, farther and farther away from home, thinking the sun and his parents had forgotten him.

Joshua took off his jacket as the sun passed noon. Trails of sweat coursed down his face and darkened his shirt.

One more bucketful, he said to himself, *then I'll stop for a rest.*

Only days prior, he and Giles had moved the heavy sluice a few yards farther upriver, almost in the shadow of a rock precipice that loomed above the shore. Tendrils of tree roots dangled, and patches of moss grew on the rock face that saw little sun.

Joshua used the shovel to chip the rock, then scooped and dropped the gravel into the bucket, as he had done for months. He lifted the bucket with a grunt, tipped it into the sluice, and let the water rush the debris away. As he rocked the contraption to help separate the chaff from the glitter, he thought he saw a glint as the rocks washed down the wooden chute.

That's odd, he told himself. *We never see the gold until it reaches the last section. Flakes and tiny nuggets don't glint in the sun.*

He hurried to complete the wash. He stepped quickly to the end of the unit and reached into the cold murky water.

What he retrieved he could scarce believe. His eyes saw it, and yet the image was as surreal as any dream—or nightmare.

In his hand, filling his entire palm, was gold . . . not a nugget, but a rock. It was a solid handful of gold, the size of a plum in August. Joshua lifted it, feeling its pull, feeling its weight.

As he held it closer to his face, the gold glistened in the sun like a thousand prisms.

This is the largest gold rock I've ever seen.

Joshua stared at the ground. And then he saw it—the glint of other such rocks in the shallows, in the murk, in the gravelly debris that lay within a stone's toss from where he stood.

His eyes froze in shock.

The body of his friend, only hours buried, was forgotten for those golden minutes. All his mind could concentrate on was what his eyes saw—the dazzle and dance of gold in the river.

<hr />

With Giles gone, Joshua worked as a man possessed. The narrow stretch of riverbank yielded gold that did not require jars for measurement but rather buckets. Barely disturbing the surface,

Joshua found more gold in two weeks' time than he and Giles had unearthed in all the months they had spent hunched in cold waters and freezing winds.

As soon as the sun rose, Joshua would gobble up cold johnnycakes with a cup or two of coffee, then hurry down to the river's edge, often just at the first hint of dawn.

He awoke looking forward to his labors.

The work offered Joshua freedom. For as he toiled, he did not think of his dead friend, or his disappointed parents, or broken-hearted Constance, or Hannah, or his Harvard friends, or of the burden to God.

Joshua dug, carried, sluiced, separated, and dug some more. He seldom stopped at noon as was the custom when Giles was alive. He simply ignored what hunger he felt and continued to work. He would prolong his efforts until the golden rays of the sunset turned to purple and then to black. Carrying the day's yield in a bucket—sometimes in two buckets—he would feel his way back the narrow path to the camp. He would set a quick fire and scurry to the edge of darkness. There he buried his gold in stout canvas sacks. Tamping the earth down and marking the spot with an old bottle or empty tin can, he would return to the fire and heat a plate of beans, gobble them down, and fall into an exhausted sleep, only to wake and repeat the process on the morrow.

As he lay balanced on the spot of consciousness that lay between awareness and deep sleep he worried about his treasure. Would he be able to mine all the riches in this stake? Would he be able to find what he had secreted away in the darkness? Would he receive a fair price for the gold? How much should he send to Giles's parents? How would he manage to carry the gold to town?

He'd attempted to write a letter to Giles's parents several times, then discarded each attempt. He wanted to offer them a tribute to their son, a tribute that might erase the angry division. As he wrote, he tried not to think of the same division separating him from his parents and everyone in Shawnee.

But as he wrote, his words did disservice to Giles's memory. So he decided to wait until the snows came to finish the letter and send Giles's part of the gold on home. Perhaps the parents of his dead partner might use the riches to do something in their son's memory.

For much of the fall, Joshua remained a recluse, only traversing between the river and camp and his hidden gold. Only twice did he venture into the nearest tent city, once to turn in part of his gold and once in order to purchase supplies. Halfway there he found his arms aching from the weight of the metal.

He stopped at the assayer's office, had his treasure weighed and converted into U.S. greenbacks, and stuffed the wad into his pocket.

Down at one end of the street was a corral that was home to swaybacked horses, braying mules and donkeys, and a motley assortment of cows—all of which had seen better days. He stood at the rail and looked in, unsure of the mechanics of picking a pack animal. His parents had never owned a horse or mule but had used oxen to plow and harvest. And he had never had a horse until he became pastor of the church and needed one for visitation.

"How's that one there, the one with the white mark on its muzzle? She a good pack animal?" he tried to ask confidently.

The owner, a wide, greasy man, stepped out of a canvas-and-plank shanty, smiled, and spit. "She's a worker all right. You got a good eye for mule flesh."

"How much?"

The owner squinted and spit again. "How much you got?"

"Depends," Joshua replied, "on what you're asking for it."

After more than thirty minutes of back and forth queries and replies, they agreed on a price, and Joshua took a bridle to the animal.

The mule was docile compared to what he had seen of other mules as miners tried to lead them upstream, braying and kicking. This old girl was as obedient as a house dog.

He turned, hiding his billfold, and counted out the amount. As he handed the bills over, he saw a battered leather satchel near the shanty door. The edge of a thick book stuck out from a corner.

"Those your books?" he asked the man.

The owner laughed until he doubled over, coughing with a rumbly thunder. "Land sakes no. I couldn't abide that much reading. Another fellow left 'em as a sort of payment on a mare. Said they're worth a lot." He scratched at his gut. "You kin read 'em?"

Joshua bent down, opened the case, and pulled several books out. Plato, Voltaire, Chaucer—all in handsome leather editions.

"I'll give twenty dollars U.S. for the lot."

"Sold!" the man barked out. "And you can keep the satchel if you'd like."

That afternoon Joshua led the mule, loaded with supplies and books, along the narrow path that followed the curve of the river.

Come the first frost of fall, Joshua reasoned, he would gather up his gold and transport it to town. And as he walked, he began to lay plans for the winter.

After exchanging the gold, he'd return, against the tide of other miners heading to the ocean. He'd spend the winter in the hills. Leaving such a rich vein unguarded would be foolish.

Especially a vein that already cost one man his life, he thought solemnly.

FROM THE JOURNAL OF JOSHUA QUITTNER
WINTER 1849

I have scarce put pen to paper these many months. Now that the snow is falling and the winds are snapping at the edge of my snug cabin, I have little else to do. I will endeavor to fill in the missing months.

The day of Giles's death, a black day, for he was a true friend and comrade, also marked the start of my great riches. The river yielded so much gold with such ease, I felt as if nature were repaying me for the loss of my friend: buckets of gold, stashed now in bulging canvas bags.

I'm now a rich man. Though my wealth is still in the form of gold, it's a fortune nonetheless.

As autumn descended on these hills, I faced a hard decision. Most miners leave their claims and return to San Francisco or the flatlands where it's warm. I was tempted again, but if I leave my claim and others hear of my success—which is nearly inevitable—then would the claim be mine when spring returns? I've heard stories of miners disappearing for much less fertile diggings.

No, in order to honor Giles's memory, and to preserve what we've worked so hard for, I decided I must stay by the river.

In the nearby canvas city, I found a group of layabouts, including two red men who promised sobriety if employed. I requested, offering a nominal sum of gold, to have them construct a sturdier shelter than Giles and I had built—a shelter fit for winter, complete with a fire pit and a working door. And they did so, complete with windows made with real glass and a door and close access to a privy.

The new shelter is not overly spacious, but it is sturdy and draftfree. The fire burns well, and they have provisioned me with a large stock of firewood. Supplies, I have purchased in abundance. Many shopkeepers sold out to me much of their remaining stock at reduced prices, for they know there will be no new customers until spring.

My bed is a thick cushioning of pine straw and native flowers, aromatic and claimed to be vermin-free by one of the Indians. I also purchased the tanned skin of a large bear, which I use as a bed covering. It is exceedingly warm and enveloping.

Open water is as near as the river's edge. An old native to this area claims that the river never truly freezes so solid that water cannot be drawn from a hole chopped in the ice. I trust him to be accurate. However, if the river freezes thick, I can always melt snow and ice.

On my last visit to town, I witnessed the steady stream of miners heading downhill with their pick, shovel, pan, and bedroll toward the ocean and warmer weather. They all seem to be wearing what has become part of a miner's uniform in these parts—a red flannel shirt. Some look pleased; others have a drawn look of quiet anguish.

That's the difference, I've deduced, between a man who has found treasure and a man who has found only hard, backbreaking work.

Some miners have begun their riotous living on the journey down. The taverns in the nearby town are filled day and night. Whiskey at a dollar a single gulp is the norm, and men will drink twenty to thirty such gulps in quick succession. They often leave staggering and near blind, but when a clear head returns, they are again found at the same tavern to repeat the same inebriation.

The brothels are as numerous as the taverns. They do a brisk business as well, offering all manner of evil debauchery.

Yet while I condemn such degrading practices, I understand the lure. It has been months since I've laid eyes on a female form. In the town's only respectable restaurant, a young woman, not comely in the least, asked of my meal selection. Just being in a woman's proximity caused me to babble for minutes before I could articulate my wishes.

How many other men have succumbed to the same pressure and been led by their evil desires to sin?

Men are devoid of companionship for months and months. I realize that some came to forget a lost love, others to escape the past, and still others, to start a new life. Will I become one of those lost souls?

Last night I knelt and offered a prayer to God. I was not sure if he would listen. Yet I prayed for wisdom and guidance, and most of all, a companion. I do not want to be alone forever.

Russian River
Christmas 1849

The winter days passed slowly. By Christmas Eve, the forest was quiet, draped in white. The pristine snow squeaked when Joshua stepped out along his path to the river.

He had let his beard grow as well as his hair. In town, if he could make it through the drifts, were any number of barbers. And every miner was self-sufficient enough to handle such a task. But Joshua knew that if he tried, hair would cascade down and lodge in his clothing. He resolved that until the waters ran warm enough to bathe completely, he would abandon shaving for the winter.

On the last trip to his claim, he had found a mirror framed in polished brass. Too heavy and unnecessary to carry any longer since it was used only for vanity, it had been discarded by a miner on his way upriver.

As Joshua picked up the mirror and rubbed it dry with the sleeve of his jacket, he recalled the stories of other miners who spoke of vast graveyards of unused and unwanted equipment that littered the setting-off points. When packing the first time, a book or a brass mirror seemed like a logical, sound inclusion. But when, after traveling for a hundred miles with the object's weight resting on tired, pained shoulders, it was often more logical to lighten the load. That's why diaries, images of lovers and wives, books, even Bibles were said to be discarded in great quantities.

One miner quipped that a man might make his fortune simply by gathering the discards of recent arrivals and reselling them.

Another miner added that the San Francisco harbor was all but impassable due to the burgeoning flow of ghost ships. Even three fancy new clipper ships were left to gather barnacles and rot in the fog and damp by crews headed to golden pastures.

As Joshua touched the mirror, he thought of those who were following him and those who came before, leaving all they held dear to pursue a dream—of gold and ambition. Some may have seen the gold as a way of escape—escape from a lifeless marriage, a hard job that offered no promise, or simply from what was normal and expected.

And so far away from home on Christmas, he thought sadly.

Joshua still puzzled over what had driven him here. He looked in the mirror and saw a stranger. The face was faintly lined now, with streaks of worry and hardship just beginning to etch their way into the flesh. The straw-colored hair had lightened in the sun and now was peppered with strands of white. The beard was red and full.

The image was that of a rich man—with eyes that looked cold and alone.

The longer Joshua stared, the lighter he felt. He began to smile, then laugh. Smoothing a hand through his hair, he said out loud, "There is no way I can make this creature staring back at me look presentable."

He lifted his head as his mule brayed in the distance.

"The only one around here who sees me is the mule, and I've heard no complaints from her."

Slipping on his jacket, he stepped from the cabin into the crystalline air. The mule, tethered to a tree in a cleared area, had wrapped the rope tight. This occurred several times a day, and for Joshua it was a welcome diversion. He tramped through the snow, broke the ice off the trough, kicked the snow from the hay, and knocked the icicles from the tidy mule shed. He reached into his pocket and pulled out a withered apple.

"Merry Christmas," he shouted. The mule took the fruit greedily and munched it down, then looked up with pleading eyes.

"That was the last of the apples, friend. You need to eat the hay." Joshua sniffed at the air. "Only another few months and we'll see the last of the snow."

He patted the mule's side, now thinner but not gaunt.

"And when it does . . . maybe we'll both take a walk to town."

March 1850

Joshua did not bring a calendar with him, but according to the last visit to town, he figured the date to be near the end of March. The snow had ceased falling weeks earlier, and what remained on the ground was slowly receding.

"March is early for a thaw, but it's not unheard of," Joshua said to himself.

In the long winter months, he had more and more often slipped into dialogue with himself. He would spend hours in discussions for two, imagining what another might say in response.

Joshua did not know much of the patterns of this land, but he saw the portents of a warm spring—birds on the wing, the liquid sound of snow, a warmer wind from the west. He ventured out several times, testing the trail to town. He wanted to name the town with a proper appellation, but so many of these temporary cities had no such naming. Miners simply pointed and called it "town."

Joshua walked for half an hour, finding the trail snow covered but very passable. Hurrying back to his cabin, he began to harness the mule. He would also carry a heavy topcoat and a large sheet of canvas in case of an unexpected snowfall.

As he packed the mule, he listened to the increasing roar of the river below. The early snow melt had filled the broad ravine with a rush of cold water. It would be several weeks, Joshua figured, perhaps even a month, before any new work could begin. A broad band of dry land lay just north of the rock precipice. That was where Joshua had stored the sluice for the winter. He knew that if the river remained high for longer than a few weeks, he could set up operations there as well.

The trip to town was uneventful. He knew, from the untrampled snow, that he was the first active miner heading downriver. It would be weeks before others made their way upriver to their claims.

The tent city was slowly shaking off the cold and snow and coming alive again for the spring. Not all the merchants and shopkeepers had returned. Some may have found greener pastures; some may have returned to their original homes. Yet even at this early date, twenty establishments had begun operation. A second and third street had been added to accommodate the arrivals. Bundles of wood planking lay along the entrance to the town. The lumber would be used on walls, sidewalks, and probably for furniture, too.

At the end of the street, Joshua found what he had been dreaming about for weeks and weeks. The sign above the massive tent read: "Haircuts, Shaves, Hot Baths, All Manner of Tonsorial Delights and Gentlemanly Pleasures."

Joshua opened the door and stepped into a well-heated establishment, scented with oils and colognes. Above one corner of the room, cordoned off by a series of panels, floated great clouds of steam.

As Joshua entered, blinking in the dim light, a short fellow with slanting eyes scurried over to greet him.

"Ahh, good sir, you most welcome," the man said, his words spiced with a lilt.

Joshua asked, "You said you have baths. Is that true? A hot bath with soap?"

The man bowed. "Indeed, sir, we have such luxuries. You wish bath?"

Joshua nodded, a big smile on his face. "Yes, I wish a bath." Then, as he said those words, a cord tugged about his heart. "This is not one of those . . . you know . . . those houses, is it?"

The little man shook his head quickly. "No, sir, this honorable place of business. None of that here. We offer just bath and haircuts and the like. No more."

Joshua relaxed. "Then lead me to the bath. And don't spare the hot water."

"No, good sir, you get all the water you want. Only ten dollars."

Joshua heard the amount, an astronomical sum for hot water and soap, but he did not even hesitate. "Lead on."

As he lay in the soapy water, feeling civilized and human for the first time in a long time, he wondered how much he would have paid, given his new wealth, to feel normal again.

"A gift beyond cost," he said to himself, used to his solitary dialogue.

"You want, good sir?" the little man asked, thinking his customer required attention.

"Nothing," Joshua replied, "just thinking out loud."

And then his heart jumped. He sat bolt upright in the tub.

From the other side of the screen flowed a clear voice in a strange tongue. There was a hint of laughter in the words. The voice was like the flight of doves in spring. It was the voice of a woman.

CHAPTER TWENTY-ONE

Russian River
April 1850

THE winds warmed the valley only for a short time. After teasing Joshua with a hint of spring, the winds shifted, presenting a blanket of fresh snow.

Joshua paced nervously in his cabin. He told himself he had enough gold for a lifetime and did not need to return to the river. He could wait for the first thaw and head back home, back to Ohio. And when he argued these points with himself, he agreed with them.

"I'm not eager to find more wealth," he said aloud. "But I cannot tolerate this inactivity."

Yet as he pondered one particular thought, the more unsettled he became.

Could I ever go home again? The words home *and* Ohio *seem to be running from each other.*

He paced harder and faster, turning every few seconds to avoid a wall or bed or door.

One morning, early in April, the weather changed again. The sun rose, unfettered by clouds, and reflected the whiteness of the snow. Joshua awoke to the sound of icicles melting from the roof with a steady *drip, drip, drip*. He made his way to the mule shed and saw to it that the animal was fed and watered.

Then he walked toward the river to get water for himself. As he bent to the water's edge, the ice creaked as an old man might, waking from a long nap.

It will break in a few days, he thought, *and then I'll be able to return to work—to doing something productive.*

Back in the cabin, he picked up a book and attempted to read. With every page, he heard the groaning death of the ice on the river. And with every creak, the words on the pages became more jumbled, as if their meaning was melting from his mind.

He slammed the book down in frustration, then jumped up and walked to the door. The sun continued to stream down, warming his face. He paced back to the fire, stirred the ashes, then hurried back to the door.

"I have no need to go to town," he said aloud. "I have all the supplies I need for months. And I truly do not require another haircut so soon—especially at those inflated prices." He walked back to his chair.

"Ten dollars for a haircut and ten dollars for a bath," he continued, mimicking the incredulous tone his mother used at describing high costs. "For twenty dollars back in Ohio, I could have five years' worth of haircuts." He went to the door again. "But then again . . ."

His shoulders sagged for a moment. Then, in a flash, he sprang into action. Although there was no need to make the long trek to town, no logical reason whatsoever, he found himself lacing his boots and buttoning his coat.

Within a half hour of wrestling with his inactivity, Joshua was leading his mule through the wet snows, with both of them slipping on the trail that led to town.

"After all," he said to the mule as they walked, "it's too cold to dig. The ground is frozen. The water is covered with ice, and it will be weeks until anyone can run it through the separator."

The mule offered no reaction to Joshua's rationalization as she plodded along.

"And if I cannot work the river, I should read and study," Joshua said, arguing with himself. "But I find I have no ability to concentrate. Perhaps I've been alone too long. I can understand why man is not meant to live alone."

And as he walked, he remembered the sound of the young woman's voice from beyond the screen in the barbershop. Just the memory, the recollection of that voice tinted with beautiful laughter, was enough to calm his thoughts.

Without realizing it, Joshua played with the lovely image in his mind. The sounds were so pure, so innocent. After she spoke, there was a pause, and then the lilting, musical laughter. To Joshua, who had lived without laughter for so long, the sound was that of an angel.

Plodding along for hours in the sunshine with such warm thoughts made the trip go more quickly. Before he knew it, Joshua found himself nearly at the edge of town. Startled, he looked up. The sun was just past overhead, and he had not been aware of the passage of time or geography.

"I could use a hot lunch," he whispered to the mule. "Then maybe . . . a haircut and shave. After all, I do not know when I'll be returning. Once the weather clears, I might not see this town again until summer."

Deciding such a plan was sound, Joshua's steps hastened a degree, and he found himself pulling harder at the reins, urging the mule to keep pace.

Angels Camp

The "town" now had a name. It was unofficial, of course, since the area lacked any form of basic government or legal system. The federal government of the United States might offer a judicial system, yet there were no federal representatives this far into the mountains. Washington, D.C., was so far east that it all but did not exist. And if there were any federal agents in the territory, they would have more pressing duties—more pressing than providing names for tent cities.

As Joshua cleared the last ridge and rocky outcropping, then turned a last corner, he saw the crudely painted sign, nailed face high on a tall pine at the trail's edge. It read: "Welcom to Angels Camp," complete with misspellings.

"Angels Camp?" Joshua said as he read the name. "This place is as far from heaven as I could imagine."

His heart twinged.

Suppose a clergyman had come over the last month or so and set up a church? Suppose he named it Angels Camp to let everyone know that a church is here? As that thought came to mind, Joshua felt a stab of guilt. *And all this time I said I'd be witnessing . . . and I've done so little of it. I hardly even spoke God's name to Giles, except at the very end.* He shut his eyes hard, forcing that reflection away.

Another sign farther into town read: "All manner of provisions and necessities at Angels Camp Provisioners."

Then it's just that the town is named by a merchant. That makes sense, Joshua thought with great relief. There were many such settlements dotting the gold fields that borrowed their name from the first, or largest, emporium in the community.

By midafternoon, Joshua had taken a lunch, left his mule at the livery for reshoeing, and exchanged another canvas bag of gold nuggets at the assayer's office. He realized that holding his new riches in paper money offered no greater security than holding the same amount in gold. A single miner, he was at risk to be overtaken in the darkness by those less honorable.

During his last trip, he had inquired as to how to send funds to a reputable bank in San Francisco. It was an easy matter to accomplish, he found out. His gold was weighed, the amount certified, and that figure then communicated by bonded messenger to the National Bank of San Francisco. That bank would hold such funds on deposit until Joshua claimed them. Officials there could also send, for a fee, funds to any bank in America.

Joshua left the assayer's office with a small bundle of bills and a notarized paper stating his most recent bank balance. It was a most impressive figure.

As he waited for his business to be concluded, Joshua scanned a New York newspaper now more than three months old. A caustic editorial mentioned the graduation and certification of a female physician from Philadelphia, from the Boston Female Medical School founded in November of 1848. The article went on to state how such things harkened an ominous period in America. "When women take to education to know the secrets inside a male form and abandon their roles as mothers and wives, then we cannot guarantee the sanctity of this great nation any longer. How low we have sunk to admit the weaker of the species into such a horrid profession. Where are the hearts and minds of the misguided founder Samuel Gregory and his professors and deans?"

The article mentioned no names, but Joshua could not help but wonder if the woman referred to was Hannah. He thought not, since too little time had passed, but Hannah was a woman of rare abilities.

This is the first time her name has come to mind in so very long, he thought, glad her image no longer brought a stab of hurt to his heart.

His mind lost in a reverie of his Harvard days, Joshua took a leisurely stroll along the growing retail district of the newly named Angels Camp. Since his last visit, numerous shops, restaurants, gaming halls, and taverns had opened. None had the look of permanence about them. Most were not much more than large canvas tents with wooden floors, rickety wooden frameworks for doors, and perhaps oilskin windows. Then Joshua saw a large gilded sign standing high above a massive canvas and wood structure.

A theater—so far from any other cultural activity? Hardly seems as though they'll have any customers seeking out such an experience.

As he walked closer, he quickly understood. Just below a banner that read "Open Soon" was a painted canvas scene that claimed to be an accurate representation of their first offering. It was a woman, dressed in a most revealing costume, and singing. The closer Joshua came to the poster, the redder his face became and the more revealing the illustration. The artist who produced such a work must have needed a great quantity of flesh-colored paint to produce such a portrait—and an almost embarrassing acquaintance with the female form.

Obviously they are not producing Shakespeare.

Then he smiled in spite of his moral stand, for underneath this revealing portrait were listed additional attractions: "We will present, with Skilled Thespians, scenes from Shakespeare's Most Provocative Plays."

Shakespeare? Provocative? Joshua wondered. *Yet if the lady drawn in this poster is the star of such an event, I imagine any play might be made most provocative.*

He refused to stare as he shuffled past, his boots clumping on the wooden sidewalk.

I'm sure this theater will be successful.

Soon he entered the barbershop, and its steam and scents once again enveloped him.

"Ahh, good sir, you return to most humble establishment of Sun Yat-sen. I honored," the owner called out in singsong. "I take pleasure in greeting you again."

Joshua smiled. He was sure Yat-sen's memory was aided by Joshua's large tip for services rendered.

"You desire a bath today, sir? We have plenty hot water. Haircut? I have my best for you. Perhaps a manicure as well? A miner must treat his fingers with care."

After an entire winter of solitary confinement, Joshua reveled in the sheer pleasure of words spoken aloud, regardless of the odd accent or mispronounced word.

"My daughter most skilled at such pleasures. It be her honor to serve you," the owner added.

Joshua's heart leaped.

It must have been his daughter that I heard last time.

"Your daughter?" he asked.

"Yes, good sir. She young, but she most proficient. You will see."

Struggling to contain his excitement, Joshua nodded to the owner. "Yes, after a bath and haircut, I would like a manicure."

"Quen-li!" Yat-sen shouted.

There was no response.

"Quen-li!" he shouted again, then added a string of harsh words in a foreign tongue. In a heartbeat a girl of about seventeen slipped out from a room at the back of the shop. Her head was bowed as she entered. Her father yelled again and raised a hand as if to strike her. She cowered in response.

"You must treat women firmly," he said as an aside to Joshua, who had almost raised himself from the chair as if seeking to defend the girl from a beating. "A woman who does not respond from first order is a woman who needs to feel the sting of pain. Pain a great teacher."

Joshua was about to offer a sharp reply when Yat-sen turned away to a new customer who had just come through the door. Quen-li had not lifted her head. She knelt at Joshua's side and bowed again, murmuring soft words. When she extended her fingers and lightly touched Joshua's hand, he almost jumped. Keeping her head bowed, she took his hand and began to massage it, adding drops of a scented hot oil to his skin. Then she spread a thick towel at her knees and laid out a series of files and tiny scissors.

Joshua had never even imagined what a manicure might feel like. He knew certain wealthy women might have such a thing done, but to his knowledge, no man had ever felt such wondrous sensations. Quen-li looked only at Joshua's hands and the task before her. For twelve minutes she filed, cut, and massaged Joshua's left hand.

Then finally she looked up at him and whispered, "This hand finished."

Joshua was enchanted.

Quen-li's hair was the color of the sky on a moonless night, dark and shimmering. Her eyes, the shape of almonds, were black, and her features as delicate as those of a doll Joshua had once seen in a store window. Her hands and limbs seemed to possess a silky power.

She smiled briefly, then hid her teeth quickly again behind serious crimson lips. She bustled around him and began to minister to his right hand.

Joshua watched her work. It was the closest he'd been to a woman in more than a year. He felt intoxicated. After a few minutes he found his tongue.

"Your name is Quen-li?"

She nodded without looking up.

"How long have you been in America?" he asked.

"I . . . the words . . . from China . . . three years, is how said?"

Her words were thick with accent, but Joshua knew what she meant. "Three years," he repeated. "Do you like it here?"

Quen-li did not respond.

Perhaps she did not understand.

"Quen-li," he repeated, "do you like it here? Do you enjoy being in California?"

She did not raise her head. "Not question for Quen-li. Obey father. Father here. Quen-li here. No more, please, sir. No more."

From the corner of the room, Joshua looked up at Yat-sen. The short man narrowed his eyes, and Quen-li shrank farther into a tight kneeling bow. "Quen-li," he snapped. "Work. No talk!"

"But Mr. Yat-sen, I asked her a question. She was answering me, that's all."

"No matter. Quen-li a stupid girl and no talk. No talk!"

Joshua did not choose that moment to respond harshly to Mr. Yat-sen. After all, he thought, it was a matter between father and daughter.

Mr. Yat-sen stalked away, tripping as he crossed over an uneven floorboard. The bottle of scent he held bounced into the air and bobbled up and down between his hands, stumbling and twisting and turning. His face a mask of horrified concentration, he spun and then fell backward, sliding on his posterior, the bottle firmly clenched between his hands.

Joshua could not help but laugh, so comical were the actions. Even Quen-li smiled, then let a sweet hint of laughter escape even as she bowed her head, her shoulders trembling in her attempt to hide her amusement.

And as that laughter again swept the air, something in Joshua's heart stirred.

Was it because I have thoughts of Hannah? he wondered. *No, it was something I heard my father say. Didn't he say that when he heard my mother laugh, he knew she was the one? He said hearing her laughter was all it took.*

He looked down at Quen-li, who had kept her face hidden.

But . . . why now? Her father is Chinese. This can't be. I can't be feeling what I think I'm feeling.

But as confused as Joshua was, he also knew his feeling was real. He glanced over at Yat-sen, who was struggling to get up, fuming and waving his arms in anger.

She needs to be rescued, Joshua thought. *And I know what being trapped feels like. She is trapped serving a mean-spirited father. She needs to laugh.*

Yat-sen spun about, glaring at his employees while trying to smile to his customers. It was not an easy task. He barked out a string of angry words, and Quen-li's smile disappeared as she returned to her tasks.

Joshua sat in hot silence.

Perhaps things are done differently in China. Perhaps this is simply the way a Chinese man treats his family.

※⋙◈⋘※

Quen-li finished without saying another word. Before she left, she wrapped his hands in steaming towels and slipped out of the room into the back. As Joshua sat with the towels warming his hands, another man entered and took the chair next to Joshua. Mud clung to his boots and dirtied his legs to the knee. Cleves Rayston, a miner with whom Joshua had a nodding acquaintance, took off his dirty coat, let it fall in a heap, and sighed.

"Been waitin' all week for this day. Us menfolk need a little pamperin' now and again, ain't that right, preacher boy?"

Joshua rued the moment when he had told this man he had left his church to come to California.

"You know, I ain't been touched by nothin' soft for so long I forget what it feels like. Pretty nice, ain't it, preacher boy?"

Joshua remained silent.

"Though I didn't think a man of the cloth would go for such nice-ties as this. I thought you preferred a hair shirt and an uncomfortable bed. I guess not all preachers are the same, now, are they?"

Mr. Yat-sen sidled over and turned to Joshua. "That right? You a preacher man?"

Joshua knew he had to tell the truth. "I am. I'm ordained. I had a church at one time. . . . But I left to earn money for God's work."

Cleves roared with harsh laughter. "Earn money for God, that's rich! The way I hear tell, you earned a lot for *yourself*, preacher boy. I see you makin' regular trips to the assayer's office. I don't see God getting his cut."

Joshua ignored his leering comments. Mr. Yat-sen leaned in closer. "You a preacher man–like Bible people who come to China?"

There must be people who have traveled to China with the Bible, Joshua surmised, *though I don't know of them.*

He nodded. "If they teach about the Bible and know Jesus Christ as Savior, then I guess they are like me. I believe in the God of the Bible as they must."

After all this time of hiding–or at least not admitting–the fact of my seminary training and my faith, it feels good to have it out in the open.

Mr. Yat-sen pursed his lips tightly and muttered some foreign words under his breath. "You come back for haircuts–but you do not come back with this God. He is not welcome. He is a god of devils."

And from the back of the room Joshua heard a narrow wail, then silence.

⚜

Before he left Angels Camp that day, Joshua saw to two other tasks that had weighed on him for months.

The first was writing a letter to Giles's parents. He had success-fully talked himself out of dashing off a letter immediately following Giles's death.

It would not arrive back east until just before Christmas, and I do not wish to break their hearts so close to such a celebration, he had reasoned. *The facts will not change if I wait till spring to mail the news.*

He purchased a packet of paper and envelopes and wrote a two-page letter. He spoke of Giles's wonderful qualities and how he'd mentioned his parents so many times with warm memories. Joshua knew this was a lie, but told himself the news was so painful that such prevarication would provide a soothing balm to his parents' broken hearts. He mentioned how faithful Giles had been and how he had renewed his service to God. Joshua did not mention that Giles's decision had been on his deathbed.

He also included a bank check for just over seven thousand, five hundred dollars—Giles's share of the gold they had collected as a team. Joshua would not keep it and knew of no other person to whom it should go.

Perhaps the money will show them Giles did accomplish something in his short life.

The second task was a letter to his own parents. This was a shorter matter: On one page, he wrote that he was fine, that work was hard, that he had found some gold. He did not inquire as to the state of the church or about Constance. The guilt was too overwhelming. In order to ease the blame he felt, he included a bank check for the same amount made out to his parents. It would be staggering to them. They could live in luxury, if they chose, for the rest of their lives. They could build a big house with elegant furnishings.

They could forget about their son's abandonment.

Joshua sealed both letters and sent them off with a messenger who operated the regular express service to and from San Francisco.

As he watched the man ride off, Joshua had hoped he'd find relief. But the dull throb under his heart remained.

Finally, Joshua began his walk to the stable to retrieve his mule and prepare for the journey back to his cabin by the river.

Russian River

When a warm wind blew strong from the west, the ice and snow receded so fast that a man could almost watch them slip from frozen state into liquid. The river churned and lapped at the base of Joshua's sluice. He visited the river's edge every day, measuring the water's crest, hoping it would soon begin to recede.

While he waited for spring to fully arrive, Joshua spent his time digging at the steep banks of the river, washing the gravel in the water at the river's edge. The return was slight, compared with last year's effort, and as he worked in the roar of the water, he worried that the gold in his claim might be washed downstream.

If that happens, then perhaps I'll get the gold from upstream, he thought, comforting himself.

The claim upriver from him had been taken over by men from upstate New York. Their arguments and shouts carried down to Joshua by the breeze. None of them looked as if they had ever taken shovel or spade in hand, and Joshua wondered if they would survive the work.

Downriver were six men from Virginia. They had brought with them an elaborate tent, big enough for twenty men, and a complete cookstove. They built two devices while waiting for the waters to recede: a large sluice and a still to produce whiskey from corn. The acrid odor mostly wafted downstream, and for that Joshua was grateful.

FROM THE JOURNAL OF JOSHUA QUITTNER
SPRING 1850

I have sent my two letters with the money. I hope the money will help ease the pain that Giles's parents will face. And while I write that, I know no treasure on earth can cover such a loss. But perhaps it will enable them to establish a memorial for their son or ease their burden of work.

I hope the same is said for my parents. Thoughts of Shawnee find their way into my mind at all hours, and I struggle to keep them from overpowering me.

The past is too painful, and I've given away too much.

Perhaps when this season is done, I will make my way back. If my heart heals, then perhaps the fine people of Shawnee will forgive me as well.

From a Letter Addressed to Joshua Quittner, San Francisco
Postmarked December 1, 1849

Dear Son,

Your mother remains shattered. The elders of the church, who were at first sympathetic with our embarrassment and loss at your leaving, have now grown angry. I've heard rumors that they'll ask us to repay the moneys you wasted going to Harvard. The church sacrificed much and received nothing in return.

If they ask, I'll use what you left us. I'd be glad to be rid of such money. I feel it's tainted somehow and you left because of it, or you felt you could leave and such money would be a solution to your inconsiderations.

Son, I pray every day that you will come to your senses. You have left a wonderful girl, Constance, with a broken heart. She pines for you—yet numerous young men stand waiting for her to recover.

Please send word that you will return soon. We'll try to forgive you.

Your father

The envelope was tattered and water-stained. The messenger said it was a miracle the letter had made its way into Joshua's hands. It had arrived by boat in San Francisco, and a messenger there had recalled Joshua's name from his latest correspondence and knew on which river he resided.

Joshua read the letter only once, then tossed it into the fire. It blazed quickly into a white ash.

CHAPTER TWENTY-TWO

Russian River
Summer 1850

HARD work became the only successful method for Joshua to truly escape the guilt that poured on his heart every time he thought of Shawnee, his parents, and the church. Each physical pain kept him in the present and let his past slide farther away. As the sun rose and set on the river, Joshua toiled without ceasing. When he stopped working, harsh words drifted into his mind. The more he tried to forget his father's letter, and all the events that caused such anger to develop, the more he remembered.

His heart pounding from the exertion, he leaned against his shovel. The silent argument began again.

Everything I did my whole life was to honor my parents–to show them that I loved them. I did what they requested. I became a preacher for them. I went to Harvard because of their dream. I came back to Shawnee for them. Never once did they ask me what I would choose to do with my life. Never once did they ask if leading the church brought peace to my soul. Never once did my father ask if I loved preaching as he did. Never once did my mother ask if what I felt for Constance was love. All I ever had was a desire to please.

Almost as a testament to his emotional turmoil, the river bore deep scratches from his work, as if a giant had clawed his bony fingers through the pebbly earth, violently grabbing for the gilded treasure that lay beneath the surface. Weeks went by, and mounds of discarded dirt and gravel pocked the riverbank on both sides. Every two days or so Joshua would strap a makeshift harness to his back and strain to move the sluice contraption a yard or two upriver.

But I've abandoned them . . . and left behind all they've taught me. God does call us to honor and love our parents. Is seeking my fortune so wrong? If it is so wrong, then why has God blessed me with such riches?

Joshua's claim continued to be productive beyond all expectations. Last fall he'd emptied his underground caches of gold, and this spring, he was filling them back up. At the end of every day he would climb up the riverbank in the dark, stumbling as he hoisted a bucket heavy with the shiny metal. Miners both up and downriver had no such luck. They were finding gold, to be sure, but from their descriptions Joshua knew that at the end of the year they would barely cover expenses.

At night, before he fell into a dreamless, exhausted sleep, Joshua would try to quiet the daylong arguments he'd had with himself. He'd attempt to pray, asking God for direction and guidance, but would quickly despair. Would God listen to a prodigal such as he?

FROM THE JOURNAL OF JOSHUA QUITTNER
JULY 1850

I've worked hard these past months. Spring was late, but the river's flow diminished sufficiently so that I was able to begin work almost the day the ice broke up. Our claim—my claim now—continues to produce gold in abundance. I have no need for more, yet I wake every morning and plod to the river's edge to continue. I'm not sure what drives me. When I used to pick up a nugget and toss it into the bag, that rich, earthy *clunk* would thrill me.

Now it has become only another noise.

I yet have hope that my sporadic prayers for guidance and wisdom will be answered. Yet I sometimes despair over having God respond to any of my feeble–and often hypocritical–prayers. I abandoned my family and my calling to seek riches, and I still expect God to listen to me. Is that not hypocrisy? Am I not as bad as the worst described in the Scriptures? Those people were doomed to hell. Have I also gone too far for redemption?

I've reserved one day every week, not for spiritual matters as we are commanded–such is the depravity of my condition–but to make my way to Angels Camp for a newspaper, a hot meal, a hot bath . . . and a manicure. That has become my preferred church.

The moments when Quen-li ministers to my hands are the most precious and wondrous of the week. When she's there by my side, my pain and turmoil vanish. Had I the ability to increase such blessed unconsciousness, I would do so in a heartbeat. It is there that I find solace and true kindness. I speak to her as best I can, and she responds as best she can–when her father is not there, that is. She smiles and laughs at my efforts to tell her of Ohio and my work on the river.

Ahh . . . to see her smile, to hear her laugh . . . such experiences are truly incredible.

Twice in the last few weeks, I have actually managed to be alone, such as it was, with Quen-li.

The first time was accidental.

Darkness was near, and I had yet to return to camp. After a wonderful hour at Yat-sen's, I spent most of the rest of the day in a tavern. I was not drinking–other than several cups of bitter coffee that tasted of seawater–but simply enjoying the sound of voices, music, and laughter. The laughter was fueled by strong drink, no doubt, but such was my thirst for company.

I realized that to return upriver at night would be foolishness, so I determined to seek out a night's lodging. As I made my way down the rickety sidewalk, I was nearly bowled over by someone scurrying out from an alley. We picked ourselves up, and to my surprise the one who had knocked me to my knees was none other than Quen-li.

She bowed and sounded near to tears as she tried to apologize.

I told her no harm was done, then asked why she was out so late. She looked up at me with those deep eyes.

"Father asleep. I hurry to buy food for . . . for next day."

"Tomorrow," I said, helping her with the word.

"Tomorrow," she said, smiling.

"He angry if no food on table."

We spoke for only a moment, but I found much pleasure in our words. I saw her smile as we talked, and my heart stirred when something I said brought her laughter, and in that laughter was the sound of gentle music.

She bowed to me, asked my forgiveness again, then hurried off into the shadows.

The second time we met was no accident.

Leaning against the awning post of the assayer's office, I watched the shadows lengthen. I had a clear view of Yat-sen's. As shadows swept along the streets, I saw the back door open and a slight figure slip out onto the street. It was Quen-li. I hurried to match her pace. I caught her off guard, and her halting words were evidence of her confusion. At my insistence, I accompanied her to the market and watched as she quickly selected provisions to fill her basket.

I continued to speak to her as she returned to Yat-sen's—though she remained silent.

A block from her home, she stopped and turned to face me. My heart beat wildly as she placed her delicate hand on my forearm.

"Why you talk to Quen-li? Quen-li not white woman. She Chinese."

There was a moment when everything became crystal clear for me, when my world changed.

I decided that after so many years of telling others what I thought they wanted to hear, I would at last be honest—totally honest with my emotions—and tell Quen-li the real reason for this "accidental" meeting.

I inhaled deeply, then spoke.

"I like you, Quen-li. I like who you are. I like hearing you laugh.

I like your smile. I like being with you . . . that's all. I like being with you."

For a minute, I believe Quen-li forgot about China, her father, and the cultures that stood in our way.

She smiled up at me and let her hand linger on my arm.

"I like . . . I like . . ."

Then, like a cloud passing before the sun, her smile vanished, and she turned to run home.

Before she did, she whispered, "Father will kill me if he know."

***

I've found out why Mr. Yat-sen holds God in such contempt. From other customers at his shop I've learned that "foreign devils" with Bibles came to his village in China. Quen-li's uncle–Mr. Yat-sen's brother–fought with these people and somehow was killed. I cannot believe any man of God would do such a thing. Perhaps it was acci-dental or caused by negligence on the part of Quen-li's uncle. In any regard, the family was now one income short and at the brink of starvation. Mr. Yat-sen had been forced to come to America to seek his fortune so that he could send money back to China.

The work here is hard, he says, and he is sad to be so far from family and anything familiar. It's obvious Mr. Yat-sen holds a deep grudge against all things having to do with God. And I cannot blame him for it, knowing what he's enduring.

***

The town continues to grow. Canvas buildings and tents are replaced–daily, it appears–with solid wood structures, some of local rock and stone. Many covered wooden sidewalks have been constructed, and now a man might traverse the entire town without stepping in mud or being soaked by rain.

Several hotels have sprouted up like mushrooms. They are not large or ornate but are packed with recent arrivals who crowd the streets and fill the nights with raucous behavior and optimistic shouts.

Provisioners have arrived with varied equipment and tools. Modern sluice units, built of metal with proper gears, are displayed alongside barrels of shovels and picks. A store owned by GD Enterprises is the largest provisioner, and I've taken time to walk among the displays of shiny merchandise.

Had I arrived this year instead of two years ago, I would not have attempted to stake a claim, for the cost of equipping such a venture would have appeared to be beyond my means. Yet more and more people arrive with money borrowed from friends and family. They speak of striking it rich and finding gold enough to repay their creditors tenfold.

Those who do poorly seldom announce their departure, though I've observed several slinking out on the road that leads down the valley to the plains and coast. Their faces are sullen, and they leave with no more than the clothes that rest on their bodies.

Life is hard, and the treasure of the earth offers itself in a most indiscriminate manner.

The theater is open, and a line of patrons snakes along the street almost continually, waiting to view the next performance. One day I even found myself standing in line to purchase a ticket.

The theater was large, surprisingly so, and several acts performed amusing skits and songs. Serving as an orchestra was a single piano player who made up for his lack of polish with bouncing enthusiasm.

The absolute highlight of the performance was a trio of quiet songs offered by the star of the show—a Miss Nora Wilkes, according to the poster out front. In contrast to earlier singers, she wasn't painted, and her attire was demure. She sang such plaintive songs of loss and heartache that hardened miners began to weep at the beauty of her voice and the words. She reminded us all of how much we've left behind to chase this illusive treasure. As she reached the last note of her all-too-brief performance, the entire crowd was in tears.

I, too, miss what society has to offer. What I find here seems counterfeit and predatory. The miners, both successful and unsuccessful, are often a dreadful lot, intent on only one thing: earthly riches. All other pursuits be damned, they would say. Yet, is that not why I'm here as well?

⚜

Two weeks have passed since I've put pen to paper. Much has transpired. I continue to work hard, and I continue to be rewarded–although I believe that the amount of gold I've found is declining from its peak of some months prior. It does not matter, truly, for I have more than I could use in two lifetimes, as well as do my parents.

Some might call this guilt money, but it's money nonetheless.

But that's not the reason for my excitement. Last week I made my usual trek into town. After six days spent in lonely silence, I yearn for even crude and unpolished conversation. Man is indeed a social creature, and I am no exception.

I'm also a creature of habit, although this week, because of a chilling, persistent rain, I rode to town a day earlier than usual, on a Sunday. (Sundays seem not to be any different than any other day of the week here. Provisioners, taverns, theaters, and the rest remain open regardless of whether it's the Lord's day or not.)

I stopped at the usual restaurant for a hot lunch and newspaper. The headlines shouted "PRESIDENT TAYLOR DEAD." The place was abuzz. There was much talk of Zachary Taylor's short half year in office and what the prospects are for our new president, Mr. Millard Fillmore.

Afterward I walked to Mr. Yat-sen's Tonsorial Emporium, as he has now taken to calling it. The crush of customers was much lighter than I'm accustomed to; only six were waiting ahead of me.

I knew I would see Quen-li today at her father's shop. She and I have shared only a few brief moments together away from her father's presence–yet I desire more contact. I took a seat near the window and read through a newspaper printed in San Francisco only two weeks prior. I noted with relish the news of the migration west. The reporter stated, if he's to be believed (I'm always dubious now after Jamison's comment about reporters' truthfulness), that San

Francisco has increased tenfold in the span of eighteen months and is expected to continue such growth in the years to come. I wonder how large it will be, since I have not seen that city's hills and bay for a number of months now. The article continued, saying that California would soon become a state of the Union. Perhaps with statehood would come more law and order.

As I read the news reports, a younger fellow next to me struck up a conversation. He was new to the area—and not a miner—for his attire was neat and prim, and his hands were white, smooth, and uncalloused. (Mine look meaty now, and are rough and often bleeding. They are not the hands of a preacher . . . or are they?) He asked of my home, and I mentioned Shawnee. He was from a town in the western part of Pennsylvania—Ligonier, I think he called it. He said George Washington had built a fort there some hundred years prior as he fought the Indians and the French.

I asked if he was staking a claim, and he laughed.

"No, that work is much too hard. I'll make more money with my head than my hands."

He went on to say that he's a reporter for a newspaper from Boston, of all places. I inquired if he knew of Jamison Pike.

The lad lit up and said that indeed he did and had crossed paths with him on several occasions. He admitted to a bit of envy of Jamison's success and his acceptance into the cream of New York society.

I thought to myself—is that *our* Jamison? I scarce believe it.

The lad claims it was Jamison's story on the original gold strike at Sutter's Mill that led him to Angels Camp. I said the same, and we shared stories of our travels and the events that led us to this place. He is sending a series of stories back to his paper—stories about the men who took upon themselves this great vision of opening the west.

This time I laughed. "I had no vision of opening the wilderness. I'm no pioneer. It was the lure of gold, plain and simple," I said. I told him of my departure from the church and the pain it had caused all whom I abandoned. This was the first time I shared such remorse with another soul—and he is a stranger. But the words flowed from my mouth. I saw him take a pad of paper and pencil and begin to write. I knew he was taking notes for a story, and I did not care.

Perhaps another might learn from my mistakes.

At the end of twenty minutes of conversation, still waiting for his turn in the chair, he paused and lowered his notes. "You said you left the church thinking you would use whatever treasure you found to further God's work. Have you done so? Are you building a church here? Or is there a church here already?" he asked.

I was speechless.

I have not used the treasure I've found for God. I have not redeemed my time. It's interesting. While those thoughts have occurred to me in the past, I dismissed them simply as idle thoughts.

It took a stranger to verbalize them and make them real.

I left Shawnee for a dream. I promised to serve God wherever I found myself. And I have not.

No bolt of lightning struck me. No voice from heaven called my name.

I just knew then and there that things would change.

We were both called over to the chair. (Mr. Yat-sen has installed a second chair, served by a young Chinese girl–his niece.) From her station Quen-li looked up as I approached and set to work.

She smiled, longer than was usual, and bowed more deeply. Her eyes sparkled with a jewel-like intensity. But her father hovered at her back, and we could not exchange more than a cheerful greeting.

I sighed, resigned to a mute communication for the moment. I looked back to the newspaperman.

"You asked about a church. Do you want to attend one? Are you a religious man? A man of faith at all?" I asked him.

He laughed–the same cynical laugh that I've heard come from Jamison's lips many times.

"Not likely. I've seen too much–even here in Angels Camp–for me to think that God has made it this far upriver. No, I was just curious. I have no need of a religious crutch. No offense, you being a man of the cloth. You still are a man of the cloth, right? You didn't give that up forever, did you? I mean, can you give that up? Or do you fellows take a vow for life–like the Jesuits do?"

It was then that I knew I could not give up my calling. I may have been confused and forgotten that calling, but I could not give it up.

And the words began to tumble from my lips as if a dam, long closed, burst open. The pressure of holding back the truth was so great that I could no longer contain the words of joy from my heart.

"No, God doesn't give up on anyone. If he didn't give up on me, then he won't give up on you."

At that instant I realized for certain that God *was* holding me in his hands–like he'd done for so many long months. What a fool I'd been! What a foolish man, to ignore God and his blessings!

"Me? I'm too much a sinner. I'm no angel, especially when I'm not being a reporter. Like I said, even in Angels Camp, there's plenty that can lead the pure–and not so pure–astray."

"That may be, my friend," I responded, "but God loves you no matter what. He truly does. He sent his Son, Jesus, to die so we wouldn't have to. Jesus went to hell instead of us–and came back victorious over death and is now in heaven. And if you believe that, when you die God will take you to heaven to live with him forever. There will be no more pain or tears or worry. It will be paradise. All you have to do is take the free gift of salvation."

"You know, I've heard the story before," the reporter admitted. "Heard it a lot. Just don't reckon I'm good enough for heaven, that's all."

"No one is," I said. "We are all sinners. Just believe in him. That's all it takes. You believe in Jesus–let him be your Lord–and that's all there is to it. You pray, and he'll answer. Call out his name–Jesus– and he'll listen."

"Sorry, friend. But I can't do that. It would mean giving up too much. And I like what I'm doing now," the reporter answered.

"But he'll free you from all that. He'll give you a new life of joy. It may not happen all at once, but you'll see. He'll make a new heart inside you. He will."

"You make a good preacher, friend. But, right now, this is one customer who isn't buying."

"I'm not selling anything. And the only cost is your heart."

"You ought to start a church, my friend. That's what you ought to do."

Sun Yat-sen's niece took a hot towel and wrapped it about the reporter's face.

And at that moment, Sun Yat-sen scuttled into the room. I did not want to stir up harsh memories, so I reluctantly let the conversation end and prayed that my words had an impact this day. While I have neglected God and my faith for a long time, this conversation allowed me to taste the sweetness of the truth again.

Upriver, several miles north of Angels Camp, was a wide, deep pool, nearly a half mile in length. Joshua scrambled and thrashed his way through the thick underbrush, pushing aside the heavy brambles that at times obscured the path. He stopped at the water's edge and cut down a green sapling. He trimmed the branches and tied a thick thread to the top. He carefully tied a hook at the end of the line. He had only three hooks remaining. There were none to be had in town, so he made certain the knots were tight.

Fastening a bit of meat to the barb, he lowered the hook into the water. Joshua had tried fishing up and down the river with little success, yet found that this quiet pool teemed with fish. The waters by his claim ran too swiftly, he thought, for fish to stay. He looked about at the green thickness on both banks. No miners had yet disturbed the scene. Joshua knew that the deeper the water was, the harder it would be to extract what gold might be found. He was sure that in the future, some miner would try it. Until then, once a week, Joshua would spend a few hours fishing at the spot. He had grown so tired of dried meats and camp bread that a fish would be a most tasty diversion.

After only a few minutes, Joshua turned to the bank. He pulled the hook from the water and set the rod at his feet. There was a loud rustle and snap from the bank to his left. He turned quickly to face the sound. It was never wise to be unprepared. Joshua reasoned that if it was someone wanting to rob him, he could leap into the cold waters and swim quickly downriver.

The brush parted and for a moment, Joshua thought he was seeing an apparition.

A shaft of light fell upon the intruder.

Quen-li stumbled from the underbrush into the bright sun. A moment later, she saw Joshua, and she attempted to stifle a scream of fright as she turned to flee.

"Wait!" he called out. "Quen-li! It's Joshua! I won't hurt you."

As she spun about, she slipped on the moist earth and stumbled, falling to her knees.

Before she could stand, Joshua was at her side, holding out his hand, bending to offer her help.

She raised one hand to her mouth and one to her chest.

"I not to come . . . if this is land of . . . for you," she said pointing at Joshua.

Joshua took her hand and helped her up.

"This isn't my land, Quen-li. I just come here to fish."

She took a step back, trying to peer around Joshua. It was obvious she did not know what he meant.

"Fish. You know . . . catch the fish that live in the water. Cook them."

He tried to imitate a fish with his hands and then pointed to the water.

After a short moment, Quen-li smiled broadly and nodded.

"You call . . . fishing?"

"Fishing," Joshua repeated. "See there, on the riverbank. That's the pole I use to catch them."

Quen-li nodded, then softly repeated, "Fishing."

Neither spoke for a moment or moved.

Joshua stared while trying his best not to be obvious or threatening. Her black hair was tied at her neck with a deep green ribbon, and the hair glistened and flowed over her shoulders. She wore a dress made of the plainest cloth—the color of dust, Joshua thought. Yet in its simplicity, Joshua found it enticing. The garment buttoned at her throat in a most delicate manner, and perhaps because of the warmth of the day, the top two buttons were undone. A small triangle of her throat was open to the sun. She had pushed the long sleeves of the dress up past her elbows, and her skin, white as a china cup in a fancy restaurant, stood in stark contrast to the greenings all around her. Her dark eyes found Joshua's for a long moment.

As she stumbled through the brush, she had dropped her woven basket. Handfuls of leaves and berries had tumbled to the ground.

Joshua saw the spilled basket, knelt, and began to retrieve the contents of the basket.

"Oh no," Quen-li called out. "Not for man to do. For Quen-li."

She knelt beside and tried to snatch the spilled contents before Joshua could.

In a moment, the leaves and twigs and berries were back in the basket. Quen-li stood and cradled the basket in her arms and looked down at her feet.

"Quen-li," Joshua said slowly, "I am just trying to help. I mean no harm."

Without looking up, she replied, her voice not more than a whisper, "Man work. Woman work. This woman work."

Joshua bent over to see her eyes.

"Women's work? What is?"

She pointed to the basket.

"Here," she said, indicating the riverbank with a sweep of her hand, "gather plant and berries and . . . for . . . for not sick."

He screwed up his face for a moment, then nodded. "Oh, you're collecting plants to make medicines."

Quen-li nodded.

Joshua pointed to the basket.

"And what are they for?"

She pulled out a red berry.

"Boil in water . . . drink."

She touched her head and offered a pained look.

"For headaches?" he asked, and she nodded.

"These for . . . ," she said, holding up a shock of leaves and patting her stomach.

"These for . . ." she bit at one leaf, then offered it to Joshua. He took it and tasted.

"Mint," he said with a smile.

She nodded, then looked away.

"Quen-li must go. Quen-li not here with man."

She turned to walk away.

"Wait," Joshua called his heart quickening. He suddenly realized that he was alone with Quen-li, without interference of customers and her irate father. "Do you come here often?"

She stopped and turned, a puzzled look on her face.

"Here," he said, pointing to the river. "Do you come here to gather plants every day?"

She narrowed her eyes.

"Not next day. Next day again," she said holding two fingers up. "Two days, then I come."

And with that, she slipped back into the brush, leaving Joshua to stare after her, all but forgetting about his fishing for the day.

And just as she turned, Joshua thought that he saw a smile light upon her face.

FROM THE JOURNAL OF JOSHUA QUITTNER
AUGUST 1850

I am perplexed and amazed and delighted. Quen-li stumbled onto my fishing hole, and my world seems transformed. Seeing her at her father's shop is like seeing a beautiful creature trapped in a small cage. Seeing her by the riverbank is like seeing that same creature wild and unfettered. We spoke for only a moment, yet I am certain that she would like me to be there as she gathers her plants and berries. I know I want this as well.

As I write this, I am aware, well aware, that she is a Chinese woman. I know that the mere thought of being with such a person would cause gasps of shock and despair back in Shawnee. And the same type people would cluck their tongues in California as well.

But to me, Quen-li is no "Chinawoman." She is just a woman of great grace and beauty and innocence. I know what my father and mother would say, but I do not care. I have let my heart harden after these long and painful months. I believe that a person like Quen-li can break that hardness.

Am I simply hoping for too much? Am I looking at this like a greenhorn looks at a vein of fool's gold? Am I seeing too much in Quen-li's eyes?

Perhaps.

But my heart is thawing. And I believe it is because of her.

***

Two days later, Joshua paced the shoreline. His timepiece no longer worked, so he was not certain how long he had been waiting.

Did she come here early? I've been here since nearly dawn. I couldn't have missed her. Perhaps she didn't know the right words to tell me a different date.

Joshua fretted and worried as he paced.

After all that I have been through and endured, the few minutes I have spent with Quen-li are the most precious and meaningful.

He stopped, tilted his ear, willing the snap of twigs and leaves to fill the air. And to his delight, he heard the sound of someone approaching. In a moment, Quen-li emerged from the dense underbrush, her basket nearly filled. She turned to Joshua immediately, a smile on her face. Perhaps by habit, she averted her eyes as she approached.

"Good sir, I am . . . happy today."

It was Joshua's turn to brighten.

"Quen-li, it is I who am the most happy. I was worried that you might not be here, and I would have been most sad if I could not see you today."

He realized that his words were hurried and that Quen-li might not understand them all. But he could not easily contain his joy.

"Are you finished collecting your plants?" Joshua asked. "I see that your basket is nearly full."

She paused for a moment. "Yes, basket is full. I done."

She turned to him and looked in his eyes.

"You want me leave . . . now basket full?"

Joshua waved his hands. "No, Quen-li, I do not want you to leave. I am happy that you are done. Perhaps we can sit and talk more today than we did the last time we were here."

Quen-li finally smiled.

"Good. I like talk. More time."

Joshua pointed over to a shaded spot on the bank. He brought a thick blanket and laid it on the ground.

"Over here, Quen-li. Perhaps we can talk. I brought some food for lunch."

As he spoke, he realized that the rough food he brought—beans and day-old biscuits and two bottles of cider—were unrefined in comparison to the more delicate Quen-li.

But she smiled and nodded as he showed her the food. She sat down on the edge of the blanket. Joshua was reminded of a butterfly alighting on a flower.

The next hour passed in a heartbeat, Joshua thought. Despite the obvious problems in language and ability to communicate, he felt that she knew him better after this short time than did any woman anywhere. She laughed with an unexpected ease.

Quen-li brushed a few crumbs from the blanket. She looked away for a long moment.

"Quen-li wrong to be here. Father would be angry," she said softly.

"Your father does not know about this?" Joshua asked, already knowing that her father had no knowledge of this meeting.

"No, he not allow you and me. Quen-li know this wrong. Quen-li a Chinese woman. This wrong."

Joshua felt his heart break. He reached out, and without considering the gravity of what he was doing, he took her hand in his and, with his other hand, lifted her chin so he might see her eyes. He knew his eyes were filled with joy, and for a brief moment, Quen-li's eyes were filled with the same joy. He knew that they both felt the same way about each other.

"This is not wrong, Quen-li. It is not. For the first time in my life, I am with someone who seems so unaffected and so innocent and so gentle. This is not wrong. You must believe me. You are in America now, and this is not wrong."

She tried to smile. In her eyes, Joshua could now see a dark cloud of sadness. He squeezed her hand. It was the first time he had held her hand, and it was the purest and softest hand he had ever known.

"It will be all right, Quen-li. Everything will be all right." Joshua promised her, yet he was certain that he did not know how.

FROM THE JOURNAL OF JOSHUA QUITTNER

AUGUST 1850

I am overjoyed and heartbroken at the same time. Such a swirl of feelings.

We spent nearly an hour together by the river. She looked at my humble food like it was a banquet set for royalty. She laughed, and as she tilted her head back, I felt the music that my father told me about so long ago—the music he heard when he first met the young girl who would become his wife—the music of her laughter is that what charmed him so.

And yet as I am captivated, I also see reality.

Her father would erupt if he were to know about this. I know how he views Christians and how he would view his daughter and me. What would he do if he did find out about us? Would he send Quen-li back to China? Could I follow her there?

I look back at my life and have discovered the truth in my actions.

Yes, I was in love with Hannah for many years, comparing everyone with her. She was the first love in my heart, and as I have read, no man forgets his first love. But my love for her is to be forever unrequited—and that is for the best. She and I were too different, and our paths were destined only to cross briefly.

My heart breaks over what I put poor Constance through. I viewed her as simply a loose end, and I desired to fill my life as others said I should, with a calling and then a wife. I toyed with the poor child, and I regret the pain I must have caused her.

But this is different. Yes, Quen-li and I are from two different worlds. But that matters neither to the heart nor to the soul. She smiles, and my heart leaps. She laughs, and I am lost in joy.

Does not God look beyond the skin and eyes of a man and woman? Does he not see only the heart and soul? If that be true—and I know it to be so—then God will be pleased at this love that is forming in my heart.

I have stared at these words for many moments.

I pray that what I have written is true.

The days between our meeting are like an eternity, yet the moments we have together rush past like a cooling summer breeze. I help her gather her plants and leaves. We talk. We laugh. Every moment, I grow deeper and deeper in love with this woman. . . . Yet for all my passion, I have not spoken of it to her.

I ask myself at the end of every day: Why?

Am I afraid that she will laugh and turn away? Am I afraid that she will embrace in agreement? Am I afraid of what the people in town will say—or her father—or my parents?

I suspect some of all that is true.

My heart is overflowing, yet my tongue is mute.

Perhaps today will be the day I tell her of my true feelings.

<hr />

Joshua could scarce remember a period of his life that was more idyllic, more wonderful than the past several weeks. Twice a week, he and Quen-li would meet by the river. They would share food— sometimes what she brought, sometimes what he brought. He would talk, and she would sit there, demure and quiet, listening to his every word. She would tell him of her home in China and their harrowing trip across the ocean.

Their meetings were fleeting, never more than an hour, for Quen-li had to return to her father's shop. If she tarried, his suspicions would be aroused.

They would sit, an arm's length apart, and look out at the river, watching the cold waters slip by. Occasionally she would turn to him and smile. He would look into her eyes and feel as if he were drowning in them.

One day the sun was nearing its zenith, and Quen-li knelt at the edge of the blanket, readying herself to leave.

The sunlight dappled down on her through the trees and, like diamonds, sparkled off her black hair. She looked up at Joshua. Behind her faint smile, he thought he saw a hint of sadness. Perhaps it was wistfulness.

This is the most perfect day I have ever experienced, he thought. *I have been in the company of a wonderful, beautiful woman who has neither guile nor deceit. It is the most perfect of times. My heart is as full as I can imagine it being.*

He sat up.

But she is a Chinese woman. What would others say?

His own words roiled in his heart.

Convention be done with. I will no longer wait until others approve. I will do what my heart calls me to do.

He leaned over, took her chin in his hand, and lifted her face to his. Her eyes were wide. Her lips parted. He bent and touched his lips to hers. She let herself fall against him, and he wrapped his arms around her surprisingly small frame. He held her tight to him for a long moment. Her arms nearly encircled his broad back.

Then he leaned toward her again. He kissed her again, and her hands grabbed at his shoulder, pulling him tight. The magnificent silence of their kiss was interrupted by a haunting shriek. A hawk plummeting from the heavens swooped down on the glassy river and plucked out a fish, snapping and swinging, and carried it off to its nest.

Quen-li watched the hawk circle higher into the sky, then turned to Joshua. She averted her eyes.

"Quen-li must go. Quen-li wrong. Father most angry."

⚜

The skies were gray and overcast the next time they met. Quen-li quietly emerged from the brush to a waiting Joshua. He reached out to her. She took his hand, yet did not look at him.

295

"Good Joshua," she said, "I have big . . . question."

"You can ask me anything, Quen-li. Anything at all."

He looked down at Quen-li. Her eyes were brimming with tears.

"I think about this when I first heard you talk about your God. When you talk to that man."

"What man?"

"The man in shop . . . man who writes in papers."

Suddenly Joshua recalled the conversation. He had urged the young man to reconsider God and faith. He had no idea that Quen-li had been listening.

She did not raise her head but whispered so Joshua had to strain to hear. "My father hate your God. But I do not. I see your eyes. I see joy. I see . . . future. I see happy. I see man who is . . . content . . . is that word right? . . . I see a man free from want. That is what I want. I do. Is that promise of your God?"

Joshua nodded.

"It is, Quen-li. I know I have not spoken much of God to you–because of your father–but I try to live my life as God would have me live."

"That is what Quen-li see. Quen-li want that too."

She looked up at Joshua, her face aglow. "I think God put his hand on my heart. I feel warm there first time ever. Like a new heart. I pray like you said. It was that day. I remember that day."

She looked away, then back at him.

"I want to ask–is that all I must do? To go to heaven like you said? Is there more to do? I want to be in heaven if you go to heaven, too."

Joshua suddenly realized again why God called him: so that others would see God's truth reflected in him. So that others would come to knowledge of him–all Joshua needed to do was to speak his name.

He leaned closer. "That is all you must do. Accept him and his love, and promise to serve him."

She smiled. "I can do, good sir . . . Joshua. I can do."

Joshua embraced Quen-li tenderly, feeling like a great protector. She nestled her head against his chest and slipped her arms about him, drawing him closer. For many moments they stood still in that embrace, holding onto each other, drawing strength from their brief union.

She looked up at him with a grateful smile. She blinked away a tear.

Then darkness passed over her eyes like a thundercloud preceding a storm. She looked away, her eyes staring at the ground.

"You not tell my father," she said in a small voice, pleading and tearful. "He beat me for dishonoring ancestors. You not tell him."

Joshua struggled for a word, any word.

How could this be kept a secret?

Then he nodded.

Angels Camp
September 1850

As Joshua made his way to town, he was whistling.

God has been working on my heart all this time. He has not forsaken me. And I shall not forsake him. All I ask is that he guide me and show me what to do now.

Strapped to the mule were two large canvas bags—nearly all the gold Joshua had unearthed over the last two months. He'd wire most of it to his bank in San Francisco and exchange the rest for bills.

His thoughts swirled.

Should I begin a church here? Could I go home, and will anyone be able to forgive me for what I have done? he asked himself over and over.

A small Bible lay in his pocket. It was one of two copies that he had carried with him from Shawnee. It would be his gift to Quen-li. Even though she could not yet read English, he reasoned, he would have the time to teach her. Everyone had the right to read God's Word.

As he turned along the last bend in the river before town, he thought of the arguments Quen-li's father might have to this arrangement. *Well, if she can read,* Joshua reasoned, *she will be more valuable to the business. She could write letters for him and do those sorts of things. And if needed, I could pay for the time I'll need to teach her how to read.* He smiled to himself. *After all, when a man leads a person to God, there is a sort of responsibility that follows. You can't just show a person the Truth and then leave her alone to figure it out.*

As he made his way on the mule, worry crossed his thoughts.

She did say that her father would be angry about this, that what she did would be dishonoring to her ancestors. But what do they have to do with it? It's not as if one needs to consult with the departed to approve of one's plans and beliefs.

Then he stopped walking.

Maybe they do–in China. Maybe they believe in some strange practice like that.

He flicked at the reins. The mule snorted, and they continued.

No . . . that cannot be. After all, this is America, and we don't have to believe in superstitions like that. Quen-li should be able to believe as she sees fit. And if she believes in God Almighty, then her father will have to accept that.

Joshua made his way to the assayer's office. In a short time the gold was weighed, and Joshua was several thousand dollars richer.

"What are you goin' to do with your gold, son?" the assayer asked. "Of all the miners in this town, you're the only one who ain't spent what he found on drink and women. You savin' it up for some big carryin's on, maybe? You goin' to spend it all at once?"

How do I answer him? Joshua thought. *Do I tell him the truth?*

"I'm looking for a way to use this to serve God. I worked hard for this, and I lost a good friend finding it. I want this money to amount to something important."

"You goin' to build a church?"

Joshua's voice was light, but his words were serious. "Maybe I will. Angels Camp needs a church, doesn't it?"

The assayer laughed. "That it does, Mr. Quittner. That it does."

A crowd had gathered outside Yat-sen's Tonsorial Emporium. Joshua gauged the Chinese man's success by how ornate and gilded each new sign became. This newest one was as tall and wide as a man and was painted in reds and golds with great flourishes.

But the sign was not the reason for the crowds. Joshua elbowed his way toward the front door, the crowd now three or four men deep. He craned his neck. They were all gathered about a hand-written poster, plastered to the store's front wall.

"Did you hear what that crazy Chinese fellow's goin' to do?" a man asked of no one in particular.

"Can't believe it myself," came an answer.

"You goin' to be here for it?"

"Wouldn't miss it for anythin'. May do some biddin' myself. She'd be a pleasant little morsel to have for dinner."

Joshua called out, "Bidding? Bidding for what?"

A short man with a fox pelt wrapped about his neck turned and spoke. "The Chinese fellow . . . he's sellin' that girl. Quen-li, she's called. The pretty one. Well, it ain't sellin' exactly. He's offerin' her as a wife for a man who brings the highest dowry."

"Land sakes! Ain't that backward?" someone asked. "Ain't the woman supposed to be offerin' money for a man?"

"You wish it were that way," another voice called out. "Ain't the way Chinese do it, I guess. And as for that pretty one—well, I bet she's worth an awfully big dowry."

"But ain't she his flesh and blood?"

"Them Chinese don't figure like that. Boys are worth somethin'. Girls ain't worth much at all. Yat-sen makes a few dollars, and he gets happy."

"But ain't that illegal, like?"

"Here? Who's goin' to stop him? You seen any sheriff ridin' by lately?"

Crude laughter answered the question. Joshua's gut tightened. He scanned the poster.

TO THE HIGHEST BIDDER AT FAIR AUCTION
A WIFE OF THE HIGHEST STANDARDS

Midway down a list of more than a dozen names, one stood out like it was on fire.

QUEN-LI: A MOST BEAUTIFUL AND TALENTED
CHINESE WOMAN. AN EXCELLENT WORKER, SKILLED
IN PLEASURE. IN GOOD HEALTH AND SOUND MIND.
A BARGAIN FOR THE HIGHEST PRICE.

In an instant, Joshua's joy crashed about him like a falling star in
the night sky. He knew there was a great shortage of women in this
region. He was certain no one would think asking for a dowry would
be considered slave trading. At least no one was calling it that—but
that was what it was. Joshua knew no one would truly care if a Chinese man sold a daughter or not. She would be a rare prize, and Mr.
Yat-sen would be thousands and thousands of dollars richer.

As Joshua stood there in the knot of men, each jostling him,
Joshua felt a tremor in his heart—as if the very muscle were breaking.

CHAPTER TWENTY-THREE

Angels Camp
September 1850

QUEN-LI! *Auctioned as a . . . as a concubine! That
cannot be!*

Joshua shouldered his way into Yat-sen's shop. Despite the crowd
outside, there was no more than a handful of men inside. Mr. Yat-
sen was nowhere to be seen. Normally Joshua would have stood at
the entrance and waited. He was not a man who bustled into places
ahead of others. Yet today he knew he must. He walked toward the
rear of the shop and pushed past the silken curtain. Quen-li would
always come through this curtain when called.

She must be back here.

There was no sign of her. In the corner of the dark room was a
carved figure on a small table. A stick of incense burned, and the
smoke snaked its way through the air. A single silk robe hung on a
nail. A pair of slippers sat side by side next to a thin padded mat. A
coarse blanket, no finer than a horse covering, lay neatly folded at
the foot of the bedding.

"Quen-li!" he called out. The room owned no hiding places, no
spot where she might be secreted.

A narrow door opened. Quen-li entered from the outside, causing the smoky incense to swirl.

She bowed.

"You do not have to bow to me, Quen-li. I am not your master," Joshua said softly.

She remained bowed as she closed the door behind her.

"I am servant to you. I must bow," she answered.

He touched her shoulder lightly, feeling her slight frame tremble beneath the weight of his hand. With the lightest of pressure, he raised her from her bow.

"Look at me, Quen-li," he said with a velvet whisper. "Please do not bow to me."

Her dark eyes found his, and she offered the barest of nods to indicate that she understood.

"You a noble man," she replied. "And kind. Most good of any man Quen-li know."

Joshua struggled to find the words to convey his outrage and yet hide his concern over her fate.

"I am just a simple man, Quen-li. And I want to say . . ."

"Do not speak now. Quen-li speak. Quen-li's new heart make her tell father of God inside. I pray to my God, and he say that I must tell father. Father angry. He beat Quen-li. Now he will send Quen-li away."

Joshua held her hands tenderly. Tears welled up in her eyes.

"Father right to do this. Quen-li with God. Quen-li happy now. You good man, Joshua. You show me God."

Joshua felt close to crying.

"Quen-li . . . I cannot allow this to happen. It was all my fault. Your father must not do this. He must not."

"It is right of father to do as he wish. Quen-li only simple girl."

Quen-li bowed her head. "I thank you, Joshua sir. You save me. You talk of God, and Quen-li hear. What you say is true. Jesus now in Quen-li's heart. Quen-li see heaven someday. Quen-li know joy not found here . . . found in heaven."

She looked up and smiled through her tears. Then slowly she lifted her hand and reached out to Joshua.

"I am filled with joy by what you say, Quen-li. That you know Jesus is such wonderful news. There can be no better words that anyone can hear."

She nodded, her tears coming freely now. She took his hand in hers tightly, her fingers barely stretching to contain Joshua's bigger palm. Next she placed her other hand over his, as if she were praying.

"You save me, good Joshua sir. You save me."

He shook his head. "It is not me, Quen-li, but God. God is the one who saved you. I only said the words."

She bowed, drawing his hand to her cheek. He felt the warmth of her flesh and the wetness of her tears.

"You say words, and my soul saved. No matter what happen to me. I thank you, good Joshua sir."

Overwhelmed with emotion, Joshua knew he'd never experienced anything as tender and heartfelt as this moment. Others had come to Christ at his urging, yet none had seemed as sincere and childlike as Quen-li. He put his hand under her chin and lifted her head.

As he looked into her face, another emotion exploded within his chest. It was not simple gratitude to God for allowing him this privilege. It was something more personal.

Is this what real love feels like? He tried to dismiss the thought. *I'm just grateful and overwhelmed. How could I love this woman? . . . But if it's not love . . . then what is it?* Joshua's heart called out.

A door crashed open. From the other side of the curtain came a torrent of foreign words, cutting the silence harshly. A glass jar smashed to the floor.

Then there was a shout and another crash. Quen-li dropped Joshua's hands and cowered backward until she was in the corner of the room.

With a shriek, the curtain was torn and fluttered to the floor. The diminutive Mr. Yat-sen seemed to fill the entire doorway. His coat was unbuttoned, his face red and florid, his long black hair unkempt, as if tossed by the wind. His eyes were glazed with venom.

"You!" he shouted, pointing a trembling finger at Joshua. "You devil! You leave here and never come back!"

Joshua held up his hands, palms open, his face a mask of surprised panic.

"But I have done nothing, Mr. Yat-sen. I was only looking for Quen-li. We were just talking."

Mr. Yat-sen seemed to expand even larger as he jumped inside the tiny room.

"Talking! Talking!"

"I did not touch Quen-li. I have done nothing to dishonor her," Joshua replied, his words coming fast. "We have only been alone for a moment!"

Mr. Yat-sen glared at Joshua.

"You not touch her like man touches woman," he spat out. "You touch her heart. You devil!"

Mr. Yat-sen stepped closer, and Joshua edged sideways toward the back door.

"You preacher man, no?"

Joshua stammered, "I am."

"You tell customer about this God?"

Joshua's thoughts spun. "Yes . . . yes I did."

"You tell Quen-li about this God? You tell her? She say this God in her heart! You devil!"

Joshua bowed his head slightly. "Yes, that's what happened. But it is not from a devil, sir. This is from God—it is a good thing."

"You devil. I tell you not talk of your God in my shop. Your God destroy family. I lose brother to your God. My family in great disgrace. I must leave home and come to this terrible place. Now you come here and tell daughter of your God. That right?"

Joshua nodded.

"Then you devil."

Mr. Yat-sen raised his hand as if readying to strike his daughter. She whimpered, cowering further, but did not attempt to flee.

"I not strike you again," he snarled, aiming a bony finger at her. "You not worth to strike." Then he spun back to Joshua. "Your God is why she must leave. She dishonor me. She dishonor family and ancestors. I let another man have her. He not be disgraced like me."

Mr. Yat-sen smiled bitterly.

"Your God cause this. Your God no god but devil."

And with that Quen-li slumped to the floor. Mr. Yat-sen stepped between Joshua and his daughter.

"You leave this place. You never return. Never!"

"But . . . but . . ."

"I shoot you for trespass. I buy gun."

He lifted up his jacket and displayed a shiny black revolver, stuck in his waistband. Unaware that the gun grease had stained his shirt, Mr. Yat-sen put his hand on the butt end and pulled it out, waving its barrel in the air.

"I shoot devil if you come back."

Joshua looked hard at Quen-li, who had not moved, then back into the blackness of Mr. Yat-sen's eyes. The man pulled back on the hammer of the pistol. Joshua heard it ratchet into place. He saw the man's finger tighten about the trigger. Joshua swallowed once, then stepped back, feeling for the doorknob behind him. Seconds later he was in the alley and alone.

Russian River

Joshua made his way back to his claim as if navigating through a dense fog. He did not see the sun or the blue sky, nor did he hear the river's constant grumble or the sound of the birds. He did not even answer the miners who called out a greeting to him from the riverbank below.

Images of Quen-li being towered over by a sweating, grunting, hulk of a miner who bought her narrowed his vision to the mere step in advance of where he stood.

The words echoed in his mind, like the clarion call of a bell on a cold night when its vibrations would hang on the air for minutes and minutes.

Joshua was certain these words would linger, not for minutes, but for every day that he drew breath upon this earth.

As he stumbled into the cabin, a fat moon hung over the river, reflecting the sparkling waters and illuminating his footsteps. But his eyes saw no beauty that evening. His body felt no rest as he found his bed. His mind found no peace as he closed his eyes and willed a dreamless sleep to swallow him.

The days following saw Joshua shuffle to the river, his eyes locked in a dazed stare, his movements slow as if underwater. He was work-ing by rote, doing what he had done for months and months. He was not aware of the passage of time or the amount of gold flecks he tossed into the bucket. If some missed the mark and fell back to the earth, Joshua did not see the loss, nor did he care.

Nearly a week after being confronted by Mr. Yat-sen, the images of a stricken Quen-li still danced before his eyes. Joshua finally turned from the river, crawled up the bank, and sat, staring off into the distance until the crimson light of a setting sun alerted him to night's approach.

He looked skyward.

"God," he whispered in a broken voice, "have you truly forsaken me? Was I not supposed to tell Quen-li of you? I have not mentioned your name for so long, and then when I do so, a young woman will suffer for the rest of her life. I spoke your name to Giles, and he died. That does not seem fair to me. It doesn't. It isn't."

Joshua stood up.

"I know what the Bible says. I know it all too well. But why punish Quen-li? She is an innocent, God. You must know that. Punish me, not her. Punish me."

The wind carried Joshua's voice down the lonely river.

"A sign, God. Can you give me a sign?"

Falling to his knees, he cradled his head in his hands and began
to weep.

❧❦❧

The "sale" of Quen-li would not occur immediately. Mr. Yat-sen was
a clever merchant. Word would spread quickly. Rich miners from
numerous rivers might be in attendance. Bidding would be acceler-
ated if the sale wasn't held until the full bloom of spring, the time of
thawing over and the season of the inflaming of men's passions.

The moon had risen by the time Joshua returned to his cabin that
night. He had waited, with the evening chill creeping into his bones,
for a celestial sign, and no sign became visible. He had listened to the
sounds of nature—the cry of the wolf and the shrieks of smaller furry
creatures. He had hoped somehow that God would use his creation
to show him the way.

But nothing had happened. So he'd trudged back to his simple
house and thrown himself wordless onto his bed.

❧❦❧

The following morning a clap of thunder awakened him. He did not
wash or change his clothes but hurried outside. Gazing skyward, he
saw a drab gray covering the sky like a cloak.

He shrugged. *If it rains, I'll get no wetter than I usually do,* he
thought to himself as he slowly made his way to the river.

The thunder and flashes of lightning lit up the sky east of him, and
the rain fell only in angry pockets.

Nearing noon, he shouldered his sluice twelve yards upriver,
almost in the shadow of the tall precipice at the far edge of his claim.
Previously, working under the rocky outcropping had made him nervous, but now Joshua did not care. Mindlessly he picked at a loose
rock, and a cascade of gravel and mud fell at his feet. He chipped at
the surface of the precipice wall.

A peal of thunder, miles upriver, echoed down the canyon. Joshua
stopped as the vibrations of the clap washed over him. He bent,

gripped the pick, and swung again. Another torrent of rock fell to the river's edge.

The bank was narrow here, with only ten or so feet of dry ground remaining between the river's edge and the rock face. There was enough room for one man to walk on both sides of the sluice, but not much more than that.

Another boom shook the canyon. A handful of fat raindrops splattered downward, then no more. Now the sky was the color of wet slate. Again a flash lit up the sky to the north, followed a few seconds later by another rumble of thunder.

He turned away from the river and swung again at the rock face. With this chipping a greater torrent of rock and stone tumbled down. Joshua dropped the pick, then ducked and covered his head with his arms. A handful of stones rattled about his shoulders. There was a stonelike groan, then a watery silence. He evaluated the rock face towering above him.

It has been here for years and hasn't fallen yet was his only thought.

He swung again, and a rock dislodged and fell toward his feet. He jumped to one side. As he turned, from the corner of his vision he saw the unmistakable glittering of gold from the wall of rock, about as high as his shoulder. He scrambled back to the wall and scraped off a thin covering of rock.

There, beneath his palms, pulsed a vein of gold. The nuggets and flakes were as wide as a man's two outspread hands, and ran for almost twelve feet.

Joshua's heart quickened. While he had found gold before, it was never in such abundance and so densely packed. He ran to retrieve his bucket and began to claw the nuggets from the wall. Soon he had filled the bucket to the brim.

He had taken no more than a quarter of the exposed gold.

And how much more must lie behind this? This is the Midas vein! There must be buckets and buckets of gold here!

Scrabbling at the loose wall of rock exposed more and more of the vein. Joshua dropped the nuggets at his feet, the bucket overflowing. As he worked, beads of sweat formed at his brow in spite of the now chilly air. He worked on, breathing hard, but didn't stop as he usually did. Such a find made a man's pulse race. And, while Joshua's soul was in pain, the lure of the glistening gold began to wash the hurt away.

Some time later, he leaned back, trying to catch his breath. The bucket now stood at his feet with a large tumble of gold beside it. As his breath slowed, he wiped his brow with a dirty and wet sleeve.

Just then he turned his head. From the very edge of his hearing he began to notice a liquid rumble. He almost felt it through his boots.

It's just the thunder, he told himself.

But the rumbling grew louder. He faced the wall and grabbed at a nugget the size of a large apple. His fingers dug into the nugget. He felt the soft metal almost give way to his fingernails. He pulled and tugged, struggling with the rock around it.

Finally, with a cascade of loose rocks, the nugget gave way, and he had his prize.

Almost without thinking, he lowered his arm and let the nugget drop near the bucket. There was more gold to be taken.

But the nugget did not clink as expected. It splashed.

Joshua blinked once, then became aware. The river had risen to his boot heels in the matter of a few minutes. The watery hiss grew louder. He leaned out and looked upriver as best as he could. The sky to the east was darker and now pocked with flashes of angry light. The dirt-laden river churned about his feet. And in the brief time it took to look upriver, the river rose past his ankles.

In that moment, he knew. He had heard of flash floods before but thought they only happened in dry riverbeds in the desert. Such a calamity could not happen here–especially since it was not raining where he stood.

But it could be raining upstream!

He jumped a foot farther into the rising water. Upriver, perhaps a half mile away, there was a boiling edge to the river.

It's a wall of water!

Joshua bent and grabbed two things: the bucket of gold and the apple-sized nugget. He slipped the nugget into his pocket and began to tug at the sluice, trying, with one hand, to edge it higher along the riverbank.

If I lose this, my mining days are over, he thought wildly.

Now the river was at his kneecaps, and the sluice was knocking its way downriver, an inch at a time at first, then faster as the river rose.

He gave it one last tug, and then the river simply lifted it from the bank and swallowed it.

The water was waist-high now, even at the outer edge. Joshua held the bucket above his head and tried to head downriver–toward the path that led from the riverbank. He stepped out, and the water torrents pushed him back to the rock wall. He pushed again, his feet fighting to stand on the graveled bank. A tree trunk bobbed along in the water, its roots twisting out of the muddy surface, clutching at the air. A root caught Joshua on the shoulder and spun him around. He grabbed at the bucket with both hands.

As he lurched for the gold, the river entered his coat and dragged him closer to the center of the raging maelstrom. He fought back, kicking and panting, both his hands above his head, the bucket raised above him.

A surge of water crashed over him and he began to fall backward, sputtering and thrashing under the violent water. He pulled the bucket to his chest as he went under. He kicked out, and his feet found a slight hold on the ground beneath him. Pushing hard, he bobbed to the surface, but the gold began to drag him back under. He gasped, gulping in air, and looked around.

The river was boiling faster, carrying trees and branches and mining equipment. He turned to the bank, toward where his cabin was, and kicked his legs desperately. Even though he was only a few yards from shore, he made little progress toward safety as the water crashed around him.

A current caught the bucket, as if the river were attempting to reclaim the gold. His shoulder was pulled under, then his head. He yanked back, the muscles at his side screaming out in pain.

"It's my gold!" he shouted at the river as it clawed at him, dragging him farther into the center. Another dozen yards, and he would be in the harshest and deepest part of the river. He ducked under, letting his feet touch the river bottom, then lurched with all his might toward shore. He bobbed to the top, but the current caught the bucket again and turned him around.

"It's my gold!" he screamed again over the wind and lightning.

Just upstream, where he had been digging, the floodwaters tore at the rock, tumbling boulder-sized pieces into the waters. Joshua shook his head to clear it and kicked, using his one free arm to head to shore.

Just a few more steps!

Then, above the shriek of the water, above the powerful liquid cry of the deluge, came a groan, then a splitting, shrill scream. Joshua spun about to see the rock precipice begin to tremble. A second later, the trees atop the cliff began to sway. With a jagged bellow, a rent tore through the rock and earth, and thousands and thousands of tons of rock and earth and trees and stone began to tumble, slowly at first, then more rapidly, into the river below.

Joshua knew he had but one chance. The rocks were already beginning to send out huge waves up and down the river. If he could find a foothold, he could push himself toward shore and save himself and his gold.

He dug down into the water, pushed hard again, and aimed toward shore. As he neared the surface, a submerged limb caught his arm and inched down his bone, cutting through his coat and tearing at his flesh. It nicked the bucket, then caught on the handle.

If I can hold on one minute more!

The bucket began to drag him under. His fingers screamed out in pain. His shoulder pulled and lurched against the current.

If I can just hold on!

The bucket and the limb were dragging him farther into the center of the river, yet he refused to let go. In a moment the surge from the rock slide would be on him, and there would be no way he could fight his way to the safety of the riverbank.

If I can just hold on!

He was yanked under the churning water one more time. He

gasped as his lungs filled with foul liquid. He wanted to cough and come to the surface, but he grappled for the bucket handle with his other hand.

A jagged bolt lit the sky with an angry line, and the air bellowed a response.

As Joshua's head submerged beneath the waves, he screamed out one last time: *This is my gold! This is mine!*

Then all was lost to the storm.

CHAPTER TWENTY-FOUR

Russian River
September 1850

LATER, Joshua would recall this one moment with absolute fidelity–as if the scene were captured in intricate detail on canvas that somehow included the sounds and feelings as well.

He had a vivid sense of being apart from his body and staring down at the boiling river. He saw himself grabbing below the water, holding onto a bucket filled with a yellow metal. He saw the gold swirling about in the river. He watched as he reacted to the pull of the water, as it called him deeper and deeper.

As Joshua watched the scene unfurl, he recalled thinking, as the water caved in about him, *This is my gold. I cannot abandon it.*

And as that thought entered his mind–that he would not abandon a bucket of metal even though holding on would mean his death–he felt a supernatural calm come over him and enter his heart.

Am I willing to give up my life for gold? Does this treasure mean that much to me? Will I die for riches?

He opened his eyes as he turned, trying to swim to the surface. He could go no farther. The water's surface was several feet above him, and he only felt the downward tug on his arms.

He had a singular choice to make.

The dirt-ridden water stung his eyes, and the debris carried by the current bounced off his body, bruising him from head to foot. He closed his eyes, feeling the substantial pull of the gold. He felt it drawing him down, farther and farther.

And he released his fingers.

The gold bucket was carried off like a kite in a March wind. He let the waters carry him, almost effortlessly now, without the heavy weight of the gold. He spun about, pushed his feet underneath him, and kicked against the river bottom.

It took only a moment as he stroked and kicked his way to the shore. He grabbed at a stout limb wedged into the rocks on shore. A huge surge swept over him—the surge caused by the rock slide. For a minute the waters cascaded over him, tearing at his arms, slashing at his legs.

He clung more tightly. The limb strained and bent but held against the pressure.

Slowly the surge washed downriver, and the torrent eased. Joshua marshaled his strength, grabbed at the limb, and with one mighty pull, threw himself toward the riverbank. Splashing and kicking, he found himself in knee-deep water about a mile downriver from where he had been lost to the angry current. The water ran dense with debris. Joshua thought he saw a body carried at the surface—a flash of leg and trouser, then nothing. A horse careened his way past in mute agony, his head lurching to stay above the swollen current.

Joshua shut his eyes, trying to clear the image from his mind. He dragged himself to higher ground and stopped midway up the riverbank. He bent over and threw up a great amount of brackish liquid—the liquid he'd swallowed while refusing to let go of the gold.

Battered and bruised, he wiped his face and mouth with a tattered sleeve. His arm throbbed, and blood oozed from a gash beneath his wet coat. He had lost his boots, and his legs ached from the effort of fighting the water. His eyes stung and burned. And when he touched his cheek, his hand came away bloodied.

But I'm alive!

He crawled farther up the bank and threw himself on a patch of wet moss in the lee of a pine. The river would never come this high, he thought, so he lay back and draped his hands over his face.

For a long moment he simply rested. Then what had almost occurred began to become more real.

He had almost squandered his very life for one more bucket of treasure.

He had almost given up his life for gold.

As he imagined what they would have found—a dead, bloated corpse with his hands fused about an empty bucket—Joshua began to tremble. Then he began to sob; great heaving cries racked his body.

He got up on his knees, every muscle crying out in pain, and gazed skyward.

"Thank you, God, for letting me live. Thank you for letting me see how foolish and arrogant I was. Thank you for giving me life once more."

Then he tottered and collapsed onto his side, sliding into a black nothingness.

***

Some time later, Joshua finally found the strength to rise up from his mossy refuge and stumble toward his cabin. The rain, which to this point had fallen upriver, now began to pelt Joshua in earnestness. The large drops began to wash the grime from his body. As he walked, he felt a sense of being reborn, of cleansing from above.

He ached so, and his head spun from the beating the river had issued. But he was alive, and on that fact, his heart rejoiced.

The last hints of sun were slipping from the west as Joshua walked into the clearing. The mule, her eyes wide with terror, saw him and began to bray and kick. Joshua made his way over to her, grabbed the reins, and pulled the mule close, stroking her face. In a moment, the animal settled down.

Joshua turned to his cabin. Before the flood, the cabin had been thirty yards from the edge of the cliff. Now the rock slide had brought the edge of the precipice to within a foot or two of the west wall of the structure. Since the racing river still slammed against the narrowed banks, Joshua realized he must save what he could, for his house could be swept away at any time.

It took less than thirty minutes for Joshua to clean out the cabin. He grabbed his books, his few changes of clothes, his father's Bible, his journal, and a case of personal items. He made numerous trips from the cabin to the mule shed, stacking everything inside. Each time the mule would lean forward and sniff. Not finding food, she would rock back and watch Joshua make another trip.

Night had fallen, and a weary Joshua wrapped himself in the bear-skin and leaned against a wall of the mule shed, protected from the rain by the canvas overhang. Lightning continued to flash, and thunder rumbled about the clearing. Rain would fall in great sheets for an instant, subside to a gentle patter, and then the cycle would continue.

Joshua thought it was near midnight when the lightning began to dance about them. In its staccato light, he saw his cabin shiver. He heard an earthen groan, then a stonelike shriek. With a wooden scream, the cabin tore in half. One part of the structure tumbled into the river. Twelve lightning flashes later, Joshua watched with faint emotion as the rest of his cabin fell into the hungry flow.

As rain pelted his face, he looked heavenward.

"You gave me my life back, Lord. And you have taken my old existence from me. Lord, let me know where you'll have me journey. Show me where I should serve you."

Thunder bowled down the valley, and lightning lit up the hills. Then there was silence—save the splash of the last raindrops.

He whispered, "Show me the way, Lord. Show me the way to go home."

A minute later the mule nudged Joshua in the back with her nose.

❧⚬◈⚬☙

The trip back to Angels Camp was agonizingly slow. The storm and flood had taken perhaps half of the well-worn path that snaked through the trees just above the river. The powerful surge of rain and wind had torn a new course for the river in spots, widening the bends, cutting deep into loose banks of gravel and stone. Trees had been toppled by the wind and water, and for every step downriver, there were a dozen steps of detour–through the woods, down to a new riverbank, up to the ridge.

Until now it had been an easy trip, but within a day it had become a perilous adventure. Joshua knew he'd been blessed with God's protection. He was bruised and cut in a number of places but had suffered no grievous or life-threatening injuries. As he trudged downriver, he worried about the miners who worked upriver. If they were injured, there would be no easy access to doctors or aid. Those needing help would be on their own for weeks or perhaps months, until the trail was improved.

Joshua had searched for the fellows immediately up and down the river from his claim after the storm. He found no sign of any of them. When the water subsided, all traces of sluices and camps and man's digging had been erased, as if a giant had simply wiped his hand and made man's frail scratchings disappear.

At the outskirts of town, in a meadow that up until now had been devoid of all but wildflowers, tents had appeared. The canvas structures looked disheveled and dirty. Joshua discovered that these were the remnants of the river miners. Of the five hundred men who had journeyed upriver from Angels Camp to find gold, only a score or so was still alive.

Angels Camp

Joshua walked slowly through the tent city, nodding to the men he'd known. Their eyes were glazed, as if they saw and comprehended nothing. Usually such a gathering would be loud with boasting and jovial camaraderie. But in this camp hushed conversations started up for a minute, then slipped back to silence again.

The common refrain was, "We lost everything we had. We lost friends. We lost equipment. We were lucky to escape with what you see here. What gold we found is buried under tons of rock and mud."

He sat with a few and offered words of encouragement. He offered to pray, and they gratefully accepted.

As he knelt in that meadow and bowed his head, most everyone else stopped to listen.

Joshua closed his eyes.

"Lord, we offer thanks that these men's lives have been spared. We offer thanks for your protection. We pray for those who are lost. We do not understand all your ways, but we know that if we believe, then our lives are yours to do with as you will. We grieve for our losses. We grieve for families who await the return of the good men who are dead and will only know heartbreak. We ask that you provide them comfort and peace. We know that your treasure is not to be found here on earth. You offer a different reward–an eternal one–to all those who will serve you. If this is a way of telling us not to pursue earthly treasures, then so be it. Let those who will hear, understand. Let those who understand, obey."

Joshua tried to think of more words that might be needed or appropriate, but none came. So he softly said, "Amen."

A chorus of rough amens followed. He looked up and found tears in many eyes. A man kneeling close to Joshua clapped a hand on his shoulder.

"You're Joshua Quittner, right?"

Joshua nodded.

"Then I know you're a preacher man who ain't preachin' anymore. I heard Cleves go on and on about you. You know that Angels Camp ain't got a preacher–and we surely need one now. We could all use a word from the Good Book. Would you think about doin' a sermon here come Sunday?"

"What day is it?" Joshua asked. He had no idea.

A man in back called out, "I believe it's Wednesday."

"I'll be honored. Come Sunday, I'll be back here to say a few words. Maybe kind of a memorial to those who aren't going home."

Even during the flood, when Joshua's life hung in a precarious balance, there was one thing that hung heavy in Joshua's heart. He knew he had to try and set things right with and for Quen-li. He knew he had to attempt to dissuade Mr. Yat-sen from sacrificing his daughter in the name of honoring the past.

Joshua acknowledged that having the cold fingers of death about one's body, and then breaking free, gave a man a true sense of boldness and freedom. He was focused on that one task as he walked into town from the meadow.

He had to talk to Quen-li, if only for a second. He had to tell her how sorry he was for what was happening to her. He had to tell her that God would provide for her needs. He had to try and give her a copy of the Bible.

That's what he *had* to do.

What he *wanted* to do is tell her how much she meant to his heart—even though they were from different cultures and had shared only a few moments together.

He knew it was foolish, but he could not deny his heart. After coming so close to death in the river, Joshua knew that every minute left to him needed to be savored and treasured. He would not have his soul in pain over this as well as the turmoil he'd caused his parents and his church.

That Wednesday, as he made his way to Yat-sen's Tonsorial Emporium, Joshua began to pray—for wisdom, for guidance, for resolution to this sordid affair.

No father should sell a daughter because of religion. That's wrong, and I need to set the impetuous Chinese man straight. Her faith cannot be compromised for the ways of their culture.

His boots sounded loud as he made his way up the steps. He opened the door, and the familiar scents of jasmine, pine, and other exotic fragrances assailed him. Joshua could not help but close his eyes and breathe deeply, trying to wash away the smell of death.

Then he heard a click. He snapped his eyes open. No more than twelve feet away was Mr. Yat-sen, a pistol wavering in his hand.

"I said you never return. I said I shoot if you come back!"

"Mr. Yat-sen, please," Joshua pleaded, "I simply want to talk to you. What you are doing with Quen-li is wrong. There is no need to do such a horrible thing."

Mr. Yat-sen's face twisted into a grimace. A vein in his neck pulsed. "Horrible thing *I* do! *I* do? I do no horrible thing! *You* do horrible thing!"

Joshua held up his hands at shoulder level and placed his palms outward. From the corner of his eye, he saw Quen-li kneeling at the side of the chair where he had spent so many pleasurable moments. He watched a smile light up her face as she saw him, then be replaced with sheer panic as her father raised the weapon and pointed it at Joshua.

"Mr. Yat-sen," Joshua continued, "I did not attempt to do anything wrong with Quen-li. She innocently overheard me talking as I explained about our God and finding one's way to heaven. I did not do this intentionally to lead your daughter astray. Surely there is a way that Quen-li can stay with her family. Doing this to your daughter is a most terrible thing."

Mr. Yat-sen bellowed like a wounded animal whose foot had been snapped tight in a toothed metal trap. He pulled the trigger back and thrust the pistol forward at Joshua. The barrel wavered in the air like a mad bumblebee.

"She no daughter!" he screamed. "You make her turn back on ancestors. I lose face. Family disgraced. No child spits on parents and grandparents. You think that not horrible? It worst thing child can do—dishonor ancestors. There no cure. You cause her to be dead to us. She of no use."

Joshua wanted to fall to his knees and grovel. "But Mr. Yat-sen, surely there is another way."

"No other way," the man yelled, then closed his eyes and pulled hard on the trigger.

The gun discharged with a loud bark, and the bullet whizzed so close to Joshua's ear that he could feel the air rush past. A lamp on the wall behind him exploded in a shower of glass fragments, scattering shards of deadly rain about the room.

"I say I shoot you for trespass. I mean it. I shoot again if you not leave now!"

Quen-li burst into a wail. "Please, good sir Joshua! Please leave! Do not be shot! Do not be shot for Quen-li!"

Unlike the rest of the customers and employees who had slumped to the floor at the gun's sound and were cowering there, Quen-li stood, one hand to her heart, one hand to her throat.

"Please leave! You must!" she implored him.

Mr. Yat-sen spun about and pointed the gun at his daughter.

"Silence!" he screamed. "You not say one word! You have no right!" The man looked over his shoulder at Joshua. "You not leave, and I shoot her as well!"

Joshua hesitated only a second, then stepped backward and bolted to the door, scrabbling for the handle, hoping and praying he could get away before Mr. Yat-sen shot him or his daughter or both of them.

Joshua had never felt less like preaching a sermon. After facing Mr. Yat-sen, he ran to the edge of town, until he was nearly out of breath. It took an hour before he regained a sense of calm. He found another establishment that offered hot baths and a room at one of the new hotels. It took a long scrubbing, but at last he felt a slight return to normalcy. He changed into clean clothing and returned to his room.

During the next few days he prayed, read the Scriptures, and worked on his short sermon. Yet even as he did this, his soul and his heart were in confusion and anguish. He realized with a start that, since Harvard, nothing in his life had truly felt right and ordered. He had turned to God, he told himself, and God had rewarded him with another serving of bewildering chaos. This time it was not simply hurt feelings or a jilted romance. It was that a woman's life truly hung in the balance because of his claims about the power of God.

That Sunday Joshua stood before a gathering of seventy-five. Virtually all the men whose claims had been washed away by the flood were in attendance, as well as a number of citizens from the town, including some of the women who worked in the taverns and gambling halls.

He imagined that in such a small town, word quickly spread. Angels Camp could claim many luxuries and sophistications, but it could claim nothing even resembling a place of worship.

As Joshua looked out over his odd congregation, he knew that many had not darkened the doors of a church for years, even if they had had the opportunity. The painted faces on a few of the women-folk gave clear indication as to how they earned their money.

He realized that some who stood before him needed a balm for their loss, some needed a cure for their emptiness, and others might require a lesson in the worth of God's treasure versus man's treasure.

Joshua despaired. A lump formed in his throat. He recognized it from his early days as a pastor in Shawnee when he tried to present the wrong message to an uncomprehending congregation. The sermon he'd prepared was much too erudite and sophisticated for such an assembly. In fact, any message that explained the Scriptures might be too much for this group. He realized they were not seeking knowledge but answers.

He smiled at them. Many had brought blankets and formed themselves into a semicircle facing him.

Joshua thanked God for the warm morning and the clear skies as a rustle worked its way through the crowd. It was obvious they did not know what to expect.

In the lined faces of the miners he saw a nobility of hard work and sacrifice. He saw their calloused hands and knew they were only here seeking their share of the American dream. In the painted faces of the women, he saw masks that hid both pain and great shame. In the expressionless faces of the townsfolk he saw a blank slate on which no good word had been written.

Joshua prayed for wisdom. Then he introduced himself and began to tell a story.

It was the story of a boy who grew up in Ohio. He saw a few nods—obviously people who had grown up in Ohio, or at least nearby. He told how the boy tried hard to please his earthly father and followed in his footsteps, yet never felt that he measured up completely. Again, Joshua saw more nods. He told how the small-town boy came to the big city and how its allure beckoned and came close to consuming him. More nods. He told about how that boy turned his back on family and friends and set off to find a fortune, then came within a breath of losing his life over a pail of yellow metal. He told how God stepped in and showed the way, the truth, and the life.

It was a simple story.

As he finished, he asked if they might join together, first in prayer, then in the well-known hymn "Rock of Ages."

When the warbly praise sang out in the meadow, Joshua felt, for the first time, that a corner of his heart was at peace.

"Rock of Ages, cleft for me, let me hide myself in Thee. . . . "

That night in the dining room of his hotel, while still basking in the glow of appreciation from those who had listened to his story, Joshua reviewed what he'd said and recalled how he'd felt.

If this is what real preaching is, he thought, *then I need to reconsider what I offer to God as my gifts. This was a wondrous experience.*

From the table behind him, Joshua heard the name *Quen-li.* He leaned backward, not wanting to appear obvious.

"I hear she's goin' to sell for a pretty penny," one man slurred.

"I wouldn't mind biddin' myself, but I hear that brothel from San Francisco has thousands. I could never match that."

"But think of the pleasure she would bring."

"Maybe we can pool our money."

Another man laughed caustically. "You louts ain't got nearly enough. A beautiful girl like that—inexperienced and all, if you fellows know what I mean, and I bet you louts do—she's goin' to go for top dollar—which none of you have. And at the rate you're drinkin', ain't none of you ever goin' to have."

Another round of coarse laughter followed.

"Yeh, but I can dream of strikin' it rich by then, can't I?"

"And if you do, might as well spend it now. How much does a man need? All those fools that drowned upriver–not a one of 'em took anythin' with 'em."

Loud comments of "That's right" and "Amen to that," ended their discussion.

Such a bitter ending to a wonderful day, Joshua thought.

He slumped in his chair after hearing again about Quen-li's fate. It was obvious that if a brothel in San Francisco was in the bidding, Quen-li would sell for a great deal of money. Mr. Yat-sen would be rich, and his daughter would live a life of horrible degradation and sin.

As suddenly as a bolt of lightning flashes through the darkness, Joshua sat upright.

He knew. He knew then what he must do. His destiny became as crystal clear as mountain air after a storm.

CHAPTER TWENTY-FIVE

Angels Camp
October 1850

THE first chill of the coming winter snaked down from upriver and covered the meadow in frost. What wildflowers had been left withered and died on the stem. Flocks of geese cruised overhead, alive with calls and flapping of feathers. The leaves turned from green to gold to brown to falling in the span of but a few days.

Joshua kept his room at the hotel until midweek. He watched from his window as merchants began to board up windows for the winter. He saw pack animals and wagons being loaded to overflowing. Most merchants and provisioners took all remaining inventory with them, not willing to trust their goods to a lock and key.

While Angels Camp fell under the jurisdiction of the territory of California, the land was young and rugged, and lawmen had not yet made an appearance. A circuit judge stopped by twice in the fall of 1850 and heard thirty-some claim-jumping cases. If the judge sentenced anyone to jail, Joshua did not hear of it, though he knew the closest jail was in San Francisco. With no constable to guard the prisoner, it was unlikely that any sentence could be enforced, save a quick, angry hanging.

Some merchants planned on remaining in town for the winter. Dismantling a store and hauling inventories could be most troublesome. Only a handful of miners might arrive in the winter, yet they would need supplies and equipment. So some hotels and restaurants would remain open, often inhabited by the merchants who remained.

Angels Camp, while still a temporary town, was gradually becoming more permanent. Houses had been constructed. Joshua knew of six homes that successful miners had built. Some were also constructed by the merchants and shopkeepers. Streets were being added to the town, and there was talk of extending a rail spur along the river.

Every town dreamed of being on the railroad as a mark of its success and permanence. There were a few miles of railroad now, mostly from mines to the valley, but it was a matter of time before more track was laid.

On Wednesday Joshua did two things. First he gave his mule to three Ohio men. They were broken-spirited, near to hollow as any men Joshua had ever seen. They had given up and were returning worse off than when they left. The mule would make their hard journey easier. Joshua would have kept the animal but had no place to board her where he was going. Second he packed his bags for his trip back to San Francisco. What he did not carry, or did not need, he arranged to be stored at the hotel.

"If I don't make it back," he said, smiling, "the rest of this stuff is yours."

The hotel clerk eyed him closely. "You hide any gold in your gear?"

Joshua laughed and said no.

"Then I don't rightly care if you do or don't make it back. Just remember that your gear will be sold by the first of April if you ain't back by then."

Joshua knew that gold fever affected not only miners but everyone in town to some degree.

"I'll be back by the end of March," he answered.

The clerk offered a wry sneer. "That is, if you don't drink up what you found. I've seen hayseeds like you before. You may have some gold in your pocket, but it'll be gone before you leave the bar."

Joshua knew men like that as well. "Won't happen to me, my friend. Not now. I have something much better to do with it. Much, much better."

"Hope you're right. Like I said, April first, and I sell what you got here."

San Francisco
Winter 1850–1851

All during December, Joshua could not get warm. The damp sea air ate its way inside a man's bones, even if the man was nearly sitting in a roaring fire.

He took a room at a modest San Francisco hotel–modest in space and amenities, not price. He arrived at the bank that was holding his funds, and to his surprise, was ushered into the office of the president and offered refreshment.

"Cigar? Brandy? Lunch?" Sheldon Belmont, the whiskered bank president, suggested in a hopeful voice.

Joshua shook his head no. "I just came to check on the status of my deposits. I have records from the assayer's office and your correspondence, but since we have never met in person, I thought it would be prudent for me to introduce myself."

Mr. Belmont beamed. "And I'm so glad you did. You honored us by selecting this bank as your depository–sight unseen and all. And as you know, you have a substantial sum in our vaults. A substantial sum indeed."

Joshua did not know what to say, so he merely nodded.

"And I take it this all came about by your prospecting the famous California gold? Just one man?" Mr. Belmont asked.

Joshua's face grew dark. "I had a partner at the beginning, but he passed on."

"Sorry to hear that, Mr. Quittner. From what I am told, prospecting is indeed a hazardous business."

Joshua looked away and out the window. The bank was built into the first hill by the harbor, overlooking the expanse. Joshua could not begin to count the ghost ships lying still in the water. New arrivals kept appearing in the harbor on almost a daily basis. They would stream into town from the piers, plodding up the steeply pitched hills, carrying huge bundles of equipment, shovels, and other furnishings, looking as if they expected the gold fields to be at the crest of the first hill. When they saw California stretch away to the east with its vast rolling geography, their eyes widened, their arms weakened, and their resolve almost visibly wore away.

"And the reason for your visit?" the banker asked.

Joshua snapped back to the business at hand. "I need to transfer two sums of money back East. I imagine you can arrange such a transfer."

Mr. Belmont blanched. "Not all of it, I hope, Mr. Quittner."

"No, Mr. Belmont. Just a portion. No need to be concerned."

At least not just yet, Joshua thought. *At least not yet.*

<hr />

Back in his room, Joshua sat at a desk and wrote two letters by candlelight. Included in each one was a notarized form indicating that a sum of money would soon arrive at a bank in Cleveland and that the bearer of this note would be entitled to use those funds as they saw fit.

One of the letters was addressed to his parents. He wrote a short note, once again asking for their forgiveness. He wrote that he could offer them no reason, no logic that would explain his actions and make them fully understand. He wrote that he had done as his heart dictated.

Perhaps it was the Lord who allowed me to do this foolish thing, for I have now come back to true faith and am rededicating my life to his service. Too much has transpired for me to return to Shawnee. I am not so presumptuous or arrogant as to think that the church, or Constance, would wait so long for my return. If I were to arrive in Shawnee tomorrow, every move and action that I might make during my lifetime would be held with some suspicion, lest I change again and depart without warning. A church needs to know that its shepherd will remain loyal. A wife must know that a

*husband will never leave her. In Shawnee, such assurances are forever lost
to me.*

*I beg your forgiveness. I include this small amount of money so that your
final days may be a time of ease and free of worry. This is not tainted
money. I worked as hard as any man might work for it. I lost a friend in
the process.*

*Please tell Constance I'm truly sorry. I did not mean to toy with her
affections. Tell her I wish her all God's blessings on her life, but I will not
return to Shawnee, and that she must forget me—if she, in fact, has not
already done so.*

*Use this money as you see fit. What might be unneeded should go to
God's work.*

I remain, your devoted son,
Joshua Quittner

He read the notarized form once more. The words *Five Thousand
Dollars U.S.* brought him no true pleasure—or pain. He carefully dried
the ink and folded the letter. Slipping the notarized form inside the
sturdy envelope, he sealed it with a drop of wax.

He had one more letter to write. It was a very brief letter to the
elders of the Shawnee Church of The Holy Word.

Gentlemen,

*I am sending to the church, through a Cleveland Bank, an amount of
five thousand dollars. The bank will contact you when the money arrives.
I wish that you use this money to fund the scholarship program of which I
took advantage and because of which I caused such a great disappointment.
I have included a separate amount of one thousand dollars to be used for an
organ or any other church repairs that might be needed.*

This money was gained through honest work.

Again, I apologize for my shortcomings and ask for your forgiveness.
Joshua Quittner

Joshua heard the low moan of a foghorn, calling out from the harbor as he stacked the two envelopes on the desktop. He would seek
out the first ship headed back East in the morning and place the letters with the captain for delivery.

329

He thought that, by spring, both letters would arrive in Shawnee.

He blew out the candle, smiled to himself in the darkness, and for the first night in months, enjoyed a deep and nearly dreamless rest.

⁂

Joshua spent January in San Francisco. The weather remained bleak, and he knew heavy snows would render travel into the mountains and Angels Camp most dangerous. Rather than risk being lost in a blizzard, Joshua determined to wait until the weather warmed before returning.

The days passed slowly, even though the town constantly hummed with activity. Up to twelve men would share space in a hotel room that would be cramped for one. Joshua had the luxury of money, so he kept his small room all to himself. At dinner one night a fellow suggested that Joshua could simply triple his money and then some by letting others sleep in his lodgings during the day.

For a moment, Joshua considered it. It would be a means of adding to his riches. Then he realized that doing so would rob him of the privacy and quiet he needed to study and pray.

He had become bolder about his faith. Sitting at a cramped dining table, he would always offer grace, then strike up a conversation with his tablemates to discover how they lived their lives. He would tell them about his relationship with God and how God was the only treasure worth having. He was not strident or so zealous as to offend, but he was earnest and persistent.

Most of his words fell on deaf ears—especially when Joshua offered them cautions concerning the dangers of prospecting. It was a warning none wished to hear. They wanted to believe they alone would defy the odds and find that golden treasure. While Joshua warned of the physical dangers, he also warned of the impermanence of earthly treasure. Yet as he talked, as he offered prayer, as he offered advice, he saw all too often that burning gleam in their eyes. It was the gleam of gold, and there was little he could say to dim the fever.

At the end of February, Joshua rejoiced, for the winds shifted and a warm breeze flowed strong off the ocean. As the weather improved, Joshua knew that within weeks the trail to Angels Camp would be cleared of snow and new arrivals would sweep into the hills.

The date for the "auction" of Quen-li was set for the first of April. Joshua knew no power on earth would keep him from that event.

He began his journey back to the hills with that warm breeze at his back. While snow was still abundant, Joshua found his way along the trail without much hardship. The trails, roads, and rivers inland were often more congested than a busy Boston street—except the traffic here was all headed in a single direction.

Angels Camp
March 1851

He arrived back at Angels Camp by mid-March. A thick pad of snow remained, preventing the streets from becoming a sea of slush and debris. As Joshua walked about the town, he began to understand what God might be calling him to. He allowed the thoughts no internal articulation, for he was willing to wait until God clarified his will and showed brightly the path on which Joshua should walk.

The town continued to pulse with those returning to their claims and with the arrivals that joined the prospecting wave. Merchants brought out new equipment and supplies, all advertised as being essential for a man's success.

Joshua returned to the familiar hotel, claimed his possessions, and waited.

While the "auction" was not a legal event, word had spread wide. Besides Quen-li, obviously the most beautiful of the women involved, a number of other Chinese merchants had brought with them young girls to include in the offerings. Joshua happened to see several of these young Chinese women as they were marched from one large tent to a bathing parlor to ready themselves for the date of the auction.

It was apparent that none were daughters offered by fathers but instead were girls taken from villages in China and brought here, unaware of their fate and unable to alter it if they were. If a peasant faced starvation and a wealthy sea captain offered a small fortune for her servitude, how many would refuse? They could not, especially if such a sacrifice would save the rest of the family. What price they brought in China was most likely pennies compared to what price they would bring in the rich goldfields of California.

Joshua, while at dinner, heard six men, all giddy with newfound wealth, claim that they arrived in town specifically for this one event.

"It's cold up on the river," one gruff man explained. "I can't cook worth beans, and I want someone to keep me warm at night. I figure a Chinese woman is well suited for that. And she don't know the language, so they'll be no back talk for certain."

The group around him laughed rudely.

Joshua had tried several times to see Quen-li beforehand. Once he was stopped by Mr. Yat-sen's employees, who feared bloodshed, and once he was met midstreet by Mr. Yat-sen himself, who cursed at him in Chinese while waving the pistol in the air.

It was obvious a winter's passage had done nothing to alleviate the man's anger.

Late one night Joshua saw one of Mr. Yat-sen's employees—a young man called Chang—scurrying across the street. Most Chinese men did not venture out at night, not wanting to be a convenient whipping boy for a drunken miner.

Joshua grabbed at Chang's collar, and the man cowered in fright.

"I'm not going to hurt you. I just want to get a message to Quen-li," Joshua explained in a whisper.

The young man shook his head. Joshua could feel his fear. "I not listen. Mr. Yat-sen shoot me. He crazy man. Your God drive him crazy. Quen-li not stop with this God. She crazy too."

Joshua yanked him into the shadows and answered, "No one is crazy, and God doesn't do that."

"No listen! Leave me!" Chang shouted.

Joshua clamped a hand over the man's mouth. With his free hand, he reached into his pocket and withdrew a twenty-dollar gold piece. It was more than Chang would earn in a year.

"You can have this—for one favor."

When Joshua felt the man relax, he removed his hand. Chang nodded, his eyes fixed on the sparkling gold coin. "I want you to take a message to Quen-li."

Chang quickly shook his head.

"I not carry letter. Mr. Yat-sen find out and shoot me. He crazy."

"No letter. Just remember what I tell you."

Chang eyed Joshua for a moment, then the coin, and finally nodded.

"Tell Quen-li that Joshua says, "Do not be afraid. God will protect you."

The young man stared back.

"You understand? Will you remember?" Joshua asked.

Chang nodded. "No afraid. God protect. Joshua says."

Joshua handed Chang the coin and watched him scuttle off into the deeper shadows.

April 1851

The day of the auction arrived. There were no advertising handbills passed out. There were no signs posted on the sides of buildings. There was no one walking the streets, calling out the time or location.

Yet at noon on the first of April, a hundred men gathered in the main room of the Gabord Hotel. It was the only space in town large enough to contain a group of that size. Such a gathering demonstrated the power of word of mouth. One man told another and another, and soon the event was as well known as any advertised activity.

What made this auction especially enticing was its patent illegality. Even observing the transactions provided many with a vicarious thrill, a quivering sense of watching evil unfold.

Such a lure, such an exotic and powerful seduction, drew both the interested parties and the voyeuristic ones.

Joshua slipped in and sat in the back, hunched over, his hat pulled down. He wanted no one to notice his appearance. Most everyone in town knew Joshua's role in this event.

From up front, a large, gaudily dressed man stepped up onto the stage. He was wearing a bowler hat that barely perched on top of his big head. He called for the crowd's attention. A tense hush spread, and the crowd found chairs or leaned against the walls.

"I'm Mr. Foster Grote, and you all know why we're here," he called out.

Muffled hooting and raucous laughter was the response from the crowd.

"We all know what the government says about this–but we're talking about Chinese here. That's a different matter, right?"

A weak chorus of "Right you are" greeted his question.

"Then we'd best be starting. I know a lot of you have a hot pocket filled with gold, just ready for spending."

Nervous, anticipatory clamor rocked the room.

The first Chinese girl, no more than fifteen years old, was pushed, almost roughly, to the stage. Grote took her by the hand and pulled her farther to the front. Her head was bowed, but anyone could see the fear in her eyes. She hunched her shoulders and tried to become invisible. Grote reached under her chin with his fleshy palm and lifted her face to the crowd. There was a hint of a tear on her face.

"Now this gal, whose name I can't pronounce, is a hard worker and a good cook. She's young and not poor looking at all. No doubt she'll keep one lucky miner warm when the sun goes down."

A series of soft hoots echoed from the crowd.

A man in front raised his hand. "Twenty bucks!" he called out.

Grote wiped at the sweat on his forehead and laughed. "That ain't going to get you a meal, my friend, let alone a banquet. I say we all get serious."

Several minutes later the bidding had gone to a thousand dollars. After calling last bids, Grote slapped his hands together.

"We got ourselves a deal, mister. You pay that man by the table, and you claim the purchase behind the stage."

Joshua winced at what he was watching. His heart hurt for the young girl, but there was nothing he could do to stop it. At one point he'd considered bringing a judge or a constable with him from San Francisco who would stop the illegal transactions. But if he did, the event would simply move to another location, or moneys would exchange hands secretly and people would look the other way for a few hours.

Joshua was realistic enough to know that hard cash would win over the cause of justice.

In the span of an hour, ten other women met the same fate as the first. The amounts increased as the physical charms of the women became more defined and pleasing.

The last woman to face the process would be Quen-li.

Joshua now understood. Quen-li, compared to the women who preceded her on stage, was a rare flower in a parched desert. Joshua knew that every man in the room would claim her to be the most beautiful Chinese woman they ever laid eyes on—and perhaps the most beautiful woman ever—white or Chinese.

There was a fragile quality of her features, her inviting yet mysterious eyes, her full lips, the sheen of her hair, the gentle and responsive curve of her body. She was like a precious crystalline figurine one would hold in a trembling hand.

Joshua saw her as she walked to the center of the stage and stared out, no hint of fear in her eyes. The word *exquisite* came to his mind. She had an almost painful, body-numbing beauty that transcended all others.

Joshua could not fathom why her great loveliness was not more apparent to him before. Perhaps it was because now he saw her in comparison with the others. As she had knelt before him in the past, her beauty had been dazzling, but there had been no other to compare her to.

Now he had that comparison, as did every man in the room.

A tense and eager silence spread out like a brisk wind.

Grote stepped back, then opened his palm as if offering every man another moment to gaze upon Quen-li's beauty.

"Good sirs," he began, "let us not sully this ravishing creature with miserly amounts. Let the truly worthy gentlemen begin with an appropriate figure."

A callow man stood to the challenge and barked out, "Ten thousand dollars."

Everyone in the room, including Joshua, inhaled with surprise.

Ten thousand dollars–for a opening bid!

A portly man stood, glared at the first man, then called out, "Eleven thousand dollars."

A man beside Joshua whispered, "I thought I knew them fellows. The fat one–Rollins, I think he's called–and the other skinny guy are from the two biggest brothels in San Francisco. I can bet this pretty one ain't goin' to spend no time in a miner's shack, that's for certain."

The man on the other side whispered back. "You know she'll earn all that back in a month, for every man in town will want the ten-thousand-dollar woman!"

The first man licked his lips and nodded. "Or the eleven-thousand-dollar woman."

The first bidder barked back, "Twelve thousand dollars!"

The crowd gasped again.

Joshua knew twelve thousand dollars was an immense sum of money. Everyone knew that.

Grote appeared stunned as the bid continued to be tossed back and forth between the two men, each adding a thousand dollars with each call.

At nineteen thousand dollars, both men appeared to be sweating. No doubt their job was to win. But it was also apparent that they wanted to win the game but not at any cost.

Rollins wiped his face with his sleeve, stared hard at his opponent, then at Quen-li. He lowered his face as if he were mentally counting the bills in his purse.

He looked up and shouted, "Twenty thousand dollars!"

The crowd breathed in as one. Then silence.

Grote waited, then looked at the callow man on the other side of the room. He muttered angrily under his breath and sat down.

No one spoke.

"Twenty thousand dollars . . . going once . . . going twice."

Rollins, his face streaked with sweat, allowed himself to smile. He did not disguise the fact that this may have been his highest bid possible.

At that moment, Joshua stood up. His chair squealed loudly, and much of the room turned to him with astonishment. Silence greeted him in a wave.

Grote stared out.

Joshua called out in a clear voice, "Twenty thousand dollars."

It was all the money he had. His bank account was empty. Besides the bank draft for twenty thousand dollars, he had a single twenty-dollar gold coin.

The barker smiled, then called out, "Needs to be higher, my friend. That's how this works."

Joshua blinked.

He heard in his mind two words: *Surrender all.*

"Twenty thousand dollars," he repeated, "and this."

He pulled from his pocket the single, apple-sized gold nugget. It was the only gold he'd saved from the flood.

"That rock real gold?" Grote asked.

"It's real gold," Joshua said. "I've got the letter to prove it."

The crowd looked at Joshua, then Grote. Grote stared hard at Joshua, then turned to Rollins. After a long moment, the portly man cursed and slumped to his chair.

"And the man in back with the fistful of gold and twenty thousand dollars takes the prize!" Grote called out.

Before he slapped his hands together, the room broke out in a pandemonium of calls, shouts, whistles, and hoots.

⚜

The crowd parted about Joshua as he made his way to pay his money and hand over his gold nugget. Men called out to him as he walked his way to the front, offering broad hints of their envy.

Rollins hissed over at him, "If you want to reconsider, friend, my offer of twenty thousand stands–as long as the merchandise does not get spoiled."

Joshua shook his head. "No, I'm not changing my mind."

"Well, if you do–and being poor has a way of changing things– here's my card."

The card read: "Wilbur Rollins, Esq. Madame Lavores's Gentle-man's Club."

Joshua took it and slipped it into his pocket.

He fought his way through the well-wishers and leering onlookers to find Quen-li standing alone behind the stage.

⚜

He took her by the hand and slipped out the back door of the hotel. They hurried down the street, Joshua trying his best to ignore the stares and whispers and catcalls from those they passed.

He pulled Quen-li into a dark and quiet restaurant. He had one twenty-dollar gold piece left. It would buy them a good meal. Joshua thought that while they ate, they might have a chance to discuss Quen-li's future.

They were seated near the back of the room, in the shadows. Joshua was not sure if it was because he was a white man with a Chinese woman, or if it was simply the next available open table. He did not care and was grateful for the seclusion.

Neither he nor Quen-li was aware that just beyond a curtain sat William Rollins.

The waiter fussed with their order, then scampered off toward the kitchen.

Quen-li looked up at Joshua, but it was only the tracing of a true smile. She had not spoken a word since the auction.

"I am now yours," she said, averting her eyes.

"No, Quen-li," Joshua said. "I did not buy you. I bought your freedom."

Her face could not hide her surprise. "You bought Quen-li. I am yours," she said, her voice shaking.

"You belong to no one. You are free," Joshua replied. "I cannot own you."

"You not want me?"

"That's not what this is about. I do not want to own you. As a Christian, I can't. I bought your freedom. That's all."

Quen-li looked confused as tears began to stream down her face. "You not want me?" she repeated.

"Quen-li . . . that's not what I did here. I cannot own you. You are free to do anything you choose."

The waiter brought their food, but neither Joshua nor Quen-li possessed much of an appetite. They sat in silence and picked at the food for several long moments.

Quen-li laid down her fork and looked into his eyes, her hand now by her throat.

"You not want Quen-li. You ashamed of Quen-li. You say your God is happy with Quen-li, but you not happy with Quen-li. You pay fortune and throw me out. I not understand. You must hate Quen-li. Maybe father right. Maybe your God is crazy."

Joshua struggled to find the right words.

"Quen-li, God is not crazy. I am doing what a Christian must do. I cannot own you. I have no right to own another human being. That isn't right. I spent that money so you could be free. You are free to do anything you want. You don't have to be afraid of your father anymore. You are free."

"Free?" she sniffed. "Free to go where? Free?"

Her tears began to fall in earnest. She sobbed, stood up, and began to run from the restaurant.

Joshua stared after her for a moment.

That's not what I needed to say, he chided himself.

He called out as he leapt to his feet, "Wait, Quen-li, wait! Let me explain!"

And as he did, two burly men appeared out of nowhere and shouldered into him, knocking him to the floor. A table overturned, and a crash of dishes and goblets filled the quiet room. Stunned, Joshua jumped to his feet again. As he did, one of the hefty figures turned to him and swung his fist into Joshua's stomach. Joshua doubled over and fell to his knees as the second man swung his fist at the back of Joshua's neck.

After that, there was only darkness.

CHAPTER TWENTY-SIX

April 1851

JOSHUA shook off the fog that rattled his thoughts, pulled himself to his feet, then wobbled out in pursuit of Quen-li. There was no sign of his attackers, and no one in the restaurant appeared to be ready to offer aid.

Clouds rolled up the valley, and a light mist began to fall. Joshua stood in the light rain, his eyes scanning the street. He then ran toward the site of the auction. He was certain he had been unconscious for only a moment or two, but Quen-li had disappeared like a wisp of smoke in a strong wind. As he neared the hotel, he encountered an almost solid wall of people. Many had been at the auction or stood in the street, watching the spectacle of men exiting with their new, and obviously unwilling, companions.

A swarm of laughter flew up as Joshua looked wildly about, his eyes searching for a hint of the color of Quen-li's green silk dress. All he saw were the rough, muddy clothes of miners and the odd finery of the town's painted ladies.

"She went that way, preacher boy!" one man yelled out, hardly able to control his mirth.

Another cried, "No, this way!"

And then another yelled, and another, all offering different directions.

"You scare her off so soon, preacher boy?" hooted one man.

"That ain't supposed to happen till the sun goes down," said another, smirking, and the crowd shouted out its agreement.

"The preacher boy ain't got any gentlemanly sense," another offered. "He done offended his prize, and she took off like a colt from a fire."

"She's over here with me!"

"No, with me!"

Joshua heard a mixture of anger, jealousy, and crude lust in every shout and taunt. In that crowd were men who had worked on the same river as Joshua for the same amount of time, who had worked just as hard, suffering just as much as he had—and who were left with mere pennies at the end of a year. How Joshua found such wealth was cause for instant and bitter resentment, and their catcalls and hooting gave strong evidence to such emotions.

He spun about, pushing his way through the crowd. He knew she could not have gone far. He needed only to fully explain his intentions to her. He needed to tell her that he did care for her but, as a Christian, would have no part in "buying" a woman—or any human being. Perhaps, as she enjoyed her newly purchased freedom, Joshua might call upon her, but he would command no special favors.

I know I was to surrender all. I know it, the voice in his head repeated. He pushed and struggled and then shoved himself mightily onto the main street.

I need to find her and tell her. She'll understand. I know she will. I will find the right words.

He ran a dozen steps in one direction, feeling the hot stares of everyone who watched him go past. He saw no sign of Quen-li. He turned around and ran the other direction, calling out her name: "Quen-li! Quen-li! Where are you?"

He heard laughter follow him as he peered about frantically. There was still no sign of her.

Would she have gone back to her father? That makes no sense.

Breathing hard, Joshua spun about, trying to find that flash of green silk in the crowd. But he could see no such color. He ran down another street, then another. Time was passing, and with every second, Joshua became more and more worried.

Suppose someone apprehended her and took her with them? Suppose a jealous miner grabbed her and spirited her off?

He wiped his brow, beaded with sweat.

Then, out of the corner of his eye he saw a flash of green and a figure nearly at the end of the main street. Joshua gave chase, calling out, "Quen-li! Wait!"

He jumped a man-sized mud puddle and caught his foot at the end, slipping sideways into the muck. He scrambled to his feet, struggling to regain his balance and footing. On his knees, he lifted his head and shouted again, "Quen-li!"

Dripping with mud, he began to run, clumps of wet earth falling from his knees and boots. The green slip turned another corner, and Joshua slowed this time to turn without falling.

The alley led to the blacksmith shop. There he discovered that the green fabric was not Quen-li but Chang, the young Chinese man of Mr. Yat-sen's employ.

"You there!" Joshua shouted. "Chang! Stop!"

Surprised, the young man stopped still. "What you want! Go away!" He was carrying a broken razor. "Mr. Yat-sen send me. This need repair. You go. He know I talk to you, he shoot me."

Joshua ran closer, then doubled over, his hands on his knees. Nearly out of breath, he asked, "Why did you run from me?"

"I not run from you. Mr. Yat-sen say we must run when he send us on job. He crazy man."

"Where is Quen-li? Did she go back to her father's shop?"

"Quen-li? Back to father? No. You crazy now. She dead to him. She go with fat man to San Francisco."

"Fat man?"

"Big man with whiskers. He have big horse. They ride away."

"But . . . but why?" Joshua wheezed, overwhelmed by surprise and anger. "I paid for her freedom."

"He not buy her from you? We think you make money on Quen-li. You no sell Quen-li?" Chang asked, confused.

Joshua shook his head.

"Then you spend money for nothing. You crazy man."

Joshua straightened up, brushed off his knees and elbows, and raced toward the livery stable.

They have to have a horse I can buy, he thought frantically, then stopped in his tracks. *But I don't have any money. I spent every dollar I had.*

In that instant, the color drained from his face, and a moan escaped his lips.

❦

Joshua knew he could not keep pace on foot with a fast horse—even a horse bearing the weight of two riders. He could run for a while, but they would soon be miles ahead. All his desire would not give him the speed of a good horse.

He ran to the hotel and gathered up his possessions. There was not much left—leather-bound books, his father's Bible, some clothes, a razor, a hand mirror, a sharp knife, and an assortment of plates, pots, spoons, and forks.

He encircled the pile with his arms and, as fast as he could walk without spilling, made his way to the livery stable. He lowered his possessions on the floor in front of the owner.

"I want to trade this for a horse," Joshua said with as much confidence as he could muster.

The owner looked at Joshua, his odd assemblage of things, then back up. He smiled. "And I want to fly, but the good Lord didn't give me wings."

"But I need a horse."

The owner nudged a book with his toe. "What you need and what you can get with this pile of stuff are two different matters."

"But I have to get to San Francisco! I need to leave now!"

"That so?"

Lord, help me, Joshua prayed.

The owner nudged at the Bible, resting on the top of the pile, with his toe. It slipped and tumbled to the floor. When it hit, the pages spread open, and a fluttering of bills fell to the floor.

Joshua did not remember hiding the currency in the Bible. It was the last few dollars of Gage's gift to him from so very long ago.

The owner bent down and retrieved them. "These real?" he asked. "Tell you what, my friend. Even this ain't enough to buy any horse that I own. But I can see you're a Christian fellow. How about I take this money and you promise to bring the horse back in a week's time–that long enough for you?"

Thank you, Lord!

"Yes, more than enough."

"Then I'll let you have that roan mare over there. She ain't all that fast, but she'll walk night and day if you ask her nice."

Joshua was already on his way to take her reins. "She'll do fine," he called back. "I'll return for my goods at the end of the week."

And with that, he spurred the horse's side, and she trotted west, down the valley road and toward the sea.

On the Road to San Francisco

Joshua had no idea of how far they might be ahead of him. Every mile down the road, he passed more miners working their way up the trail. Some claimed to have seen a rider and a Chinese woman; some did not. But then, not every miner was paying attention to what came down the trail, what with them loaded and straining to shoulder their equipment upriver.

Joshua rode the mare as hard as he dared that day. Despite the fact that the stableman said the horse would run all day and night, come nightfall the horse started to whinny and nudge to the side of the trail.

"I know you're tired, girl," Joshua said, patting at the horse's neck, "but can you give me another hour? Just an hour."

Unmoved by Joshua's pleading, the horse started to buck with each step. In the dim moonlight, Joshua could see why the horse pulled back. Part of the road had given way to the recent flood. A narrow tramping path led into the brush, the darkness all but hiding it from view. To continue, Joshua knew, would be to risk hobbling the horse with a twisted leg or worse.

"All right," Joshua said as he pulled back on the reins. "Then we'll stop here for the night. But we leave at first light. Is that a deal?"

A cold breeze flowed downriver from the hills to the east. Joshua built a fire and huddled by it, drawing the horse blanket about his shoulders. He knew Rollins and Quen-li had had to stop for the night, as he did. He knew that they could not be more than an hour ahead of him. He also knew that they could not go much faster than he. Joshua knew that Tallen's Mill was only a little farther down the trail. He figured that the two of them may have found rooms there for the night.

Joshua built a small campfire. The fire hissed and cracked. Red sparks leapt into the night, then disappeared. Joshua watched the fire for over an hour, trying to calm his heart and thoughts. Finally he bowed his head.

Lord, let my prayers ascend to you tonight. I've done what I thought you led me to do. I've offered freedom to a poor, innocent girl. And yet, even in that, I've managed to stumble. Am I forever doomed to listen and act and then face disappointment?

I heard your voice . . . I know for sure. You told me to surrender all. And that is what I did.

Yet Quen-li is still on her way to a brothel, and I'm certain I'm a culprit in forcing her on this path of destruction. That's not what I want, nor do you. I've paid a dear price for this woman. I will not let her be sullied. You must help, Lord. Please help me.

When the fire burned to a bed of hot embers, Joshua fell asleep.

He did not awaken until the first shafts of light crept over the eastern hills.

⁂

Quen-li and Rollins had indeed stopped at Tallen's Mill. The innkeeper described them both.

"Came in late. Paid in gold coin. Took two rooms. Left before dawn, I reckon. Didn't even stay for breakfast. For a big man like that to skip a meal—well, I bet he had some pretty pressing business. And with such a pretty Chinese woman, I can guess at his business."

Joshua spurred his horse on, but despite any urging, the horse refused to move faster than a steady trot.

The hills gave way to the broad, flatter valley. If Joshua stood in the stirrups, he could see the first edgings of the blue ocean. San Francisco lay hours to the west. The trail widened here to a more proper roadway, though the spring rains had left it a quagmire of ruts and mud.

Joshua spurred his horse to the side, and they trotted through higher grass and brambles. The road meandered, following the contours of the hills. Joshua could smell the ocean before he saw it—an acrid, biting scent of salt and fish and pine. He knew he was a few hours from town, yet darkness fell suddenly, and clouds obscured the moon. There would be no more riding this day.

Joshua knew that by noon of the following day, he would reach San Francisco. He prayed that Rollins and Quen-li would not be riding through the night.

San Francisco

As the horse neared a gallop, Joshua held tight to the saddle horn with his left hand and withdrew Rollins's business card from his pocket. The address told him nothing. Yet if tradition held true, Madame Lavores's establishment would be in the same neighborhood as other similar establishments. Joshua had never walked down that street, but he knew where it was.

The city, its buildings, and its people tightened around him. Wooden structures gave way to stone, and every block bore evidences of a new establishment rising from an empty lot.

Joshua turned right once, then again.

If it's anywhere at all, it's along this street.

As he turned the last corner, his heart leapt. The sheer bulk of the man's frame on the horse a block ahead of him indicated that it had to be Rollins. And behind rode a slight figure, clad in green.

Joshua spurred the mare for one last gallop. He pulled her to a breathless stop just as Rollins was hoisting Quen-li from his horse.

Rollins saw Joshua, and his right hand went to his side, feeling for the pistol that lay holstered there.

"You got no claim to the woman, Quittner," Rollins called out. "She said you set her free—and you didn't want her—and she made her own choice to come with me." He pushed his coat away from the handle of the pistol. "Sounds to me like she's capable of deciding what she wants to do with her life—and that don't include you, Quittner. Now I'd be most obliged if you get out of my way and let us pass."

A small crowd gathered in the street to watch.

Joshua all but ignored Rollins and his gun. Dismounting from his horse, he looked at Quen-li. Her eyes were red and hollow from crying.

"Quen-li, I made a terrible mistake. I said the wrong thing to you."

She raised her head. "You hate me. I understand. You buy me to laugh."

"Laugh? I did not. I bought you so you wouldn't have to come to a place like this."

Her lips shook. "But I have no place to go. I cannot go to Father. I cannot go with you. Only place I go is here. Where else for a woman who has no family? I know no one in America."

"Quen-li . . . I didn't say what I meant to say. You didn't understand me. Let me explain."

She bowed her head and, in a velvety voice, whispered, "Why do you hate me?"

Joshua was stunned by her words. "I don't hate you. . . . I think . . . I know . . . I love you."

"Then why you turn me away?"

"I'm not turning you away. But I'm allowing you to leave me if you choose. I hope you don't, because I want to ask you to be my wife."

Her face showed her great surprise.

"It is not because I bought you, Quen-li. It is because I love you. I think I loved you from the first day I heard you laugh. I cannot buy your love, but I can live my life trying to earn it. Please say yes."

"Your words true? You not laughing?"

"I am not laughing. I mean every word of what I say."

Like the sun breaking through the clouds, a smile flooded Quen-li's face. Through her tears, she ran into Joshua's arms and embraced him, her arms twined about him tightly with an intensity that almost took his breath away.

"I've never been more sure of anything, Quen-li. I want to spend my life with you," Joshua softly said.

Rollins put his hand to his gun, and Joshua saw the man's fat fingers tighten around the grip. He lifted his head.

"You have no legal standing here, Rollins. You tried, but you failed. I have the receipt of purchase, and Quen-li has decided."

His eyes clouding, Rollins slammed the gun back into his holster and stomped away, throwing open the gate to Madame Lavores's with a metallic boom.

Joshua at last sighed with relief. Looking into Quen-li's eyes, he saw they were awash with happy tears.

Slowly, he let his lips find hers. As they met, she clung to him, and he welcomed the urgency of her embrace.

CHAPTER TWENTY-SEVEN

San Francisco
April 1851

JOSHUA and Quen-li were to ride together back to Angels Camp, not as buyer and bought, or rich man and slave—but as husband and wife.

No more than an hour after finding Quen-li with Rollins, Joshua had found a city judge willing to perform their marriage.

Before he began the ceremony, the judge had pulled Joshua aside and whispered into his ear, "You know you're marryin' a Chinese woman, don't you?"

Joshua had said, his tone close to anger, "Yes, I do. And is there some concern about that?"

Flustered, the judge had hemmed and hawed that there was not.

"Just checkin' to see if you ain't liquored up and didn't see the difference—that's all. Don't want any dissatisfied customers."

Angels Camp

It took Joshua and Quen-li three days to make it back to Angels Camp from San Fransisco. For a moment Joshua thought of staying in town, but without money, he knew that was impossible. *There is my claim on the river,* he reasoned.

They rode while there was sunlight and slept by campfires at night. They arrived in Angels Camp early in the morning.

"I still have the full week with the horse, don't I?" he asked the man at the livery. "I can bring her in two days, right?"

The livery owner rubbed his chin, then nodded.

When they plodded down the main street, Quen-li almost dozing as she hung onto him, her arms threaded about his waist, Joshua realized with finality that he had no money—only his claim on a river and the remnants of a mule shed.

Maybe I left a few things there that we could use to exchange for a few nights' lodging. I could find work here with another claim company. . . . Somehow we'll get by.

Russian River

He spurred the horse, and by late afternoon they stood in the clearing that had once held Joshua's cabin. The river had quieted, and the forest seemed to absorb all sound. Quen-li watched as he walked to the edge of the precipice and looked down at the peacefully flowing waters.

Perhaps I could go back down and dig for a while. Maybe I could find enough to build a cabin again.

He looked back at Quen-li. She was now leaning against a tall pine. Her eyes slowly fell closed. The trip back had been hard, and they were both very tired and hungry.

All Joshua wanted to do was fall into a bed and sleep.

But if I work the river, where will we stay? I cannot even buy a tent. Quen-li will be forced to sleep in the open. He looked to the sky. *This is not the way to begin life as a husband and wife.*

He turned and stepped noiselessly toward her, trying not to awaken her. *And what of my promise to serve God? If I prospect, that dream is gone.*

Then his toe caught on a small outcropping, and he stumbled, falling to his knees. He turned to see what had tripped him.

There among the rocks was a glint of yellow, flashing in the afternoon sun. His heart lurched. He scrambled about, digging at the sparkle as hard as he could.

In a moment he saw it—a gallon-sized glass jar of gold flakes and nuggets. It was one of the many jars he and Giles had buried so many months ago.

He sat there, dumbfounded, as he held the heavy container in his hands. It was by no means a fortune, but it would be enough to make a new beginning.

His thoughts raced.

In that single heartbeat, in that simple fall to his knees, he knew, without question, what he should do.

Just to the south of Angels Camp was a wide, open meadow, sprinkled with lovely flowers and grasses. Joshua quickly reasoned that he could purchase those acres, raise a few chickens and cows, perhaps grow some vegetables and wheat. Why, if Angels Camp kept growing, a farm close by would be a sound investment.

This jar of gold would probably cover the cost of the land and enough supplies to get started. Joshua knew that land far from the gold fields came at a very fair price.

He crawled over to Quen-li. Her hands were folded like two doves nesting together. He touched her shoulder and whispered, "Quen-li . . . Quen-li . . . wake up . . . I have some wonderful news."

Angels Camp

That night they enjoyed a hot bath, fresh sheets, and a comfortable bed—as husband and wife—as lovers. It was not the most luxurious room in town, but to both of them it seemed like a bedroom in the castle of a king.

One day later, Joshua exchanged most of his gold and purchased thirty acres of meadow land.

That afternoon, after buying some new clothing, he and Quen-li were walking along the main street in Angels Camp. A paper sign, freshly printed, had been tacked to the side of a building at the southern edge of town.

"For Rent. Reasonable. Contact GD Enterprises."

He turned to Quen-li. "This town does need a church. Maybe it's time one got started."

She squeezed his hand, smiled, and nodded.

⁂

The rent was most reasonable.

Joshua had a small wooden sign painted that read: "The Bible preached here. All are welcome."

The first Sunday twenty-four people sat on the pews Joshua had made from the wood of his land. The next week, stiff and sore from building a cabin on his farm, Joshua preached to nearly fifty people. The following week, the room had over one hundred miners, clerks, trappers, and merchants.

As he worked his new land, he prayed almost continually, thanking God for his blessings and guidance.

⁂

Joshua and Quen-li still garnered stares and snickers as they walked together down the streets of Angels Camp. Yet each day, the stares grew shorter, and the crude remarks and calls grew fewer.

One day, as Joshua and Quen-li stepped out of the church, Mr Yat-sen hurried past them. He did not stop or exchange a word with them, yet he turned his head, and his eyes found Quen-li.

She stopped and bowed as he passed.

Joshua told Quen-li later that the slightest of smiles passed his lips, and his eyes widened at the sight of his daughter.

For that slightest of gestures, tears came to her eyes.

October 1851

By the time the first leaves began to take on their fall color, Joshua had erected a small cabin complete with a puncheon floor, a henhouse for his chickens, and a corral for his cows. He purchased simple furnishings—a bed with a comfortable mattress, a chest of drawers, two upholstered wing chairs to place by the fire, a sawbuck table with four wooden Windsor chairs, and a cast-iron cookstove. The money from his last gold find was nearly gone, but by spring, the sale of eggs, milk, and crops would begin to pay the bills.

One morning Quen-li burst from the cabin and ran out into the pasture, where Joshua was digging fence holes. She wrapped her arms around him tightly. He smiled and returned her embrace.

"A most welcome diversion," he called out, laughing. "But what's the occasion?" Joshua often forgot that Quen-li understood only perhaps half of what he said. It was clear that today she understood even less.

It did not matter, however.

She took his hand and placed it on her belly. Joshua turned his head in puzzlement. Quen-li was reserved and prim. This was most unlike her.

Her radiant smile told Joshua all he needed to know.

"A child . . . ?"

She nodded.

"But . . . when . . . how?"

She blushed and softly said, "In spring. A baby. Baby boy. It is feeling—but more. A mother knows. It will be a boy. I will give you son. My father will have a grandson."

Puzzled no longer, he picked her up in his arms and spun her about. He knew she wanted to present him a son. He knew, even though their marriage was young, how important a son was to the Chinese.

Boy or girl—I will be overjoyed.

"I guess we'll have to find a Boston rocker to buy," he said, tenderly kissing his wife, soon to be a mother. As they danced with joy in the field, Joshua took in his entire world with a new perspective. Thirty acres, the cabin, a few animals, a church in town—all the things that he once scorned were now his whole life.

He set Quen-li down, took her hands in his, and gazed into her eyes.

He was at peace.

At last Joshua had found the complete joy that had eluded him for so long. Finally he realized that true contentment comes from family, hard work, having peace with God, and serving him—and all the gold in the world cannot buy these treasures.

As he bent down and kissed his wife again, Joshua's heart flooded with love and happiness.

⁂

That day Joshua walked to town with a single mission. He walked straight to the Tonsorial Parlor. Mr. Yat-sen stood in the middle of the crowded room, which was filled with steam and scents.

Joshua stood in the doorway. For a moment, Mr. Yat-sen allowed anger to cloud his eyes, then he softened.

It was the time for Joshua to speak.

"Mr. Yat-sen, your daughter is with child. As grandfather, you have the right to name the child. Quen-li says it will be a boy child."

With that Joshua bowed deeply as Quen-li had instructed and repeated the words in Chinese that meant "honorable father."

Joshua straightened up to see Mr Yat-sen try to hide his smile, yet his sparkling eyes betrayed him.

Again, in Chinese words taught to him by Quen-li, Joshua repeated, "Honorable father, you will always be most welcome in our home."

December 1851

As the first winter weather set in, Joshua ventured into town to purchase a week's worth of supplies. Quen-li's belly was growing big, and he could not look at her without smiling. Her father had not yet visited, but they had spoken for several minutes while on an errand in town. Quen-li was certain that God would be at work on her

father's heart and that the new child would be the key to his future
as well.

Stepping into the General Mercantile Store, Joshua pulled out a
long list of items that they would need. Before he could ask for any
item, the owner reached under the counter and rustled about.

"Quittner—you got a letter. Someone dropped it off here yesterday
... or was it the day before ... no, it was yesterday. I remember
'cause them miners from Virginia stopped in askin' for new picks ...
or was that two days ago?"

All the while the man talked, a pale envelope wavered in the air.
Joshua finally reached out and took it.

It was postmarked *Monterey*.

The clerk never stopped talking, even as Joshua tore the envelope
open and unfolded a single sheet of stationery.

The letterhead read, "GD Enterprises, Inc."

That's the landlord of the church building.

Joshua gave a start, and his eyes jumped to the end of the letter.

Could "GD Enterprises" stand for ... ?

At the bottom of the letter was a distinctive signature: Gage Davis.
His eyes leapt to the top again.

Dear friend,

*I hear you are in Angels Camp and were once a rich man. Don't be
surprised by what I know. I'll be in town in the spring. I need to check up
on my holdings. Hope to meet you then. I have much news of our friends.
You'll be shocked and surprised.*

I trust you'll hold an open bed for me.

Your friend,
Gage Davis

Amazed at God's working of such intricate details, Joshua stared
out the window, watching the first of winter's pure, clean snowflakes
swirl in the air.

Midnight is upon us now. The moon, full and yellow, has crept into the eastern sky. The breezes have calmed, and the blackened ocean hisses, gentle and quiet. Salt and pine scent the darkness, heavy and sweet. The lantern is lit, and I sit, in its pool of golden light, on the porch of my home by the sea. I am only footsteps from the tranquil water. Far down along the beach I see a dozen torches dance above the surface of the sea. A trio of fishing boats has slipped into the shallow waters, with nets trailing behind in their wake. In the morning, we will dine on their catch.

It is a simple life I lead. But it has not always been so.

This new state has proved an epiphany of sorts to each one of us—Joshua, Gage, Hannah, and myself. Not as an ending, but as a beginning. As my mind fills with the memories of all that has happened, I have retrieved a single volume from the tall stack of books on my desk. It is a Harvard University yearbook from the year of my graduation. Pressed between these pages are newspaper clippings, letters, photographs, programs, notes, a flower or two—flat mementos from our lives, entwined over the years.

I have witnessed the beginning of our stories, our joinings and fractures, our steps and missteps. I have seen our joy and wept at our hurts. I am retelling these stories—of our four individual lives—not because I seek to recolor our past in pleasant umbers and soft gilding—but because they, my friends, my comrades, each insist that I am the only fair witness to our past, and now, our present, and indeed our future as well.

I speak the truth—these lives, these stories are worth the retelling. As each of us began our friendship within the aged walls of the

Destiny Café in Cambridge, Massachusetts, each of us carried a dream. We've asked ourselves and each other, did those dreams come true? Did reality match what we imagined as callow and feckless youths? Did the journey of our lives bring us the happiness we hoped for?

I have asked myself this question many times over the years: When a dream does not come to pass, are we lying to ourselves when we say we are happy? Is a dream denied something worse . . . or something better?

I have told you of Joshua and his life—as he abandoned his service to God only to find his heart once again at God's throne and in his service.

I will not now tell how each of our stories end, for to do so would diminish the worth of these pages. It would be like knowing what lay beneath the fine wrapping paper and bows on Christmas morning. And is not the enjoyment of travel to be found in the traveling itself, rather than the tired rest at the end of the journey?

I smile as I write this. I will rest as the moon continues her journey, and begin the incredible story of Gage Davis on the morrow.

With God's help,

Jamison Pike
Monterey Bay
The State of California
January 1860